Julie Caplin is the international bestselling author of the Romantic Escapes series. Her books have hit the bestseller charts in Italy, Germany, the UK and the Czech Republic and have sold over a million copies worldwide. Her uplifting romantic comedies are set in gorgeous destinations across the globe, providing her readers the ultimate escape.

Formerly a PR director, for many years Julie swanned around Europe taking top food and drink writers on press trips to sample the gastronomic delights of the continent. It was a tough job but someone had to do it. These trips have provided the inspiration and settings for her novels.

Julie also writes romantic and historical fiction as Jules Wake.

juleswake.co.uk

 x.com/JulieCaplin
 facebook.com/JulieCaplinAuthor

Also by Julie Caplin

Romantic Escapes

The Little Café in Copenhagen

The Little Brooklyn Bakery

The Little Paris Patisserie

The Northern Lights Lodge

The Secret Cove in Croatia

The Little Teashop in Tokyo

The Little Swiss Ski Chalet

The Cosy Cottage in Ireland

The Christmas Castle in Scotland

The French Chateau Dream

A VILLA WITH A VIEW

JULIE CAPLIN

One More Chapter
a division of HarperCollins*Publishers* Ltd
1 London Bridge Street
London SE1 9GF
www.harpercollins.co.uk
HarperCollins*Publishers*
Macken House, 39/40 Mayor Street Upper,
Dublin 1, D01 C9W8, Ireland

This paperback edition 2024
4
First published in Great Britain in ebook format
by HarperCollins*Publishers* 2024

A catalogue record of this book is available from the British Library

ISBN: 978-0-00-857926-5

This novel is entirely a work of fiction. The names, characters and
incidents portrayed in it are the work of the author's imagination. Any
resemblance to actual persons, living or dead, events or localities is
entirely coincidental.

Printed and bound in the UK using 100% Renewable Electricity
by CPI Group (UK) Ltd

To Michael Doherty (aka Isle of Man, Sales Director) and his lovely wife, Kate, may your life be full of sunshine and love x

Chapter One

They say bad things come in threes. As of now, Lia Bathurst was officially up to five. She pressed the intercom embedded into the rough stone wall again.

For the second time, the disembodied voice floated out of the speakers. 'This is a private residence. You need to leave.'

Desperation tightened her vocal cords. 'Please, I'd just like to speak to Signor Salvatore. It will only take a minute. I promise.' All she had to do was tell him that Mary Bathurst née Harding had sent her and she was sure he'd see her. He had to. After all, she'd come all the way to Italy to see him.

'If you wish to speak to Signor Salvatore, you should book an appointment with his business manager, Signor Knight.' The intercom cut off with a finality that suggested if Lia buzzed again there would be no pick-up this time.

Sodding hell. She slumped against the wall and wiped a hand over her sweaty forehead. Back in London the far too handsome Mr Knight had been Mr Extremely Unhelpful, which is why she was now on the doorstep of Ernesto Salvatore's picturesque pink villa.

Now what? She'd just flipping walked for an hour up a road with more hairpins than Marge Simpson's updo, in thirty-degree heat, to get here. Her calves were killing her, her toes were rubbed to hell and her throat was drier than Death Valley. A sensible person might have set off with a bottle of water, but when she'd checked on Google maps, the Villa Mimosa hadn't looked very far. Technically it wasn't – if you were a crow. What she'd failed to factor in was the one-in-five slope of the tarmac ribbon that wound its way around the hillside of the Amalfi Coast.

With another sigh she eyed the stone wall enclosing what she guessed was a substantial property. It was foolish to expect anything else. Ernesto Salvatore's summer home was bound to have tight security. If she'd tracked him down on the internet, his many fans no doubt could do the same. The wall, complete with razor wire on the top, stretched along the dusty road into the distance. On the other side of the property were steep rocky outcrops that a Himalayan goat would be hard pressed to scale. Even without the sharp wire deterrent running along the top of the wall, Lia doubted she could have climbed onto it. Certainly not in her flip-flops, which had proved another totally impractical decision.

She was all out of ideas.

Coming to Italy had seemed such a good plan at the time, right up until she'd walked into her friend Luca's dilapidated studio, with sunlight streaming through the gaps in the roof, and seen the lumpy sofa bed she'd be staying on for the next few weeks and the miserable excuse for a kitchen. As for the bathroom, she didn't even want to think about the last time it had been acquainted with anything approaching bleach. Probably not in the last decade.

Uncharacteristic self-pity threatened to overwhelm her. How could everything go so wrong at the same time? This time two weeks ago, life had been peachy. Then, like dominoes falling, everything seemed to collapse. With a sniff she bent down to rub at the sore between her toes and the white liquid-filled blister that had erupted on her right foot. It was her own stupid fault for being so impetuous, and there was no bloody phone signal up here for her to even call for an Uber.

She began to limp down the road but after a couple of hundred metres had to stop. She knelt on one knee to wind a much crumpled tissue, unearthed from the bottom of her messenger bag, around her big toe to try to alleviate the rubbing. It was going to be a long and slow journey home in the heat of the mad-dogs-and-Englishmen midday sun. A battered Fiat tore past, the driver taking the corner on two wheels with all the panache of Lewis Hamilton, scattering gravel around her ankles, the backdraft lifting dust, making her cough and splutter. She caught sight of the driver and for one quick moment thought she'd seen him somewhere before. With an unexpected, and exceedingly unwelcome, jolt of her heart, she remembered a pair of vivid blue eyes and then told herself she was imagining things. Wiping her face, thinking she must look a complete sight, she straightened and watched as a pale blue Vespa put-put-

putted towards her. It was so cute and so very Italian, and despite her discomfort the sight made her smile. The scooter slowed and to her surprise stopped. The driver put down his feet on either side of the scooter and drew off the bowling ball helmet to reveal a shock of white blond curls. He resembled an angelic cherub, apart from the lively grin on his face.

'*Parla inglese*?' she asked hopefully.

'Sure do.' To her relief his accent was English, although she shouldn't have been surprised. With that mop of hair, he definitely didn't look Italian. 'You look like a damsel in distress. Can I help?' He beamed at her.

'I'm trying to get back down to Positano. Do you know if there is a bus route round here? Or how I might get a taxi?' She waved her phone. 'There's no signal.'

'Where are you headed?' he asked.

'Anywhere near the seafront.'

With alacrity, he flipped the kickstand down, hopped off the scooter and opened up the storage box on the back to pull out a helmet, which he held out in front of him as he dropped into a low bow. 'Your chariot awaits.'

She laughed.

'It's okay. I've always wanted to rescue a damsel in distress.' Dimples appeared in his cheeks, the cherub replaced by naughty choirboy. 'Here you go. I'm headed to the beach. I can give you a lift.'

'That would be brilliant,' said Lia. 'Thank you, so much.'

'No problem,' he said with an easy shrug. 'I'm going that way.' He watched as she did up the chinstrap.

'I'm Leo, by the way.'

'I'm Lia.'

'Pleased to meet you, Lia.'

'I'm very pleased to meet you. Thank you for the lift.'

'You haven't seen my driving yet.' His dark eyes sparkled with mischief. Everything about him seemed golden and sunny.

'Is it that bad?'

'Terrible, but I haven't killed anyone yet,' he said cheerfully. 'And round here everyone's driving is pretty shocking. You can't do too much damage with a Vespa.'

'It's very pretty,' observed Lia admiring the colour again.

'I know.' He winked. 'The girls love it. My brother says it's an insult to masculinity but he's very old-fashioned that way. But, hey, he doesn't have as many girlfriends as I do. What does that tell you?'

Lia wondered if perhaps he just wasn't as pretty as Leo, who exuded easy charm and happy self-confidence. He was one of those people who just made you smile.

'Come on, hop on.'

'Thank you again, this is really kind of you.'

'I know but it's all right. You can buy the ice-cream.'

'What ice-cream?' she asked with a wry smile. He really was a charmer.

'I know this lovely little gelateria on the way. I think it's probably just what you need.'

'And how do you surmise that?' she asked.

'Because everyone needs ice-cream and you were looking like you wanted to throw yourself off a cliff. Honestly, it's far too nice a day and it would make a terrible mess. You can tell me all about it over ice-cream and coffee.'

'Coffee as well now?'

'Why not?' His grin widened.

Managing a conversation from the back of the scooter was difficult and Leo seemed happy to accept her silence as she clung to the Vespa with her thighs, gripping the luggage handle with her hands. It seemed a little too personal to put her arms around the waist of a complete stranger, no matter how much he resembled an adorable puppy. She made the most of enjoying the scenery. On the arduous climb up the hill, she'd been too busy putting one foot in front of the other to appreciate the dramatic landscape of the towering rocky peaks and the houses nestled into their crevices on the side of the hills. Terracotta-tiled roofs ran across the landscape like strata in rock, as the buildings slotted into every level spot. The whole valley side reminded her of an elaborate wedding cake with hundreds of tiers.

From this height above the town, she could see right out over the bay and the huge crescent of deep, dark navy sea against the brilliant blue sky. Her heart lifted at the sight of the sun glinting on the cresting waves and she felt a little ashamed. It was a beautiful day and she should be grateful she was here. Not everyone got to spend the summer in Italy or had virtually free accommodation – even if it did leave something to be desired.

Determined to focus on the positives she concentrated

on the here and now. Leo drove with typical Italian panache, weaving in and out of the traffic, navigating with snappy precision around cars that looked more abandoned than parked, barely missing wing mirrors and the occasional car door when they were suddenly thrust open. Although the traffic through the narrow streets had slowed to the speed of treacle, Leo maintained a constant pace, veering round corners and changing direction so often that Lia had no idea where the sea was in relation to them anymore. It was hidden by the higgledy-piggledy lines of buildings hugging the contours of the steep hillside.

When Leo braked suddenly and swung the scooter onto the pavement outside a gelateria, she very nearly fell off.

'Here we are,' he said taking his helmet off and putting his feet down, balancing the scooter between his legs as he waited for Lia to dismount. 'I'm going to have a Stracciatella. Double scoop. With chocolate sauce and nuts.'

'*Per favore*?' suggested Lia, who'd been brought up with very good manners and was slightly disconcerted by his blithe assumption that it was all right to order extras when someone else was paying. Or was that a very British attitude?

The cherubic grin reappeared on his face. 'Yes, please. Come on.'

As soon as she stepped away from the scooter, he swung the helmet onto his arm and led the way into the shop.

She followed more slowly, immediately aware of the cooler air and the delicious smells of vanilla and chocolate. A glass chiller cabinet ran the whole length of the shop, filled with deep containers of different flavours of ice-cream, beautifully swirled into creamy peaks although many were marred by substantial craters indicating their popularity. Descriptions were written in neat italics in English, German and Italian: Strawberry Sunburst, Lemon Delight, Chocco Chocolate, Madagascan Vanilla, Deluxe Stracciatella, Nutella Supreme. Lia's mouth watered.

'*Ciao*, Gina,' Leo greeted the dark-haired girl behind the counter, and launched into a stream of Italian, pointing and gesticulating. Lia noticed he was in constant motion, his head bobbling as he spoke and his foot tapping as he indicated the vanilla with shavings of dark chocolate ice-cream he'd chosen.

'What are you going to have, Lia?' he asked. 'The chocolate is very good and so is the strawberry. Gina, this is Lia; she's new in town.'

'Hi,' said Gina.

'What do you recommend?' asked Lia, bemused by the choice. It all looked good and she realised she hadn't eaten since the boiled egg she'd had for breakfast. To give him some credit, Luca had at least left her some basic supplies.

'Stracciatella,' said Leo. 'I told you it's the best.'

Gina laughed. 'He never tries anything else. I suggest you should try the Nutella Supreme, it's chocolate and hazelnut. It's my favourite. But everything is good. It's all made here,' she indicated the back of the shop and a set of double doors, 'by my father.'

'Stracciatella is best,' muttered Leo again rolling his eyes good-naturedly.

'I'll try the chocolate and hazelnut,' said Lia taking the easy option but determined not to give in to Leo's quiet insistence. She really wasn't that much of an ice-cream aficionado. Ice-cream was ice-cream.

That view changed the minute she took the first taste from the overladen cone that Gina handed her.

'Oh my God, this is heavenly,' she murmured.

'Told you,' said Leo, taking a huge slurp of his own. 'Thanks, Gina.'

They wandered out onto the small sloping deck clinging to the pavement just in front of the shop, passing narrow troughs of vibrant red geraniums, the bright colour contrasting sharply with the white-painted decking. There was just room for a couple of pretty white bistro tables and chairs with heart-shaped backs.

'Mmm, that is wonderful,' said Lia as the rich chocolate swamped her tongue. It might just have been the best ice-cream she'd ever tasted, although how could it not be, sitting in bright sunshine in Italy with a handsome companion.

'Told you. But next time you should try the Stracciatella.'

'Has anyone told you that you're like a dog with a bone?' she teased.

'No,' he replied airily. 'I just know what I like.'

She laughed. He was very easy company and – she realised – the first person she'd spoken to properly in a couple of days.

'So do you live here?' she asked.

'Just for the summer. My family have a place here. We always come. But it's no hardship. Positano is the most beautiful town on the Amalfi coast.' He stopped with a wicked grin and then added, 'Apart from Minori, Ravello,

Amalfi, Cetara and Furore, to name but a few. Have you seen any of them?'

'Not yet. I only arrived two days ago.' She'd barely had time to get her bearings in Positano. 'I'm still trying to find my way around. It's quite confusing.' The steep hillside was riddled with tiny narrow lanes that twisted and turned at regular intervals, teeming with boutiques and little shops spilling their wares onto the street.

'But you like it?' he asked.

'I love it!' She beamed at him.

'So you are on holiday?'

'Not exactly.' Lia decided that it was probably best to be circumspect with the truth for the time being. She suspected that the locals might be quite protective of their famous residents. 'I'm an artist. I've borrowed a friend's studio for a couple of months.'

'An artist. You don't look like one.' He tilted his head to one side. 'You're far too pretty to be starving in a garret.'

'What does an artist look like?' asked Lia, laughing.

'I don't know,' admitted Leo, his eyes crinkling. 'Starving and gaunt? And maybe covered in paint. That's a very lovely dress.'

Lia smoothed down the pale sage fabric, fingering the delicate embroidery she'd spent ages completing. It was one of her favourites. 'Thank you,' she said, deciding he probably wouldn't be that interested to know she'd made it herself.

'So how long will you be artisting here?'

Lia sighed, her mouth turning down. 'Good question.' She thought ruefully of the very basic creature comforts of the studio she'd borrowed. On the plus side, it had a lot of the equipment she needed and the space to work.

'You don't know?' The sympathy in his eyes made her open up.

'I'm looking for inspiration for a new commission and I don't know if I'll find it.'

'That sounds bad. You can't be unhappy in Positano. What do you need to be inspired about? Maybe I could show you around?'

'That would be great.'

'We have so much beautiful scenery, I'm sure something will come to you.'

Lia nodded, relieved that he didn't ask any questions. It still stung that the Braganzi restaurant had rejected her initial designs for the commission for its new restaurant in London. After the restaurant's phenomenal success in New York, the London venue was due to open in September and the Italian husband and wife owners were looking for exceptional artwork to dress the walls. Lia had been thrilled to be invited to submit some initial designs. She'd been less than thrilled by the feedback.

She screwed up her face as she recalled the verdict relayed via her agent. 'Not aspirational enough', 'needs to be more visceral', followed by 'frankly a bit dull.' They hadn't pulled any punches, and what the hell did 'not aspirational enough' mean? Thankfully they were still interested in her work and were willing to wait a few weeks for her to submit some new ideas. Unfortunately that deadline had been like the kiss of death, sucking every creative thought out of her head. Since then she hadn't been able to think of a single idea. It was as if her brain had been wiped clean of anything new or different.

She realised she was pulling faces and that Leo was staring at her with bewildered fascination.

After a moment, he said, 'It might never happen, you know.'

Lia gave him a rueful smile. She had a feeling that Leo didn't really want to know about her problems.

'There's lots to paint around here. I'm sure you'll find something.'

'I don't paint.' She smiled; it was a common misconception. 'I'm a textile artist. I create pieces from different fabrics, so they have texture and depth.' She loved talking about her work and was proud that she was garnering growing interest, but she wanted commercial recognition as well. That damn commission would be the icing on the cake, if she could just secure it.

'Oh,' said Leo, clearly uninterested.

'What do you do? Are you a student?'

Leo laughed. 'No. I'm older than I look. I'm spending the summer paddleboarding.'

That explained the sun-bleached hair, although Lia hadn't realised it was a job. 'What? You teach paddleboarding?'

'No, I'm a complete layabout, but I'm trying not get too worried about it. You only live once. I'll work out what I want to do eventually. Did you always know you wanted to be a … what was it? A material artist? I mean how do you get into that? I didn't even know it was a thing. It is a thing, isn't it?'

'It is a thing,' she agreed, smiling at his slightly worried look. 'And no, I didn't know I wanted to be a textile artist until I was at art college and I discovered it. I fell in love.'

'How wonderful. I've been in love loads of times. It never lasts,' he added with such weary sadness that she burst out laughing.

He grinned. 'My brother says I'm incredibly shallow but then he's a miserable git. I suppose someone in the family has to be the sensible one. It's never going to be me.'

Lia could relate to that, being the only arty one in her family. Although now she understood why she was the odd one out.

'So how old are you?'

'You're not supposed to ask a lady how old she is.'

'I'll tell if you do.'

It wasn't a big deal for Lia. At thirty, she was … well, until recently, she'd always been comfortable with who she was and where she was going. In fact, until that stupid email two weeks ago, her whole life had been terribly simple.

Chapter Two

The cooing of the pigeon in the roof woke Lia the next morning and she stretched, trying to unknot the kinks in her back, convinced Luca's bed was half mattress and half abandoned bricks. She rolled to her feet and stood on tiptoe. Over the roofs of the surrounding houses, she could just see the sea. It was still there, she mused with a smile. Despite her complaints about Casa Dia's accommodation, as a studio it was perfect. The light streamed in over the well laid out tables and equipment and, given that it was perched on the top of another building like a rook's nest on a ship, it was ideal for her work.

Today she was going to start work, or at least play around with a few bits of fabric. Perhaps if she immersed herself in the beauty of this place, her brain might relax and cough up an idea or two.

She made do with a quick cup of coffee – thank you,

Luca, for the freshly ground coffee and the French press, which was about the only piece of catering equipment he possessed – promising herself she'd go out for a pastry and a cappuccino down by the beach mid-morning. She might also hunt Leo down as he'd said he'd be on the beach all day. Given he was fun, cheerful company and the closest thing she had to a friend right now, it wouldn't do any harm. Perhaps he might even have an idea of how she might meet Ernesto Salvatore. Leo clearly knew the area well, so it was possible he might know which restaurants or bars Ernesto frequented.

With a little frisson of hope and excitement, she laid her suitcase on the large draftsman board. Customs would have been surprised by the contents, she thought as she opened it, the fabrics spilling out in rainbows of colour, myriad shapes and an extensive array of textures.

Her original designs had incorporated elements of famous Italian buildings – the windows and tiers of Ponte Vecchio, the spires and domes of the Vatican City, the fountains of Rome, the wedding-cake tiers of Pisa – but the Braganzis had said they weren't evocative enough of Italy.

An hour later, the table was covered in combinations of materials but nothing felt quite right. When it was, she'd know. It was a gut thing that she found impossible to explain to anyone else.

After a quick shower, she put on a flowing silk dress – another one of her own designs – and skipped down the steps to the narrow street directly below Casa Dia. Thank goodness Luca's sister had met her at the bus stop when she'd arrived, otherwise she'd never have found this place. After several sharp twists and turns, the alleyway brought her out just near the beach. The row of restaurants on the front was already busy with people and she sauntered along past the tables inhaling the aroma of coffee and listening to the happy hum of chatter. The sun warmed her skin and the sensation brought back some of her usual optimism.

Lia grinned to herself, enjoying the swish of the turquoise silk around her legs and the weight of her hair hanging down her back in a long plait. There were plenty of admiring glances as she walked along the front, probably due to the white blond hair, which she'd inherited from her mother's Scandinavian genes – all twenty-five per cent of them – and the olive skin – an unusual combination – along with her green eyes. She now knew the latter came from genes that did not belong to the man she'd always called Dad. Her expression hardened. It was hard to discover that your whole life had been a lie.

'Hey, Lia!'

The bellow from the café she'd just walked past made her turn and she saw Leo waving to her from one of the small tables at the front.

'Hi, Leo.'

'I was hoping I'd run into you today. Have you had breakfast?'

'No.'

Leo pushed a chair out with his foot. She gathered it was an invitation. 'This place does excellent *cornetti al cioccolato* and *cornetto alla marmellata* – that's with apricot jam.' Before she'd even taken the seat, he hailed a waiter. 'What will you have, Lia?'

'*Cornetto alla marmellata* and a cappuccino, *per favore*.'

'I'll take a *cornetto al cioccolato* and a double espresso.'

The waiter nodded and as he left, Lia leaned forward and whispered conspiratorially, 'And what is a *cornetto*? I'm guessing we're not having ice-cream for breakfast.'

'No! That is an abomination. A real *cornetto* is a traditional Italian pastry. *Cornetto* means horn but it is not like a croissant, which is a common mistake. The dough is sweeter and softer. Much better,' he added with a defiant lift of his chin.

'I wouldn't dare argue,' teased Lia.

'So what plans do you have today?' asked Leo. 'It's a good day to spend on the beach.' He gave her a hopeful grin. 'I could tell you all the best places to visit.'

Lia wrinkled her nose, sorely tempted.

'Go on, you know you want to.'

'Your English is very good.'

'Ha! That's because I am half English. You don't think this hair came from my Italian side, do you? I can tell you're English,' he teased tugging her plait.

'Actually I'm half Italian,' she said, skimming over the angst the unexpected discovery had caused. 'I did one of those DNA tests. Fifty per cent Italian, twenty-five per cent Norwegian and odd bits of English, Welsh, Irish and Northern European.'

The casual words belied the world of upset that had

followed the discovery. Her whole life turned out to one big fat lie and she couldn't even claim it was a relief to find out why she had always felt different from the rest of the family. Understanding the basis of that gnawing ache of not quite belonging brought no satisfaction. She wondered what Leo would say if she told him she was actually the daughter of the famous Italian film star Ernesto Salvatore.

'Like me,' Leo exclaimed delightedly, completely oblivious to Lia's inner turmoil. She couldn't bring herself to speak to her mother at the moment; there was so much stored-up anger that she was scared would spill over and she might say something she'd regret.

'No one ever believes I'm Italian,' Leo continued. 'Although sometimes it's quite useful.' He gave a naughty wink. 'Especially when I don't admit I speak Italian.'

Lia could quite believe it. With that mop of golden surfer-boy curls, he probably caught the eye of all the local Italian women.

Leo showed no further interest in the DNA test, which was actually a bit of a relief. The results had blindsided her, turning everything she thought she knew upside down. How could her mum have lied to her all this time?

Having lived with the drama, and shared the shock with her closest friends, it was actually nice to be away from it all, to just be herself and not worry about what it all meant. Avoiding her mother, father and sister on the phone was probably a bit harsh but she just needed some time, and in her last conversation with her mum she'd asked that they give her that. Learning that your dad wasn't your dad at all took some getting used to.

Would she ever get used to it?

She glanced down at her phone and almost laughed out loud. Her dad had sent her a GIF of that horrid child from *Finding Nemo* tapping on the fish tank in the dentist's waiting room, with the caption: *Are you still alive?*

Quickly, she sent him one back with a caption *I'm not dead* and then put her phone down as the waiter reappeared balancing a tray on one hand. He slid the plates of *cornetti* in front of them along with their coffees, and her stomach let out an inelegant rumble of appreciation at the sight of the small, curved, egg-washed pastry. The dinner of bread, cheese and salami the previous evening hadn't been terribly substantial.

'Maybe you should have ordered two,' said Leo, laughing at her.

'A gentleman wouldn't have commented,' said Lia reprovingly, which made Leo laugh even more.

'You don't think I'm a gentleman, do you? That sounds very boring.'

Lia shook her head. She doubted anyone had ever called Leo boring. With his lively energy and sunny nature, he was probably the life and soul of every party.

Suddenly he jerked his head up. 'Hey, Raph!' He jumped to his feet waving. 'Over here!' Lia turned to see who he was calling over as Leo supplied, 'It's my brother.'

A tall dark-haired man began to weave his way through the tables.

'Morning, Leo. How…' His voice died as he spotted Lia, who was doing her best to sink through the floor.

'You!'

'Mr Knight.' Lia gave a curt nod. She did not flipping believe it. Of all the crap-bad luck.

'Oh,' said Leo, with a delighted smile. 'You two already know each other.'

Chapter Three

'Not exactly,' drawled Raph, irritation prickling through him like a nettle rash. 'What are *you* doing here?'

The cool blonde lifted her head and gave him a direct look that said she wasn't the least bit intimidated by him. More was the pity. 'Having breakfast,' she said.

'Small world,' burbled Leo, oblivious as always to the undertones, and Raph bit back a snort of annoyance. His younger brother breezed through life on a golden sunbeam. Everything in his world was perpetually happy. Which on one hand was great, but Raph nurtured a concern that if something truly bad did happen, he'd not have the resilience to cope with it.

'We're going to the beach after this. Do you want to come with us?' asked Leo through a mouthful of his pastry.

'Yes, do. That would be so much fun.' The woman smirked as she put down her coffee cup.

'Although you'll have to lose the suit, bro.'

Raph ignored his brother and stared down his nose at the woman. For some reason she disconcerted him. She'd got under his skin the first time they'd met in his offices in London, and since then he hadn't been able to put his finger on what it was that caused the low-level buzz of awareness of her, which consequently pissed him off even more. It had been like a thorn needling him. He didn't like not being in complete control.

He narrowed his gaze at her oh-so-innocent face. She sat there as serene as a Madonna, her lovely eyes meeting his with a touch of disdain, as if she felt sorry for him.

He knew he'd been a bit harsh with her, refusing to listen to her story, but she was one of many women who'd claimed Ernesto Salvatore was their father, and now here she was sucking up to his brother. She was clearly yet another one hoping to convince him to pay her off, to avoid a paternity claim against his stepfather.

'Bro?'

Raph realised he'd missed something Leo had said and now his brother was getting to his feet.

'I said, keep Lia company while I...' He indicated the toilets at the back of the bar area.

'Certainly. It will my pleasure,' he replied grimly.

'Why don't I think that it will be mine?' murmured the woman.

As soon as Leo was out of earshot, he turned to her. 'What the hell do you think you're playing at? Stay away from my family. That includes Leo.'

'I didn't know he was anything to do with you.' Two bright spots of colour burned on her cheeks.

'You seriously expect me to believe that you travelled all the way to Italy and you just happened to bump into him?'

She caught her lip between her teeth and stared up at him. 'I know what it looks like, but it's the truth.'

'Go home. You're wasting your time. I won't allow my stepfather to be blackmailed again.'

'Your stepfather? I thought you were his business manager.'

'Not officially, no.' Although sometimes he felt like he was. 'He's married to my mother so I help with some of his business affairs when they're of a more personal nature. I have my own work.'

'So you're related to him.'

Raph sighed. 'Only by marriage.'

'You're very protective of him,' she said.

'I've had to be.' He glared at Lia again. 'I've told you already, the only way you'll get within ten feet of Ernesto is with a DNA test.'

'That will take months,' she said, 'and I wouldn't put it past you to delay things or lie about the results.'

His temper flared. How dare she? 'I wouldn't need to lie about the results.'

'So you think. Have you even spoken to Ernesto?'

'Do you have any idea how many women have claimed he's their father?'

'You told me in your office, remember? But if you'd just talk to him, you'd know this is different. Just tell him my mother's name. Mary Bathurst née Harding. They had a relationship in London in the nineties – 1993, to be precise. Ask him.'

'Ernesto isn't the sort of man that would abandon a child. He would have taken responsibility.'

'Well, he didn't. If I do a test, will you let me speak to him?'

'Only if the test results prove your claim.'

She glared at him. 'Like I've already said, that will take ages.'

Raph gave her insolent shrug. 'What's the hurry?'

Her mouth settled in a mutinous line before she said with some heat, her bright eyes burning with conviction, 'How would you feel if you discovered you had a father you didn't know? Would you be content to wait? You have no idea what it feels like.'

He had to give her credit, she got an A star for persistence and for acting ability. It almost tugged at his heartstrings. Almost.

'I presume you've relayed this sob story to Leo.'

'Of course I haven't. I didn't even know he knew him.'

'Well, now you do. But I'm warning you, you won't get anywhere near Ernesto through Leo. If I were you, I'd pack my bags and go back to London.'

She gave him the sort of sweet smile that suggested she'd just as soon slide a dagger through his ribs. 'Does everyone do what you tell them to?'

He almost laughed out loud at that one. If only his bloody family did. It would make his life so much easier.

He stood for a minute, loath to let her have the last word, and then he spotted Leo coming back and hurried forward to intercept him.

'Leo, do you know anything about this woman?'

'What, Lia? I know she's an artist. Spending the summer here for inspiration.'

God, Leo could be obtuse at times. 'I might have known.' Because anyone with a proper job wouldn't be able to drop everything at the chance of meeting their very wealthy alleged father. Not that he believed it was true for a minute. 'Where did you meet her?'

'Near the villa. She was limping down the road so I stopped and offered her a lift.'

Raph cast his eyes heavenward. 'And you didn't think it strange that she was loitering outside the villa?'

Leo thought about it for a moment. 'No, not really. She smiled at me.'

'And…' There was no understanding Leo's logic sometimes.

'She looked a bit lost and I was going into town anyway.'

'Stay away from her. She's another one after a paternity claim.'

'No,' said Leo scornfully. 'She's really nice. You are so paranoid. I told you I just bumped into her.'

'And she didn't mention she'd already been to see me in London?'

'No. Why would she? She didn't know who I was.' Leo's smile dimmed and Raph felt a little guilty spoiling his illusion.

'Sorry, Leo, she was using you.'

Leo swallowed and Raph felt like he'd kicked a kitten.

'Do you want a lift home? I can send Marco down for

the Vespa in the truck,' he suggested, knowing the gardener wouldn't mind.

Leo looked over his shoulder towards Lia, his mouth twisting ruefully. 'I'd better pay the bill.'

'Serves her right if she has to pay.'

'She paid for the ice-creams yesterday.'

'I bet she did. Reeling you in.'

'And what if you're wrong? Not everyone has an ulterior motive. What if she does just want to meet Ernesto? What if she's been told he's her dad and she believes it, even if it's not true?'

'None of that explains why she came haring out here after I'd told her that the best thing would be to arrange a paternity test.'

Leo sighed. 'I'll go back on the Vespa later. I'm going out on the board for a little while.'

Raph watched as with slumped shoulders his brother walked back to the table. He exchanged a couple of words with Lia, she laughed and they both looked over at him as Leo opened his wallet and pulled out a couple of Euro notes, which he placed on the table. Lia shot Raph a pitying smirk, waved goodbye to Leo, who grinned at her, pulled her sunglasses down over her eyes and picked up her phone, focusing all her attention on the screen. Raph allowed himself a small smile, amused by her cool dismissal. He wasn't going to let her go without finding out how long she planned to stick around.

He sat down at the table in the seat vacated by Leo.

She ignored him for a moment and he took the time to study her. That buzz of awareness was back, the hairs on the back of his neck rising. Today her blond hair was in a loose plait with tendrils escaping in every direction around her face as if they couldn't bear to be confined. He wondered if it mirrored her personality. She struck him as impulsive as well as dogged and determined. He couldn't decide whether he was impressed or annoyed by her persistence.

'How long do you plan to hang around?' he asked, finally frustrated by her ability to remain unperturbed by his presence.

She grinned at him. 'What, like a bad smell?'

'You're wasting your time.'

'Who says I'm wasting my time? It's already proving productive.'

'You mean leeching on Leo.'

'Actually no. You have a one-track mind – and you don't seem to have a very high opinion of your brother, do you?'

He bristled. 'I never said that.'

'No, but you clearly think he's too weak or stupid to spot a gold-digger.'

'Leo's a nice guy. He tends to see the good in people.'

'Whereas you, Dark Lord, see the bad? Are you always this suspicious of people or is it just me?'

Raph considered her words. Something made him reply honestly. 'I tend to be suspicious of people, but based on previous experience, it's justified.'

'Really? How depressing,' she said, propping her chin in her hands and giving such a mournful sigh that he almost laughed.

The quick irreverence and sense of fun made him warm to her, even though he didn't want to like her.

'How old are you?' he asked suddenly.

'Thirty, why?'

'Why now? Why do you suddenly want to contact … your father?

'You were dying to put those air quotes round "your father", weren't you?' She grinned up at him. It was a tough job to try and stay on track with her.

He didn't say anything, just left her to fill the silence, which he was confident she would. Nothing seemed to daunt her but to his surprise her face saddened and he saw her throat move as if she were swallowing hard.

'I didn't know before. I only just found out.' There was a wealth of pain and sadness in her soft words which tugged at him and he found himself wanting to comfort her. Especially as he knew there was only further heartache ahead when she discovered that Ernesto really wasn't her father. There was no way he could be, of that, Raph was one hundred per cent sure.

She lifted her head. 'I ought to get back to work.'

'Where are you staying?'

She laughed. 'I haven't a clue. I only know how to get there.'

As she rose, he fell into step beside her.

'Are you going to escort me home?' she asked.

'No, I'm headed this way. I parked down the road.'

She tilted her head and looked at him. 'I can't see you on a little blue Vespa. Please tell me yours is black with decal flames on it.'

Now he did laugh. 'How did you know?'

'Call it intuition,' she said with a smirk, her brown eyes dancing with mischief.

He suddenly wanted to lean down and kiss her – just to see what her reaction would be, of course, nothing more. Because Lia really wasn't his type. He preferred glossy, sophisticated women who were cool and contained, or at least … he always had done in the past…

Chapter Four

R aph arrived back at the villa to a full-scale shouting match. As soon as he stepped out of the Ferrari onto the paved driveway in front of the villa, he could hear his mother's voice at an unusually loud volume coming from the side of the house. What's more, Ernesto was shouting back at her. What on earth was going on? He hurried towards the source of the commotion, rounding the building to find the two of them standing toe to toe on the vine-laden veranda.

He winced as the loud Italian words coalesced into meaning.

'Don't think you can leave me, you bastard. I will chop you into little pieces and feed you to the fish.'

'You think,' said Ernesto with scorn.

Raph stopped dead and shook his head. Some days it was like living in Bedlam. Today was clearly one of them.

'I know,' yelled his mother, Aurelia, with all the melodrama of a third-rate actor murdering appalling lines –

though she was no actress. She waved a fist in Ernesto's face 'You're a two-timing rat bastard with a very small...' With her forefinger and thumb, she intimated her meaning and then broke off into giggles.

Ernesto caught her hand and kissed it and the two of them began to laugh uproariously together. Raph caught sight of the sheaf of curled papers they each held in their other hands and sighed.

'Ah, Raph,' Ernesto greeted him. 'We were just trying out Matteo's latest masterpiece. What do you think?'

'Dreadful. I don't know why you keep humouring him and offering to read his stuff. Wouldn't it be kinder to put him out of his misery? He's never going to write a decent script.'

'What, and kill all his hope?' Ernesto shook his head. 'I will give him some constructive feedback and...' – he sighed – '... hopefully he will try again and maybe—'

'Darling,' interrupted Aurelia. 'Maybe Raph is right and you should stop encouraging him. I don't think he's got what it takes. He's much better behind the camera.'

'You're right, my love. He's the best Head of Photography I've ever worked with. I need to remind him of that. Perhaps you can help me write him an email, Raph. You're so good at that sort of thing.'

'An excellent idea.' His mother bestowed a sweet smile upon him. 'You always know the right thing to say and you're very diplomatic. Which reminds me, do you know if all the invitations have gone out? Signora Cavalli says she hasn't received one.'

'That's because you took her off the guest list,' Raph

pointed out. As usual he was helping to organise the annual Salvatore summer party.

'Well, I think she should go back on,' said Aurelia. 'What happened last year wasn't her fault. Would you mind making sure an invitation goes out today?'

'Mamma, you do remember you and Ernesto have a secretary for this sort of thing? She's still able to work remotely.'

'Yes, darling, but she's nowhere near as efficient as you.'

Raph rolled his eyes. 'Maybe you should get rid of her then.'

'Raphael Knight. How could you say such a thing?' his mother scolded. 'Esther is part of the family. The only reason she isn't here this summer is because her niece is being christened.'

'I'll see to it,' he said with resignation, turning to head for the little salon he used as an office whenever he was here. Over the years, it had acquired more and more equipment and he could run his business just as easily from here as from his official office in London.

'Before you go...' his mother started. He turned. Ernesto was earnestly checking the flagstones. 'Will you be bringing anyone to the party?'

'No,' he said.

'You're very welcome to, if there's anyone you would like to invite? They could stay. There is plenty of room.' One didn't snort at one's mamma, but her understatement was breathtaking. The villa could sleep twenty-two quite easily and that didn't include either of the two self-contained guest suites in the grounds – one of which he'd taken up residence in, as he liked to maintain a semblance of independence whenever he visited. It seemed only fitting at the age of thirty-one.

'Mamma, there is no one I would like to invite to the party or to stay at the villa.'

Ernesto risked looking up and exchanged a wink with him. Unfazed by his short reply, his mother simply said, 'You will join us for lunch, won't you?'

'Yes, Mamma.'

'Good boy.' Her eyes twinkled at him and before he could make his usual protest she held up her hand and said as she always did, 'You'll always be my boy.' With that she sailed off inside the house.

Raph expelled a quick breath.

'She only wants what's best for you,' said Ernesto with a smile.

'I don't see why she's not holding out for Leo.'

Ernesto patted Raph on the arm. 'He's still a baby himself.'

'No, he's not. He's a grown man … or rather he would be if you all let him be.' Leo might be twenty-seven but he still had a lot of growing up to do.

'Would settling down be such a bad thing?' asked Ernesto, a frown marring his forehead. 'It made a man of me. I can't imagine my life now without your mother and our family. It has brought me much joy.'

Raph clapped him on the shoulder. Ernesto had been like a father to Leo and him and had treated the two brothers and their subsequent four half-brothers and sisters equally.

'And you have brought my mother much joy, for which I can never thank you enough.'

Ernesto's eyes welled with tears and he embraced Raph. 'We are family.'

Raph nodded. While he rarely said it out loud, there was no denying that he loved his family fiercely … even though they all drove him crazy most of the time.

'Now –' Ernesto draped an arm around his shoulder '– let's see what your mother has cooked for lunch today.'

Chapter Five

L ia tossed down her pencil. Enough was enough. She
wanted to go out and play. The idea she'd been
working on all day just wasn't doing it for her any more.
She was bored by it and if she was bored then how could
she convince anyone else it was any good? Despite working
every day for the last week – playing with bits of fabric,
sketching ideas, walking through the narrow lanes and
drinking far too much coffee – she was still waiting for
inspiration to strike. She needed a break, from her own
company as much as from anything else.

Her dad had sent her another one of his GIFs. A man of
few words, it was their way of communicating. For a
moment she dithered about where to go, before deciding
she'd head to the beach – not the main one where she'd
seen Leo paddleboarding in the distance a couple of times,
but the one at Fornillo, which was a ten-minute walk. Leo
had told her that her brother thought she was using him
and she was determined to prove Raphael Knight wrong.

The problem was that now she knew Leo was connected with Ernesto, she did want to use him, but she couldn't bear the thought of the disappointment in Leo's puppy-dog eyes.

———————

It actually took considerably longer than ten minutes to reach the beach because she was distracted by the shops that opened directly onto the narrow streets. Bougie dress boutiques with glamorous sundresses, gorgeous potteries with brightly painted earthenware, and family-run shops selling olive oil. Her favourite was one dedicated to lemons, with bright white dishes, napkins and tablecloths embellished with the shiny yellow fruit, and bottles of cloudy Limoncello. The smell was clean and fresh, and as she prowled round the shop touching the embroidered lemons and examining coasters with cross sections of the inside pulp, a glimmer of an idea began to float in the back of her head. But like mist, when she tried to grasp it, it vanished. Before she left she treated herself to a lemon-scented soap and one of the sweet little dishes covered in lemon fruit.

Satisfied with her purchases, she vowed not to stop again until she reached her destination. She was itching to get to the beach and make a couple of sketches, and her enthusiasm made her want to hurry, but it was impossible in the busy streets, which were crowded with tourists, all of whom appeared to have all the time in the world as they meandered across her path. When her phone rang in her bag it was a bit of a relief, something to divert her impatience. Until she looked at the screen.

Mum. Again.

Lia's conscience poked her – hard. She ought to speak to her mother but she really didn't want to. In their last conversation, Lia had told her she needed some time to come to terms with her new reality. She still had nothing to say that they hadn't already said. Worse still, her mother would know from the ringtone that Lia wasn't in England. Her heart nose-dived to the balls of her feet; her mother was going to be so hurt that Lia had gone off to Italy without discussing it with her.

A world of guilt swamped her, which she tried to resist. It wasn't her fault her mother had lied to her all this time. She shoved her phone to the bottom of her beach bag, swung it over her shoulder and picked up her pace, brooding as she walked.

The day the DNA results came back would be forever branded into her head. Her friend Izzy had been writing an article about the numbers of people who were using DNA tests to discover more about their heritage and long-lost family members. Izzy had asked Lia and three other friends if they'd be willing to do the tests to see what sort of results came back among a group of people who'd grown up together from the same part of London.

It was supposed to be a laugh and provide some material for Izzy's feature, but instead a bombshell had blown up in Lia's face when that email arrived. Her DNA was fifty per cent Italian, which hadn't made any sense. Curious rather than alarmed, Lia, who was having lunch with her mother that week anyway, brought it up over their first glass of Prosecco.

'Did you know I'm half Italian?'

All the colour leached out of her mother's face.

'Mum?' Lia leaned over and touched her mum's cold hand lying limply on the marble table top.

Her mother stared at her but didn't say anything.

'I don't quite understand how it all works but Izzy says it's really unusual to have such a high percentage of a single nationality these days. Did you know you or Dad had Italian ancestors? Mum? Are you all right?'

Her mother was concertinaing her napkin between her fingers, looking off into the middle distance.

Then the penny dropped. If there was no Italian ancestry in either her mother or her father…

'I'm not adopted, am I?' The words popped out before she could stop them, before she was able to pick through the idea to examine it properly. But that couldn't be right. Lia looked just like her mother, with the same blond hair, the same shaped eyes, albeit green rather than blue, and the same small, neat chin. But her olive skin was different and she suddenly realised she couldn't attribute it to either parent.

'No, you're not a–dop–ted.' The word was split into telling syllables as her mother's eyes pleaded. For what?

In that moment, Lia knew that a chasm had opened up right beneath her feet.

'Not adopted but…?' She stared at her mother, a little lump of uncertainty lodging itself firmly in her chest, growing colder by the second, like the coming of an ice age. 'Dad?' That couldn't be right. Simon Bathurst was her dad, always had been. He taught her to read before she even went to school, he always made home-made crinkle-cut chips with a pastry cutter for Saturday evening tea, he brought her cups of hot chocolate when she was revising for exams.

Lia wanted to shake her mother, dislodge the truth from her with a Heimlich manoeuvre.

'Mum?' she prompted, fearful now. 'Were you … assaulted?'

'God, no.' Her mother grasped her throat in shock. 'No, no. You were conceived in love. Never doubt that.'

'But not with Dad.'

Her mother shook her head so slightly that her hair didn't even shift.

Lia stared at her, the sound of the restaurant around them receding to a dull buzz. She felt disconnected, cut off from reality and the rest of the world. Lia stumbled to her feet, almost tripping over the chair legs.

'Lia!' Her mother's sharp cry barely pierced the weird shell around her. She needed air.

On shaking legs she manoeuvred her way through the tables, heading for the door with singled-minded focus. Once outside she leaned against the wall, the sound of the traffic loud in her ears.

'Lia, darling.' Her mother had taken her arm. 'Lia.'

Her mother steered her back inside and ordered two brandies.

'Drink this.'

She knocked her own back in one gulp as Lia sipped at the fiery liquid, which burned her insides.

'So who is my father?'

With a heavy sigh her mother, toying with the brandy glass, began, 'He was an Italian actor working in London. We went out for four months and I accidentally got pregnant. I discovered just after he'd been offered a part in Hollywood. It was a big deal. Really big. He had to go but he said he would send money and stay in touch.'

'Let me guess. He didn't.'

Mum smiled a little ruefully. 'Actually, he did. He was very good. But when I met your father, a few weeks later, we knew straightaway that we were in it for the long haul. He was quite happy to take me and you on and once we were married everyone assumed you were his. Your birth father wanted to stay in touch and to see you but I told him it was fairer on everyone if he stayed away. Over the years it just didn't seem important … and by then we'd left it too late to tell you.'

Maybe not important to them, but it mattered to Lia.

The familiar pang of emptiness brought on by the memories made her stop in the street, the other tourists tutting as they were forced to steer their way around her. A couple of days after that lunch, her mother had posted an old photograph to her. The black and white picture showed a considerably younger Mary and an extremely handsome man with a head of dark curls, a broad build and limited height. The Post-it note on the back read: 'This is your father – Ernesto Salvatore. He can be contacted via his business manager, Raphael Knight.'

Lia met with Raphael Knight the very next day. It didn't go well. Hence her impulsive trip. And now here she was in Italy and no further forward. She needed to get that photo into the hands of Ernesto, and though she currently had no idea what her next step should be, she wasn't going to give up.

Chapter Six

Even though it was four in the afternoon, the sun warmed her skin as she hit the beach. Supine, languid, oiled bodies lay on their towels grouped around parasol sticks buried in the sand. Lia chose a quiet spot a little closer to the sea and marked out her territory with her towel, beach bag and a little cooler bag with a couple of cans of Coke and a small treat of one of the *sfogliatelle ricce* stuffed with hazelnut praline she'd picked up at the bakery this morning because she couldn't resist them. With their layers of crisp puff pastry they resembled lobster tails. The first one she'd eaten with her morning coffee in the studio and this one she'd saved as an afternoon snack

She stripped off her scarlet jersey beach dress to reveal an orange bikini she'd had for ages. She loved this colour, as bright as citrus and as warm as sunshine. Sadly, the requisite feminine curves had bypassed her: she was almost as straight as Leo's paddle board, with barely any waist. Her sister had a proper curvaceous figure, just like her mother's, with boobs, tiny waist and rounded hips, which Lia envied, but Stacey never stopped criticising her own shape or complaining that Lia had it so much easier because she could eat what she liked and never change. She'd always wondered how they could look so different but now she knew: Stacey was only her half-sister. The familiar pang of pain twisted inside Lia's chest. And Dad wasn't her dad. They were the family, not her. Everything had changed and she didn't belong any more, despite what her sister had said last time Lia had seen her.

Of course you're still my sister,' Stacey had insisted, when they'd met in the café around the corner from their family home. 'I just know where the weird comes from now.'

'Thanks,' Lia had replied, lifting her shaking hand to drink her coffee. The news had rocked her world but Stacey didn't seem to see it the same way. 'Thanks a lot.' The bitterness in her voice had been apparent.

'Oh Lia. I'm only joking. It's a shock to me, too, but I don't understand why you can't just carry on as normal and why you're so mad at Mum. I think you're being a bit unfair on her.'

That accusation had been like a punch to the stomach.

'Unfair!' Lia had cried. 'How can you say that?'

Stacey had shrugged. 'There are two sides to every story.'

Lia had blinked back furious tears. 'You don't understand. It doesn't impact you.' The ugly resentment spilled out. 'You're all still family. I'm the outsider. Simon is not my dad. He's your dad.'

She banished the memory, determined not to let self-pity drag her under.

Lia took a deliberate bite of the *sfogliatella*, savouring the loud, satisfying crunch of the crisp pastry shell and enjoying the sweet filling as it oozed over her tongue. She closed her eyes and sighed. Focus on the good things in life, she told herself, pushing away the negative thoughts. When she opened them to scan the horizon, she spotted Leo carrying his board down the beach towards her on his way to the water's edge. He saw her at the same moment and lifted a cheery hand in greeting, very nearly dropping the board under his arm.

'*Ciao*, Lia,' he called. 'Haven't seen you all week. Where've you been?'

He came straight over and dumped his board, sitting down next to her, his elbows perched on his knees.

'Working,' she lied. She'd been avoiding him but now after spending nearly a week on her own she was desperate for company.

'You know what they say about all work…' He gave her a mischievous grin.

'And it's true,' she agreed mournfully before smiling back at him. 'I'm bored with being dull.'

'I've seen you a couple of times on the other beach. In the distance. Why didn't you come over and say hello?'

'Because I needed to work,' she said. *And she didn't want him to believe what his brother thought of her.*

'Fancy going for a drink in an hour's time? I know a great place that does a wicked Aperol spritz. You have to try them.'

'Who doesn't love an Aperol? But I thought you were supposed to stay away from me. Your brother seemed quite clear.'

Leo waved an irreverent hand. 'Do I look like I ever do what I'm told?'

Lia grinned back at him, although she had a feeling that when Raphael Knight cracked the whip everyone jumped. He had that commanding air, which normally wouldn't appeal to her at all, but there was something reassuringly solid and reliable about him, which she (annoyingly) found attractive. Maybe it was because everything she'd once thought solid and reliable had been pulled out from under her feet, all the things she'd once taken for granted proven to be lies.

'I'm just going out on the board,' said Leo, oblivious to her inner thoughts, 'but I'll swing by and collect you when I'm done.'

'Perfect,' said Lia. The evening was looking up.

She watched him as he loped over the sand to the sea and set up the board before towing it out with strong swimming strokes. She noticed quite a few admiring glances from some of the younger women on the beach and looked afresh at him. In his tropical board shorts with the light gold tan across his lean body and that crowning glory of golden hair, she could see he was quite attractive. Funny she hadn't thought of him in that way at all, unlike the man coming across the sand away to her left. Now *he* was something to look at.

Dark sunglasses framed a masculine face with a strong square chin, his deep brown hair was slicked back, and in plain navy shorts he cut an altogether earthier and sexier figure. From behind her own sunglasses she studied him, watching his muscular legs, sprinkled with dark hair, cover the sand at a steady pace. His skin was burnished with a deep mahogany tan and his broad chest was subtly defined by muscles. He sauntered with an innate self-confidence – clearly a man who knew who he was, what he wanted and where he was going.

He dropped his towel and sunglasses onto the sand just before the water's edge and strode into the sea, diving into the water, his body a sleek arrow. Lia almost wanted to fan herself. When he crested the waves, he shook the water out of his face and she smiled to herself appreciatively. It was rather like watching an expensive after-shave ad, except so much better because she was seeing it in the flesh. He looked familiar and for a moment she wondered if he were someone famous that she hadn't recognised out of context, but at this distance she couldn't see his features in enough detail to figure it out.

She turned her attention back to her book but curiosity had her checking the shore every few minutes. She was rewarded five minutes later when he rose out of the waves and began to walk out of the water. *Daniel Craig, eat your heart out*, she thought as the sun turned the drops of water on his skin into sparkling diamonds. Then her heart did a funny flip of recognition. Bugger, it was Raphael Knight. Man, he looked even better out of clothes. Shame he was such an arse. Lia felt a genuine sense of aggrieved disappointment but continued to keep an eye on him as he scooped up his towel and slid his sunglasses back on.

Damn, he was coming towards her. Surely he hadn't seen her watching him among all the people on the beach? He stopped a few metres away from her, dropped his towel on the sand and lay down on it, propping himself up on his elbows to survey the scene. The position emphasised the musculature of his chest and Lia felt herself having totally inappropriate thoughts about said chest. How was that possible when she didn't even like the guy? Her hands *did not* want to run over those pecs, or skim that tanned skin. Oh God, she was getting hotter. A dip in the water was suddenly very appealing indeed, but she lay still, not wanting to draw his attention to her. Again, she repeated to herself, she did *not* like Raphael Knight.

Any hope that she could escape his notice was dashed when Leo came bounding over to his brother.

'Hey, Raph, look who's here.' He pointed to Lia. 'We're going for Aperols at Franco's. You gonna come? Ready, Lia?'

Raphael – she couldn't call him Raph – looked over at her, his mouth tightening very slightly as the now familiar disapproval emanated from him. Convinced he'd refuse, she turned her head away, not wanting to give him the satisfaction of snubbing her, but to her surprise he said, 'Sure, why not?'

Annoyingly he clocked her automatic double-take and gave a slow smile.

'Are you ill?' she asked, mortified that the childish response was all she could come up with.

'No,' he said mildly, rising to his feet and shaking the sand from his towel.

She busied herself gathering up her bits and pieces and slipped on her flip-flops. Taking a couple of steps away from the water, Leo stopped her. 'No, we'll get a water taxi from the dock. It's quicker. I'll just dump my board with Guido at the bar.'

Lia and Raphael watched as he ran lightly across to the nearby bar.

'He has friends everywhere,' said Raphael, shaking his head.

'Better than having no friends,' said Lia.

Raph raised a supercilious eyebrow, which he did rather well. 'I have plenty of friends.'

'None you'd prefer to be with this afternoon?'

'Plenty, but I'd rather keep an eye on you.'

'Should I be flattered?' she asked with a flirtatious smile, knowing he didn't mean that at all.

'No,' he growled.

She grinned, pleased to have the upper hand.

The water taxi took them round the bay and in no time they were docking on the jetty in Positano. Leo had talked enthusiastically throughout the trip, seemingly oblivious to the stony-faced stand-off between Lia and his brother. Being very British about it, Lia smiled and nodded, pretending there was nothing amiss as she focused on the calm, flat dark blue sea around them. Raphael spent the whole time scrolling on his phone, tapping out responses and pulling a gamut of expressions, the rainbow of emotions communicating annoyance, irritation, exasperation, satisfaction, indifference, impatience and back again.

'He is worse than a teenager. Always on his phone,'

teased Leo as he jumped nimbly out of the boat and turned to offer Lia a hand.

'Some of us have businesses to run,' observed Raphael idly, finally looking up from the screen, his eyes hidden behind his expensive shades.

Franco's was only a short walk away and Leo greeted the head waiter with a quick hug and jokingly insisted they were shown to the best table out on the terrace. Half the wait staff seemed to know him and called out greetings as they were led out to the terrace.

'How do you know everyone?' asked Lia, as Raphael leaned back into his chair.

'Went out with the boss's daughter for a while,' said Leo with a cheerful grin, waving over at a young woman on the other side of the room whose face lit up when she spotted him. 'There she is, that's Claudia.'

The young woman came hurrying over wiping her hands on the small black apron at her waist. '*Ciao*, Leo,' she greeted him and he stood to kiss her on both cheeks. After a quick conversation in rapid Italian, Leo introduced Lia. 'She's an artist, you know,' he said.

Claudia nodded with an easy friendly smile, her dark eyes dancing. 'And you are here for the best Aperol in town, Leo tells me. He might forget to call and say hi, but he always remembers where the best drinks are, don't you, Leo?' She gave him a teasing nudge in the ribs. Clearly there were no hard feelings there.

Lia beamed back at her, delighted by the warm uninhibited welcome. It seemed Leo's sunshine extended to all those in his orbit.

'And you know my brother, Raphael,' added Leo.

Claudia gave Raphael a wary nod and a more sober greeting. 'How are you?'

Interesting, thought Lia, and while she should have been pleased that he'd received a more frigid welcome, she actually felt a little bit sorry for him. Claudia hadn't done it deliberately but her instant reserve made it feel as if Raphael was the outsider here. Lia automatically felt sympathy for him – after all, she could relate to that feeling. It reminded her of the way she always felt that little bit out of sync whenever she spent time with her family, particularly with her mother and sister, both of whom set great store by appearances and couldn't understand why she preferred to set her own agenda when it came to style.

Even in casual gear, Raphael still had an aura of power about him. He'd pulled on a white Ralph Lauren polo shirt over navy-blue cargo shorts and wore slightly battered deck shoes. There was a stillness about him that set him apart from Leo's non-stop movement and laissez-faire geniality. Claudia dashed off to get their drinks and they settled at their table on the edge of the terrace, which made the most of what had to be one of the best views in town. On the opposite wall, making quite a statement, was a mustard-yellow painted baroque fountain that contrasted with the royal blue tables and chairs. This place, along with the kaleidoscope of pastel-coloured houses on the opposite hillside, had to be an Instagram favourite. Lia could almost guarantee there would be a #francospositano.

'A bit touristy,' observed Raphael, as a group of young

Italian girls jostled with each other to take selfies with the view behind them.

'*Sì*,' said Leo. 'But Lia is a tourist.'

'So she is,' said Raphael with a twisted smile as if to remind her of her place.

Lia shrugged. It was too nice a day to pick a fight with Raphael.

An older man, whom Lia had caught sneaking glances their way, rose from his table on the other side of the terrace and approached. 'Raphael. We haven't seen you here for a while. How are you? And how is Ernesto?'

'He's fine, thank you, Giò.' Lia immediately noticed that Raph's voice was toneless, almost uninterested, even as he asked, 'How's business?'

'You know. Not always easy. We're hoping for a good summer but things have been difficult. We could do with a boost to the local economy.'

'I'm sure.'

'I hear Ernesto is starring in a new movie with Julia Roberts. Will there be a première in Italy? Will she come to the party?'

Raphael gave her a brief smile. 'I'm not sure yet.'

'It would be so exciting if she did, it could create quite the buzz in the town.' Giò smiled winningly at Raphael. 'We could create a cocktail in her honour. I'd love to talk to Ernesto about it. Perhaps you could mention it?' He produced a card from his wallet. 'Maybe get him to call me.'

'Sure,' said Raph, tucking it into his pocket. Lia wondered if it would ever reach Ernesto.

'You know, that would be awesome,' said Leo as the

man walked away, tapping his hand on the table with a quick drumbeat, just as Lia said, 'Does that happen often?'

Raphael turned to her, ignoring Leo's sarcastic teasing response. 'Enough.'

'Julia's already said yes, hasn't she?' said Leo.

Lia's eyes widened at his casual use of the actress's name and was dying to ask if it were true, but worried it would make her look completely gauche.

'Oh look, our drinks,' she said, grateful for the distraction.

They all turned to watch as one of the waiters brought over a tray and presented the drinks with a flourish, handing the first one to Lia. She held it up to see the light fizz bubbling through the autumnal orange drink and when she took the first sip she sighed with pleasure as the bubbles hit her tongue with the citrus zest of orange. Whether it was being here in Italy or being relaxed at the end of the day, it tasted like the best Aperol spritz she'd ever had.

'Oh look, there's Tonio,' said Leo, suddenly jumping to his feet with his drink in his hand and almost knocking the table over in his haste. Then he was gone, joining a group of young men who'd just emerged from the restaurant onto the terrace.

Raphael sighed and pursed his mouth slightly.

'And then there were two,' Lia observed with a wry smile, thinking he must be hating this, being stuck with her.

'Yes,' said Raph, his voice so dry that she burst out laughing.

'I'm really not that bad. In fact some of my friends quite like me.'

His mouth quirked very slightly. 'I'm sure they do. How's the drink?'

'Delicious. Leo was right. This place is wonderful.'

'It is but it's not my favourite.'

'I could have guessed that,' said Lia with a cheeky grin. 'I think you'd be more at home in a high-backed leather chair with a glass of whisky and *The Financial Times*.'

'You know me so well,' he quipped. 'So, how are you filling your days? And where are you staying? It's expensive in Positano, especially at this time of year.'

Lia almost snorted Aperol out of her nose. 'You're not very subtle, are you?'

Raphael tried to look affronted and then had to the grace to give her a gracious smile. 'I was trying to be.'

'Well, you failed. Badly. I'm planning to stay as long as it takes. And I've got excellent accommodation.' She crossed her fingers under the table. As long as it didn't rain in the next month.

He sighed. 'Look, I don't know what you've been told but I promise you, Ernesto is not your father. Still, if you insist on persisting on this course, then you might as well go through the proper channels. There's a DNA testing company in Milan that is very reputable. I could put you in touch with them.'

Lia tilted her chin. 'My mother wouldn't lie to me. In fact, she didn't want to tell me about Ernesto in the first place.'

'Okay. Then why didn't she ever tell Ernesto she had his child? He's a famous, rich movie star. Why wouldn't she?'

JULIE CAPLIN

Lia curled her lip. 'My mother isn't interested in fame or fortune. Besides, she did tell him.'

Raphael shook his head vehemently. 'And that is where your story falls down. If Ernesto knew he had a child, he would not turn his back on them. He loves children and family is everything to him.'

'I'm telling the truth.'

'I'm sure you believe it, but I know Ernesto.'

'You're impossible. Just ask him. He'll tell you.'

Raphael tilted his head to one side and studied her. Then he shook his head. 'Sorry. No can do. Like I said. Do a DNA test and we can go from there.'

'Why are you being so stubborn about this?' she cried.

'Why are *you* being so stubborn?'

Lia's fingers curled into her palms. 'You're just being deliberately difficult.'

'I'm just looking out for my stepfather, who doesn't need to be bothered by this sort of thing again.'

'So we're at stalemate,' said Lia mutinously.

'It would appear so.'

Chapter Seven

They sat in silence for a minutes, Raphael gazing out at the vista. Even though he'd seen it a thousand times before, it never got old.

'It's a lovely view,' Lia suddenly said as if determined not to dwell on their disagreement. 'The colours at this time of day are just gorgeous.' He watched her profile as she tilted her head, absorbing the sight, entranced by the panorama spread before them. 'That peach house there, it looks like it's glowing from within. And that one there in the shade is almost purple. Look at the shadows, mauve and lilac with pale grey.'

She was right. The low afternoon light softened the picture and lent the pretty pastel houses an otherworldly magical aura, something he'd never appreciated before. They sat in tense silence, both of them studying the view.

After a little while, Lia turned her gaze on him, her face softening as she looked at him. 'It must be a wrench leaving here and going back to London.'

He frowned, pausing for a minute. 'Not really. I enjoy it here but it's not my life.' He never had a moment to call his own when he was here, constantly on call to sort out some problem and offer an opinion on something. He loved his family, but he found it exhausting never to have his own time. Much as he loved the sunshine, the food and the atmosphere, he missed the peace and routine he had in his own home in Notting Hill, as well as his friends and their dinners and their Saturday five-a-side football games.

Lia suddenly frowned, her eyes screwed up with intense concentration.

'Are you okay?' he asked after a minute, fascinated by the mobility of eyebrows semaphoring what appeared to be a dozen different emotions.

'What?' She jerked her head, her smile a little dreamy as if her world was still out of focus.

'Are you okay? You looked…' He wasn't sure quite what the right word should be.

Her dazzling smile hit him like a firework illuminating the sky, her whole face lit with inner joy.

'I've got it,' she said, deep contentment radiating from her. 'It's perfect.'

'And we're talking about…'

'An idea. I've been invited to submit a commission to a restaurant, and I've been trying to come up with—'

'Hey, guys.' Neither of them had noticed Leo approaching. 'Tonio and the others are off to Sorrento. And then on to a club. There's probably room in one of the cars if you fancy it, Lia.'

Raphael almost laughed out loud at Lia's confused

expression as if she'd just woken up and Leo was speaking Martian.

'Count me out,' he said. 'I'll see you tomorrow. Don't wake the house when you get in. The kids get grumpy if they don't get a good night's sleep.'

'All right, Grandad.'

Raph gave him a tight smile. There were only three years between them, something Leo seemed to prefer to forget.

'Coming, Lia? There's a really cool club we go to. It's ladies' night so you'll get in free, and the first drink is on the house. I bet you could squeeze in the back of Tonio's Jeep with me.'

'I don't think so. It sounds like a late night.'

Across the terrace, Tonio called impatiently to Leo.

'Sure? You'll have fun,' wheedled Leo.

Lia shook her head. 'No, thank you. Go have a good time.'

Leo kissed her lightly on the cheek. '*Ciao, bella*, see you soon. I'll be on the beach again tomorrow.'

'Bye.' Lia watched him leave with a fond smile that surprised his brother. She'd turned down a golden opportunity to get closer to Leo and inveigle her way into meeting Ernesto. They both rose and, once outside the building on street level, she said rather formally, 'Good evening.'

'Good evening. Do you have far to go?'

'No. Are you going to be a gentleman and offer to see me home?' Her eyebrow quirked with that look of amusement that seemed to hover around her face so often.

He suspected she smiled more often than not, and it was only around him that she looked so serious.

'Do you want me to?'

'No, you probably only want to find out where I live so that you can unleash a horde of cockroaches or something unpleasant to see me off.'

'You think so little of me.'

'Yes,' she said, her eyes dancing mischievously at his expense. It was a novelty. Most people treated him with respect, aware of his wealth and status.

'I shall leave you to it. Have a pleasant evening, *signorina*.'

He was intrigued as to where she was staying but he left her to it and meandered up the hill towards the scooter he'd ridden in on. This one was a sensible black, one of several at the villa that guests could use to zip back and forth to the town and the beach from the house, which was a few kilometres out of the town to allow for peace and privacy, although the paparazzi weren't above hanging about at the gates for the odd candid shot.

Raph stopped at the top of the hill and parked the scooter at the viewpoint. Lia puzzled him. She'd been quite open about her determination to meet Ernesto and equally honest that she wouldn't give up trying. But contrary to his expectation, she didn't seem to be using Leo to accomplish her goal. Or was she just playing a long game?

Raph knew from experience that people couldn't be trusted. They always wanted something from you. When Ernesto had first married his mother, life had changed so much for the better. They took a car to school instead of the bus. They had new clothes instead of the neighbours' hand-me-downs. They moved across town to a much bigger house. But as well as the material things, other things had altered. He was suddenly more popular with his peers. He was invited to people's houses more frequently. He wasn't stupid; he knew that his newfound popularity was directly related to Ernesto.

Raph wrinkled his nose and returned to the scooter, revving the little engine with more force than necessary. A plume of smoke belched from the exhaust in protest and he eased back, continuing the journey more sedately. He'd been fooled before by people he'd allowed close – and he wouldn't let it happen again.

'Raph, darling. Come and join us for a glass of wine on the terrazza,' called his mother when he entered the villa. 'Ernesto and I have just opened a very nice bottle of Valpolicella.'

'Thanks, Mamma.' Suddenly he felt really old and dull. Too old to be settling down for a drink with his parents and his half siblings who were scattered around the room, each occupied with some sort of technology.

'Raph. Raph.' One of the twins jumped up. 'See this. I won a trophy.' Michael waved the gilt trophy while his twin sister Bianca, eleven going on eighteen, rolled her eyes. 'They gave them to the whole team, not just you,' she said, with the sort of withering scorn only a sister could summon, and went back to her mobile phone. Luciana, who was thirteen and thought having a brother as old as Raph was acutely embarrassing, didn't even look up from her phone.

'Raph, do you know I'm the only one in the whole family who doesn't have a phone?' announced eight-year-old Giulia, coming to lean against his leg, as he sat down in a chair across the marble coffee table from Aurelia and Ernesto, her dark eyes looking up at him with all the sad desperation of a Labrador puppy.

There was a sudden stillness as everyone looked at him, as expectant as the bomb disposal squad. Once again, he'd walked into a domestic crisis – the sort the rest of the Salvatore family thrived upon – and he'd drawn the referee straw.

How come Leo was out partying and he was stuck with the part of peacekeeper and older brother role model?

Back in London, his life was so far removed from this that it resided in another galaxy. Someone somewhere was having a huge joke at his expense. At his Notting Hill home, he'd have been drinking red wine and sharing overpriced posh crisps with a bunch of friends before heading out to a local restaurant. For some reason his thoughts veered to Lia. He'd bet she wasn't knee-deep in siblings, destined to say the wrong thing and bring the wrath of some member of the family down on herself. Was she alone in her artist's garret or was it part of a community and she was sharing a bottle of wine with like-minded people?

'Don't you think it's really, really, really unfair, Raffy?' Guilia's lower lip trembled and her eyes swam with tears. She'd have put any Oscar-winning actress to shame.

Raph glanced around him.

'Me and Michael had to wait until we went to high school even though everyone in LA has cells. It's not fair if she gets one now,' interjected Bianca. The family lived in Los Angeles for most of the year, spending their summers here at the Villa.

'But I want one,' cried Guilia. 'What if I go out on my own and I see a wolf and it wants to eat me?'

'*Cara*, there are no wolves here,' said Ernesto.

'I'd say it could get on with it,' muttered Luciana.

Michael laughed and Giulia lifted up her nose and sniffed. 'Papa, you want me to be safe, don't you?'

Raph looked at Ernesto and hid a grin. Young Giulia was a smart cookie.

'Of course, I do but…'

'Why do you need a phone, sweetheart?' asked Raph as his sister climbed up onto his knee and made herself comfortable.

'Oh, lots of reasons,' she said sounding so grown-up that he had to stifle another laugh. 'Everyone in my class has one, you know.'

'Do they? Everyone?'

She nodded solemnly. 'Well, apart from Noah.'

'So you're not the only one,' Raph pointed out.

'No, he has two.' Giulia jutted her chin out and looked up at him, her eyes bead bright and focused with unnerving intensity as if she was attempting some kind of mind magic. It was like being under an interrogator's light. 'I could Facetime you when you're in England and we're in America.'

'But you do that already, with Mamma and Papa.'

'But not when I'm sad,' she said, her lip quivering.

Michael, Bianca and Luciana all burst out laughing.

'I get sad sometimes,' she said with great dignity.

'Not very often,' said Raph. His youngest sister was a sunny, confident child who rarely got upset about anything. She was putting on quite a show this evening.

She tutted and huffed out an annoyed breath. 'I really want to play Minecraft. Everyone at school does.'

'But can't you play on…' Raph's voice trailed off.

'If I had my own laptop, yes.' Giulia's seraphic smile held a touch of triumph. 'But I don't.'

'How about' – Raph caught his mother's eye to check he was doing the right thing – 'I give you my old laptop?'

She nestled against him, her body relaxing and he smelled innocence in her apple-scented hair. 'That would be all right. Wouldn't it, Papa?'

Ernesto laughed. 'I'm not sure I have any say in the matter.'

'Course you do. You always do what Mamma says.'

Raph had a feeling that he'd just been manipulated by a master, especially when she suddenly slithered off his lap. 'I'm going to get my book. You can read me a bedtime story.'

'Not just now, Giulia,' said Aurelia. 'Raph would like to sit and talk to the adults and enjoy his wine.'

Giulia gave her a sweet smile and disappeared.

'I'm going to watch a film,' said Michael.

'*Guardians of the Galaxy 3*?' asked Bianca hopefully.

'I'm up for that,' said Luciana.

After a chorus of chaos, the room fell silent.

'She's a pickle, that one,' said Ernesto, chuckling into his wine. 'I'm not going to have to worry about her. She will be telling the boys what to do. No one will boss her about.'

'Giving her your laptop is a very good compromise. I think she is too young to have a phone,' said Aurelia.

'Me too,' said Ernesto.

Raph poured himself a glass of wine and took a hefty swig. He deserved it.

'I saw Giò Dutti while I was out. He was asking after you. He's rather keen that you invite Julia to the party.'

Ernesto laughed and shook his head. 'That man would sell his own grandmother if he thought it would make him any money. What did you tell him?'

'I told him I'd mention it. And now I have.'

Ernesto's eyes twinkled. 'Thank you. And now I shall ignore it. I have enough to think about with my family, especially Giulia.'

'By number six you'd have thought you would know how to manage them,' Raph pointed out to his mother, bringing the topic back to Giulia.

'I do. It's her father. He spoils her.' She cast a stern look at Ernesto, who waved her words away with an airy hand.

Ernesto shrugged his shoulders. 'What can I do? I love all of my children.' He paused and caught Aurelia's hand. 'And, of course, my beautiful wife.'

Aurelia's brilliant smile reminded Raph why he put up with them all. Ernesto had made his mother the happiest woman in the world, changing her single-parent existence of drudgery, endless worry and financial fear into one of partnership, love and happiness. They adored each other and while Raph didn't enjoy some of the elements that having a famous stepfather brought to his life, he was extremely grateful for all the positives. He just wished he could have some time off for good behaviour every now and then.

Chapter Eight

Lia put down her sketchbook, dropping the lemon-yellow pencil with a satisfying clatter on the table, her heart dancing with that indefinable excitement that came with creativity. This was it. Admittedly it was only one element of the design she had to come up with, but it was a start and she was confident that this one was a winner. She also had an idea for a picture of Positano that excited her and she would start work on right away.

She envisioned the image of half a lemon glistening with moisture, which she would create with an intricate design of crystals and tiny bugle beads. She would embroider the subtle dimples on the lemon skin with tiny French knots in almost but not quite the same shade of yellow.

With a joyful laugh she snapped shut the sketchbook, pleased that she finally had something to focus on. Now she was going to celebrate and treat herself to lunch and enjoy the sunshine.

She ordered *linguine alle vongole* drizzled with lemon-infused olive oil and a glass of Pinot Grigio and sat at a table tucked in the corner with a very attentive waiter, who also brought her a dish of Nocellara olives and fine *grissini*. It had never bothered her to eat on her own as she always brought a bit of embroidery with her and she was happy to watch the other diners in between stitches. It was quite handy as a way of advertising because people often stopped to ask her about it and then went on to buy her work via a gallery.

As she drank her wine, she observed the busy festive atmosphere with lots of families having lunch together. She noticed one large group of different ages arriving, and felt a momentary pang of envy. They were so obviously a family, the children all with their mother's dark hair and their father's strong features. At the centre of it all, the mother, a slim woman in an immaculately tailored fuchsia-pink dress and matching jewelled flip-flops, with her hair piled in a messy bun of curls exploding at various angles, laughed and chided them. There was a lot of laughter and teasing. The youngest girl, in a flame orange sundress, pranced around the table like a little show pony and came to stand next to her father, wrapping her arm around his neck. Her colourful dress contrasted beautifully with his emerald-green linen shirt and white chino trousers. This family wasn't afraid of colour, that was for sure. Fascinated, Lia watched as he turned to face his daughter, cocking his head to hear what she had to say. Her hand froze in mid-air and she almost dropped her fork.

Ernesto!

She couldn't believe it. Sitting there right in front of her. For a moment she thought maybe she was imagining it. Could it really be him? Was he the man in her mother's photo? As much to stall for time as to reassure herself, she rummaged in her tote bag to pull out the photo of the pair of them at Ronnie Scott's. There was no mistake. It was definitely him and now, after everything, she was only a few feet away.

Her stomach turned a dozen somersaults, the pasta churning round like a washing machine on a slow spin. For a moment her body refused to respond to any of her commands, unable to do anything but covertly study him. He looked every bit the handsome film star with tiny silver streaks at the temples of his swept-back dark hair. Oh God. Lia swallowed; his life was a world away from hers. What had she been thinking? She couldn't just approach him, a random stranger claiming to be his daughter. It was ridiculous. And there was no way she could go over and interrupt the happy family party.

Suddenly, insinuating herself into his life didn't seem such a good idea. In fact it was a dreadful idea. Truly dreadful. How naïve she'd been, with her simple fantasy of calling at his house and meeting him. Coming almost face to face with him, with his family all around him, brought home a very different reality.

Her flight instinct kicked in. She had to get out of here. Right now.

JULIE CAPLIN

Pushing her half-eaten pasta dish aside, she gathered up her scissors, needle, threads and the fabric square she'd been working on and with uncharacteristic haste shoved them into her workbag, not bothering to put the items into their allotted slots. When she rose quickly, the chair shrieked across the wood, drawing a dozen diners' attention, including Ernesto's wife, who shot her a sympathetic smile as she hurried off.

Then, as if things weren't already bad enough, she spotted Leo and Raphael coming through the door at the front of the restaurant. Luckily Ernesto had also seen them and hailed the pair with a wave and a delighted smile. She darted towards the exit and took the stairs as fast as she dared. Once in the street she hurried down the lane, not really thinking about where she was going, just desperate to put as much distance as she could between her and … – she winced – her and … her father.

She found herself down by the main beach, which was full of tourists, but she welcomed the crush. She needed to surround herself with other people to stop her feeling so alone. When she sank down on the dock at the water's edge, she swallowed a huge lump. She'd chased an impossible dream, imagining that she would miraculously feel like she finally belonged when she met her real father.

Hauling in a heavy sigh she concentrated on the outbreath, waiting for the thudding of her heart to slow. She'd never felt so alone or so lost. Worse still, she was stuck here in a ratty studio for the next month because her pride wouldn't allow her to go home just yet.

She just had to secure that commission. It was the only thing that was hers now. Proof that she was someone in her own right. Not an outsider. She had no other option – it was going to be a very long summer.

Chapter Nine

Raph caught the flash of scarlet in his peripheral vision and that quick poke of awareness. Turning, he was in time to see Lia disappearing through the doorway that he and Leo had just walked through and running full flight down the stairs as if she had the hounds of hell on her tail.

The horrified expression on her face had him instinctively taking a step after her, a surprising stab of concern making itself felt. What could have upset her so much? For some unfathomable reason, he felt responsible for her. Was it because he knew he could have done more to put her off in London? Maybe if he'd just insisted on a DNA test there and then, it would have appeased her. Rushing out here to Italy was only going to end in disappointment and for that he was genuinely sorry.

'Raph, Leo. You made it,' Ernesto bellowed, immediately commanding their attention.

Raph gave the staircase one last look before following his brother toward the family.

'Of course we did,' said Leo with a touch of unjustified indignation. Raph had to supress the urge to kick his brother. It was he who'd dragged Leo out of bed and forced him into the shower. 'Would I miss this?' Leo asked as he kissed his mother and sat down next to Bianca, immediately teasing her about the T-shirt she was wearing – 'Not still into that death metal crap, are you?' – which of course prompted the usual fallout, her passionate defence and Michael's perennial complaints that she had no taste.

Raph smiled to himself. Business as usual. Sunday lunch at Capaldi's was a family tradition during summers in Positano. They'd been visiting the restaurant from the very first year that Raph and Leo had come to the villa with their mother, just after she'd married Ernesto, and coming here always reminded him of the dramatic change in their fortunes. He had so much to be grateful to his stepfather for, despite the downsides: the press intrusion, the hangers-on, the wannabes.

'Did you bring the Ferrari?' asked Luciana. 'Can I go back with you? Leo can walk. I bet he's got a hangover. It will do him good.'

'Who, me?' asked Leo, all innocence.

'What time did you get in?' asked Aurelia, a teasing twinkle in her eyes. 'Was it five or six?'

Leo grinned. 'Five, but don't worry, I've caught up on my beauty sleep.'

'I don't doubt it,' said Ernesto. 'It's a good job Raph has more sense.'

Raph took his seat next to Ernesto. There were times when he'd have loved to kick back and behave irresponsibly and do what he wanted to do instead of being the 'sensible one' and the role model to his younger half-siblings – who all, of course, hero-worshipped Leo – but that was not to be.

'Did you go dancing, Leo?' asked Giulia.

'I certainly did, *piccola*.'

'I like dancing. I think I should go with you next time,' she announced.

Leo grinned. 'Everyone would want to dance with you, *cara*.'

'I know,' said Giulia, picking up a crayon and going back to her drawing. Mobile phones were banned at mealtimes. It was a rule that Aurelia upheld religiously and that even Leo adhered to.

Menus were passed out and even though they knew the dishes off by heart, they all began to study the pages as if there might be an exam coming up. The usual discussion and bickering ensued and Raph found himself smiling again. Ernesto might be a Hollywood star, used to having people at his beck and call, with the money to cater to his every whim, but his family came first.

A waiter approached and spoke in Italian to Ernesto. 'Er, excuse me, Signor Salvatore. But is this yours? It was left on a table.'

The waiter slid a black and white photograph from his tray.

'I don't think...' Ernesto stopped and picked up the

photograph, studying it. '*Madre di dio*. It *is* me. When I was nineteen. In London. Where did this come from?'

'It was on the table over there. The young lady sitting there dropped it.'

Ernesto frowned.

'What is it, darling?' asked Aurelia.

'Me and an old girlfriend. The one I told you about,' he said a touch urgently to his wife, his eyes widening with some private message. 'You know.'

Aurelia nodded.

Raph felt a frisson of unease. Why hadn't his father ever mentioned any of this before? 'What girlfriend?'

Ernesto beamed. 'Mary Harding. She's married now. Mary Bathurst. We were madly in love and then I went to Hollywood.' Then his smile faded and he sighed, exchanging a look with Aurelia. Raph frowned.

'So you know this woman?'

Ernesto nodded, his brows drawing together to form a deep furrow of concern. Raph watched, increasingly puzzled, as his mother patted Ernesto's arm in what looked like a consoling gesture. Ernesto gave her a sad smile.

'Can I have a look, Papa?' asked Bianca. Ernesto nodded and handed the picture over the table.

'Look how young you were,' she said, amused, showing the picture to her sisters.

'Ugh, that lady looks all loved up over you,' complained Michael.

'That was before I met your mother,' Ernesto reminded him. 'And before I was famous.' He turned round to look back at the now empty table. 'I wonder where the photo came from and who it belongs to and what they were doing here?'

Raph's heart sank, hard and fast. No! What was going on? Had Lia been telling the truth after all? And why, after she'd been so adamant that she wanted to meet Ernesto, had she fled when the opportunity had presented itself?

———————

'Ernesto, is there something you'd like to tell me?' Throughout lunch Raph's unease had increased and he'd barely been able to eat. He stood with his stepfather on a small private balcony away from the rest of the family as they tucked into dessert. 'About the photo?'

Ernesto leaned on the ironwork balustrade and gazed out over the deep sapphire blue of the sea. 'Mary had a daughter. Mine. Her name is Lia.'

Knots twisted Raph's stomach. He felt he'd stepped off a cliff. This couldn't be true. It undermined everything he thought he knew about his stepfather.

'You know for a fact she's yours?' Raph's question was sharp with underlying accusation.

Ernesto paused for a moment. 'Mary wouldn't have lied to me.'

'But you have no proof. Blood tests or anything.' Still he hung on to the hope that he hadn't been wrong.

'No.'

'And you never thought to tell me?' He closed his eyes and muttered, 'God give me strength.'

'I didn't need to tell you because there was no scandal. It

was all sorted out. Mary decided to keep the child and I accepted responsibility, but I'd just got my first job in Hollywood and I didn't want to give it up, and by then Mary had met someone else. He was prepared to adopt the baby and at the time it was a simple solution. We stayed in touch and she sent me updates. It was only when I married your mother that I was ready to meet her ... but by then it was too late. Mary said it would be wrong to upset Lia and that if it came out publicly it would be difficult for Lia to lead a normal life. At the time I could see you struggling to make adjustments with the change in lifestyle—'

'You mean being papped all the time,' Raph suggested.

'Yes. I saw how it affected you, and Lia was so close in age to you ... I wanted to spare her some of the trouble you were having. I know you found your teenage years difficult because of me.' He patted Raph on the shoulders. 'And I'm sorry for that.'

Raph scowled. 'Don't apologise for something that was out of your control.'

'Even so, seeing your holiday snaps splashed all over the papers the day you went back to school after the summer break can't have been much fun.'

'I survived,' said Raph. It had been excruciating. Whereas Leo had managed to shrug it all off, Raph couldn't get over the constant attention.

'It was bad enough that you had to go through that. Imagine a daughter turning up out of the blue. The press would have loved that. So I agreed with Mary that I would stay away and that if Lia ever wanted to make contact she would let me know.'

'So Mary knew how to contact you?'

'Through our solicitors, yes.'

Raph's stomach constricted. So why hadn't Lia contacted the solicitors? Part of him was pleased that he'd read Ernesto right and that he wouldn't have abandoned his child, but another part of him was sad for Lia that she'd never known her father.

'Why didn't you tell me any of this?'

'There didn't seem much point, especially when I assumed she didn't want to see me.'

'She came to see me. I didn't believe her. She'd only just discovered you were her father.' And now he was going to have to eat humble pie.

'She's here?' Ernesto's voice was eager.

'Yes,' said Raph, resigned to the fact that Ernesto would want to see her and that he was going to have to make that happen. Lia was just going to love that. 'She came here looking for you.'

'So she wants to see me.'

'I think she might just want to do,' he said but his sarcasm flew right over Ernesto's head. It didn't occur to his stepfather that Lia might take advantage of him. He was an extremely wealthy man, after all, and Lia was ... well, she was an unknown quantity. What if she did want money? She was an artist, and unless they were famous they didn't make much money, did they?

'I want to meet her.'

'Okaaay.' He looked through the French doors back to the table. 'What about Mamma?'

Ernesto snorted. 'You think I would keep something like

this from her? She's always known. It has made us both sad over the years.'

That explained her response to the photo. It appeared everyone had been keeping secrets.

'You should invite her to the house. Tomorrow. She could come for lunch.'

'I could but I don't know where she lives.'

'What do you mean?'

'I met her by accident. She was...' He sighed. 'She was with Leo when I first saw her here. She'd picked him up near the house.'

'And Leo didn't tell me.'

'I asked him not to because...'– Raph held out his hands – 'because we didn't know who she was or what she wanted.'

Ernesto shook his head. 'You are too suspicious. She is family. Your sister.'

Raph shook his head vehemently. 'She's definitely not my sister. We're not related by blood in any way.'

'She's family. You're family. We're all family. You're going to have to find her.'

'Why me?' asked Raph, though he knew the likely answer: because it was always him.

'Because you sent her away in the first place.' Ernesto patted him on the arm. 'Now, I am in need of a Limoncello.'

Chapter Ten

O f course now that he wanted to find the damn
woman, she'd vanished off the face of the earth.
He'd tried emailing her but had had no response, and
stupidly he'd refused to take her mobile number when
she'd come to his London office.

'Are you sure you haven't seen her this week?' he asked
Leo as they backed their scooters into a tiny space between
two cars, his skin already tingling at the thought of a plunge
in cool sea water. He'd had enough of sitting in the study in
the villa on such a glorious day and needed a clean escape
to the beach. The ultra-stylish black mosaic tiled pool at the
villa, while perfectly adequate for cooling down, never
brought quite the same exhilaration as being in the sea. Leo
had needed no second invitation, and they left the villa
before the younger children realised their plans and insisted
on coming too, even though they'd already spent the
morning at the beach. Despite its dark sand and pebbles,
Fornillo beach was the firm family favourite.

As soon as they arrived, Raph scanned the beach looking for a lone female with a floppy hat and an orange bikini, which is what she'd been wearing last time he'd seen her here. Not an easy task when there were so many people enjoying the fine summer afternoon; some swimming, others paddling in the shallows, while many more gathered in groups, camped around parasols and colourful beach towels. The solo visitors tended to be lying down, their faces shaded by books, magazines, hats or sunglasses, making it difficult to work out who they were without being intrusive.

'Can you see her?'

'No,' said Leo, his hand shading his eyes as he glanced down the beach.

'And how come you don't have her number?' Raph asked as they staked their claim on a small patch of sand, dropping their towels and shoes.

'She never asked.' Leo stripped off his T-shirt and dropped it onto the ground. Raph shook his head and carefully folded his own and placed it on top of his shoes so it wouldn't fill with sand.

'Besides I don't take my cell to the beach. Chicks know where to find me.'

'Chicks? As in your female acquaintances?' Raph asked, slightly incredulous. 'What do they see in you? Neanderthal man is born again.'

They walked side by side in the rolling, bandy-legged walk demanded by the soft sand enveloping their feet with a sharp sting of heat, down towards the water, an azure blue that merged with the seamless edge where sky and sea met.

Leo shrugged and grinned. 'Hey, I can't help it if women find me irresistible.'

'Does Lia?' Raph hated that the question had popped out before he could stop it, as involuntary as a cough or a sneeze.

'Why? Do you like her, bro?' Leo turned to look at Raph, wiping his long hair out of his eyes, grinning like a loon.

'Don't be ridiculous.' Raph hoped his response was airy, indifferent. 'I don't even know her.'

'You don't to have to know someone to know.' Leo grasped his hands over his heart – he was so bloody childish sometimes. And extremely irritating. 'What about a *coup de foudre*? Love at first sight. Felled by Cupid's arrow.' Leo turned and walked backwards into the shallows, water lapping his ankles as his teasing gaze latched onto Raph's face.

'Load of nonsense. Never lasts.' Raph ducked his head and waded into the water, welcoming the quick chill on his calves.

'No, not for everyone,' said Leo, the expression on his face sobering. 'But don't forget Mamma and Ernesto.' Leo had him there. Their relationship really was a love affair of the heart, even fifteen years on.

'That's the exception. They got lucky in that they actually liked each other and have stayed together.'

Leo threw up his arms in disgust. 'You don't have any romance in your soul.' He dived into the water, surfacing quickly. Raph wasn't about to let him get away with that.

'And you do? Which is why you have a revolving door of girlfriends,' yelled Raph across the surface of the sea.

'I don't have any problem in falling in love.' Leo grinned, floating on his back. 'It's staying in love I have trouble with. There are so many lovely women out there. It would be a crime to deprive myself of the chance of finding the right one.'

Raph launched himself into the water, the cold flowing over his shoulders and back, and took a couple of quick, fierce strokes to warm himself up. As soon as he submerged his body, he felt the tension leave his shoulders and the worries of the day fly free. Ernesto and Aurelia, wary of being tarred with the self-entitled tag of celebrity, were quite happy to pass any difficult jobs over to Raph. Already this morning he'd solved a dispute for his mother with the people who installed the kitchen last year, spoken to the swimming pool maintenance company who hadn't done a good enough job cleaning the pool, and helped Ernesto with his email account, which he'd managed to lock himself out of, again.

Drawing alongside Leo, he asked, 'Have you ever considered that all those women are drawn to the idea of you? Famous star's son, young and wealthy.'

'Harsh, bro, harsh.' Leo snorted. 'Have you seen this?' He indicated his bare chest and the surprisingly well toned abs. 'And of course, there's my sunny personality. You should try smiling a bit more. That would attract the ladies.'

'I don't have any problem attracting the ladies, and unlike you, I'm a little more self-aware as to their motivation.'

'Bro, you sound like a jaded old cynic. Let loose, have a good time.' To demonstrate his meaning, he kicked his feet hard, sending splashes of water dancing into the air, glinting in the sunshine. 'So what if they want you for your money rather than your monkey ugly looks, you can still have some fun. It's not like you have to make any promises. Transparency, man. That's the watchword.'

Evidently boring of the subject, he changed the topic. 'What about Lia's mum? I thought you said Ernesto knew how to get hold of her. Doesn't she know where Lia's staying?'

Raph shook his head. 'Ernesto had the mother's number. I phoned her. She didn't even know Lia was in Italy.' Speaking to Mary Bathurst had left him disconcerted. He hadn't wanted to pry or get involved, really, but self-recrimination and regret were clearly evident in her carefully chosen words, as was the fact that Lia wasn't communicating with her. Despite that, she wasn't prepared to give out Lia's number without permission.

'I wouldn't worry about it; she'll turn up.' With that Leo turned and dived under an oncoming rippling wave.

Raph shook his head. Leo's outlook on life was so simple. So easy. They swam for a little while, Leo relaxing and floating while Raph powered through the water with a fast crawl. When he'd swum far enough out, he turned and swam back, feeling the pull and burn of his muscles.

Once he drew level with Leo, he floated on his back, at ease with the world. Nothing like the sea to put things in perspective. He gave the beach a casual perusal and then … damn. Just a few metres from where they'd left their clothes, he spotted a familiar figure. How had he missed her? It was Lia and it looked like she was packing up and leaving. He immediately picked up speed, moving from a lazy breast stroke into another fierce crawl, and as soon as his feet hit the sand, he strode up the beach, his eyes blinking with the salt as he shaded them with a hand, shaking the water out of his hair. Where was she? He couldn't see her anymore.

Figuring that she was likely to walk back along the cliff path, he hurried over to his pile of belongings on the sand and scooped them up, shoving his sandy feet into his deck shoes and wincing as the sand scraped his skin at the heel.

Glancing back he saw Leo, still in the sea but now chatting to a couple of bikini-clad girls – no surprise there. He'd understand – in fact he probably wouldn't care – that Raph had abandoned him. Having his older brother around no doubt cramped his style anyway.

Walking as quickly as he could, while sinking on the soft surface and the skin on top of his foot being sand-blasted in his shoes, he weaved through the towels and parasols, earning looks of irritation from carefree sunbathers, as if his urgency spoiled their enjoyment of the day. When he reached the path, he thought he saw her up ahead but several people blocked the way, clearly happy to amble in the heat. It was too hot to rush and he felt like an idiot as he squeezed past them, apologising. Once through them there was no sign of Lia and he picked up his pace, hoping he'd catch up with her. She couldn't have got very far, could she? To be on the safe side he checked the shaded stopping points under the trees.

Ten minutes later he reached where the path turned and began to go back down to the main beach. There was still no sign of her, which left a vague disquiet within him. He ought to have caught up with her by now unless she'd sprinted off, which he thought was highly unlikely. Had she walked a different way going up into the town? Why had he just assumed that she'd take the cliff path? He groaned, wishing he'd brought some water with him to wash away the dust in his throat and the salt residue from his face.

As he pushed an impatient hand into the stiff saltwater peaks of his hair he realised there was nothing for it but to empty the sand from his shoes and walk back to Fornillo.

Lia was turning into the bane of his life.

There was a choice of bars on the beach and, out of habit – for good reason – Raph headed to Da Ferdinando. It was run by the children and grandchildren of Ferdinando, and there was always a friendly face there and a warm welcome. It was as much a hit with the tourists as it was with the locals.

Just as he was about to sit down, he felt a prickle down his neck. Turning, he found Lia's cool-eyed gaze on him. Bloody hell, she'd been here the entire time. Shaking his head at his own stupidity he crossed to her table. 'Mind if I join you?' he asked.

That smile of hers did it every time. Slightly smug but at the same time with that hint of mischief that told him she was amused by him. It sent his stomach in a loop.

'What would you do if I said no?' She cocked her head to one side, the cheeky challenge notching his pulse up a beat.

'I would respect your wishes,' he replied gravely, feeling horribly formal.

She laughed and at the sound of it he found himself relaxing. 'No, you wouldn't. You'd probably look round wondering why the sky hadn't turned green. Everyone does as you tell them. You're a born people manager.'

'Not by choice,' he muttered. 'Can I buy you a drink?' He nodded towards the dregs of her Aperol spritz and the solitary slice of orange at the bottom of the glass.

'That would be lovely. Thank you.'

He caught the eye of Guido, one of the young waiters, and ordered a beer for himself, 'and the same again for the lady'.

'You're being very friendly all of a sudden,' said Lia, her eyes narrowing.

'I can be a friendly sort of guy,' he said, unable to resist sparring with her as the apology he'd intended to start with was vanquished by the quick burst of energy that flowed between them.

She spat out another laugh. 'No, Leo is a friendly sort of guy. You … I haven't figured out yet.'

'I can be friendly,' he repeated.

'When you want something,' she hazarded, cocking her head again. Bang on the button. Did she have to be so damn intuitive? He didn't want to admit straightaway that he'd been wrong about her, even though he knew it was the right thing to do. He was enjoying the back and forth between them too much.

'That looks interesting,' he said, with a deliberate change of subject. He was intrigued by the embroidery hoop in her hand, which was fixed in a length of material into which she was hand-stitching tiny black lines. He thought it an extraordinarily sedentary and patient pastime for someone like her, who always seemed to be on the go and on the verge of leaping into action.

'I hope so,' she said, surveying it, catching her lip between her teeth. 'It's been a bit of a pig. I've spent all week in the studio trying to get the dyes right but I'm there now.'

The colours – peaches, pale pinks, shadowy mauves and lilacs – looked familiar and his brain sifted through trying to make sense of them. It took a moment and then it clicked.

'Positano. It's the hillside in Positano.' The view from Franco's came back to him and so did the memory of her face in profile and the quiet careful examination she'd given it.

'Give the man a prize.' Despite her flippant words, a fierce glow of pride lit up her face.

'Can I see?' He held out a hand, pleased and surprised when she moved to hand it over. But at the last minute she changed her mind.

She held the needle and black thread aloft but rather than place it in his outstretched hand, she shunted her chair round to his side to share it with him as if she couldn't quite bring herself to let go of the work.

'May I?' He reached out to skim the surface of the taut fabric captured within the embroidery hoop. Something about it called to him and begged to be touched.

She gave a small half-smile and a barely-there nod.

The colours of the fine silk were so subtle, the shades

between them infinitesimal and their depth giving a curious 3-D effect. The optical illusion was further deepened by the tiny black stitches that defined sections of buildings – a window here, the outline of a door there, the scalloped edge of a roof.

Words escaped him, floating just out of reach like a balloon caught in a breeze. It seemed impossible to capture the right ones to describe it. The image was more about what wasn't there than what was, leaving the beholder to fill in the gaps.

'Are you pleased with it?' was all that he could come up with. Anything else he might have said felt inadequate.

'Very,' she said and snatched it back, this time putting it away into a work bag at her side. He sensed he'd disappointed her but to try and say something now would sound insincere, as if prompted purely by her dissatisfaction with his response. Trying to explain would feel too intimate, as if he'd seen into a little bit of her soul.

And when had he turned into a fanciful romantic? There was no room for being like that in his life. Everyone relied on him to be the pragmatic one.

'It was a smart move, leaving the photo.' As soon as he said it, he regretted his knee-jerk reaction, allowing the words to intrude into the unexpected moment of sensitivity. He hadn't meant to be that blunt or accusatory. What he wanted to say was that it had been effective without making it sound like she'd been cunning or devious.

'Sorry?' Her head snapped up, shock and disbelief imprinted within her expression.

Way to go, you idiot. He'd well and truly spoiled what

might have been a rare moment of connection between them. Maybe he'd done it on purpose. A deliberate act of self-sabotage. This girl unnerved him and he'd been fighting it since the day she walked into his London office, crackling with life and energy. Even so, he couldn't give up his original position. Even if she really was Ernesto's daughter, it didn't mean her motives in wanting to meet him were pure.

'The photo of Ernesto and, I presume, your mother.'

'You found it.' He could see the flicker of relief in her eyes. 'I must have dropped it.'

This time it was Raph's turn to raise an eyebrow. 'In the very restaurant where he dines every Sunday? How convenient.'

'I didn't know that. I was already there,' she protested.

He wanted to believe her, she sounded genuine, but then again it was common knowledge that the family always ate there when they were in residence.

'Don't you want to know how the story ends?' he asked.

'I'm sure you're going to fill me in.' He'd annoyed her now. He could see her tongue poking none too subtly into the inside of her cheek.

'A helpful waiter brought it over to Ernesto. Did you pay him?' Okay so maybe he was being an ass but it was just too much of a coincidence. Surely she could see that.

Twin spots of colour burned on her cheeks. Her eyes narrowed in anger and she sprang to her feet, both hands on the table. 'How dare you?'

Raph had never registered the colour of emotion before,

but this was an incandescent flame of scarlet consuming Lia.

'I was in the restaurant. Having lunch. Your family walked in. At first I had no idea it was them. Then, when I did – and I don't give a shit if you believe me or not – I panicked. And I left. Just gathered up my stuff and left.'

She leaned forward, her face mere inches from his, and he was oh so conscious of her heaving chest, the tide of red flushing the skin on her neck and the well-targeted disdain echoing through every syllable of her words, hitting the bullseye. 'Do you honestly think I'd have left my only evidence, my sole leverage, behind in the hope it might just fall into the right hands?' Her mouth twisted and the look she gave him would have withered an entire tree, curling its leaves to crisps.

Even though there was no coming back from this and he was faced with this flash flood of shame that he'd misjudged her, his stubborn mouth carried on, as if it hadn't quite dug itself into a deep enough mire of trouble. 'So why didn't you go up and speak to him?'

'Because…' She glared at him as if he were too stupid to live. 'Because … I didn't want to disturb a family lunch. Not with his wife and children there.'

'Noble of you.' It was as if he'd got into the role of the villainous character and couldn't get out of it. What was wrong with him?

She gave him a mutinous glare. 'It might not have occurred to you but I'm not in the habit of trying to upset people. Take a note, Mr Knight. What I *was* trying to do was to be discreet, spare innocents public embarrassment and go through the right channels, but you … well, you were the one that put a stop to that. I was left with no option.'

'I didn't stop it; I just told you it would take some time. But *you* didn't have the patience to wait.' Now he was trying to blame her when it was his own distrust of people that had deliberately kept her away from Ernesto.

'Because I knew full well *you* didn't believe me. It was obvious you were reluctant to tell Ernesto anything. How could I trust that you'd actually share DNA results with him?'

She had a point. He wouldn't have bothered submitting the test to the lab because he'd been there too many times before. He knew better than most that there were always people trying to claim a connection to Ernesto to get something from him.

'Well, you're in luck because he wants to meet you.'

'He does?' Lia's body stiffened, and it gave him a certain satisfaction. Lia might well be Ernesto's daughter but the question he kept coming back to was: why was she here now?

Raph didn't know what might have motivated her but he did know there was always a good reason.

Chapter Eleven

W hat did you wear to meet your long-lost father? Lia had pondered this question for the last twenty-four hours. Ever since the moment Raphael had texted her a time to come and visit Ernesto at the Villa Mimosa for morning coffee.

On this occasion, she'd taken a taxi so that she didn't arrive looking like a dishevelled wreck who needed a handout. Contrary to Raphael Knight's belief – he really did have a dim view of humanity – she wanted to find out more about who she really was. All she knew was that she no longer felt quite whole anymore. Her mother's admission had bored a hole in her and, like the hull of a ship, she was taking on water. She was listing, unsure of who she was.

She'd plaited her hair in a French braid, and after much deliberation, rather than opt for the safe, smart option, she'd chosen another of her own dresses, a very plain shoestring-strappy empire line dress in fine lawn cotton that she'd dyed in a spectacular shade of brilliant kingfisher blue with tiny fissures of pale lemon that darted up from the hem creating a flash of contrasting colour as she walked. She loved the way the dress emulated the flash of a kingfisher diving into water. It always garnered compliments and comments. As her mother said, it was very much a 'Lia' dress – although she wasn't sure if that was a good thing or not. Both her mother and her sister – half-sister, she amended quickly with the familiar stab of hurt – were keen fans of the capsule wardrobe vibe, favouring muted tones: taupes, mushrooms and creams, bookended with navy-blue or black.

She raised an unsteady hand to press the silver intercom button.

'Lia Bathurst here to see Signor Salvatore,' she said, her voice a little shaky, expecting the hydraulics to buzz and the gate to swing wide with an open sesame immediacy. For a moment she felt in limbo as the silence extended, punctuated only by the hum of the nearby cicadas. Standing outside the pale pink walls of the property, she glanced around, taking in the elaborate wrought-iron gates in front of the drive as she stood by the smaller gate in the wall. Waiting. Was she on CCTV being weighed up?

Finally the door opened.

'*Buongiorno*,' said a voice and Lia found herself looking at one of the younger children from the restaurant. 'You are Lia. Our new sister. I'm Giulia.'

'Giulia!' The slim woman Lia recognised as Ernesto's wife placed her hands on the girl's shoulders, shaking her head slightly with exasperation. 'I'm so sorry, the little one has jumped the gun. Please do come in. We are very pleased to meet you.' The excessive formality and slight admonishment of the girl made Lia's heart sink a little. Clearly the child's mother wasn't so pleased to welcome her into the fold. It must be difficult to discover that your husband had fathered another child before your own children.

'Thank you. And thank you for inviting me. It's very kind of you.'

The woman shook her head. 'You are most welcome. I'm Aurelia, Ernesto's wife and mother to this impatient little one.' She still had her hands on her daughter's shoulders as she steered her ahead of them into a loggia that ran along the length of the outside wall, skirting gardens filled with beds of vibrant flowers. Verdant green vines trailed up the pillars of the pale stone gothic arches as their feet padded along on polished stone flags. Lia could smell the pungent aromatic fragrance of the rosemary bushes from beneath the low wall.

'It's very kind of you to invite me,' said Lia again, wishing she didn't feel so intimidated.

'We thought we'd have coffee on the terrace by the pool. There's a lovely view and the children are all dying to meet you. They're a bit much if we're all inside.' Aurelia rolled her eyes.

At that moment Giulia skipped off, running outside through a wooden doorway at the end of the long stone walkway.

'I'm sorry about that. We did try to warn her that this must all be strange for you, meeting all of us at once –

discovering a whole new family – but she was so excited to have another sister. I hope you don't mind.'

'Mind?' Lia's thoughts were so scattered, she didn't know where to start picking them up.

'Yes. Her assuming that you would want to claim more siblings without even knowing us.' Aurelia gave her a gentle, sympathetic smile and then added with a touch of mischief that immediately made Lia relax, 'You might not even like us, once you've met us, which would be a terrible shame because we're really quite nice.'

Lia laughed and Aurelia grinned at her.

'I can see where Leo gets his smile from.'

'Oh yes, he's all me. I was blond as a child – now the hairdresser helps.' Aurelia patted her the sun-streaked highlights that ran through her light brown hair. 'And you must tell me where you got that divine dress.' Aurelia stopped and touched the fabric of Lia's skirt. 'It's beautiful.'

'Thank you,' said Lia and beamed at the other woman. 'I made the fabric myself. It's what I do.'

'You made this! It's wonderful. How clever. I wish I had a talent like that.'

'You have plenty of talents, *cara*.' Ernesto stood in the wooden doorway, a wide smile on his handsome face. He might have been in his early fifties but he could easily have passed for mid-thirties. 'Lia, welcome. I'm Ernesto. I'm so pleased to meet you after so very long.' He stepped forward and kissed her on each cheek, holding on to her forearms to study her. 'You have the look of your mother, but I think but there is a little of me, too.'

'Yes, she has your beautiful eyes.' Aurelia winked at Lia. 'You will find that the way to Ernesto's heart is flattery.'

'Of course. Always,' boomed Ernesto, laughing delightedly. 'But seriously we are very happy to have you here.'

'Yes,' chipped in Aurelia. 'It has been preying on his mind for many, many years. We are so pleased that you are.'

'You knew about me?' Lia was surprised that he'd confided in his wife previously.

'Oh yes, I've always known,' said Aurelia, patting her husband's arm. 'It has been a source of great sadness for both of us. Now you are here we really want to get to know you.'

Lia's heart expanded at her gentle words. After Raphael's constant suspicion and determination to keep her away from his stepfather, this open expression of pleasure completely floored her. It hadn't occurred to her that she'd be welcomed with such warmth.

'That's very kind.'

'Nonsense. Now come. Meet everyone. I think it is easier to dive right into the water. Get the shock of it over with,' said Ernesto and he took her arm, guiding her into a hallway. The walls were filled with photographs of him with leading ladies, as she might have expected, but there were equal numbers of him and Aurelia with their family, with lots of candid family holiday shots of the children at different ages. Against one wall of the room by the huge arched doorway opening out into the garden was a pile of inflatables, swimming goggles, snorkels and foam pipes, next to several baskets of bright pool towels.

From outside Lia could hear shrieks of laughter and when they stepped out into the sunshine she could see three children playing with a ball in the huge oval pool, which was surrounded by jacaranda trees. A large patio was filled with very expensive-looking teak sunloungers with striped cushions. In the shaded areas hammocks were strung between wooden posts, and egg-shaped wicker chairs suspended from some of the larger trees, each filled with a nest of bright primary-coloured cushions.

This was what real wealth looked like, she realised, but there was also a casual ease about everything, strewn about rather than carefully arranged as in a show home.

Ernesto headed for a little summer house to the left of the pool. Not that it was that little, as it could easily have seated fifteen around the table inside, which was laid with a large coffee pot and delicate white china coffee cups, as well as a tray of the most gorgeous-looking miniature pastries.

'Come, sit down. Aurelia has had lots of fun baking this morning.'

'You made these?'

'I love to cook.'

'That is one of her talents,' said Ernesto proudly. 'You have to try her Lemon Delight. They are the best in Positano – but don't tell anyone. We like to keep them to ourselves.'

Aurelia actually blushed, which was very sweet.

'He is exaggerating. But I do enjoy spending time in the kitchen.'

Lia was surprised. She would have expected them to have a chef or a housekeeper or a cook or something.

She must have shown it – or maybe Aurelia was a mind-reader.

'This is our family home. Where we can be ourselves for the holidays. We don't have any live-in staff here, although Patrizia and Marco live in the cottage next door. Marco was at school with Ernesto. They look after the house when we're not here and when we are, Patrizia does the housekeeping and Marco manages the gardeners and acts as driver if we need him to. I do most of the cooking though. It is my treat. The time when I can truly look after my family and nurture them properly. Food speaks the language of love.'

'She loves me so much. She tries to make me fat,' complained Ernesto, patting his almost flat belly.

Aurelia giggled and shook her head. 'Pay no heed to him. He talks a lot of rubbish.'

'But you love me anyway.' He snatched up her hand and kissed it.

'Papa! Please.' The teenage girl approaching with wet hair leaving a trail of drips behind her mimed vomiting. 'You're so embarrassing. Hi. I'm Luciana. You can call me Lucy. All my American friends back in LA do.'

'You live in LA?'

'Yes,' said a terse voice and Lia turned round to find Raphael studying her. 'Maybe you should come see us out there.'

The sight of him gave her that usual step-off-a-cliff sensation. But it wasn't just those dark, striking looks that turned her stomach liquid; her whole system was tuned into the quick burst of anticipation at the prospect of them sparring again. Around him she felt like a fencer, primed and ready to go. It was liberating. She could say what she felt to him. When he was about, there was no ducking behind a mask of manners.

'Oh yes. That would be lovely,' said Aurelia, clapping her hands, oblivious to – or maybe in spite of – Raphael's sarcasm. 'You could come for Thanksgiving. We always have a family party then. Leo and Raph fly in from London.'

'I can't wait,' drawled Raphael and Lia gave him a docile smile, ready to strike.

'I'm sure you can,' she said. 'But try to contain yourself. You can enjoy me being here.'

'I can,' he said and disarmed her with a quick smile of appreciation and by sitting down next to her. She wondered if payback might include a swift kick of retribution under the table … or was he softening towards her?

Aurelia served tea and coffee to everyone and urged Lia to fill her plate with the pastries. 'These cannoli are only small,' she insisted, pushing the roll of crisp pastry stuffed with pistachio cream and nibbed hazelnuts onto her plate.

'They look beautiful. What is this one?' Lia pointed to one that was unfamiliar.

'That is bocconotti filled with hazelnut cream. It is an Italian shortbread.'

'So, Lia, tell us all about you,' said Ernesto. 'Me, everyone knows about. I am very boring. You are the surprise package on a birthday.'

Beside her Lia heard Raphael's quick snort of derision. 'Ernesto loves to pretend he's very modest. He's not.'

Aurelia grinned. 'No, he isn't. But then he's an actor. Everyone tells him he's wonderful.'

'Except my family,' mourned Ernesto with a twinkle in his eye. 'They like to remind me that I am a mere mortal and that I have lots of flaws. That I'm actually quite useless.'

'It's true,' piped up Lucy, now sitting cross-legged on the floor in the sunshine. 'Papa is very bad at DIY. We have to get a man in to do everything, unless Raph and Leo are here. Raph is very useful. He mended the light in my bedroom … although I think it was Papa that broke it in in the first place.'

'And there you have it. My family, my biggest fans.' Ernesto lifted his shoulders in a self-deprecating shrug, which Lia found quite charming. The man had charisma by the wheelbarrow-load. 'Ah, here are the twins. Lured by the promise of treats.'

Lia was introduced to the eleven-year-old twins, Michael and Bianca. All the children had impeccable manners but were not above teasing their dad, who seemed to set himself up to be the butt of their good-natured jokes.

Aurelia sat serenely, watching her family interacting, making the odd interjection while Raph, next to her, felt like a buzzard ready to pounce – although on what, Lia wasn't sure. He disconcerted her because he was giving off an on-edge vibe, but more so because his tanned thigh was almost touching hers and if she shifted so much as a centimetre, the dark hairs on his legs would brush across her skin. This close she could smell him, a beguiling mix of coffee, lemon, pine and man – that musky masculine scent. Her nerves jangled with the awareness of him and the strange desire to lean into him and press her nose to the column of his neck and inhale the scent of him.

He glanced down at her, a half-smile playing at his lips as if he knew exactly what she was thinking.

'How are you finding Amalfi?' asked Ernesto and she turned to him, grateful to break the odd connection between her and Raphael. 'Have you been here before? Have you been to Italy before? There is so much to get to know about you. About your life.' Sadness crossed his face. 'We have so much time to make up for.'

'And we will,' said Aurelia, taking his hand and patting it with her other hand. 'We have the whole summer. There is plenty of time.'

Aurelia gave Lia another one of her gentle, sympathetic smiles, as if she understood that Lia felt overwhelmed by the magnitude of having to share a whole life. Did she want to expose so much of herself to someone who was still very much a stranger themself? She was the outsider here and she didn't want to unpick herself in front of them all.

She focused on Ernesto's question. 'It's very beautiful and yes, it is my first time here, but I have been to Rome and Florence before for weekends with friends.' She'd always wanted to go to Italy when she was younger and now she had an inkling as to why her mother had been so reluctant for her to do so.

'Maybe you could learn Italian while you are here. We will all help you,' said Ernesto. 'You are half Italian after all.'

'I can try,' said Lia with a laugh. 'I was never very good at French.'

'Pah!' dismissed Ernesto. 'You have good strong Italian blood in your veins. It will come easy when you spend time with the family.'

'Not everyone is so happy to be with family all the time,' Raph pointed out. 'She might have better things to do with her time.'

'And she is right here and quite capable of speaking for herself,' Lia murmured so that only he could hear it, as the twins began suggesting things that she could do with the family.

'We could go to the beach. Can you swim, Lia?'

'I can swim,' she said with a laugh at Giulia's serious question. Actually she'd swum a lot as a teenager, getting up at five every morning to train before school for several years.

'And sew,' said Aurelia. 'Lia made this beautiful dress.'

Giulia's eyes widened. 'It's like a princess dress. Can you make one for me? With silver stars?'

'Now Giulia, that isn't very polite.' Aurelia shook her head. 'You have lots of lovely dresses already.'

'I do,' said Giulia complacently, reaching forward and stroking the fabric.

'Where did you find the fabric?' asked Aurelia.

'I made it. Well, I bought the fabric and dyed it to create this effect. That's what I do.'

Ernesto frowned. 'What you do?'

'Yes, I'm a textile artist.'

'That sounds interesting,' said Aurelia. 'Do you make lots of clothes?'

Lia shook her head. 'Only for myself and then it's quite

often just to practise something. I create art from textiles.' She picked up her phone and flicked to one of the albums on her phone.

'This is the sort of thing I do.' It was always easier to show people than try to explain.

Ernesto and Aurelia took the phone and peered at the screen, scrolling through with ahs and ohs of appreciation. Lia shot a look at Raphael – as if to say: see, I'm good! – but to her surprise she found he was studying her with sharp-eyed intensity. Her heart stuttered under that thoughtful assessment. What was he thinking? She wasn't about to try and seek approval from him but at the same time she didn't like the way he assumed the worst of her.

'These are gorgeous,' said Aurelia.

'Yes,' Ernesto agreed, peering at the screen. 'I would like to buy one. This one.' He turned the screen to her. He had good taste; it was one of her favourites. An autumn woodland scene of fallen leaves and lean tree trunks in a golden glow of late afternoon sun.

'Nice one,' muttered Raphael under his breath, his cynicism burning a little hole in her chest.

'Yes, that one,' said Aurelia. 'It is beautiful. I can almost hear the crispness of the leaves when you walk through them, kicking them up.'

'That's it. Exactly,' said Ernesto excitedly. 'I would very much like to buy it.'

'You don't need to do that,' she said, a little hitch in her heart at his enthusiasm. It was the sort of thing her own dad – or rather Simon – would have done. Except Raph had spoiled the moment. She knew that he thought she had an ulterior motive for showing them the website.

'Besides, all of these have been sold already. They're just examples of my work.'

'Sold? All of them?' Raphael looked incredulous. If she hadn't been in front of Ernesto and Aurelia at that moment, she might have put him in his place and explained that her work was highly sought after.

'How do you do all this?' asked Aurelia, her hands drawn to Lia's dress again and providing a welcome change of subject. For a moment Lia wondered if the woman had picked up on the subtext between her and Raph.

'I have a studio in London where I work. And I've managed to borrow a studio here in Positano for the summer.'

'So you could make a dress for Bianca?' suggested Giulia suddenly with a sly look at her sister.

'Yes, that's a good idea,' agreed Luciana with a smirk.

Giulia nodded enthusiastically. 'She never wears dresses and she needs one for the party.'

'No, I don't,' snapped Bianca.

'Ah, yes! You must come to the party,' said Ernesto with another sudden change of direction that made Lia's head swim. She wasn't used to being part of such a big group. She had yet to understand the dynamics and the pecking order. 'Raph, make sure Lia gets an invitation.'

'Oh no, I don't need—'

'But you must,' said Ernesto. 'We hold it every summer and everyone who's anyone in Italy comes. George and Amal came last year and the year before De Niro.'

'Oh, right,' said Lia faintly, having a strong suspicion he was referring to the Clooneys and Robert.

'It's always a great evening,' said Aurelia. 'You really must come. Raph, tell her.'

'Oh yes. You must come,' said Raph in a monotone that said anything but.

'That reminds me, Ernesto…' Aurelia and Ernesto began talking party details and Lia took a moment to ground herself. She felt like Dorothy tossed into the tornado. Although at least she could give a little credit to Raphael. She knew where she was with him – his hostility was actually quite reassuring.

'Don't you like Lia, Raph?' Giulia piped up, fixing him with a hard stare, elbow on the table, one hand propping up her chin.

Next to her, Raph started and Lia almost laughed at the panicked widening of his eyes, which looked every which way but at her. When he did finally manage to look her way, she shot him a she's-got-you-there smirk.

'Of course I do.'

Lia could swear his teeth were gritted. He'd have made a great ventriloquist.

'Then why do you look all cross?' Giulia leaned over and with a sharp jab prodded the crease between his eyebrows, which had drawn together in two dark slashes.

'I'm not cross,' he denied, and Lia gave him a knowing grin. 'Just thinking. Organising the party takes a lot of thinking. I have to remember all the people to invite.'

Lia winked at Giulia. 'Just as long as he doesn't forget

me, eh?' This was fun. Winding Raphael up was highly amusing.

'As if I would,' said Raph, in a quiet silky voice, his nostrils flaring slightly. The low timbre of his voice and its suggestive challenge made her catch her breath. When she glanced up at him she couldn't look away from his steady gaze.

'Lia?' She hadn't even noticed Ernesto moving from his seat to stand by her side. 'Perhaps we can go for a walk. I'd like to show you the grounds.'

Her breath sighed out silently and she turned to give Ernesto a bright smile, relieved by the interruption. She found Raph far too disturbing. 'That would be lovely,' she said.

———————

With great pride Ernesto led her through the grounds.

'This is a classical Italian garden,' he said, pointing out the neatly trimmed cypress and laurel hedges laid out in perfect symmetry as well as the white marble sculptures and the water features. 'And this' – he pointed to the path that meandered throughout the greenery – ' is the promenade.' He gave a chuckle. 'Rather appropriate. The promenade was to both see and been seen in the garden, which is the stage. When Aurelia read that, she insisted we restored it when we bought the villa.'

'It's very … restful,' said Lia being diplomatic. It was too regimented and formal for her taste. She preferred wild, untamed gardens with lots of blousy flowers bursting with colour.

Ernesto laughed. 'Well said, my dear. It's not my favourite area of the gardens nor Aurelia's, but it's part of the image and it's also private, so a good place to get away from the children on occasion.'

'Like now?' asked Lia.

Ernesto smiled approvingly at her and she smiled back. Although she didn't know him at all, it felt like they were on the same wavelength and that he got her. It was a relief to find that he was so normal. Not a hatchet-faced mafia godfather, nor a middle-aged con artist, a temperamental chef, a dodgy security guard or a grieving widower. They were all characters from the films she'd watched avidly since she'd discovered who he was. She hadn't told anyone that. It had been her guilty secret. Ten in three days had been quite the cinematic marathon.

'I'm not sure what your mother has told you.' He moved to a stone bench set in a shady alcove. 'I wanted to explain. No disrespect to your mamma but I promise you it was not my choice to have no place in your life. But … she was your mamma and she had her reasons.'

'I know a little,' said Lia.

'I loved her, you know. Very much. But it was young love, young and desperate.' He laughed at himself. 'When I got the call from the producer in Hollywood, it was one of those life-changing moments. I had to go and Mary, she wanted me to go. She was very supportive, but I think perhaps she was much wiser. She knew ours was the sort of passion that would burn out.'

Lia bit her lip, allowing Ernesto his artistic licence. She couldn't imagine her pragmatic mother voicing the words let alone talking about passion burning out.

'She called me to tell me she was pregnant but that she'd also met someone else. I'm afraid at the time it was rather too easy for me. I was on set in Hollywood in my first film, doing what I'd always wanted to do. She handed me a fait accompli and I'm ashamed to say I agreed without too much soul-searching.

'A few months later, when the filming finished, I went to see Mary, but by then she had her Simon and I could see that she was happy. Happier than I'd ever seen her. I met him, you know – a good man.'

Lia swallowed. He *was* a good man, and she missed him.

'He promised that you would be his own. I offered money to support you but your mother … she didn't want anything that would create a tie.'

Ernesto gave her a sad smile. 'All neat and tidy. That was Mary. Not that I blame her. I … took the easy way out. At least I thought it was easy, but as the years passed, I always wondered about you. When I married Aurelia I told her about you and I got in touch with Mary. She… I don't want to speak ill of your mother. She only wanted what was best for you.'

'Mmm,' said Lia, unconvinced. It hurt that her mum had lied to her, because that's what it was: one huge, massive lie. Everything that Lia had known wasn't true. Her dad wasn't her biological father, and her sister was actually her half-sister. Inside her there was a huge black hole of empty chilliness, and if she dwelt on it too long it would suck her into nothingness. It was the most horrible feeling she'd ever had in her life. A sort of bereavement that she wasn't allowed to grieve over.

Ernesto laid a comforting hand on hers.

'Your mother is a good person.' He smiled. 'She has brought up a beautiful young woman. I can sense you are beautiful all the way through.'

Lia's natural good humour couldn't let that one go. She snorted. 'You hardly know me.'

He shrugged. 'I know these things. And,' he gave her a twinkly smile, 'you do have the most excellent genes.'

'If you say so.'

'I am your father,' he intoned in a Darth Vader voice, which made her burst out laughing. His face softened. 'Now you have two fathers.'

Suddenly Lia was choked. It was extraordinarily generous of Ernesto to acknowledge that but also it brought home how much she missed her dad and how heartbroken she'd been when she'd discovered the truth about her parentage. It had taken away all the bedrock of who she thought she was.

'Thank you. I feel I've lost him.'

'No, *cara*. You just need some time to adjust. So why don't you enjoy getting to know us and give yourself that time?'

Lia nodded. She liked this man. Liked him a lot.

'And I must return the photo to you. But I would like to perhaps have a copy.'

'I'm sure Raph could arrange that,' said Lia with a cheeky smile.

'That's a good idea, I'll ask him.'

They walked and talked a bit longer before ambling back to the poolside.

'Lia!' Leo's irrepressible grin lit up his face. 'You're here.'

He came bounding over and Lia relaxed just a little. She realised she'd been holding herself quite tightly, wanting to be on her best behaviour in front of Ernesto and Aurelia but also desperate not to give Raphael any reason to support his view that she was here for what she could get. He was so bloody transparent. If he'd had the chance, she knew he'd have stamped *gold-digger* on her forehead as a warning to his family.

The younger children immediately crowded round Leo with cries of 'Will you come in the pool with us?' 'Please, Leo.' 'Yes, Leo.'

'I will if Lia will,' he declared as Aurelia and Ernesto looked on indulgently.

'I didn't bring a swimsuit,' said Lia, wishing she had as the pool looked so inviting.

'That's no problem,' said Aurelia. 'We always have a selection for guests. You can take your pick. There's a shelf in the pool house next to the guest towels.'

Of course there was.

'Just help yourself and then you should stay for lunch,' continued Aurelia.

'Thank you but I really should head out soon. I need to work,' she said, touched by their open welcome.

'You can work this afternoon,' said Ernesto, leaning back in his chair, one arm draped across the empty chair next to him. 'Raph can run you back after lunch.'

'Yes,' enthused Leo. 'Mamma is making her special pasta for lunch. You *have* to stay and try it.'

If she hadn't seen it, Lia wouldn't have believed it, but the whole family suddenly turned dewy-eyed – even Raph, although his attention was diverted as his phone rang.

He drew his mobile from his back pocket, rising from the table and walking a few steps away to take the call. Lia heard him issue a curt '*Sì*.'

A few moments later, he returned. 'I'm afraid I need to go and make some calls in the office, if you will excuse me. See you later.'

As he walked away Lia couldn't decide if she was relieved or disappointed.

Chapter Twelve

'Here, here, Lia,' yelled Bianca, waving madly, sending a quick splash towards her twin as he tried to mark her.

Lia, squinting into the sun, tossed the beach ball towards her, laughing when Ernesto made a ridiculously over-ambitious dive to intercept it, sending a wave of water surging across the pool.

'Papa!' Lucy jumped on him when he came back to the surface and Michael took advantage of Bianca's inattention to snatch the ball from her grasp.

The already chaotic game descended into further mayhem as the four younger children ganged up on Ernesto, splashing him with wild giggles, while Leo and Michael wrestled over the ball. When Lia finally hauled herself out of the pool, she flopped onto one of the sunloungers, still laughing.

'They're all mad,' she said to Aurelia, a little

breathlessly, wondering what on earth she must look like but then deciding she didn't much care. The ice had been well and truly broken. Thank goodness for Leo.

'I think Ernesto is the biggest kid of all,' Aurelia replied with an indulgent smile. 'He's a good father. It's very important to him that we're all here for the summer. And Raph this year. Usually he only comes for a weekend or two. Ernesto worries about him. I do too.'

'Raph is a big boy, Mamma,' said Leo, water sloughing from his body as he padded over. 'That was fun,' he said, sitting on the sunlounger next to Lia. 'I'm knackered.'

'Me too,' said Lia.

'Imagine being their mother,' said Aurelia before adding with a teasing smile aimed at her husband who was clambering out of the pool, 'Not to mention wife to the biggest child here.'

'You don't mean that, *amore*,' said Ernesto, draping his wet body all over as she shrieked and pushed him away.

'I … live … in a madhouse,' she said, giggling between the kisses Ernesto peppered her face with. She finally fended him off. 'I'm going to prepare some lunch.'

'Would you like a hand?' asked Lia.

'No, but I'd love the company,' said Aurelia.

The kitchen was vast with a vaulted ceiling and marble surfaces everywhere. Lia stared, fascinated by the eclectic mix of old and new, which looked as if it came straight from the pages of an architectural magazine. Despite the light pouring in through a series of bifold doors that lined three sides of the modern section, the old kitchen area was deliciously cool. Bisecting the two spaces was a large marble-topped island, almost the size of a double bed, with a double sink on one side with a high-spouted copper tap. Dark blue cabinets lined the walls with white porcelain knobs on the doors and drawers. Copper pans hung on white tiled walls interspersed with shelves filled with herbs spilling from dark glazed pots.

While the kitchen area had minimalist simplicity and style, the dining area was modern and bright with a distinct sense of comfort. A huge pale wood table with long sleek lines dominated the space along with ten stylish dining chairs, each one with a different ikat-patterned cushion and a piping of colourful pom poms – blue and green on some and orange and yellow on others. A sunshine-yellow L-shaped sofa, which looked large enough to seat the entire family, was scattered with more pom-pom-decorated cushions, these in solid primary colours. Outside the bifold doors was a terrace shaded with a vine, around which were arranged bulbous terracotta pots containing leggy agapanthus swaying in the breeze, and beyond that a rustic wooden fence framed the view of the sea.

'Take a seat,' said Aurelia, pointing to the raffia-topped bar stools, which immediately reminded Lia of old-fashioned Italian restaurants in London. 'Would you like a glass of wine? I'm going to have one.'

Before Lia answered, she'd produced two elegant glasses and poured white wine into them.

'*Salute,*' she said and raised her glass.

'*Salute*,' replied Lia.

'It is so nice to have some adult female company for a change. And someone that is not always looking at Ernesto and wanting his attention. It gets very tiresome.' Her mischievous twinkle belied her words. 'All these gorgeous young actresses thinking that because I chose to stay out of the limelight, I must be some frumpy old woman.' She grinned at Lia. 'They always seem quite affronted when they meet me. I have never worked out at what age I should have become invisible. Do you cook?'

'When I remember,' said Lia, a little guiltily. 'I don't really have the time to cook.' Food was fuel in between everything else and was invariably on the hoof.

'Time isn't essential but taking care is: when it comes to cooking you have to devote what time you have to the task in hand. Whenever I try to rush, the food is never as good. There is a difference between food taking little time and food being made quickly. It's all about the attention. The love and care you give it. Don't you agree?'

Lia shrugged. 'I wouldn't know.'

Aurelia tutted. 'I will show you how little time a really fantastic dish takes – *dieci minuti*. Like Leo said, this is the family favourite. I made the pasta earlier, but you could buy that.'

'You made the pasta?'

'*Sì*. I am Italian.' Aurelia gave another one of mischievous grins. 'But only when I'm in Italy on holiday. In LA we have a cook and Ernesto has a personal trainer and a nutritionist. Life is different there. Here I can be myself again.'

'Do you like living in LA?' asked Lia.

'I love living in LA. We have a beautiful ranch just outside Santa Barbara and we have a place on the beach in Carmel. But this is home, where we can be just the family. You live in London?'

'Yes. I've got a flat in Wandsworth, which I share with someone.' Her current flatmate, Jane, worked as cabin crew for a budget airline.

'Next time we're in London, it will probably be for the première of Ernesto's next film, which is in post-production at the moment. We must meet up. In fact, you should come to the première. I'll let you know as soon as I have a date.'

'Thank you,' said Lia, a little stunned. That would certainly be an experience.

'Now. Pasta. This is my favourite Amalfi Lemon pasta. Fresh, light and so, so easy to make. Not that I normally tell anyone that.' She pushed the large pottery bowl of lemons that Lia had been admiring towards her and a seriously heavy-duty long, slim grater. 'You can zest three lemons for me while I infuse the garlic in the oil.'

Lia watched as she poured unctuous dark green olive oil from what had to be a two-litre glass jar into a large stainless-steel frying pain.

Using the zester, Lia sliced tiny yellow shavings onto a pretty painted plate, the fragrant citrus smell filling her nose. It imprinted on her brain and in that moment she was a little overcome by the feeling of being at one with herself. She was convinced that for evermore she would associate the smell of lemons with the very Italian-ness of this moment: Aurelia's unfussy bustle around the kitchen, the simple pleasure of preparing food, the touch and feel of the lemons beneath her fingers and the gentle companionship between two women who had nothing more than one man in common. Lia's heart blossomed with a feeling of well-being and simple happiness.

Aurelia, who was now peeling garlic cloves, exchanged a quick smile with her, almost as if she'd felt Lia's change in tenor, and tossed a handful in the frying pan while switching on the kettle. With grace and the ease of familiarity, she darted around the kitchen gathering the next ingredients – some fresh chillis and a pot of anchovies from the fridge, and the earthenware bowl of pasta hiding under a tea cloth.

'Here.' Aurelia gave her a white ceramic lemon juicer. 'Could you squeeze them now.' It wasn't a request, she was in sergeant major mode, not that Lia would have refused. She was fascinated by the process. Already the smell of garlic filled the air as Aurelia removed the pan from the heat, leaving the garlic cloves in situ.

'Good, eh?' she said. 'You just fry the garlic a very little. You don't want to make it too dark; it'd taste bitter. We leave it in the oil to give it flavour but not to overpower the dish.'

As soon as the water in the kettle boiled Aurelia emptied it into a large saucepan and set it on the biggest gas ring on the large hob.

Lia juiced the lemons, relishing the ache in her muscles as she twisted them around the reamer.

A sudden hiss alerted them to the water boiling over in the pan. Whirling like a ninja, Aurelia whipped off the top and then tipped the bowl of fresh pasta into the boiling water before returning to the chopping board, where she quickly sliced her way through a small pile of anchovies and then deseeded and chopped the chillies.

Halfway through she opened the oven, put in a pile of flat-bottomed pasta bowls and danced her way to the big American-style double-doored fridge, where she removed the biggest piece of parmesan Lia had ever seen.

'Can you grate some of this? At least three big handfuls?'

While Lia was doing that, occasionally pinching a stray curl of the pungent, acidic cheese, Aurelia disappeared and returned with a bunch of flat leaf parsley in her hand.

'I love the smell of parsley,' said Aurelia. 'So clean and fresh and it cuts through the lemon beautifully. I think we're almost there.'

She fished the garlic cloves out of the oil and then added the anchovies, lemon zest and juice, along with the chillis and parsley, gave it a swift stir and then drained the pasta and returned it to the saucepan. Next, she tossed all the ingredients into the pan, stirring it with a big wooden two-pronged fork.

'And that's us done. Now I just have to call everyone.'

Lia wondered how she was going to round everyone up and then laughed when Aurelia sent a voice message via WhatsApp.

'Phones are useful sometimes, but *not* at the meal table. It is my rule. Food should be enjoyed together, not with distractions. When we eat together, we eat together.'

'My … m-mum's the same,' said Lia, her voice cracking

a little. A tug of homesickness twisted her insides as she pictured the family kitchen back home. Lia tried to swallow the blockage in her throat as her eyes blurred.

'She … she only told me about Ernesto two weeks ago.'

'*Cara.*' Aurelia wiped her hands on a tea towel and drew Lia to a seat at the table. 'I didn't realise. This must be difficult for you,' she said taking Lia's hand. 'Quite a shock, I'm sure. I had no idea and then today we come at you like a herd of bulldozers. If I'd known, maybe we would have been a little more … gentle with you. I just assumed you had always known, at least that you … you had a different father.'

Lia wiped back a tear. 'I'm sorry. I didn't mean to get emotional. I've fallen out with my mother.'

'I'm so sorry. But I'm sure she will forgive you. That's what mammas do. We always love our children even when they are difficult.'

Lia gave Aurelia a limp smile. The woman was so damn nice. 'The problem is I'm not sure I know how to forgive her.'

Aurelia held her hand, patting it gently. 'You will find a way. Time is, as they say, a good healer – as is sunshine, good food and family. Let us look after you and your heart will heal.'

A slight tap of glass on marble made both of them whirl around to find Raphael setting down a water tumbler on the island. 'Sorry, did I disturb a heart-to-heart?' he asked, not looking the least bit sorry.

Aurelia gave Lia's hand a final squeeze and shot her a

heart-warming smile before turning to face a scowling Raphael. 'Your timing is perfect. You can open a bottle of the Tenuta San Franceso Per Eva that Ernesto likes. You must try it, Lia; it comes from a local vineyard. It's lovely and light and will make a perfect accompaniment to our lunch.'

Raphael shot Lia a suspicious look before doing as his mother asked. Too rattled to be amused, Lia sighed and took a fortifying sip of wine.

'Lia, would you mind laying the table?' Aurelia thrust a handful of forks and napkins at her. Grateful to have something to do, she jumped to her feet and began to lay the table as the rest of the children started to appear.

'I want to sit next to Lia,' announced Giulia, marching straight over to her and tugging at her dress.

'Me too,' said Leo, coming over and draping a loose arm around her shoulder. 'Has Mamma taught you how to cook my favourite dish? I could marry you now.'

'No!' squealed Giulia. 'He's stinky. If you have to marry someone it should be Raph. He's a proper grown-up.'

'Who are you calling stinky?' Leo put her in a headlock and tickled her.

'You, Mr Stinky.' She giggled. 'Stinky, stinky, stinky.' She managed to disentangle herself and ran behind Lia, using her as a barrier.

'I get no respect in this family,' grumbled Leo, clearly not the least bothered about it.

It was quickly apparent that everyone had their usual place: Ernesto at the head of the table, Aurelia on his right and the children ranged around them. Lia realised a moment too late that the empty seat next to her was reserved for Raphael. It seemed she was never going to escape the man.

Chapter Thirteen

'Are you busy this morning?'

Raph looked up from his laptop screen to find Ernesto lounging against the door jamb of the study. It was one of those leading questions that Ernesto loved to employ. Although to be fair, if he'd said yes, Ernesto would have taken his word and left him in peace.

'No. What do you...' He softened the question by adding 'need' rather than 'want'.

'I've decided to buy one of Lia's pictures. She said she was working on one of Positano. She said I could come to her studio and see her work.'

'Did she?' said Raph dryly, surprised by the swift tug of disappointment in his gut. Looked like Lia hadn't wasted any time capitalising on her new connections. 'And is this a genuine desire or an act of charity?'

'I saw her website, she is very good.'

'Hmm,' said Raph. Smoke and mirrors, he guessed. No one regulated websites – they could be a complete fabrication and no one would be any the wiser. People could make any old wild, unsubstantiated claim and there was nothing to stop them. He sometimes thought WWW stood for the Wild Wild West – lawless and untamed and inhabited by snake-oil salesmen. Although, he had to admit the piece he'd seen Lia working on had impressed him.

'Now that you know where she lives, you can take me there … when it's convenient, of course.'

Raph studied Ernesto's guileless, innocent face; people forgot Ernesto was an actor at their peril.

'And that's why you asked me to take her home yesterday?'

'Yes,' said Ernesto, his eyes turning shrewd, into the savvy operator that Raph knew him to be. You didn't get to be that successful without having some street smarts. 'You don't trust her, do you, Raph?'

Ernesto folded his arms, waiting with watchful stillness.

'Honestly, no. Sorry, I just can't help it.'

'Not everyone is bad.'

'I know, but I keep asking myself why she's here now.'

'Because she didn't know before. She's only just found out.'

'You only have her word for that.' He couldn't shake his natural caution. 'I think you should hold back a little before you welcome her with open arms. We need to get to know her and find out more about her. Especially before you go splashing the cash on the next great artwork.' His implied quote marks made it quite clear what he thought about her work. 'I also still think we should get her to do a DNA test.'

'There's no need. I know she's my daughter.' There was

a stubborn set to Ernesto's mouth that indicated he wouldn't change his mind on this.

'There's no harm in being cautious.'

'What about gut instinct? Trusting your intuition.'

Raph shrugged. 'Even the most trustworthy people can let us down sometimes. Swayed by money, the promise of fame, what they can get.'

'But Lia came all this way to meet me. Don't you think that says something about her?'

'Yes, it does.' Part of him admired that after he'd dismissed her from his office in London, she'd come to Italy. He hated people who gave up easily because things were too hard, but equally he hated people who took shortcuts trying to avoid the graft.

'She's tenacious when she wants something. Like money or to use your name for any number of things. You of all people should know better than to take people at face value.'

'You are much too cynical. What time can we go?'

'We might as well go now.' Get it over with and then he might be able to get some work done instead of giving in to the temptation to look at the woman's damn website.

———

Was it pride that made him take the throaty Lamborghini Urus? It wasn't exactly the most practical car to drive in Positano but he felt it was useful to remind Lia who she was dealing with, and the battered Fiat that Ernesto and Aurelia used to potter about in wouldn't cut it.

Luckily there was nothing coming on the narrow street where Lia's accommodation was situated. Raph had dropped her there the previous afternoon, waiting with the engine running until she'd opened the door and entered the building. It was always useful to know exactly where people lived. He managed to squeeze the Lamborghini into a tight space between a brand spanking new convertible Audi TT and an ancient Peugeot with its paint peeling from the bonnet that looked as if it might be held together with string. The back seat was filled with crates of lemons. It was part of what he loved about being here in Italy. The car probably belonged to a farmer who'd brought his lemons to sell to a local restaurant. You never saw that in London.

'Which one is it?' asked Ernesto, peering at the buildings crammed together.

'That one.' Raph pointed to what amounted to part greenhouse and part shed on top of an existing building accessed by a narrow stone stairway open on one side with no handrail.

Ernesto pulled a face at the white paint peeling from the wooden panels on the side of the edifice and gingerly took a step on the staircase. He knocked on the rickety glass door at the top, murmuring with outrage to Raph, 'This wouldn't keep a child out, let alone a thief. Why would anyone stay here?'

'Because it's cheap, I guess,' said Raph. 'Struggling artists can't be too choosy.'

'Actually it's because of the amazing light and the facilities,' drawled a faintly amused voice from behind them.

Raph winced. Why was he destined to be overheard by this woman at the least opportune time, on every single occasion?

'Lia!' Ernesto greeted her. 'I wanted to see your picture. The one of Positano that you told me about.'

'Oh.' Lia's cheeks turned pink. 'That's … that's lovely of you.'

Raph studied her, surprised by her sudden shyness. Surely her new father's opinion wasn't that important to her? They were strangers, after all. Her hands fidgeted as if she didn't know what to do with them … or was it because she'd been caught out and her starving artist act was all show? His distrust was too deeply ingrained to give her the benefit of the doubt. He regarded her with contemptuous eyes and she flushed as if all too aware of his scrutiny. He would bet she wouldn't have much to show them.

'I apologise for my bad manners for turning up unannounced, but I was very excited to see your work.' Ernesto had turned the charm dial all the way up and like every other person on the planet, Lia melted like gelato in the hot Italian sun.

'I'd love to show you my work space. It's a bit messy though.' She shot Ernesto a dazzling grin, the sun creating a halo around her hair, full of silver slivers of light.

'Messy is good. A sign of a creative mind.'

Raph almost snorted. Ernesto was continually asking Aurelia to find things for him, because his office was an absolute tip. Her superpower was laying hands on discarded scripts within seconds of being asked.

As they stepped over the threshold, Ernesto stopped

dead and Raph cannoned into him. He felt the older man stiffen.

'You live here?' he asked. Raph glanced round and could understand the chill in Ernesto's voice. The place was a dump and was that a pigeon's backside he could see through the hole in the roof?

Lia nodded with a touch of chagrin tugging at her lips. 'Just for the summer. The studio facilities are really very good. I'm very lucky to have found somewhere I can dye my fabrics.'

'And this is where you sleep?' Ernesto looked over at the alcove tucked in the corner. The bed might have been neatly made but it was a flimsy, cheap affair that wouldn't hold up to much, if any, action. Not that Raph wanted to think about Lia in that way … and damn it, if an image of her didn't flash in his head. Her hair fanning around her head on a pillow as she stared up, lips open in anticipation. What was wrong with him? It was a while since he'd split up with his last girlfriend, Layla, in London, but even so.

'Where do you cook?' It wasn't so much a question as a bark. Raph could tell Ernesto was not impressed.

Lia pointed to the counter under the window, with a sink and a small fridge tucked beneath it.

'And the cooker?'

She lifted her shoulders. 'I tend to live on salad, fruit, cheese and cold meats. It's not exactly a hardship here. Would you like to see my work?' She clearly felt uncomfortable at Ernesto's scrutiny and was already draping a swathe of silk over her arm. It was the piece Raph had seen her working on the other day, although she'd added considerably more of the fine black stitches. He had to concede that she had talent.

Ernesto studied the fabric before stepping forward slowly with obvious reverence. Raph didn't blame him. It was breathtaking in its simple beauty, the subtlety of the colours and the delicate lines conjuring up the eternal iconic image of Positano.

'*Squisito*,' he said, reaching and running his finger over the texture.

'Thank you.' Lia might not have understood the word, but Ernesto's awe-filled voice needed no translation. Raph himself itched to touch it. There was something so appealing about it.

'You created this?' Ernesto shook his head. 'You are very talented.' And like a kid in a candy shop he was already looking at the next thing. 'And this.'

He fingered a completely different piece, a lemon on a rough hessian backing, the delicate pale silk contrasting with the coarse weave. The contrasts intrigued Raph as much as the image of the vibrant lemon in its fine detail, the succulent flesh, the drops of juice and the bright waxy skins.

'I would like to buy both of these,' announced Ernesto. Of course he did. Raph almost rolled his eyes. He could have guaranteed that he'd want to find some way of giving his long lost daughter money without embarrassing her. Admittedly the pictures or whatever they were called were very good indeed, but this was standard Ernesto.

'I'm sorry,' said Lia. 'The lemon is not for sale; it's for a project I'm working on. But you can take a look again at the scene of Positano when it's finished, which' – she gave him a admonishing shake of her head – 'won't be for a little while.'

Raph gave her an ironic look. Clever. Was she denying Ernesto to make him keener?

'I will wait,' said Ernesto grandly. 'In the meantime, you cannot stay here. I insist you come and stay at the villa.'

Raph almost groaned out loud. What was Ernesto doing? They needed to keep the woman at a distance until they figured out her game. Surely it was obvious she was up to something, what with her just turning up out of the blue like this.

'That's very kind but—'

Raph's brief moment of relief – she was going to turn him down – shrivelled and died when Ernesto went into full impresario mode. 'Nonsense. It's not kind. It is important and it makes sense. You can get to know your brothers and sisters and we can get to know you.' He held up a hand. 'I have missed out on twenty-eight years of your life.'

Raph rolled his eyes. Seriously? Ernesto was playing the emotional blackmail card? He felt a little like he was on stage but had stepped into the wrong play.

'I insist. It would make me very happy. And Aurelia would want it too. She knows how much I've grieved for the daughter I'd never met until yesterday.'

Raph didn't know who to glare at first, his stepfather, for this ridiculously over-the-top speech, or Lia, because the last thing he wanted was for her to be under the same roof as him. There'd be no escaping her and she disturbed his equilibrium far too much. When he shot her a dark look, he realised that he'd made a tactical error. Locking eyes on him, she lifted her chin like Joan of Arc going into battle.

'That would be lovely, Ernesto. Thank you.'

'Excellent.' Ernesto clapped his hands together. 'Pack your things. We shall leave now.'

Chapter Fourteen

I f looks could kill, Lia would be three feet under with several tonnes of rubble piled on top. She grinned as she levered herself from the soft buttermilk leather seats of the fancy car. Raph caught her eye and his face tightened. It was his own fault. She'd been all set to say no to Ernesto, but when she'd seen that look of quick fury on his stepson's face, an imp inside had said yes just to mess with him. It had been a complete whim.

'Lia, *cara*.' Aurelia darted down from the porticoed entrance and wrapped her arms around her in an effusive hug. 'We're so happy you decided to come and stay. It will be lovely to have some adult female company for a change and we have so much to catch up on. We can drink Prosecco together and make pasta, and you can learn Italian.'

Her soft, perfumed embrace was so generous and natural that it made Lia think of her own mother and she had to swallow the lump threatening to lodge itself in her throat. She missed her.

Ernesto came and put his arms around her and Aurelia, in a group hug. 'This is going to be a wonderful summer. All my children here together. Come, Raph, you too.' Ernesto turned to Lia. 'Although he is my stepson and he tells me what to do – when he can – I still think of him and Leo as mine.'

Raph's face actually softened and Lia eye's widened at the sight of the gentle smile curving his lips as he slipped an arm across Ernesto's shoulder. 'You're a sentimental fool, Papa.'

'No, I'm the man who fell in love with your mother and her babies, and she and you boys and the bambinos we made have made me the happiest man in the world.' Tears shone in his eyes. 'Family is everything.'

'See? Sentimental old fool,' said Raph, turning to Lia, for once a quick grin on his face.

'Come, come,' said Aurelia. 'I have made up the guest suite for you in the garden. It's much nicer and you can have some privacy down there away from the children.'

'Great,' muttered Raph in a voice that she was clearly supposed to hear.

Aurelia laughed and waved a hand. 'No one will bother you down there.'

Unless Raph popped down there to murder her, thought Lia.

If the concept of a guest suite sounded grand, the actuality was deluxe on speed and Lia could barely believe it. It was the most luxurious space she'd ever seen. She had her own front door leading into a tiny vestibule with a terracotta-tiled floor, a space that contained a large bevel-edged mirror and an elegant antique console table with an enormous pot containing at least eight stems of white orchids. From the hallway a door led into a beautiful, light, airy bedroom with a white wooden floor and pale pine beams supporting the sloping roof. A huge bed with white drapes around it filled one wall, piled with crisp white cotton sheets and pale grey cushions embroidered in one corner with tiny pink French knots. A white fireplace on one wall was decorated with three fat Diptyque candles below a large gilt Romanesque mirror with chubby cherubs in each corner. It was the only ornate thing in the simple but stylish room. An ensuite led off from the left, with a bath that wasn't much smaller than a pool, and the biggest, fanciest shower Lia had ever seen in her life. In the recessed shelves were rows of rolled white towels and baskets of Officina Profumo-farmaceutica di Santa Maria Novella bath gels, body lotions, shampoos and conditioners.

'If you need anything, let us know, but we try and provide everything because we don't have a full-time housekeeper here,' said Aurelia, pointing out a substantial guest pack, which on first sight contained a proper shower cap, a white linen bath robe, slippers, a couple of hairbrushes in different sizes still in their packaging and a selection of brand-new swimsuits in differing sizes.

Aurelia opened a couple of cupboards to reveal not one but two hairdryers, one of which was the latest Dyson airwrap, as well as a set of GHD straighteners and a curling wand.

'I'll leave you to settle in. Come up to the house for dinner but you must treat it as your home.'

It was all a bit overwhelming but also a bit of a *Pretty Woman* moment, especially when Aurelia left and Lia flopped onto the bed and lay there looking up at the high ceiling. This place was A-mazing.

A sudden nip of homesickness pinched at her gut; normally she'd have taken lots of photos and sent them to her sister and mum on the family WhatsApp group. If circumstances had been different, they'd would have got such a kick out of seeing this, and her mum would have reminded her to make sure she gave her hosts a gift. Her dad would have teased her and told her to keep her room tidy otherwise they'd kick her out and she'd have sent him a jokey GIF of a hideously messy room.

Brushing the thoughts aside, Lia pushed herself up from the bed and went over to the French window.

'Wow!' Outside there was a small patio with a pair of sunloungers, a hammock and a swimming pool. She'd never had a whole swimming pool to herself, certainly not one quite like this, the turquoise mosaic tiles glittering with little veins of gold running through them. She wandered to the edge. A naughty smile crept over her face. She'd always wanted to go skinny-dipping – here was the perfect opportunity. Without a second thought she stripped off her T-shirt and skirt, whipped off her underwear and took a running jump into the pool. The cool water enveloped her and she swam a few strokes before surfacing, absorbing the shock of the cold, which wore off very quickly. After a while she slipped onto her back and floated squinting up at the bright blue sky, spreading her arms and legs out like a starfish, letting herself bob on the surface. This was absolute heaven. An idea began to formulate as she studied the depth of the cloudless sky, examining its intensity, and she wondered how she might achieve the colour.

'Well, that's not a sight you see every day,' drawled an amused voice.

Startled Lia opened her eyes to find bloody Raphael standing there in his usual attire of navy-blue shorts and white polo shirt – he must have a whole wardrobe of them.

'W-what are you doing here?' she spluttered. She had to crouch to keep her naked – totally naked – body submerged. She crossed her arms over her chest, hunched like flipping Quasimodo, wondering how much he could see from that angle.

'I live here,' he said, way too cheerfully. He was enjoying this.

'I meant in the guest suite.'

'There are two guest suites. I live in the other one.'

'You do?' Shit, why hadn't that dawned on her?

He grinned. 'I do.'

'Right. Well, this is embarrassing.'

'Don't worry,' he said, 'I'm not the least bit embarrassed.' If his grin got any wider there was a chance it might split his gorgeous bloody face.

She gave him a withering glare. 'Very funny.' Why was he just standing there, looking so ridiculously handsome? He could have stepped off the pages of a magazine. She felt herself growing hot, if that was possible in a pool. Clearly it was.

'Would you mind turning your back so that I can get out?'

'Do I have to?' he teased.

Part of her wanted to be relaxed about this and perhaps with Leo she might have just casually waded out of the shallow end and sauntered past him, but Raph was an altogether different animal.

'I would prefer it,' she said with as much haughtiness as she could manage.

'Shame,' said Raph but to his credit he turned around. With as much dignity as she could manage, she walked out of the pool, forcing herself to slow her steps as she padded around the edge back to her room.

Once she crossed the threshold of the patio doors she darted into the bathroom and snatched up a towel, glaring at herself in one of the many mirrors.

'Why are you such an idiot?' She shook her head, unsure quite how she was going to face Raph again. When she emerged from the bathroom, she could see that Raph had taken up residence on one of the sunloungers, earphones in and his phone by his side. The only other sunlounger was right beside him. Lia screwed up her face. Was he doing this deliberately to try and chase her away? Well, he could forget it. Raphael Knight was not going to scare her off. He was going to learn that he didn't always get his own way.

Unearthing her favourite bikini from her hastily packed bag, she put it on, selected a stripy beach towel and one of the expensive Lancaster suntan lotions from the guest pack and went out to the poolside.

Her mouth dried. Sunglasses were both a blessing and a curse. He couldn't see her looking at him but by the same token she had no idea whether he had his eyes open and was looking at her. She was trying to be cool and not daunted by the perfection of his muscled body – seriously, people in real life did not look like that.

'Are you going to sit down or just stand there admiring the view?' asked Raph without so much as moving a muscle.

Damn, he was so good at gaining the upper hand.

'View? What view?' she asked.

'This is supposed to be one of the best views on the Amalfi coast,' he said, still not moving.

Who said things like that? Did he really believe it? 'Whoa, you're sure of yourself,' she said, amazed by his deadpan delivery.

Raph began to chuckle. 'I didn't mean me … but I'm flattered you think so.' He sat up and waved a hand at the backdrop.

Lia felt the flush of heat race up across her chest and into her face. The view. Oh God, yes, the view. How had she not noticed? Because she was too damn busy ogling him, which, of course, he now knew.

Go with the flow, Lia, she told herself.

'You must work out a lot,' she said.

Raph shrugged. 'I find it's a good way of destressing at the end of the day and' – he pulled a moue of disgust – 'I have a dodgy back. If I don't keep up the pilates and core strength, I pay for it.'

She was surprised by the admission of weakness and immediately sympathetic.

'Ouch, that's no fun. My … dad' – she waved a hand, trying to dismiss the mistake – 'my other dad … he suffers. I know how miserable it can be. He had an operation a few years ago. An injection in the spine. Worked brilliantly. But he had to wait a while before they would refer him for it. I don't know, maybe it's not the same in Italy.' She was gabbling now.

'I live in London,' Raph reminded her.

'So you do. So how long are you out here for?'

'Why? Are you hoping I'll leave soon?'

'I couldn't care less whether you stay or leave,' snapped Lia. 'You're always questioning my motives. What have I done to make you distrust me so much?'

Raph raised an eyebrow that quirked just above his sunglasses. 'You came out to Italy. You tracked down Ernesto and inveigled an invitation to stay. I'm just trying to figure out what exactly it is that you want.'

'I don't want anything but to get to know him.'

'So you keep saying.'

'Because it's true.' Lia sat down on the sunlounger and massaged her temples, trying to ease the niggling headache that was gathering pace. 'Look, I don't want to fight with you. Why can't we call a truce? Give me a chance to prove that I have no other motives.'

Raphael pushed his sunglasses on top of his head and studied her for a moment and then he sighed. 'Ernesto is really pleased to see you and very excited that you're here. If you break his heart, I will hunt you down and make you regret it.'

Chapter Fifteen

Raph poured Aurelia an Aperol spritz and as he handed it to her, he spotted Lia walking in the dappled shade of the path from the guest suite to the main house. As she walked in and out of the shadows, he found his eyes drawn to her. She'd showered and changed since he'd last seen her and her hair was a mass of blond curls that draped over her bare shoulders. The peasant-style dress with puff sleeves floated around her ankles and the shirred bodice skimmed her breasts, which he now knew were round and high with small pink nipples. She'd looked like a floating angel in the pool earlier, with her fair hair fanning out around her, her body surrendered to the sky, and it had triggered an extremely inconvenient bolt of pure lust.

He grabbed himself a beer from the fridge tucked in the summer house, his hand shaking a little as he eased off the crown cap. What the hell was wrong with him? He couldn't possibly be attracted to this woman – a totally unknown quantity who, for all any of them knew, was out for what she could get. Landing free board and lodgings here, she was already a winner. Given the state of the place she was staying – obviously all she could afford – no wonder she'd jumped at the chance of coming to stay at the Villa Mimosa.

'You look lovely, *cara*,' said Aurelia, rising to her feet and greeting Lia with kisses on both cheeks.

'Thank you. So do you. I love your necklace. It's so unusual.'

Aurelia's hand rose to her neck to cradle the delicate golden chain and jewel-dotted pendant. 'Ernesto bought it for me last summer. For our wedding anniversary. It's very different, isn't it?'

'May I?' Lia stepped forward and held out a hand, picking up the pendant to examine it.

Raph watched as her fingers ran over the surface of the gold embellished with diamonds and sapphires – weighing up its value? – and couldn't help noticing their long, slim elegance. Or imagining their touch. Again the image of her naked body jumped into his head.

'Can I get you a drink?' he asked abruptly and she dropped the necklace.

'Er … yes.'

'What would you like?'

She looked a little nonplussed for a second, her green eyes thoughtful. 'I … er…'

'We have wine, Prosecco or spirits,' interjected Aurelia, with her innate ability to always smooth any social interaction. She had a talent for putting people at their ease and making them comfortable no matter who they were.

'Or perhaps you'd like a cocktail. Raph makes a lovely Limoncello spritz. Have you ever tried one?'

'That sounds wonderful.' A warm smile lit up her face. 'What's in it?'

'Prosecco, Limoncello and a little soda,' said Raph, still abrupt, wishing he could relax around this bloody woman. It was as if his body was at war with his brain.

Lia met his gaze and for a second he saw the brief flash of embarrassment before she lifted her chin to brave it out. 'That sounds lovely.'

'Let me make one for you. Is everything to your liking in the guest suite?' Raph asked.

'Yes,' she said, sending him a forced smile before adding, 'although I must ask, Aurelia, do you get many pests in the pool?'

Raph nearly choked as she gave him a guileless smile.

'I wondered if I might need some bug spray.'

'There are citronella candles in the room and around the pool, and I can let you have some lemon oil if you're very susceptible to bites.'

'I should be all right,' said Lia, 'now that I know they're there. Forearmed is forewarned and all that.' Her eyes never left Raph's and he lifted his beer in a silent *touché*. She'd definitely won this round, but he didn't feel bad about it. Instead he was reluctantly impressed by her sharp wit.

'Lia.' Ernesto burst onto the scene in one of his favourite Hawaiian shirts, an eye-watering yellow and green affair. Despite the lurid colours, he managed to carry it off. Aurelia gave him her usual fond smile. 'Why haven't you got a drink? Raphael, you're not neglecting our special guest, are you?'

He bounced over and gave Aurelia a huge kiss, draping an arm across her shoulders and pulling her in for a hug as if he'd not seen her for days rather than mere minutes. It was one of the many things that Raph admired about his stepfather, this absolute adoration of his wife, although Raph couldn't imagine ever feeling like that about anyone.

When he handed the drink to Lia, she murmured, 'Not spiked with cyanide?'

'Couldn't get hold of any at such short notice, but give me time.' He flashed her a grin and she laughed.

'Cheers.' She lifted her glass and took a confident swig.

He inclined his head, amused by the mischievous quirk to her lips.

'So, Mamma. What is on the menu this evening?'

Aurelia clapped her hands together. 'Ravioli stuffed with walnut and ricotta, with rucola salad and a caprese salad.'

'Did you made the ravioli?' asked Lia, leaning forward in her seat, with what looked like a genuine show of interest. He had to remember that his mother was very good at charming people, bringing out their better sides.

'But of course. If you'd like, tomorrow I will show you how to make pasta. It's very easy.'

'Okay,' said Lia. 'I'm not much of a cook but I'll give it a shot.'

'Raph is a very good cook but he takes a holiday when he is here with us, unless we have a barbecue, and then he is in charge. Ernesto is not allowed anywhere near the grill.'

'That is so unfair, my love,' complained Ernesto, turning indignant eyes on his wife.

'No, it is not, darling,' she said, giving his shoulder a complacent pat. 'You know you burn everything.' Aurelia turned to Lia, rolling her eyes. 'He starts talking or playing with the children and forgets that he is supposed to be cooking. And the next thing we know, everything is like charcoal. Raph is much more focused.'

'I bet he is,' said Lia, with a sugary smile that was sweet enough to hide the poison in her meaning.

Despite her wilful gibe, it did leave a thistle prick of irritation snagged in his skin, another reminder that he was on the outside. Relied upon to be the serious one of the family.

'Papa, Papa. Read me a bedtime story,' demanded Guilia, bouncing onto the terrace wearing pink gingham pyjamas and clutching a large white rabbit, the pink of its ears matching her pjs.

'We have a guest tonight, sweetheart,' said Ernesto. 'But I can read one now before dinner.'

Giulia pouted. The child knew exactly how to get around her father's protestations – all of them in fact.

'I thought you said Lia was family. A new sister.'

'She is. Your half-sister.'

Giulia frowned. 'And Raph is my half-brother.'

'Yes. Raph's mamma is your mamma, but I'm not Raph's papa. But I am Lia's papa.'

Unsurprisingly his half-sister looked exceedingly confused by this.

'What about Raph? Is he Lia's brother?'

'No. They're no relation at all.'

Giulia frowned.

Aurelia gave her an indulgent look. 'We're all family. That's the important thing.'

Perching her chin on the top of the rabbit, Giulia sat in one of the wicker chairs, ruminating on it all as the adults chatted about this and that.

'I can't marry Raph, can I?' she suddenly piped up. 'Or Leo?'

'No, sweetheart.'

'But Leo could marry Lia.'

Raph almost choked on his drink. He seemed to be doing that a lot of late. The thought of his brother and Lia... It would be an unmitigated disaster. His stomach twisted in violent protest – over his dead body would that happen. Throughout the sudden turmoil of emotional protest, he managed to maintain a cool silence, proud he was able to appear unruffled by this pronouncement.

Aurelia tilted her head to one side, sending a quick sweet smile to Ernesto. 'Technically she could. Wouldn't that be sweet?'

Until that moment, Raph had never experienced a genuine cold sweat, but one broke out sending a shiver through him. Leo and Lia. Lia and Leo. They were... No. That wouldn't be right. Leo was all wrong for Lia. Although shouldn't it be: Lia was all wrong for Leo? He didn't care about Lia's needs, he cared about Leo.

'Or Raph. Because he's old,' announced Giulia, coming to sit on his knee, turning her innocent face up to his, 'And you always say he needs a wife.' Her damp hair brushed his chin and her shampoo filled his nose with the sweet scent of green apples. He gave her a quick hug. She turned and gave him a wholesome smile. 'You should marry Lia. She's much nicer than Layla.'

Which reminded Raph, he really needed to find out if Layla had moved out of his place yet. Though they'd broken up, she'd been staying at his place as hers had flooded.

Aurelia let out a peal of laughter. 'Yes, you should, Raph, and then we really would all be family.'

Raph and Lia exchanged horrified glances as Ernesto joined in with his wife and began to roar with laughter. 'What a wonderful idea, Giulia. Then we could be one big happy family.'

This time, Raph really did mutter, 'Over my dead body.'

Chapter Sixteen

'What would you like to do today?' asked Ernesto, when Lia arrived at the breakfast table the next morning.

Raphael nodded at her over his demi-tasse of espresso. He reminded her of a brooding vampire waiting to swoop.

'Honestly?' she asked, casting her eye over the immaculate spread of plates of cheese, salami, rustic bread, granola, pastries and juices. How on earth did they all stay so slim?

'But of course.' Ernesto beamed at her. 'Come and have some breakfast. Coffee?'

'Yes, please.'

'Help yourself to whatever you'd like to eat.'

'Or I can make you some eggs,' said Aurelia, jumping to her feet.

'No, no. This is fine.' More than fine. At home she was lucky if she grabbed more than a coffee.

'So today. Would you like to go out on the yacht? Or we could take you to Naples. Or Sorrento. I know! Pompeii.'

Lia shook her head, wondering how to couch this without sounding ungrateful. 'To be honest, I need to do some work.'

There was silence around the table accompanied by blank looks of incomprehension.

'Work?' Ernesto frowned.

'I still have to work, so I need to spend the day in the studio.'

'But that place is...' The childish expression of disgust Ernesto pulled made her smile. It was impossible not to, not when she realised he had her best interests at heart. A quick pang squeezed her chest. Her mother had done Ernesto a disservice.

'I know it's not The Ritz, but it has everything I need there. My dye baths, my drying areas... It's perfect, even if it's a bit open to the elements.'

Ernesto waved an expansive hand. 'But we have plenty of room here. We can buy equipment and set up a whole room for you. What do you need? Tell us and we can arrange it. Raph can have everything sent from Rome or Milan or Naples.'

It would have been so so tempting to give in, just to see the look on Raphael's face. He already looked as if he'd swallowed a frog. Was he worried how much money it would cost? Or that she would never leave once she'd got her foot in the door?

'That's very kind of you, Ernesto...' She let the pause hang for as long as she dared before adding, with another one of her ultra-sweet smiles directed towards Raph, 'but Luca's studio is perfect for my work. And it has very good light.'

'Yes, I noticed that,' said Raph smoothly. Lia shot him a sarcastic smile. Yeah, right.

'To be honest, Ernesto, I like to work in peace without any distractions and I would hate you to think I was rude if I disappeared for hours on end. When I'm working I'm a little single-minded. I rarely stop for lunch—'

'You don't stop for lunch?!' Ernesto turned to Aurelia. 'Did you hear that?'

Lia caught her lip, glad that she hadn't volunteered that when she was really in the zone (pretentious as it sounded) she'd quite often work through the night without bothering with more than a cheese sandwich for dinner.

'Lia, you have to take better care of yourself.' Aurelia reached out and patted her hand before turning to Ernesto. 'Yes, darling, I heard her, but she can take lunch with her. I will make my focaccia—'

'With rosemary and the little crystals of sea salt?' Ernesto kissed his fingers. '*Bene, bene, bene.* No one makes focaccia like my Aurelia.'

Lia smiled uncertainly while Raph rolled his eyes, clearly used to the flamboyance and drama.

'Focaccia with burrata and tomatoes. I will make them for you and then you can take some arancini as well as some fruit. The cherries are really good at the moment. And maybe some of Nonna's pistachio cannoli.'

Ernesto groaned. 'My mother's cannoli recipe is the best.'

Lia was starting to feel overwhelmed. 'You really don't need to do that,' she protested. Ernesto and Aurelia were far too kind and the last thing she wanted was to presume or take advantage, or even appear to do so, especially not when bloody Raph was sitting there like a brooding hawk. He seemed determined to think the worst of her.

'I want to do it. *We* want to do it,' said Aurelia, speaking for her husband. 'We have missed out on you for all of these years,' said Aurelia, her eyes softening with the pathos of a great tragic actor.

'Yes,' agreed Ernesto, clasping his hands together.

Now it was Lia's turn to burst out laughing. 'The pair of you are terrible.' She shook her head. Terrible but rather adorable.

'I know,' said Ernesto, grinning. 'But I do like to get my own way with ease instead of making difficulties and stamping feet. It is so much better, don't you think?'

'I believe it's called being charming,' suggested Raph dryly. 'Although he can stamp his feet with the best of them.'

'I can believe it,' she joked and immediately there was that zing of awareness as the two of them exchanged a rare look of understanding.

'But making lunch is such a tiny thing,' said Aurelia, with a determined shrug and a very small stamp of her elegantly shod foot – which had a distinct look of Ferragamo about it. At art college, Lia had shared a house with a fashion major who knew about these things and had given her quite an education. 'And we want to look after you. There is so much time to make up. You must understand that.'

Lia's eyes widened at this blatant emotional blackmail, which was done so prettily that it was impossible to take offence at the outright manipulation going on.

'I absolutely promise you, you don't need to do anything. It's just lovely to get to know you.' Aurelia really was one of the kindest people Lia had ever met, perpetually cheerful and positive. How on earth did she end up with a grump of a son like Raphael?

'How about I work today and take tomorrow off?' suggested Lia, desperate to give Aurelia something back.

Aurelia threw her arms around her and gave her a big hug. 'You are delightful. Isn't she, Raph?'

Lia turned, dying to see his reaction to this, grinning at him as he swallowed his coffee quickly.

'Er, yes.'

It was gratifying to see the hunted look on his face.

———

Breakfast was delicious but Lia felt exhausted afterwards. Ernesto and Aurelia were both such live wires and held a rapid-fire conversation that veered from the Cannes Film Festival to the last Met Gala and what the standout dresses of the night had been, through to who'd written the last Oscar-winning short film. A couple of times during this conversation that veered up and down, left and right and back round in a circle, she caught Raph's eye. It was funny – they seemed to be on the same wavelength.

As Lia was thinking this, she realised that everyone was looking at her.

'What do you think, Lia?' asked Aurelia.

'Sorry, I was miles away.'

'Ernesto has suggested taking the yacht out for dinner this evening.'

'Oh,' said Lia. What did you say to that? She'd never been on a yacht.

'Would you like that?' Aurelia's gentle question was full of concern, as if all they wanted to do was please Lia.

'Please don't go to any trouble on my account,' she said. 'It's very kind of you to have me to stay. I don't expect you to entertain me.'

'Nonsense,' said Ernesto. 'We shall take the boat out and have dinner and watch the sunset. It is *molto romantico*. The sea, the sun on the water, there is nothing better. I will call Hortense straight after breakfast and get her to bring the *Elsie Mae* to a berth in the bay and we'll drive to the beach this evening.'

'Hortense?' asked Lia, thinking this sounded like a lot more than just taking 'the boat out to dinner'.

'She's our purser on board. There is no marina in Positano, so the crew stay with the boat over in Sorrento,' said Aurelia. 'She'll let the captain know and arrange dinner. She's married to the chef, Matilde, who is the most fabulous cook. Seafood, I think. Do you like seafood, Lia?'

'Yes … except oysters. I've never tried one but I'm not sure I could bring myself to.'

Raph shuddered. 'You're not the only one.'

'They're an acquired taste,' said Ernesto, a touch loftily. Both Raph and Aurelia turned on him with outraged gasps.

'You hate them,' she said.

'I know.' He gave a charming shrug. 'But no one needs to know that, do they? I'm supposed to be urbane, sophisticated and all those things.' He looked down at the tatty shirt, another lurid Hawaiian affair, which he wore with a pair of battered denim shorts, and gave an ironic grin.

Lia loved that he could still be self-deprecating and aware of himself as well as playing the movie star.

'What time do you want to leave?' asked Raph, looking at his watch as if he had somewhere to be, making her conscious that she was inconveniencing him.

'I'm happy to go as soon as you're ready,' she said.

'I'm ready now.'

Of course he was. Raph seemed to delight in wrong-footing her. 'I'll just grab my things.'

Ernesto and Aurelia had moved on to another topic and were chatting between themselves as she rose to leave the table.

'Have you got much?' Raph asked.

'Er...'

'Equipment. Bags. Materials?'

She shook her head.

'Good, we'll take the Vespa. It's easier at this time of day and some of us have got to get back to do a proper job.'

She bristled like a hedgehog. 'I can take a taxi if you're too busy with your big important job – what is it you do again? Apart from looking after your stepfather, of course.'

Raph's lips curved in an approving smile, which warmed her even though it shouldn't. Hadn't she just accused him of nepotism?

'Shall we call it a draw?'

Lia was suddenly aware of the avid, indulgent gazes of Ernesto and Aurelia and had a horrible feeling she and Raph had set off an unexpected firework, which had exploded right above her hosts' heads in a glittery shower of something – quite what, she wasn't sure, but it wasn't good.

Getting a lift with Raph was one thing; climbing on the back of a Vespa with him was entirely another. Lia stood on the little circular drive in front of the vine-covered pergola at the back entrance of the villa as he drew to a stop in front of her, the spare helmet over his arm like a basket.

'Your carriage.' He held out the helmet, which she pulled down over her messy bun. It was already far too hot to leave her hair loose. 'Jump on.'

He was completely business-like, almost impassive, but it was still easier said than done. Why was she so conscious of him? With a quick swallow, she gathered her skirts around her knees. This had been simple with Leo. A bit of a laugh. No awkwardness. She hopped on one foot with all the finesse of a pigeon, trying to bend one leg over the seat avoiding the storage box on the back. It was all very ungainly. However, Raph seemed utterly uninterested, which made her feel like a sweaty schoolgirl with a crush.

Except she didn't fancy him, she just found him a bit … a bit … unsettling. That was the word. He scrambled her equilibrium. Especially now, sitting behind him. She wanted to hold her breath so she wouldn't be so aware of the scent of him. That indefinable essence of him. He was so close, and even though they weren't touching, she could feel the presence of his body through his fine linen shirt. She couldn't banish the image of his long, lithe back, which had embedded itself in her brain that day on the beach. Her fingers twitched and she had to clench them into fists, fighting the urge to run them over the contours of his skin and muscle.

He turned and looked over his shoulder. 'All set?' That calm, indifferent expression on his face pricked her. How come she felt all churned up and he was oblivious? Irked by this, when he put the scooter in gear to move smoothly forward she slipped her arms around his waist, clasping her hands on his stomach and leaning into him. When she felt him stiffen with surprise, she couldn't resist a small smirk to herself. There was just something so satisfying about tormenting him, even if it meant tormenting herself as well.

Raph turned out onto the road between the grand wrought-iron gates, driving with none of Leo's showy panache as they overtook a parked car. Lia would have described his approach as orderly: safe and sensible.

But there was nothing safe and sensible about her pulse, which was now racketing about like the other scooters around them. The wind whipped her face and she sheltered against Raph's broad back, feeling the warmth of his skin on her cheek. As her breasts nestled into Raph's back, they felt heavy and rather sensitive, and where his bottom backed against her, she had the urge to tilt her hips towards him. Every nerve ending seemed attuned to him. Beneath her hands, she could feel his muscles bunch as they turned this way and that, curving down along the steep road.

When they arrived at the studio, twenty minutes later, he dropped her off and whizzed away without a wave or a backward glance, as if she were a parcel dutifully delivered on time, in the right place.

She let out an irritated huff. Why did she want him to think better of her? Why did his opinion matter? Pinching her lips, she went into the studio and made herself a coffee. Bugger bloody Raphael Knight.

Chapter Seventeen

The car engine was running, and the air conditioning was at full blast, although the door was still open, awaiting the rest of the passengers.

Already inside, Lia watched as Raph stood outside checking his phone. There was still no sign of Ernesto and Aurelia, even though they were due to leave at six thirty. It was now six thirty-five and after a day baking in the studio, the prospect of going out on the water and having a swim was growing more enticing by the second.

Thankfully it had been Leo who'd come to collect her just half an hour ago, running late of course, and she'd had time for a quick shower and to change into the flippy skirt and T-shirt she thought of as suitable maritime wear, and comb her hair and put it into a high ponytail, before they were due to be picked up to go to the marina.

After a further five-minute wait, Aurelia appeared. 'You two will have to go on without us. Leo has a date and

Ernesto needs to sort something out and I need to help Bianca. Marco will drop you off and come back to get us.'

'We can wait,' replied Lia, not wanting to put them out or make the driver do two trips. There was also the matter of being stuck on her own with Raph – again.

'No, no. Hortense is expecting you.' Aurelia was already shooing Raph into the back of the car with the focused attention of a collie with sheep.

When she closed the door, safely corralling him in, and they were about to roll away in the purring Mercedes, she rapped on the window, which Raph lowered.

'Start dinner without us, if it gets too late.' She knocked on the roof, waved at the driver and the car moved smoothly away, leaving Lia staring at her through the window. How long were they likely to be? It seemed a bit weird but then she didn't know them that well and they did have five children to look after.

'Good day?' asked Raph after a few minutes' silence in the car.

'Very good,' said Lia, amusement dancing in her eyes at the domesticity of his question. 'You?'

'Excellent, I did lots of looking after my stepfather.'

'Well done,' she said with a quick smile as the car curved smoothly around the contours of the hill. It was quite a contrast to the journey by Vespa earlier in the day but not quite as enjoyable. Despite the luxury of the leather seats and the cool air, Lia missed the visceral sensations of the wind on her face, the sun on her skin and the distinctive resin scent of the crooked Mediterranean pines that clung to the hillside.

'And then I did my own work. A board meeting with my executive team via Zoom lasted most of the afternoon.'

'Sounds riveting,' said Lia with a wince.

'It was productive. What about you?'

'Are you really that interested?'

'Try me.'

'I mixed up some dyes and tested them on different fabrics. Drew some preliminary sketches of another canvas for the submission to the restaurant.'

'Is it a restaurant in London?'

'Yes. They've had a very successful site in New York for the last three years, so they're bringing it over to the UK.'

'Would I have heard of it?'

'Braganzi.'

Raph gave a low whistle and his eyes appraised her. 'Very nice. Impressive.'

'You've been there?' Stupid question. Of course he had.

'Yes. It's one of Ernesto's favourites. He knows Vincent Braganzi and last time I was in New York, I went there with my then girlfriend. The food was excellent. I'll look forward to the London one opening.'

'I'm hoping that getting this commission will raise my profile in the UK.'

'I should think being an artist of any type is difficult at the moment.'

'Mm,' she said noncommittally. Actually, as an artist she was doing better than most. In recent years she'd had some significant success, but the Braganzi commission was a really big deal. Even her parents would be impressed. While supportive, they'd never really 'got' her work, but the eye-watering amount of money Braganzi was spending on the artwork was going to be headline news and put her name right up there. But she wasn't going to tell Raph that – it was much more fun to feed his belief that she was a starving artist out for what she could get. One of these days, she'd rub his nose in the truth.

'How long does it take you to … to make? Is that right? To make a picture.'

'It depends on the materials I've decided to use, the size, and how or if I'm embellishing it. Each piece I make is entirely individual. It's impossible to say.'

'So how do you know when a piece is finished?'

'That is a really good question.' She stared at him, surprised by his interest. 'I could say never because you always want to tweak or change things. Ultimately, I think that it's the artistic eye, an instinctive knowing when to stop. When something has reached its pinnacle. It's hard to explain but in your heart of hearts you just know.' Surprised by his intent expression, she flashed him a quick smile. 'Does that all sound like pretentious, artisty bollocks?' she teased.

'No. It doesn't. It sounds like freedom. If it's ready, its ready, and if it's not, it's not.'

Gosh, Raph almost sounded wistful and for a moment she wondered if she'd underestimated him. He always seemed so sure of himself, his feet firmly planted on a path.

'So apart from looking after Ernesto' – she grinned at him, making it clear she was teasing him again before continuing – 'and Ernesto's interests, what do you do?'

'I manage Ernesto's portfolio as part of my investment

company – my team and I manage our clients' portfolios to maximise their investments.'

'That does sound very official,' she observed gravely, a faint smile touching her lips, enjoying the game.

'Yes, it does, doesn't it?' he said with a quick roll of his eyes. 'But somehow I get dragged into managing other areas of Ernesto's life, pretty much anything that's outside the remit of his agent, who manages his career.'

'So you're in finance?' That explained a lot.

And she must have given away the thought because he said almost immediately, 'It's not like I'm a vampire or anything. Do you disapprove?'

'No, I just don't really know anyone in finance. My mum and my sis— Stacey … are both business consultants and my … my dad is an engineer.'

'It's all right; we're not all evil.'

'I didn't think you were.'

He raised an eyebrow rather pointedly, so she amended quickly, 'Not all the time at least.'

His sharp blue eyes met hers, crinkling around the corners. 'I've been called a catch on occasion.'

'I'm sure you have, but I'm not in the market for a shark,' she retorted.

With another laugh, he said. 'You win this round.'

The car dropped them off at the now familiar Fornillo Beach and Raph led her over to a boat tied up on the jetty.

When Ernesto had said dinner on the yacht, she'd

envisioned something slightly grander than this – hadn't there been talk of an onboard chef? – although the little white speedboat was perfectly nice with cushioned seats around the back.

'*Ciao*,' called a woman sitting in the driver's seat – Lia guessed it probably had some nautical name but that's what the leather chair in the middle of the boat looked like to her.

This must be Hortense, she decided as the woman spoke to Raph in rapid Italian. Raph jumped into the boat and then held out a hand to help Lia aboard. As she took it, she felt the tingle – that indefinable spark of attraction, which had no rhyme or reason. She didn't even like the man, did she? Although you'd have to be dead not to find him attractive.

'Have a seat,' he said, indicating one of the smart navy leather seats. She settled down and Raph sat down opposite her, his arms resting on the edge of the boat as if boarding had given him permission to relax. The change was immediate and fascinated Lia. He caught her quizzical glance.

'There's nothing like being out on the sea. On days like this, I sometimes wonder why I live in London.'

'Why do you?'

'My work is there. And...' He paused. 'I'm a person in my own right in London.'

She nodded, automatically understanding exactly what he meant. Here he was the family role model and, it seemed, fixer of everything. Although he wasn't, he might as well have been the head of the family. For a moment, a very brief one, she felt a little sorry for him. For the responsibility he shouldered. They all seemed to expect so much of him.

Hortense fired up the engine, which droned as she put the boat into reverse, casting off the line.

'What about Ernesto and Aurelia? Will we come back for them?' she asked.

'They'll catch us up,' said Raph, which made no sense at all.

'What, in another boat?' she asked, as Hortense dextrously turned the boat around, the outboard engine churning up the water and leaving a frothy wake behind them as they began to head out to sea.

'This is just the tender. It'll drop us off and go back for them.'

Lia had absolutely no idea what that meant. 'Of course it is,' she said. 'And a tender would be?'

Raph began to laugh. 'Our mode of transport to the *Elsie Mae*.'

'This isn't the yacht?'

'No, this isn't the yacht,' he said, watching her with that wry smile of his. She felt a right idiot.

'Right. I knew that.' She pulled a face before admitting, 'I so didn't.'

'I guessed.'

Less than ten minutes later they drew up alongside … Lia wouldn't have called it a yacht. The thing was bigger than her parents' house, and with six bedrooms *that* wasn't exactly small.

'Wow,' said Lia.

'Impressive, isn't it?' said Hortense, waiting for her to

step out of the boat onto the low platform at the back of the *Elsie Mae*. 'It's a beauty.'

'It is,' said Lia, reminded once again just how wealthy Ernesto and Aurelia were as the boat rocked gently beneath her feet. They were out in the bay, Positano in the distance, the colours tumbling down the hill in a waterfall of pastel.

Her gaze dropped to the sea, arrested by the colour and texture of the water, the depth of the intense inky blue, which rippled like silk in the wind, and the desire to capture it and recreate it burned fast and sharp in her. That colour so rich, so deep. The never-ending patterns and movement.

'Never disappoints,' murmured Raph, his voice soft but with an edge of gravel, sending a shiver through her. He'd come to stand next to her, his hands leaning on the steel rail of the boat. A little dazed, she looked up him. His eyes met hers, his look strong and steady, almost as if he could see straight into her head, and she could swear his thoughts mirrored hers. He understood. It was the second time she'd felt that connection. Felt that there was more to Raph than possibly even he knew.

Her heart jumped in her throat as she looked at him. 'No,' she agreed, her voice no more than a sigh. The boat swayed and he took a step closer, his hand lightly touching her waist. She took in a quick breath, her lips parting, and her pulse leapt in joyful anticipation as his unwavering gaze focused on her and he lowered his head.

'Would you like to take a look around?' said Hortense, making Lia almost jump. 'I'd be happy to show you.'

'Er, yes, um.'

She glanced back at Raph, but his face was wiped clean of any expression. Her heart sank as hard and heavy as an anchor. What had just happened there? Had he wanted to kiss her or was that just wishful thinking on her part?

'Would that be all right?' she asked him, swallowing, wanting to wipe her hands down her skirt. Oh God, it was official: she had a crush on him. One that was every bit as bad as when she was sixteen and eighteen-year-old Danny Shore moved into the house next door.

'To look round?' she added, hoping for some sort of reassurance. She had no idea whether it was the done thing to look around someone's yacht, even if she was dying to see how the other half lived.

'Yeah,' said Raph, absently turning away. 'Go ahead. I'll order some drinks. What would you like?'

'Whatever you have. Wine?'

'We have everything,' said Raph, with one of his mocking grins, which was a pertinent reminder of her place and of their combatitive relationship. It immediately reminded her that he might have wanted to kiss her in the moment, but it was just a passing fancy. He didn't even like her.

'Of course you do. I'll have a glass of Prosecco, then.' It was so tempting to say champagne, but she held back, worried it might confirm his view that she was the gold-digger he believed her to be.

Lia was fascinated by the neat ingenuity of the interior of the yacht as they made their way to the small, highly functional galley where Hortense's wife greeted her.

'Hi, you must be Lia. I'm Alessia, the chef. Ernesto has told us all about you. He says you must enjoy this evening.'

Lia frowned, unsure of her meaning.

'I'm sure I will.' She lowered her voice. 'This place is amazing. Have you worked here long?'

'Three years,' said Hortense, answering for both of them.

'What time would you like to eat?' asked Alessia.

'When Ernesto and Aurelia get here, I guess. It's up to them.'

Hortense and Alessia exchanged a quick glance. 'Oh, there's been a change of plan. They are not coming now. Ernesto called me to tell me that he wouldn't need the tender after all.'

'Oh,' said Lia. 'I hope everything is all right.'

'I'm sure it is,' said Hortense smoothly, with a secretive smile. 'Why don't you go back on deck and we'll serve the food in half an hour?'

'Fine,' said Lia. 'I'll ... I'll let Raph know.'

She made her way back to the deck where Raph had opened a bottle of Prosecco and placed it in an ice bucket. As soon as he saw her, he poured a glass and handed it to her.

As she took a sip, a surge of pleasure and appreciation at just how lucky she was washed away her reserve. 'This is heaven, thank you. I can't quite believe I'm here. By the way, Hortense says Ernesto and Aurelia aren't coming. I hope everything is all right. Do you think we ought to go back?'

Raph rolled his eyes. 'Typical Ernesto. He'll have forgotten something and he's double-booked himself. He's terrible at diary management. I've tried to get him to use his phone.' He lifted his glass in an ironic toast. 'Looks like you're stuck with me.'

'Looks like it,' she said. 'I'd better be on my best behaviour otherwise you might toss me overboard.'

'Now there's a thought,' he said with a wicked gleam in his eye.

'Actually I wouldn't mind a swim now, if that's all right. Before dinner and before I drink any more.'

'Excellent idea. I've been looking forward to one all day.'

'Me too,' she said.

'Good God, are we in accord for once?'

'Eek, it looks like it,' she said, pretending to look about her. 'Don't tell anyone.'

'I won't if you don't.' His laughing eyes caught hers as he rose to his feet, kicked off his deck shoes and reached for the hem of his white T-shirt. She couldn't help watching as he whipped it off in one smooth move and her mouth went dry at the sight of his tanned chest and the dark hair that trailed from his belly button to beneath the waistband of the navy swimming shorts. Just admiring the view, she told herself, quickly ducking her head to undo the buttons on her dress.

She followed him down onto the little platform at the back of the boat and watched as he dived into the water with a graceful arc. Unable to compete with that entry she sat down and put her legs over the edge into the water and gently lowered herself in. She welcomed the cool slide of water over her skin as she stretched her body into the first stroke. By the time she was immersed, Raph had surfaced like a sleek seal, his dark hair plastered to his head. If anything it just highlighted his chiselled face, much to Lia's dismay.

'Lovely, isn't it?' he said, grinning at her, running a hand through his hair.

'Yes,' she said, treading water for a moment and studying the coastline and the cloudless sky beyond it. Lovely was an understatement though, especially with the sun glinting off the rippling waves, turning them into sparkling diamonds.

'Want to swim out to the buoy?' he asked, pointing to one of the orange floats bobbing a little way away. She narrowed her eyes and assessed the distance. Not too far. Maybe a hundred metres.

'Sure, why not?' she said, an imp of mischief asserting itself. Without warning she launched into a determined freestyle, enjoying the pull on her shoulders and the sensation of ploughing through the water. It had been a while since she'd swum competitively but muscle memory took over and she kept up a smooth, mechanical rhythm, relaxed and easy, taking in a breath with every third stroke.

Her competitive spirit and desire to put Raph in his place for once also kicked in and she put in an extra kick and pull into every stroke, focusing on what his face would look like when he finally caught up with her.

As it turned out, he wasn't so very far behind her, but she definitely beat him.

'What kept you?' she asked with a triumphant smile, her heart pumping hard and her chest heaving.

'You took me by surprise,' he said. 'You swim well.'

'I know,' she said with a quick grin, delighted she'd outswum him.

'You're looking very pleased with yourself.'

'I'm guessing you don't get beaten at many things.' He was so damn self-assured and gave off that air of all-round competence.

Raph gave her a searching look before replying. 'I can't decide whether to agree with you or ask what's brought you to that conclusion. I'm intrigued by your opinion of me.'

Lia shrugged in a way she hoped came across as nonchalant, realising she might have given herself away a bit. The truth was that she thought about Raph and his character entirely too often.

'You don't need to be; it's not the least bit flattering,' she said.

He laughed. 'With you, I wouldn't expect otherwise. You seem determined to see the worst of me, when all I'm doing is trying to protect other people.'

'Whereas you seem determined to see the worst in other people without giving them a chance to prove otherwise.'

'Perhaps my viewpoint has been shaped by experience,' he replied with alacrity.

'With everyone?' she queried. 'Maybe it's the company you keep?'

Raph paused. 'There is always that. Do you want to swim back? I'd like to dry off before dinner. Rematch?'

'I think I'll enjoy a leisurely swim back,' she said. The burst of speed had taken it out of her, and there was no way she could reproduce that form without a much longer rest, but she wasn't about to admit it. 'It's been a while since I did any serious swimming and I'd forgotten how much I enjoy it, especially swimming in the sea. But you go ahead.'

'No, it's fine.' He began to swim along beside her, with an easy breast stroke, which she had to stretch herself to keep up with. 'I try to swim often in London but it's not the same in an indoor pool. That's why I come down to the beach most days when I'm here.'

'There's something about swimming in the sea,' agreed Lia, watching her hands, blurry and pale beneath the water as she swam. She felt buoyant and alive here in the water with Raph, but that could have a lot to do with the flood of endorphins rushing through her body after that freestyle sprint.

They exchanged a glance and again Lia felt that quick, silent click of understanding between them. Funny how in tune they were in some ways and how different they were in others. There was a lot more to Raphael Knight than she'd originally thought, but she needed to remember to be on her guard around him. He'd made it quite clear that he didn't trust her and she was sure he would find any reason he could to get rid of her. Both from the villa and from Ernesto's life.

Chapter Eighteen

Arriving back at the boat, Raph hauled himself out of the water with ease, levering himself up on his arms before twisting gracefully to sit on the swimming platform and rising to his feet in one fluid move. Lia eyed him. She doubted she had the same upper-body strength and feared floundering about like a freshly caught fish.

'Here,' he said, almost reading her mind as he held out a hand. She caught it and before she could process the logistics, he pulled her out of the water with surprising strength, the unexpected trajectory making her cannon into him, wet skin to wet skin, her body flush against his.

'T-thank you,' she stuttered, trying to disentangle her arms from around his neck and one leg from between his. The touch of his thigh against hers ignited a flash of heat that struck straight at her core and she was aware of his smooth skin under her fingers and her chest pressed against his, all of it sending her nerve endings into a tailspin.

He felt cool, soft and strong and she registered each

sensation in her brain in quick succession. She wanted to touch and taste him.

She saw his Adam's apple dip and knew she wasn't alone in that wanting. Hauling in a breath she dared herself to look up at him.

'Lia,' he murmured as she looked at his lips, that wide sulky mouth she was dying to feel on hers. 'We...' He swallowed and his gaze roved over her breasts, just barely covered by the fabric triangles of her bikini. His eyes narrowed but he didn't move. It was incumbent on her to step back or for him to push her away but neither of them seemed capable of functioning. He rested his forehead against hers, and against her hip, she could feel the hardness of him, pressing through his wet swimming shorts. It made her heart hitch with sudden feminine satisfaction. This gorgeous man wasn't immune to her. He clearly felt the same unwelcome attraction as she did, which was one heck of a relief. It would have been awful to be suffering this affliction on her own – disliking him but being crazily attracted to him at the same time.

Maybe she should just go for broke, kiss him and get it out of the way.

She lifted her head, shocked by the sudden intensity in his eyes. Sharp need swamped her and just as the words 'Kiss me, Raph' left her mouth, he put his hands on her arms and moved her away from him.

Red-hot shame doused her cheeks and she closed her eyes as if that might make her invisible and lessen the hideousness of the situation.

'It would be a mistake,' he said, his voice as husky as hers.

She nodded dumbly. 'Yes. It would. Don't know what came over me. Heat of the moment and all that.' Was it possible to die of embarrassment? 'Bet you get women throwing themselves at you all the time. Must be an occupational hazard.'

His mouth quivered, his easy sense of humour coming to their rescue. 'I think you're confusing me with someone else.'

Not with that body, she wasn't.

'Thanks for hauling me out. You obviously don't know your own strength.' She gave him a blithe smile. 'Do you have any showers on this fancy boat of yours?' A cold one would go down perfectly right about now.

'Yes, I'll get Hortense to show you to one of the guest cabins. There should be everything you need in there.'

She nodded dumbly to herself – of course there would be. As he turned and mounted the small ladder up to the next deck, she watched his thigh and calf muscles bunch with each step and cursed the curl of lust that still lingered. Quickly she turned around to look out to sea, needing a moment to regain her equilibrium.

After a couple of seconds, she closed her eyes, mentally composing the WhatsApp to Stacey. She'd get one hell of a kick out of the yacht and the villa.

You wouldn't believe this place. I've got my own guest suite with its own pool – although I have to share it with David Gandy's evil twin – the pool that is, not the guest suite. Tonight we went out on the yacht. Just about to have a shower in one of the guest cabins before dinner on deck. Seriously, it's another world. Wish you were here.

With a wince from the metaphorical jab of pain, she opened her eyes and lifted her chin. There would be no WhatsApp. She still couldn't bring herself to contact her … to contact Stacey. Stacey who had sided with Mum in the view that the discovery of a different father made no difference to who they all were and their relationships with each other. Lia swallowed as her stomach churned. She had far too much going on. She shouldn't even be thinking about the attractions of Raphael bloody Knight – he was one complication too many.

Fresh from the shower, feeling that the water had washed away her embarrassment, Lia's natural positivity reasserted herself. She needed to deal with Raph and just get it all out in the open. She certainly wasn't going to allow this episode to drive her away.

When she emerged on deck, Raph was sitting at the table looking at his phone. He looked up as she approached and gave her a small, grim smile.

'Lia…'

'Raph…'

'I wanted to apologise,' said Raph, rising to his feet, ever the perfect gentleman. He gestured towards the seat opposite. 'Can I pour you another glass of Prosecco?'

Lia's eyes widened but she nodded before asking, 'Apologise. For what?'

'For any misunderstanding.'

'Misunderstanding?' Now she was confused.

'If I was sending the wrong signals.' Raph's squirming discomfort was almost cute and so unlike him. What had happened to the man in control who told everyone else what to do? 'I didn't mean to. You're clearly … a very attractive woman. Obviously. That's … yes, it's obvious. And I … not just me … but any man would be blind not to see that. But given the circumstances, it wouldn't be wise to act on … not … you know…' He trailed off, his eyes reminiscent of a rabbit in headlights. It was utterly adorable and so out of character, and despite the circumstances, Lia felt her heart melt just a little. Raphael Knight was much softer on the inside than she'd assumed.

'No, I guess you're right,' she said, reassured by his stumbling but then going the same way herself because … apparently it was that sort of day and all of a sudden she was tripping over her words. 'Not about the being attractive because, well, I wouldn't say that about myself. Obviously I wouldn't and you are … a very attractive man … very attractive, but then you know that. I mean you should do…' She wrinkled her nose and then burst out laughing. They were as bad as one another.

'Tell you what. Why don't we just forget any of it ever happened? And this.' She waved a hand as if to wipe away the conversation. 'I mean, if we're brutally honest, it was just one of those things. It didn't mean anything, did it? There's no need for either of us to feel awkward about it. That would just be silly.' She laughed self-deprecatingly. 'Besides, you don't even like me, remember?'

'How could I forget?' he replied, his trademark smirk back in place.

'Well then. No harm done. Are you going to pour me a drink or not?'

Raph obliged and right on cue, Hortense appeared carrying two small plates and a bread basket.

'To start with, we have chargrilled squid in a salad of lemon, fennel and rocket, and a black pepper and prosciutto flat bread.' She deposited a plate in front of each of them.

Raph thanked her in Italian before saying to Lia, 'It looks delicious. I hope you like squid.'

She took a bite and then leaned forward and said in a low voice, 'I didn't think I would. I like the round crispy bits but I've never fancied the wriggly bits.' She spiked an example on her fork and waved it at him. 'But guess what? They're delicious.' She popped the squid into her mouth to enjoy the slightly caramelised, salty flavour.

'Maybe you should try oysters, then,' suggested Raph.

She shuddered. 'Maybe not.'

They drank the rest of the bottle of Prosecco, along with a bottle of Pellegrino sparkling water, and enjoyed the main course – swordfish steaks wrapped in courgette flowers with ribbons of blanched courgette served with a potato, red onion and mint salad. It was light and delicious.

'I'm sorry Aurelia and Ernesto couldn't make it,' said Lia.

'Yes, I can't imagine what kept them. Ernesto loves coming out on the boat and I'm surprised Leo didn't invite himself.' Raph shook his head. 'It's all very odd.'

As Lia didn't know them that well, she couldn't comment but she could see that he was very worried.

'Do you want to head back?'

'No. They would radio the captain if there was a serious problem. Besides, Ernesto would be very upset if you didn't stay for the sunset.'

The sun was already sinking towards the horizon, brushing the hazy white clouds with a golden blush, and the light began to change, bringing a magical glow that endless painters and photographers through the centuries had endeavoured to capture.

'And you wouldn't want to upset Ernesto, would you?' quipped Lia, wondering just how upset Ernesto would be.

'I try not to make a habit of it. Mainly because it upsets my mother.'

His words hit Lia right in the stomach like a lump hammer and her eyes filled with unbidden tears, her mouth crumpling. It was the longest she'd gone without speaking to her mum but she just couldn't get past the fact that her life had been a lie, all this time. Would she ever have told her?

'Are you okay?'

'No,' she said, lifting her head and giving him a direct look. She was all over the place this evening. 'I'm not all right. I've found out that I'm a half. I'm only half a part of one family and half a part of another.' She gazed out to sea, watching the waves. She didn't fit anywhere. The foundations beneath her feet were rotten and she was no longer sure where to step, aware that they could crumble at any point. 'You think discovering my father is a famous movie star is a bonus. But it isn't. Not from where I'm standing.

'I haven't found a father, I've' – her voice cracked – 'lost the family I thought was mine. And now I'm left in the middle, not entirely belonging with either.'

When Raph laid a gentle hand on hers her muscles tensed, surprised at the unexpected touch. 'Believe it or not, I understand that feeling. Being part of a blended family, especially with such age ranges, is not always easy.' He gave a self-deprecating laugh. 'Maybe you and I are not so different after all.' He withdrew his hand. 'But we're here now and we have good food and the best view in the world, so maybe we should just make the best of it, for this evening.'

Chapter Nineteen

Lia's words echoed in his head the next morning as he made his way out to the patio for an early swim. It was that or a bloody cold shower. He glanced towards the closed blinds of her patio doors, wondering if maybe he'd done her a disservice. Guilt nagged at him as he slipped off his flip-flops and dumped his towel on the sunlounger. It had honestly never occurred to him that she had lost something. He'd been so focused on keeping a close eye on her, making sure that she didn't take advantage of Ernesto and their relationship.

It was only half-past seven but he'd been awake for what felt like hours, thinking about her, going over and over that flash-point moment when all he'd wanted to do was ravage that kissable mouth and let his hands rove over her smooth olive skin, which really would have complicated the hell out of life. Even now his body tightened in response and he groaned softly to himself. He couldn't allow her to get under his skin. Irritated with himself, he prowled to the deep end of the pool and dived in, welcoming the immediate chill of the water as it enveloped his body. The rush of cold dimmed the remnants of desire, bringing clear-headed sense back. He swam the first length trying to process the facts in his head. There was no DNA proof that she was Ernesto's daughter. Ernesto had accepted her based only on a photograph. A bloody photograph, for God's sake. How did he persuade Ernesto that she really should do a test, just to make sure there was absolutely no room for doubt? He could be sneaky and get her DNA without her knowing – it was simple enough to take hair from her hairbrush and have it sent to the lab in Milan – but that would risk Ernesto's wrath and it didn't sit well with Raph himself.

He needed to be on his guard. So far she seemed to be who she said she was, but he knew from experience how people could be swayed by money, by fortune, by the press. The whole family had been burned when a young actress had insisted that Ernesto was her father. She wasn't the first to take her claims to the press but that time, things had ended in scandal with Ernesto losing a lucrative job when it turned out the woman's mother would have been below the age of consent at conception, which the tabloids gleefully focused on despite Ernesto's denials. No one was interested when the DNA evidence that categorically proved his innocence emerged – the damage was already done. Ernesto might have had his day in court and won, but who read the tiny paragraph of apology in the paper, and what could be done when producers had already recast the part?

As if he'd conjured Lia, when he next surfaced, she was

standing on the edge of the pool, one foot rubbing the back of her leg, her blond hair loose, looking like a lost angel.

'Morning,' he called, immediately aware of her skimpy T-shirt, which just skimmed the tops of her thighs. Thank God he was in the water and it was cold.

'You know you swim very loudly,' she complained, frowning down at him.

He almost swallowed a mouthful of water laughing at her grumpy face. 'Not a morning person?'

She scowled, wrinkling her nose. 'Does that even require an answer? Not before coffee. I couldn't find anywhere to make coffee in the room.'

His pulse quickened at the sight of her – rumpled, cross and sleepily sexy with that mane of blond hair tangled about her face.

'Sorry, it's not the Italian way. We're very fussy about our coffee. It's made in a moka on the stove or in a proper machine … or not at all.'

Her face fell and he almost felt sorry for her. She was clearly one of those people who couldn't function without coffee. 'If you give me ten minutes to shower and dress, I'll take you over to the house and make you a coffee.'

'Okay,' she said a little grudgingly.

'Hopefully you'll be a little sunnier after caffeine.'

'Hopefully you'll be less of a pompous arse,' she muttered, obviously forgetting that water amplified sound.

'There's always hope,' he said with a grin, hauling himself out of the pool and watching her eyes widen with quick horror as she realised he'd heard her.

Sparring with Lia was a whole lot of fun.

Lia watched curiously as Raph unscrewed the base of the coffee pot and put in the freshly ground coffee. It looked terribly old fashioned. Didn't people use cafetières these days? Although she guessed that was more French. Raph filled it with bottled water and then screwed the top on before setting it on the hob.

'How does that work?' she asked with a quick frown.

'The water boils up through the pressurised coffee and into the top chamber. Dead simple but very effective and the absolute best way to make coffee. Every Italian home has one of these. I have one in London.'

'Lia, good morning. Good, you're looking after her, Raph.' Aurelia came rocketing into the kitchen, bursting with colour and fizzing with energy. 'Have you had breakfast yet? There are some fresh pastries from the bakery and lots of fruit. What are your plans today? And how was the trip on the boat? Isn't it divine?'

'What happened?' asked Raph.

'Oh, it just got late,' said Aurelia with an airy wave of her hands, her eyes darting everywhere but her son's face, before giving Lia one of her warm smiles. 'Did you have a lovely time? I hope Raph looked after you.'

Lia ignored the question about Raph. The less said about him the better. She'd had a very disturbed night's sleep with a very vivid dream featuring him.

'It was wonderful, thank you, and the food was amazing.'

'So what are your plans for today? Ernesto has to work –

he has a new script – but we'd love you to have dinner with us this evening.'

Lia pulled a regretful face. 'I didn't get as much work done as I wanted to yesterday.' That was an understatement. The lemon picture fitted the bill for the commission but not in isolation; she needed more and she didn't know what that would be just yet. She huffed out a sigh. 'I'm a bit stuck at the moment.'

'Stuck?' Aurelia repeated in a very 'this-won't-do' way. 'How are you stuck? What can we do?' Barely a second elapsed before she said, 'I know, we will have breakfast on the terrace and afterwards you can tell me all about it. Talking things through can help. When Ernesto is wrestling with something, usually how he's going to approach a character, he talks me through it and every time, he answers his own problem. Maybe I can help.'

'I'll leave you to it,' said Raph. 'Some of us have a full day of calls and meetings. I need to make a start. I'll see you later.'

Lia acknowledged him with a nod, quite relieved he was leaving, and turned back to his mother.

Aurelia was looking at her so earnestly, Lia didn't have the heart to say no to her offer. Besides, what harm would it do? If she were honest, it would make a pleasant change to try a different approach. Ever since her original ideas for the commission had been turned down, she'd been stuck in a loop of doubt and fear that the inspiration for the lemon image was a one-off. Perhaps a day here on the estate relaxing might give her brain the inspiration it needed.

'Thank you, if you don't mind.'

'Of course not. Now, I'm making ricotta pancakes for the children for breakfast this morning. Would you like some?' Aurelia was already gathering ingredients together and handing her a bowl. 'If you could beat the eggs for me that would be helpful.'

Always happy to be doing something rather than watching, Lia set to work.

The minute there was a pile of fluffy pancakes on the table, along with a pot of Nutella and several jars of jam, honey and lemon curd, children began appearing from all directions: Giulia, jumping about as if powered by Mexican jumping beans, wearing a Disney princess nightie and clinging like a limpet to her father's arm; the twins with wet hair in towelling hoodies who'd obviously come straight from the pool; and Luciana in a cropped top and full make-up, which earned a discreet eyebrow raise from her mother.

'Mamma makes the best pancakes in the world,' declared Giulia through a mouthful of food, dark smears of Nutella daubing her chin as she reached for a second one. Lia had to agree that they were delicious – light and fluffy with a custardy creaminess to them, especially with the acidic bite of the dollop of lemon curd she'd spooned on top of them. And, as she'd seen for herself, so easy to make. Aurelia had simply added several large tablespoons of ricotta cheese to the batter. This was definitely one recipe she would try for herself once she got home.

The pancake pile disappeared rapidly, as did the second batch. The meal was noisy and cheerful with everyone excitedly discussing their plans for the day. It seemed the children had plenty of local friends and most of the plans involved a trip to the beach at some point, except for Giulia. 'Why can't I go to the beach?' she wailed.

'Because you're a pain in the ass,' said Michael.

Her outraged shriek almost pierced Lia's ear drums. 'It's not fair. Why can't I go with the twins?'

'Because you're not old enough,' said Bianca.

'And they don't want to have to look after you,' quipped Luciana.

'Well, why can't I go with you?' she whined.

'I'm going out with my friends.'

'And Matteo,' said Bianca with a sly dig.

'Kissy kissy,' said Michael in a typically irritating brotherly way.

'Luciana's got a boyfriend,' sing-songed Giulia.

Luciana threw a napkin at her sister and a heated discussion erupted between the four younger siblings while Aurelia calmly continued a conversation with Ernesto at the other end of the table.

Lia leaned back in her chair, watching the family, and Leo gave her a wink as he sauntered in.

'Welcome to the madhouse,' he whispered as he leaned over her shoulder and snaffled a pancake, swiping jam across it and stuffing it into his mouth. 'Wanna come to the beach with me?'

'I'd love to but I have to work this morning.'

'Work?' Leo grimaced. 'Rather you than me. If you get bored I'll be at Fornillo.'

Lia nodded, wondering if Leo had ever had a job. He

seemed to have a remarkably casual attitude to the concept of work. Not everyone had the option of getting 'bored'.

'Can I come with you, Leo? They're being mean to me,' Giulia pleaded.

'Sorry, small fry. I'll be out on my board.'

'Margot is coming over to play, remember?' said Aurelia, who seemed to have an inexhaustible source of patience.

'Yay. Margot!' At that Giulia jumped up and went running off, presumably to get dressed for the arrival of her friend.

'So what's this about a boyfriend?' asked Ernesto with a twinkle in his eye. 'Who's Matteo?'

Luciana's mouth pulled back in a snarl as she glared at the twins, before turning to her father with an innocent nothing-to-see here expression. 'He's just one of the guys – a friend.' She lifted her shoulders with an insouciant shrug.

'Do I need to meet him?' asked Ernesto. 'Tell him to behave with my little girl?'

'Papa! I'm not a baby. You're so embarrassing.'

He beamed at her. 'It's in the job description, honey.'

'You're so mean,' she said and flounced off.

'Ernesto!' chided Aurelia but his smile was unrepentant and he winked at Lia.

'The same goes for you.'

Lia managed a weak laugh. 'I'll remember that.' But inside a pang of grief hit her, for the father at home who'd been exactly the same. God, the first boyfriend she'd taken home – poor Gary. Her dad, normally the most gentle of souls, had given him such a thorough cross-examination it was a wonder he ever came back. Once again it reminded her of that feeling that she had one foot in each of two worlds and didn't belong in either.

———————

After the noisy chaos of breakfast, it was a relief to escape to the garden and to the little wisteria-clad pergola Aurelia had directed her to. Two low wicker chairs with pale pink cushions, separated by a glass-topped table, faced the sea view. It was an idyllic spot and offered the quiet that her hostess had promised her. Lia sat down with her sketchbook and sighed, inhaling the scent of honeysuckle and jasmine that rampaged over the wooden struts above her. She took a couple of deep breaths and practised a few mindful exercises, reminding herself to be in the moment and remember how lucky she was. When she opened a fresh page a minute later she sighed, a quick grab of despair catching her... So much for the mindfulness. With only days to present her new ideas, there was still nothing she felt passionate about for the restaurant. Instead, a new idea for something different popped into her head and the pencil in her hand moved quickly as she began to sketch the trailing plants, their vivid green leaves and the bright curly tendrils, twisting like corkscrews, anchoring themselves to any surface they could. It would make a fabulous embroidery design. 'Urrgh,' she ground out in frustration. The idea was wonderful and she could see it so clearly ... but it wasn't right for Braganzi.

'Not going well?' Aurelia appeared at the edge of the pergola holding a tray with a large jug of what looked like home-made lemonade and a plate of tiny sugar-coated donuts.

'I've got plenty of ideas, just not the right ones.'

'How annoying,' said Aurelia, placing the tray on the table. 'I hate when that happens. It's like when I'm cooking and I know fresh zucchini should go in the recipe and I didn't buy any. You know the dish will not be right without it… Everyone else will eat it just fine, but you'll know there is something missing.'

'Something like that.'

'So what is the problem? Please have a *zeppola*. These ones have custard in them and they're so delicious. I can never resist them.'

'Did you make them?' asked Lia, looking at the small donuts, or at least she assumed that's what they were. When did this woman sleep? And how did she keep her trim figure?

'No, Margot's mamma made them and brought them with her when she dropped her daughter off. Giulia and Margot are in the pool and Ernesto is watching them while he reads his script.'

'I'm sorry to drag you away – I know he has to work.'

'Don't be, that is why we come here for the summer, so that he can spend time with the children. When we're here we like to be hands-on as much as we can, though it is nice to have a break from them now and then.' She winked. 'I adore them but they're exhausting – especially Leo. He's such a worry … but I don't need to bore you with that.'

She reached over to take the sketchbook. 'May I?'

'Yes. Sure. They're just ideas, snippets of things.'

'I saw your website. You're very talented. I love the combination of colours and textures of your work.'

Lia smiled. 'I'm not sure Raph is that impressed.'

'Don't mind him. He's very overprotective of Ernesto and me. People occasionally try to take advantage and Raph doesn't react well. There was an awful scandal in the tabloid papers accusing Ernsto of sleeping with a minor. Utter nonsense, of course, but the newspapers don't care about the truth. When I first married Ernesto, it was a difficult time for Raph. Things changed so much and I didn't appreciate just how dramatic that change would be. We tried to carry on with our lives as normal to start with, but I underestimated the impact of Ernesto's fame. To me he was just a wonderful man who I fell in love with, and even more amazingly, he fell in love with me, but … fame makes some people act crazy and eventually Raph had to change schools. Raph is a good man. A very good man.'

She flicked through the pages. 'These are all very good. You're very talented.'

'Thank you but they're just the drawings, I work them up using fabric and thread and any other textile that seems appropriate.'

'So what's the problem?'

Lia explained how her first set of designs for an important commission for a new restaurant in London had been rejected. 'I don't understand what they mean when they say they want the pictures to be aspirational.'

'What sort of restaurant is it?

'Italian,' said Lia. 'Another reason for coming out to Italy.'

Lia nodded. Aurelia frowned and sat back in her chair, thinking for a minute.

'If I were in a restaurant, I'd want the art on the walls to share the passion of food, to convey to me how delicious the dishes are going to be. Your lemon picture is perfect – when you describe it, I can almost taste the citric acid on my tongue – but food is more than the sum total of ingredients. You need the flavours of Italy: basil, oregano, artichoke, tomatoes, pecorino, pasta, but also something else.' She tilted her head to one side considering the problem.

'I know,' said Lia despairingly, 'but I need to capture them in a different way, so that they … they…' She just didn't know.

'So that they make people want to do more than just take a bite of them. They need to convey a feeling.'

Lia rocked back in her chair. 'That's it. That's it exactly, but I don't know how to accomplish that.' She held up her hands in defeat.

Aurelia leaned forward and patted her knee. 'I have an idea. I suggest you immerse yourself in the Italian food and the culture of food; visit the tomatoes on the vine, taste the pizzas in Naples, sample the antipasti, make the pasta and everything in between. You should make a gastronomic tour.' Excitement bubbled in her voice. 'And I will help you. Show you where they grow the basil, the lemon groves, the vines, the buffalo dairy for mozzarella.' She clapped her hands. 'It will be so much fun. Raph can organise things for us.'

'Okay,' said Lia rather taken with the proposal. Research. Proper research. Instead of waiting for the muse to strike her. She much preferred the idea of being proactive. When ideas came to her normally it was when she was busy doing other things, not trying to force them into her brain.

'And the first part of that is you learning to make pasta, like my nonna taught me. We should make some for dinner this evening. There is nothing like fresh home-made pasta. And I'll show you how to make an amatriciana sauce. My favourite. And Raph's too.'

It was a great idea – not making Raph's favourite, she quickly clarified for herself, but learning more about Italian food.

Aurelia clearly relished her role of teacher. Lia wore an apron around her waist, her hair tied up in a ponytail and a notepad and pen at the ready.

'There is no trick to making pasta but hard work. Flour, eggs and love,' said Aurelia flexing one arm. 'It's all in the kneading. But I find it can be very therapeutic – especially when someone has annoyed me. And we need music.' She set her phone on the side. 'I have a pasta playlist.'

'No!' Lia shook her head in disbelief.

'But yes, doesn't everyone?' Aurelia's eyes puckered with mischief as the distinctive riff of an electric guitar burst out of the discreet speakers built into the undersides of the cabinets and The Rolling Stones' '(I Can't Get No) Satisfaction' filled the room at full volume.

With her hips swinging and her head nodding in time to

the beat, Aurelia poured what looked like a huge amount of flour onto the marble countertop, shouting over the music, 'This is double zero flour, which is a very fine flour and particular to Italy.' She took a pinch and sprinkled it down onto the mini mountain, the fine particles dancing like dust motes. Lia was surprised they weren't vibrating with the bass.

'It is very good for making pasta because it contains enough gluten to stretch the dough without breaking it.'

Lia nodded, having no idea what gluten really was apart from the fact that lots of people were now intolerant of it.

'But I also add a little semolina durum wheat flour to give the pasta a little texture.'

Again Lia nodded. The music was too loud to ask questions and she wasn't sure she needed to know about flour. Surely flour was flour.

Aurelia mixed the flours together on the marble surface and heaped it up before making a well in the middle. With a sharp rap on the side, she cracked an egg single-handed directly into the flour.

Now that was impressive. As Lia watched she repeated the movement with a second egg.

Still shimmying along to the music, Aurelia handed her an egg. 'You try. And on the drumbeat.'

Her joie de vivre was contagious and Lia found herself swaying to the music as she took the egg, tapping it in time. Unfortunately, where Aurelia managed a sleight of hand to manoeuvre the two halves of the shell to release the egg, Lia just crushed the shell in her palm, sending a shower of shell and egg to the floor.

'Oops, sorry.'

'It's no problem. Practice makes perfect.'

Without any fuss, she swiped up the mess and cracked the rest of the eggs.

'Now watch – this is the magic.'

With a fork Aurelia beat the yolks and whites until they were well mixed and then used her hands to start combining the flour and eggs.

Lia watched avidly as everything was incorporated, leaving a floury, crumbly dough. Aurelia made it look easy.

'This is where the love comes in and where you take over.' She moved out of the way. 'You need to knead the dough until it's smooth and silky, and I warn you it's hard work. You know how to knead?'

'I think so.' Didn't you just squish it this way and then that? She'd watched enough *Bake Off* episodes to have a reasonable idea.

'No, no,' said Aurelia, showing her the proper technique a minute later. 'You really have to work the dough. Show it who is boss. You need to warm it up to stretch the gluten. That's better.'

Ten minutes later Lia was still at it, but there was a certain satisfaction in seeing the dough coming together. It was like alchemy, turning the loose flour and golden eggs into something entirely different: this pliable ball that felt unctuous beneath her fingers.

'See,' said Aurelia, pointing to the smooth surface of the dough. 'That is perfect.'

'Thank goodness for that,' said Lia, feeling the ache in her arms.

'And the best thing – it's just flour and eggs.' Aurelia folded her arms and leaned back against the countertop, her eyes focused on Lia. 'Simple ingredients but they create something so wholesome and filling.'

Lia nodded, suddenly aware of the intensity of Aurelia's gaze.

'For me, it's like a family. My family. Your family. We're all separate ingredients, our personalities as different as flour and eggs – some eggs are bigger than others, some flours finer, but when we come together the disparate elements combine to make a perfect whole.' She took Lia's hand and gave it a squeeze. 'I think you should call your mamma. You might think you don't belong anymore because things have changed, but though the ingredients are not quite the same, the combination is still a good one. You are still family.'

Lia pinched her lips together, unsure what to say. Inside she felt a little wobbly and almost tearful. She missed her mum, dad and Stacey.

As if sensing Lia's swirling emotions, Aurelia straightened and pushed herself away from the counter.

'Now it's time to roll the pasta.'

'Roll?' Her arms couldn't take much more.

'*Sì*. But don't worry. In the old days, my nonna would roll it out over and over until it was thin enough, but I use a pasta rolling machine now.' She crossed herself and looked upwards. '*Scusa*, Nonna.'

Even with the roller it took another half an hour before the kitchen was decorated with several oblong sheets of pasta hung from the backs of the kitchen chairs, covered with white tea towels.

'Now we will roll them again through the cutter to make tagliatelle and then put it in the fridge for dinner this evening. How do you feel?'

'Honestly? Knackered,' replied Lia, rubbing her biceps.

'But satisfied, no?' Aurelia was still full of energy and now dancing to 'Paint It Black'. 'You have made food to feed your family. For me this is a great pleasure. And when we all eat, the food is the centre. Food brings people, family and friends together. Like I said, pasta is like family and it binds us to make us greater, like the egg and flour bind to make pasta.'

Her earnest gaze and spirited words reinforced her passion. To Lia, it was a revelation.

'That's a wonderful view. I had never thought of it like that.' The words stirred something at the back of her brain, an elusive idea, like a wisp of mist she couldn't quite grasp but it was there, shimmering just out of reach.

'I told you,' said Aurelia happily, 'you need to immerse yourself in food. The ideas will come.'

'I think you might be right.'

'Of course I'm right,' she said, tucking a floury hand through Lia's arm. 'I'm the mamma; I'm always right.'

Chapter Twenty

'What do you mean, you haven't moved out yet, Layla?' Raph rubbed his forehead, trying to contain his frustration. Layla Monroe had once seemed the perfect girlfriend, fun, good-looking and reasonably undemanding. But their relationship, if it had ever been that, had run its course and when he'd broken things off she'd been quite accepting, insisting on maintaining a friendship of sorts. She'd been so reasonable about everything and made so few emotional demands of him, he'd agreed. And when she'd needed a place to stay, it had seemed natural to offer up his empty London flat. After all, it would only be one week. However, that was a month ago and she was still there.

'Raph, darling. What difference does it make? You're not here. Don't worry, I'll be gone before you're back. It's just ever so convenient at the moment. Your place is so much closer to the theatre. I promise I'm not throwing any wild house parties.'

'That's not the point,' he ground out.

'What is the point, sweetie?'

Another thing about Layla that had worn thin: her ability to be obtuse.

'Call it housesitting. Some people pay for that. I'm keeping the burglars at bay. And potential squatters.'

Oh, the irony.

'Besides, I'm still thinking about coming out to Italy to visit Sally. Remember Sally? She had the place in Maida Vale. Anyway she's rented an Airbnb in Sorrento until the end of August. The play is finishing in a couple of weeks, so I thought I might have a little holiday until we take it on tour. I could come and say hi. I'll take you out to lunch as a thank you for letting me stay in your place.'

'Very kind,' he said dryly, knowing it was probably just another one of her plans that never seemed to materialise. One of the reasons they'd lasted as long as the year they had was because with her work and needing to take any part going – she did a lot of adverts – they hadn't actually seen that much of each other. It had seemed to suit her as much as him.

'I know,' she said chirpily. 'I'll let you go. Speak soon. *Ciao.*'

Irritated by the fact he hadn't managed to get a clear answer from her, he ended the call and saw a text from Pietro Ricci, owner of the Amalfi Lemon Grove Company, which arranged tours for tourists. He'd managed to set up a private visit for Lia and Aurelia as part of the gastronomic tour Aurelia had insisted he arrange for them. She seemed to have taken a shine to Lia – something he'd need to keep an eye on. It was one thing for Ernesto to swallow the woman's story but his mamma was normally a lot savvier than that. She was the one that could be relied upon to back him up and talk some sense into Ernesto. He really wished his stepfather would let him sort out a DNA test – just for his own peace of mind.

Expect to see your guests at eleven o'clock today. Lunch afterwards in the vines. Pietro.

Thank goodness something was going right, but he was annoyed that this gastro tour was yet another bloody call on his time. Mamma seemed to forget he had a business to run. But it was hard to say no to her. Habit rather than anything else. When she'd been a single parent all those years ago, he'd done everything he could to try and alleviate those ever-deepening worry lines on her forehead. Life had improved dramatically when she met and married Ernesto, and Raph's gratitude was so great, he found it difficult to say no to him, too. Between the two of them, his sense of obligation was digging him into an ever deepening hole.

Over the last couple of days, with quite a lot of planning and co-ordination, he'd set up today's series of visits to a buffalo farm, some lemon groves and tomato vines, rounding off with a trip to the small port of Cetara where the famous *colatura di alici*, the very pungent anchovy sauce, was made. Admittedly the latter might just have been payback to his mother for dumping the job on him.

He typed the final timings into the itinerary and emailed it to Aurelia before double-checking his own calendar for the day. Management Zoom call at ten thirty. Client check-in at twelve thirty. And a long meeting that afternoon about corporate governance, which he could well do without. It was important, but it would be three hours of his life he'd never get back. And he still had to submit the monthly report to the exec committee.

Now he was awake he might as well get up and make a start and get a couple of hours work done before breakfast.

Lia was closing the door to her room at the same moment as him, her long hair tied up in a swishy pony tail that he knew left rampant kiss curls clustering around the nape of her slender neck. Damn. There was no way he could duck back inside and pretend he hadn't seen her. Now he was going to have to walk through the gardens up to the main house with her. Something he would rather avoid. Ever since that night on the boat, even though they'd discussed – rather maturely, he thought – the attraction between them, he couldn't get those husky words out of his head. 'Kiss me, Raph.' He'd successfully avoided her for the last two days – burying himself in work at the main house, having dinner with friends in Positano, working in the study late into the night – all so that he wouldn't bump into her around the pool again. Yet here they were.

He'd also made a complete dork of himself. What the hell had been wrong with him? Layla would have laughed her gossamer-fine stockings off, if she'd seen his stuttering, schoolboy apology. In fact, she probably wouldn't have believed it was him. There was something about Lia that disconcerted him. Maybe it was because she was one of the few people who didn't seem intimidated by him when he put his game face on.

'Morning,' said Lia, a teasing light in her eyes. 'Are you going to stand there scowling at me all day?'

'No,' he said, discomposed by her as always and frowning even more.

'Phew,' she said. 'That's a relief then.'

'Are you all set for the tour today?'

'I am,' she said, swinging a bulging tote bag at him. 'All packed with provisions and supplies. I presume you're headed the same way as me, although if you like you can walk ten paces behind me and pretend you never saw me.'

Bloody woman was a mind-reader. If he could have got away with it, he might well have done.

'It's no trouble to walk with you to breakfast. Did you sleep well? Your light was on very late.' He hadn't meant to say that. Did it sound creepy? As if he were watching her? 'I was thinking of going for a swim and I didn't want to disturb you.'

'I was too hot. Funnily enough I was thinking about going for a swim too.'

'You know there's air con.'

'Yes, but I can never get it right. I don't understand how the temperature works. It's either too cold or too noisy. I woke up the other night absolutely frozen.'

'You put in the temperature you want the room to be. I set mine at around nineteen or twenty degrees.'

'Not ten then,' said Lia.

'Not ten, no.'

'No wonder I was so flipping cold.'

The memory of her sea-cold body pressed against him flashed bright and fast into his brain. The hard points of her nipples. The chill of her skin against his chest. The heat of her mouth bare inches from his.

'Mm,' he said absently through the dryness of his own mouth.

They walked along the path shaded by the twisted Mediterranean pines, their scent fresh and sharp in the cool morning, and Raph could hear the skittering feet of lizards scurrying out of reach over the crisp brown needles covering the ground. Through the bent trunks of the trees, he could see glimpses of the sea far below. The sun was already high and light bounced off the water, flashing and twinkling like a rainfall of diamonds.

London, Layla and the irritations of the day suddenly seemed irrelevant.

'How is your work coming along?' he asked, knowing she'd spent the last two days at the studio in town, reluctantly impressed that she'd insisted on borrowing a scooter to go under her own steam. Maybe she was as keen to avoid him as he was to avoid her.

'It's not,' she said with a mournful twitch of her nose, which for some reason he found rather endearing, which was a complete anathema. He didn't normally respond this way to 'cute' women.

'Maybe you should go home,' he suggested. God knew how difficult he was finding it to get any work done.

'That's what I love about you, Raph. There's no artifice. No holding back. You tell it how it is.'

'I just meant that I know how distracting it is out here.'

'Sure you did. And for your information, I'm not finding it distracting. I'm getting lots of work done, just sadly not the right sort of work. My Positano piece is almost finished. So is the lemon picture. So my time here has not been in vain.'

'Are you pleased with what you've done?' he asked, knowing the answer. The Positano picture drew him in and he was very tempted to offer to buy it except that Lia would probably refuse, just to be contrary and thwart him in some way.

'Yes,' she said and he liked the way her eyes suddenly shone. 'I am. They're a bonus, but they're not why I came here.'

Ernesto was in the kitchen when they arrived, directing operations rather badly. Giulia was eating Nutella straight from the jar whenever his back was turned and Michael was taking surreptitious looks at his phone under the table, while Bianca kept throwing cornflakes at him each time he glanced down. Mamma was missing in action – none of this would have happened on her watch.

'*Buongiorno, buongiorno,*' Ernesto greeted them, wiping his hands on the tea towel tucked into the top of his trousers. 'I'm making omelettes for breakfast. Would you like one?'

Taking in the mess of eggs and herbs on the counters, and the butter in the sauté pan blackening, Raph demurred. 'I'll stick to muesli and yoghurt this morning.'

'Lia. You'll try one of my special omelettes, won't you?'

'What's special about them? she asked with a cheeky smile. Raph liked that she already had a handle on Ernesto.

'They're special because *I* am making them,' he announced grandly, puffing out his chest. Luciana rolled her eyes and Giulia collapsed onto the table in giggles.

'They're special because they'll contain similar carbon content to your average piece of charcoal,' said Raph. 'I'd recommend sticking to yoghurt and fruit.'

'You wound my sensibilities,' declared Ernesto, wiping his brow with mock sorrow.

'Better that than you poisoning a guest,' said Raph, already handing a pot of yoghurt to Lia.

'Thank you. Who'd have thought you'd be stepping up to save me from death by burned offerings?'

'I'm not all bad…'

'Michael. Phone. Away. Now,' said Ernesto, finally spotting his son's illicit texting.

'Where's Mamma?' Raph asked. It was unusual for her to allow her husband to take charge of breakfast. It never ended well … not when unsupervised Nutella was involved.

'She's poorly,' said Ernesto, turning his back on Raph, focusing his attention on the pan on the hob. 'Not well at all. As soon as she woke up she had the most terrible headache. And she feels a bit sick. She's going to stay in bed today.'

'Oh.' Raph glanced at Lia. 'I'd better cancel the trip then.'

'No. No,' said Ernesto. 'Aurelia says you must go without her.'

'I don't mind going an—' Lia started to protest.

'No. Aurelia insists,' said Ernesto, his feet spread wide, thrusting his broad chest forward, reminding Raph of a stubborn bull. 'Raph can go with you.'

'I could go on my own.'

'No, you'll need a translator. Raph will go with you.'

'Ernesto, I have work. Meetings. I'll rearrange everything for another day when Mamma's better.'

'No,' said Ernesto. 'Remember Pietro could only do today? He is going to Tuscany next week for a month.'

'There are other lemon groves.'

'He would be insulted.'

'Then Leo can go,' said Raph, quite reasonably. That was a perfect solution.

'Your mamma wants you to go. She knows Lia will be properly looked after if you're with her.'

Raph winced, grateful that Leo wasn't around to hear that. Since his broken marriage a few years ago, the family tended to dismiss him and Leo played up to it. For all his easy-going surfer boy demeanour, Rafe knew Leo wasn't happy. But he wasn't prepared to talk about it to any of them just yet.

Lia looked from Raph to Ernesto and he felt sorry for her because she was clearly uncomfortable. Her shoulders had hunched and she looked like one of the Loggerhead turtles that were frequently seen in the waters around here. It must be very awkward for her standing here listening to this and feeling that she was the cause of the argument. He remembered what she'd said on the boat about not belonging with either family. This couldn't be helping.

'Okay,' he said. 'I'll take Lia today.'

'Please, it's honestly—'

He held up a hand. 'Mamma would never forgive me. Besides, I could do with a day off. I am supposed to be on holiday after all. Give me half an hour to rearrange things and I'll see you out the front.' And if he were totally honest with himself, it would be fun to spend the day with Lia. With her he could relax a little and be more light-hearted. She didn't expect anything of him – except to be the villain.

'Raph, I really don't—'

'Lia, it will be a lovely day,' cried Ernesto. 'Beautiful food, beautiful scenery. What is not to like? You are our guest. We want you to fall in love … with Amalfi, with our home.'

When Ernesto turned theatrical, it was bloody hard to refrain from rolling one's eyes. Raph shook his head instead.

'I don't want to be any trouble,' persisted Lia, not realising the battle was over.

'You're not going to be any more trouble than usual,' said Raph with a quick smirk.

'Oh, I don't know about that,' said Lia, her eyes lighting up with the usual glint of mischief. 'You ain't seen nuthin' yet.'

Chapter Twenty-One

'Oh, that smell.' Lia sighed. All along the terrace ahead of her was a broad row of deep green plants, blooming with silky, veined leaves, glossy in the sunshine.

Gino, their guide, helped her up the steep stone steps to the next terraced row and began telling her in his charming Italian accent how the plants were grown from seed each year. He was knowledgeable and very attentive.

The fierce sunlight beat down on the steep hillside and Lia was glad of the baseball cap she'd crammed on her head at the last minute. Raph's face was inscrutable behind his dark glasses. As always he looked like a crew member from a private yacht in his tan shorts and white linen shirt, although today rather than his usual deck shoes he was wearing trainers and she could understand why. This terrain wasn't for the faint-hearted. They'd had to climb several steep stone steps to get to this point, but for the aromatic scent of the basil alone it was worth it.

'Basil has been grown here since mediaeval times,' Gino

told her. 'It is believed that it was introduced to Greece by Alexander the Great in 350BC and then spread to the rest of the Mediterranean. In Italy it was once known as the symbol of love.' He gave her a playful smile and waggled his eyebrows. 'It was said that if a lady left a ... how you say it? Piece of basil on her balcony ... it was a sign for her man to come to call.'

Lia smiled. This man was a practised flirt, the sort that charmed as naturally as he breathed, and it was much easier to play along than take offence, even though Raph was glowering at the pair of them. Probably still miffed that he'd been persuaded into coming along, although she was still surprised by his acquiescence. It seemed out of character; while he clearly loved his mother, he was no mamma's boy.

There was only so much to learn about basil and so, with the scent lingering in her nose and the sight of those bushy young plants embedded in the picture library in her head, she was more than happy to move on. Next stop was the lemon grove run by Aurelia's friends Pietro and Anya, where they'd be stopping for lunch. Hopefully they would be chatty; Raph's silence as they drove along the winding road up the mountains was starting to irritate her.

'You know you didn't have to come, don't you?' she said.

'I know.'

'So why did you?'

Raph shrugged. 'It seemed the right thing to do.'

She raised her eyebrows. 'It did?'

'Yes,' he said simply, leaving her wondering why it had been the right thing to do.

'Have you been to the lemon place before?'

'No, there normally isn't time when I visit. Usually, I only come out for two weeks.'

'How come you're here for longer this time?'

'Just seemed like a good idea.'

She began to laugh. 'It's because I'm here, isn't it?'

Raph didn't respond. One thing she did appreciate about him was that he wasn't a good liar.

'That's so sweet,' she said after a moment. 'Protecting your family from the big bad gold-digger.'

'I don't think you're a gold-digger,' he admitted.

'What then? Are you just always predisposed to think the worst of people?'

There was a long silence and she watched his hands, solid and secure on the steering wheel. Funny, she hadn't thought about it before but she could see now that his driving was like the rest of him, reliable and steady, although, as descriptions went, these probably weren't terribly attractive. It made him sound dull and he was anything but. He was probably one of the most interesting men she'd ever met. That first meeting, she'd cast him as a ruthless, hard-nosed businessman, but since then she'd seen several sides to him – the handsome, charming sexy man who stirred things within her that she had no business feeling, and the family man who played with his younger siblings, accommodated his mother and supported his stepfather. You could tell a lot about a man from the way he interacted with his family.

What would her dad, Simon, think of Raph? He'd probably like him.

'I'm sorry. I am predisposed to think the worst just because of what I've seen over the years. People using my relationship with him to get to Ernesto, others trying to get money out of him with fake paternity claims.'

'That must be tough. Aurelia told me about the tabloid scandal.'

'That's the really bad stuff. It's more the day-to-day stuff that gets to you. Schoolfriends selling photos when they've been round to a family barbecue, or inveigling an invite because they want a selfie with Ernesto. Over the years I've seen it all, so yes, I'm a suspicious bastard.'

Walking through the shady lemon groves, the plants growing across the wooden pergolas held together with willow, was another aromatic delight. The fresh scent of the lemons wafted on the breeze circulating the hillside high above the town of Amalfi. Pietro and his wife, Anya, had greeted them with enthusiasm and were clearly very proud of their farm.

'It's very hard work,' explained Anya. 'And these days we rely as much on tourism as on the farming for our income. We have tours every day and we have a shop where we sell soap, scented hand lotions and body washes, as well our own Limoncello, olive oil and herbed vinegars.'

They'd climbed a very steep hill traversed with stone walls, which Anya explained had been there for over two hundred years. 'We are the fifth generation to farm lemons here. *Sfusato Amalfitano*. Only lemons grown in this area can officially be called Amalfi lemons because of the unique micro-climate. The sun, the sea, the mountains.'

The crop had to be harvested and carried down the steep hillside and rocky steps. Lia was fascinated by the fat lemons with their dimpled skins that hung everywhere she looked and equally by Anya and Pietro, who were both so passionate about their products and the importance that their farm played in the local eco-system.

'We're literally saving Amalfi,' Pietro told her. 'The lemon trees and their roots are anchoring the soil to the mountains. Without these lemon groves the town would be deluged with mud slides. We farmers play more than one role.'

Taking pity on Lia, whose face was now red with exertion – bloody Raph hadn't so much as broken out a sweat, Lia noticed – Anya took them into one of the cool barns near the crest of the hillside, where she served them lemon cake and freshly made ice cold lemonade.

Raph downed his in one, his head thrown back in appreciation, and Lia almost choked on her drink as those quivery butterflies took flight in her stomach at the sight of the tanned column of his neck. Every now and then she forgot quite how handsome he was and then she'd see him like this and her system played silly buggers. Like she'd told him on the boat, he was an attractive man. Too bloody attractive, she thought.

She caught Anya looking at her speculatively and took another hasty glug of lemonade.

'Raph has an effect on women, yes?' she murmured quietly to Lia.

'Not me,' denied Lia hastily, which she realised was tantamount to waving a red flag and shouting 'I fancy the pants off of him'.

Anya didn't say anything. She didn't need to – her knowing smile said it all.

———————

They enjoyed a lunch of tagliatelle drizzled in lemon olive oil, toasted pine nuts and fresh parsley, seated on a terrace along with a dozen other tourists who had also been doing a tour. When Lia and Raph joined the party under the shady pergola, they were welcomed by American, Spanish, French and German voices – and those were just the ones Lia identified.

In the centre of the table was a large carafe of crisp white wine, which Anya served as everyone settled into their seats. She insisted on mixing the party up so that people were forced to talk to people they didn't know, which immediately created a festive air around the table, making it feel like a celebration. Lia was sandwiched between a tall and very beautiful blond Danish girl, Pernille, and a garrulous American woman, Gerry, who oozed sunny positivity.

'Isn't this just delightful?' she asked as soon as Lia sat down. 'Where are you from?'

'London.'

'I'm from Connecticut and here with my husband, Chris, over there,' Gerry said, pointing him out. 'We booked this trip to celebrate our thirty-fifth wedding anniversary. I wanted to come for our honeymoon but back in the day we didn't have the money. How about you, are you on holiday?'

Lia explained that it was a working holiday and ended up talking a great deal about her art to the fascinated Gerry, who immediately looked her up online and shared her website with Pernille, who was equally interested.

Over lunch everyone swapped restaurant recommendations, the details of where they were staying and general must-dos in the area.

Across the table Raph was contributing to what looked like a lively conversation with a young Colombian man and the partner of Lia's Danish neighbour.

'Have you been to Naples yet?' asked Gerry.

'Yes. It's authentic. Quite rustic but interesting,' said Pernille.

'Can you recommend a restaurant?'

The Danish girl shook her head. 'We wanted really good pizza but everywhere was so busy.'

'Raph, my…' Lia paused trying to sum up what Raph was to her. 'Sworn enemy' sounded a bit dramatic but they weren't friends. Did they even like each other? And 'my father's stepson' sounded way too convoluted. 'My hosts' son might be able to recommend a place. His family come every summer and they know the area pretty well. In fact I was supposed to be coming with his mother today but she's unwell.'

'And the change of plan was no hardship, I take it? It doesn't appear so from where I'm sitting,' commented Gerry with a glance at Raph.

Pernille grinned. 'If I liked older men, I would not say no.' Which Lia supposed was quite a compliment given the Danish girl and her boyfriend both could have stepped out of a Marvel superhero film. They had that healthy 'life lived outdoors' glow to them, and it was no surprise when Pernille recommended kayaking along the coast.

'That sounds energetic,' said Gerry. 'We did the Path of the Gods two days ago. Now, that is a really good hike. You really ought to check that out. It's only seven kilometres but boy, is it hilly, and we do a lot of hiking back home.'

'Yes, we did it. Took some really great photos. The views are incredible,' agreed Pernille. 'You should go,' she encouraged Lia.

Lunch came to a close and everyone said goodbye as if they were old friends.

'You look like you enjoyed that,' said Raph as they walked back to his car.

'It was so much fun,' said Lia. She felt on a high after good food and great company. 'The superfit Danish couple said I should do the Path of the Gods. The title alone sounds rather epic.'

Raph nodded. 'In Italian it's *Sentiero degli Dei*.'

'That's even better.'

'I could take you on Sunday, if you'd like. It's one of my favourite things to do.'

'I didn't have you down as a hiker.'

'I'm not, but it's guaranteed peace and quiet as none of the kids ever want to go for a walk.'

'That's mean,' said Lia with a laugh at his logic.

'No, it's not. I love them all but they're not my kids.'

'Is it weird having much younger brothers and sisters?'

'What's weird is not seeing that much of them for half the year and then having the whole family full-on for most of the summer. When I've only just got used to them again, they go back to their lives in LA.'

'Do you not go out there?'

'Sometimes, but believe it or not, I do have my own life to live in London. My own friends to see.'

'You have friends? You amaze me,' said Lia, risking a cheeky nudge of her elbow in his ribs.

'What is it you said? "Some people like me."'

'Actually what I said is "Some of my friends quite like me."' She paused before adding, 'but that's because I'm nice.'

Chapter Twenty-Two

They saw long oozing twists of mozzarella being made and folded into glossy skeins of marble white before being cut into the familiar fist-sized balls, smelled the less than fragrant buffalo on the farm, who came nosing along the fence to say hello, and tasted freshly made, melt-in-the-mouth burrata at the Rocco farm high up in the craggy hills, before coasting back down hairpin bends and frankly terrifying sheer drops to the small town of Cetara.

Lia was extremely grateful that Raph was driving because although she appreciated the spectacular views, her heart spent most of the downward journey on high alert.

'Cetara is known as the world tuna capital,' said Raph as he parked the car rather precariously on the edge of a narrow road, half on and half off the pavement. There was just enough room for another car to squeeze past through all the other cars that were haphazardly parked along the street in a variety of interesting positions, including one small Fiat wedged into a space that left it hanging over someone's small garden terrace below.

'I suppose somewhere has to be,' observed Lia, although to be honest she was slightly surprised; the place looked pretty small. When they'd driven through Amalfi earlier, there'd been similarities with Positano, but Cetara immediately felt very different. When they reached the small harbour and beach area, dominated by the Vicereale Tower, the most obvious difference was that tourists had to vie for space with the painted wooden boats pulled up on the pebbly beach.

Many of the shops sold little bottles of dark liquid, which Raph explained the town was famous for: colatura di alici. 'It's the juice that is left over once the anchovies have been soaked and it's full of flavour.'

So that explained the slightly sharp fish smell scenting the air around the harbour as they ambled along eating ice-cream. With the late afternoon sun warming her skin and the seagulls shrieking as if outraged at something, she realised she'd actually enjoyed the day far more than she'd expected. Raph was excellent company, knowledgeable without being too know-it-all, and very easy to be with.

'You seem very relaxed today,' she said, after spending a moment or two wondering whether to say it or not.

'I am.' He laughed. 'For once. My family drive me insane. I love them but it's like herding kittens sometimes. Ernesto can be shrewd when it comes to his work but he's hopeless when it comes to running the house and his financial affairs.'

'That's because he knows you'll do it for him,' said Lia.

'My mum is the same. She's a very capable businesswoman, running her own consultancy – she's on top of every spreadsheet and all the profit-and-loss data going – but the minute something goes wrong at home, the dishwasher stops working or it's time to renew the TV licence, it's Dad that has to sort it out. The funny thing is, if he weren't there, I know she'd get on with it and do it with no trouble.'

Raph's brow furrowed. 'And you think Ernesto is the same.'

'Yes. You said yourself he's shrewd when it comes to his work and presumably he managed his affairs perfectly well before you were able to do it for him.'

'Yes, Mamma helped him.'

'And she managed to bring up two boys by herself before she met him. My mum does it because … well, she's slightly more successful than Dad, so it's a way of giving him some power back in the relationship. Maybe … it's the same with you. I'm not saying it's deliberate. It could be subconscious. I'm guessing before Ernesto came along, you were the man of the family? Maybe he defers to you so that you don't have to relinquish that role.'

Raph paused and they both sat down on a low wall facing the sea. It was clear that her words had made him think.

'I'm not sure if that makes me feel better or not. You're right, before Mamma married Ernesto, I was the man of the family. Things were tough but they were normal. And when she married a famous movie star, our lives were anything but normal.' He held up his hands in a surrender gesture. 'Don't get me wrong, it was kind of wonderful not to have to worry or see Mamma get that pinched look, the little twin furrows on her forehead, but our lives … boy, they were upended.

'We stayed in London at first but that didn't work, so we were transplanted to LA. That was no hardship. Sunshine. A pool. Being a novelty in an American high school. Things were good, seriously great. But I was naïve. Didn't realise at first that this wonderful new life came with conditions… And now I sound like an ungrateful git who didn't appreciate his good fortune.' Raph rose, shrugging his shoulders as if trying to shake off self-disgust. 'We ought to head back. I haven't heard from Mamma all day. I hope she's okay. It's not like her to be sick.'

Any sign of what had ailed Aurelia earlier was obviously long gone as they found her playing badminton in the garden with the twins and Luciana, while Ernesto and Giulia sat in the shade, both colouring in complicated circular patterns in a book of mandalas.

'Ah, Raph and Lia,' called Ernesto. 'Perfect timing, I was just about to organise some drinks. Come sit down.'

'Mamma seems to be feeling better,' said Raph, nodding towards his mother, who was making a frantic leap to swipe at the shuttlecock, laughing breathlessly as she did so.

'Better?' asked Giulia, her tongue poking out as she coloured in a teardrop shape with great care.

'She had a bad headache, *piccolina*,' Ernesto said hurriedly, beaming at Raph, 'but she took some tablets and made it all better. Would you like a drink, Lia? I make a very mean Negroni.'

'What's in it?' she asked.

'Gin, Campari and vermouth,' said Raph. 'And' – he nodded at Ernesto – 'he had a brief spell as a cocktail waiter, so he knows his stuff.'

'In that case, I'd love one,' said Lia.

'Excellent – and then you can tell us all about your day.' Ernesto strode off, although he paused to talk to his wife, who quickly wrapped up the badminton game and came hurrying over, scooping her wayward hair back from her forehead.

'How was your day? I'm so sorry I couldn't join you. But it's amazing what painkillers can do. I feel fine now. No matter, tell me everything. How were Pietro and Anya? Did you try some Limoncello?' She peppered them with question after question, enthusing over their answers.

Lia grinned at Raph when, at one point, they both went to respond to a question at the same time, creating an unexpected sense of fellowship. Instead of being solo, for once she'd been one of two, and that felt surprisingly nice.

When Ernesto reappeared carrying a tray of pale orange drinks, and Giulia had jumped up to join her brothers and sisters, Aurelia gave him a happy smile. 'Raph and Lia have had such a good day. I think we should plan another trip … for your inspiration, of course. This time: pizza.' She turned to Lia. 'I think you should go to Naples later in the week.'

Chapter Twenty-Three

'Hurry up, Luciana,' yelled Bianca from the back of the car. 'Otherwise, you have to go in the car with Mamma and Papa.'

Lia exchanged a quick look with Raph. It was half-past eight in the morning, following a military-operation-style breakfast, which had commenced at ten to and finished at ten past. Lia had watched the proceedings with fascinated interest as everyone was rounded up and Aurelia repeated a litany of 'Have you got's' followed by an endless list: suncream, water bottles, hats, spending money, spare plasters and sunglasses.

'Welcome to the Salvatore family,' he said, as they both observed the chaos of trying to get the entire family out of the house and into two cars at the same time.

Lia, as guest of honour on the 'official pizza investigation outing', as Michael had dubbed it, had automatically been awarded the front passenger seat with Raph in the Lamborghini SUV. Bianca and Luciana, by dint of shouting the quickest and the loudest, won the right to travel with them, while the rest of the children, including Leo, who didn't want to be left out of a trip to the finest pizzeria in Naples, would be travelling with Aurelia and Ernesto in the family people carrier. Lia had lost count of how many cars the family seemed to have available to them.

When the idea had been mooted by Aurelia a couple of days previously, it was greeted with unanimous enthusiasm and no one, not even Raph, wanted to be left out of a trip to Lombardi's in the old part of the city.

So Lia found herself sitting in the car with Raph, who seemed surprisingly relaxed, given he'd been dragged away from work for another whole day.

'Bianca.' Raph's voice was stern. 'Have you got sweets in the back of the car?'

Her eyes widened and she tried to look innocent but then respect for her older half-brother overcame her. 'Yes, Raph.'

He winked at her. 'Make sure you share them. The driver needs sustenance.'

'Yes, Raph.' Her face relaxed into a smile at his teasing and she offered a bag of jelly beans to him and Lia.

'Not just now, *cara*. And don't eat them all too quickly. If you're sick in my car I will make you walk home.'

'You wouldn't,' she said with a giggle.

He raised an eyebrow and she giggled again, turning to Lia. 'He likes to pretend he's the big bad wolf – but he isn't really.'

'Don't tell her that,' protested Raph, his hand on his

heart as if wounded. 'I need someone round here to do what I tell them.' He turned to Lia and said mournfully, 'No one has any respect for me.'

'Now *that* I don't believe for a second,' she said severely, catching Bianca's eye. The young girl, with a face full of mischief and fun, whispered to her, 'Mamma says he's a pussycat really.'

Mmm, thought Lia, but pussycats still hissed when provoked and would use their teeth and claws when necessary.

Finally everyone was loaded, the big wrought-iron gates opened and the two cars pulled out onto the road. Once they'd taken the meandering route over the headland from Positano onto the busy road to Naples, the dark shadowed shape of Mount Vesuvius dominated the skyline for most of the journey. It stood on guard, a rather forbidding sentinel above the Bay of Naples, and Lia gave it a wary glance as they neared the city.

'When was the last time it erupted?' she asked quietly, glancing over her shoulder. The two girls in the back were both plugged into their phones.

'Not since 1944, during the war, but they monitor it very carefully so that they'll get an early warning if it erupts again.'

'Is that likely?' asked Lia.

'No one knows but it's still active so there's always a chance.'

'And people still live here when it's what? Only a few miles away?'

'Twelve kilometres,' piped up Giulia from the back, not

so plugged in after all. 'We have kilometres in Italy. Miles at home in America. We did a science project at school and Papa helped me. We made the volcano explode with vinegar and baking soda. He told me all about Vesuvio.'

'I had no idea the volcano was so close to the city. My dad has always wanted to visit Pompeii and Herculaneum.' She could've bitten off her tongue for saying that.

'But he's been,' said Giulia, indignantly. 'He took us last summer. And it was really hot and boring. Did you know there were dead people there? You can see them.'

'She means her other papa, silly,' said Bianca. 'The one she had before ours.'

'You have two papas? How?' asked Giulia.

Oh God, how to answer that one to an eight-year-old?

'Every family is different, Giulia,' said Raph. 'Remember I had a papa before Mamma married your papa? Now, have you decided what type of pizza you're going to have? Pineapple and ham?'

'No!' the girls chorused, obviously well trained. 'It's an abomination.'

'The best and only pizza is Margherita,' said Bianca. 'Just tomatoes, mozzarella and basil.'

Lia shot Raph a grateful look, impressed by his distraction technique.

'What's your favourite, Lia?' asked Giulia and a lively conversation continued for the next few kilometres about what should or shouldn't go on top of a pizza. It was universally agreed that pineapple had no place, but olives most definitely did, even if they were 'yukky' according to both girls.

'I didn't like them when I was your age,' said Lia.

'Don't worry,' said Giulia, patting her on the shoulder. 'You can always spit them out on Papa's pizza when he's not looking. He never notices.'

Raph sniggered and Lia had a difficult time holding back a snort of laughter. On this occasion it was obvious that neither of them dare look at the other, as it was highly likely they'd have hysterics.

'Lia must go to Porta Nolana,' declared Aurelia as the family congregated in a small shady park area once the cars were parked near the sea front. 'You should go to the market, *cara*. They have the most incredible fish there. Raph, you can take her. The children won't want to go. We will go for a walk and we can meet you at the restaurant in an hour and a half.'

With that Aurelia and Ernesto gathered up the children and quickly departed. Leo winked at Lia and joined his mother herding the four younger children over the road.

'See you later,' said Ernesto, with a cheery wave and he too walked off.

Lia frowned. 'What just happened?'

'That's my mother. Getting everyone to do what she wants. You've heard of silent assassins? My mother is an invisible bulldozer.'

'And here I thought she was so sweet.'

'She is, that's how she achieves her aims most of the time. Before you realise what she's up to, she's charmed you into doing her bidding. I've had thirty years of it and I've still not worked out how she does it.'

Lia did feel like she'd been left in the wake of a large ferry.

'We have our orders. Let's go to the market. I understand she has taken responsibility for your food education.'

'Something like that, although I have to admit it was fun making the pasta with her and I can now add Amatriciana to my repertoire.'

'Amatriciana is my favourite, although no one makes it like Mamma.'

They wound their way through stone-flagged narrow streets bordered by tall, storied houses. Above them the balconies perched across from each other were full of the day's washing, hanging limply in the growing heat. Compared to the quiet restraint of Positano, the crowded town felt hot and stuffy, but the tightly packed streets were alive with colour and vivacity. Around her voices held hundred-mile-an-hour conversations in sing-song Italian, interspersed with the manic toots of Vespas weaving in and out of tourists with daredevil panache, leaving a plume of petrol-scented exhaust fumes that mixed with the smell of hot city.

Raph walked at a leisurely pace, for which she was grateful. It felt so much warmer here, the thoroughfares barely wide enough for the cars that honked furiously, forcing their way at snail's pace through the throngs of people. Despite a certain shabbiness, there was a vitality to the city, a sense of liveliness and authenticity. She could almost see the history here, and it was easy to imagine merchants crowded into the busy port, centuries ago, walking the same flagstone streets.

'Here we go, Porta Nolana.' Raph pointed to the arched entrance between two circular towers, one of which was built into a modern block of flats. 'This used to be one of the mediaeval gates to the old city.'

From Lia's point of view, the scene wasn't particularly prepossessing from the outside but the minute they stepped into the small lane sandwiched between taller buildings and she saw the market stretching deep into the city, she paused to take in its beauty. There were stalls selling everything from home goods to toys to electronics and of course the most amazing fruit and vegetables.

'It's all about the fish,' Raph explained. 'The fish market here is one of the best. If it lives in the sea, you can buy it here. Or so I've been told.'

The fish stalls were quite remarkable. There were large plastic tubs filled with what Lia assumed was sea water containing fresh cockles, whelks and clams. The tables were covered with deep polystyrene boxes filled with chipped ice, displaying silver streaks of whole fish like tuna, sardines and mackerel, the pinks and oranges of fillets of salmon, scallops and the delicate filigree flash of tiny anchovies along with the larger distinctive swordfish and a dozen others that Lia could only guess at. With so much seafood on display, the colours and textures immediately inspired her. She took out her phone and began taking lots of photos, asking Raph what everything was.

'Orata is sea bream, spigola is sea bass, branzino is

European bass. Good job, Mamma isn't with us. Ernesto adores sardines and she'd have to buy him some and then, knowing that the kids would complain about the smell all the way back, she'd try to get me to transport them – and they're not coming in my car.'

Lia laughed at him. 'How old are you?'

'Old enough that I don't want a fishy-smelling car. Not when she could just buy them in Positano at the pescheria.'

———

They fell into easy conversation and Lia was surprised to note that an hour had quickly passed.

'Oh, that is gorgeous.' She stopped in front of an expensive-looking clothes shop where a bright print skirt featuring old buildings that reminded her of the Positano picture she was working on was displayed in the window.

'That's very you,' said Raph. 'You love your colour, don't you?'

'Yes, it's just you that lives in navy and white, you know. The rest of your family loves colour too.'

'I like colour.'

'Since when? Even your swim shorts are navy.'

'I don't have a lot of time to shop. Besides, white and navy is smart. No one ever complained before.' His slight pout was rather endearing.

'What about that?' Lia pointed to a pink linen shirt on one of the male mannequins in the window. 'Would you wear that?'

'Yeah, I don't have a problem with pink.'

'And what about those?' She pointed to a pair of striped turquoise and white swim shorts featuring brightly coloured toucans.

'They're okay,' he said a little less confidently.

'I dare you to buy them.'

'Dare me?'

'Yes. Live a little.'

'I don't need to live a little. I don't have anything to prove. Certainly not to you.'

'So buy them. And the shirt. I think they would suit you.'

'Good God, is that a compliment?'

'I wouldn't get too carried away,' said Lia, turning to look at the skirt again. It really was lovely. 'But I think it would make you look a bit less stuffy.'

'Stuffy?' He almost spluttered over the word.

'Yes.' She liked seeing him like this, slightly outraged but also amused. 'Are you going to spend all day repeating everything I say?'

'Are you going to spend all day insulting me?'

'I've just given you a compliment. You'd look nice in that shirt and the shorts are fun. Anyway, suit yourself. I'm going to try the skirt on.'

She went into the changing room, taking with her the skirt and a couple of dresses that had also caught her eye.

Just one twirl in the mirror convinced her that the skirt was an absolute must-have.

'Very nice,' said Raph, when she stepped out into the shop to take a better look in the bigger mirror.

'I think so too.' She nodded to the sales assistant. 'I'll

take this but I'm just going to try on the other dresses.' She turned to Raph. 'We've got time, haven't we?'

'Plenty of time.'

She went back into the changing booth and the sales assistant asked her to hand out the skirt.

When she came out of the booth Raph was at the till and had a large bag in his hand.

'You bought something?'

'I bought two somethings.'

'Well done you.' She took her purse from her bag and turned to the shop assistant, looking for the skirt on the counter.

'It's all taken care of,' said the assistant with an indulgent smile, casting a hero-worshipping look at Raph.

'Saved time,' he said, holding up the bag. 'Come on. I need a caffeine break.'

'Raph. You can't buy that for me.'

He shrugged. 'Think of all the birthdays I've missed.'

'We're not related.'

'No, but Ernesto would have got me to sort out a present if he'd been allowed. He's very generous.'

'I don't need presents and I can buy my own clothes. I have to pay you back.'

'Whatever. We can sort it out later.'

'We will,' said Lia, determined that she would. Raph had assumed she was after money when she first turned up and her pride insisted that she gave him no grounds for believing it.

'Do you want to see anymore?' he asked as they strolled away from the shop.

'No, I'm all fished out,' said Lia. 'I'm ready for a coffee too, although maybe it's a bit too hot.'

'I know a place that does espresso granita and it's on the way to Lombardi 1882.'

'Sold. That sounds exactly what I need.'

Raph led her through the streets. 'And on the way I can show you the famous staircase of the Palazzo dello Spagnolo.'

'Okay,' said Lia, more than happy to play tourist today. It was quite nice to feel that she was seeing a bit more of the country and she felt invigorated and energised by the hustle and bustle of the city. That idea circulating at the back of her head was starting to weave its way into life, like a vine climbing and spreading with summer growth.

'It's near here,' said Raph. Lia had no idea how he knew his way around. It was like a maze running through tall buildings of ochre, yellow and orange, characterised by narrow wrought-iron fenced balconies filled with brightly coloured geraniums and petunias. Suddenly he stopped and crossed the road and led her through an archway to a courtyard that she'd have walked straight past had she been on her own.

It was one of those totally unexpected gems. The courtyard itself held a couple of slovenly parked cars and was nothing to write home about but on the opposite wall was the most magnificent four-tiered double staircase, which might have inspired an Escher picture. In perfect symmetry the two sets of stairs ran up either side of the palazzo. Each floor had an ornate ceiling painted in a delicate pale green and embellished with white stucco.

Simple yet stylish, the design immediately brought a smile to Lia's face.

'Like it?' asked Raph, coming to stand beside her, so close that his arm brushed hers, the touch of his soft hairs sending what felt like a static charge through her. Her body lit up in awareness and she couldn't help turning to face him, her emotions naked on her face.

'It's beautiful – and what I like most is that there's no one else here. It's a secret, serene oasis in the middle of the wild party of the city.' Like him in the centre of his family. They were colourful and unknown and she was still feeling her way with them, but with him she knew who she was.

'That's exactly how I feel.' He gave her a slightly startled smile and yet again they shared that click of understanding and shared presence, the sense of being in the moment together. With it came the increasingly familiar flip in the pit of her stomach and Lia felt so very aware of him: the faint peppercorn stubble on his chin, the smoothness of his tan skin, with its tiny freckles stretching over his cheekbones, and those thick, glossy eyebrows. Her fingers itched to meander across his features, feeling the different textures.

Oh God, she was staring at him, imagining his face in her hands.

Her eyes fell to his lips, particularly the wide bottom lip that was almost sulky but eminently kissable.

'Lia.' His Adam's apple dipped and her body responded to the husky tone in his voice with a quick internal shiver. 'Don't.'

'Don't what?' she whispered.

'Look at me like that.'

'Why not?' A smile curved her lips, satisfaction nudging her like a cat wanting to be stroked.

'Because...' His delicious pause made her heart turn in another of those feathery flips of anticipation. ' Because ... it makes me want to kiss you.'

The tension gripping her shoulders relaxed. It was finally going to happen. He was going to kiss her.

'Papa! Papa! Look, it's Lia and Raph! Hey, Raph! Lia!' Giulia's excited voice burst over them like a rain shower and they both took a step back. Lia could bet he was schooling his face as much as she was, as they both turned to greet Giulia and the rest of the family gathered behind them in the shadow of the gateway.

'Hey!' replied Lia, her voice a little unsteady as all the bright, beautiful anticipation inside her deflated like a week-old birthday balloon.

Raph scooped up the little girl who'd run straight up to him. 'We had a Coca-Cola in the park, but Papa says no gelato until after pizza.'

The rest of the family crowded round all talking at once, although Aurelia hung back and Lia caught the thoughtful gleam in her eyes. Oh God, what was she thinking? Mortification filled Lia as a hot blush coursed up her face. She and Raph might not be related but the idea of them together might seem very odd to his mother and stepfather, especially when she was staying in their house and she'd come here to meet Ernesto, not embark on a summer fling. Weren't Italian mammas meant to be very protective of their sons?

Ernesto, taking photographs of the staircase, decided to organise a selfie of the family in front of it.

'Hurry up, Papa. This is boring,' muttered Michael as Leo hauled him into the picture with a brotherly headlock. Lia found herself squashed next to Raph, his arm around her, both of them studiously avoiding looking at each other. Two not-quite-kisses had left her with a weird ache of longing and a very odd sense of despair. Knowing Raph and his distrust of everyone, he was likely fighting this unwelcome attraction and would no doubt batten down the hatches and avoid being alone with her from now on, when all she really wanted was to find out if kissing him would live up to the expectation their near misses had built.

Chapter Twenty-Four

L ombardi's was a family-run restaurant that had been in business for over a hundred years and while it was thronged with tourists in brightly coloured shorts and T-shirts, it was obviously equally a draw for well-dressed local families. One of the waiters hurried out to greet Ernesto with a shout of welcome, an enthusiastic handshake and a kiss on both cheeks for Aurelia – the family were obviously regulars.

Despite this, there was no preferential treatment, which didn't seem to bother Ernesto in the least, and they joined the queue, which thankfully wasn't too long.

'This is the best pizzeria in Naples,' Ernesto told Lia, gesturing at the building. 'My father used to bring me and my brothers and sisters here when we were Giulia's age. It has been a favourite with our family for many, many years. Enrico and Alberto' – he pointed through the restaurant towards the back of the building – 'are the great-grandchildren of Enrico who opened the restaurant in 1892. It is a Naples institution.'

This assertion was reinforced by the nearby wall, which was lined with pictures of the different generations of family as well as lots of newspaper articles about the restaurant and numerous award certificates and trophies. Lia looked around her in fascination. The bright, airy décor spoke of simplicity and taste with its white-cloth-covered tables, wooden chairs and tile floors. Black and white clad waiters buzzed about with welcoming smiles, plates and trays held aloft as they weaved in and out of the tables, delivering menus, drinks and food. The scent of rich tomato, aromatic basil and toasted mozzarella filled the air along with the contented chatter of happy customers. The relaxed, laid-back vibe made it clear that this was a restaurant where people came to enjoy being with each other as much as the food.

Lia felt that twang of synapses at the back of her brain again, another image starting to solidify. The strands of mist she was trying to capture were teasing her again but becoming clearer. Rather than force it, she took a breath, focusing on the present, and at that moment Raph caught her eye and they exchanged a quick private look. He made his way to her side.

'Are you okay?' For some reason his presence was reassuring.

'Yes. Just thinking about my commission.'

'Are you worried about it?'

'Not really. It sounds pretentious but there's something

cooking away in my subconscious. I just have to trust in the process. It will float up when it's ready.'

Raph touched her arm and she realised she was probably pulling all sorts of faces.

'I'm a great believer in sleeping on things.'

She glanced up at him, reassured by his quiet confidence, and felt the need to lighten the mood. Unable to resist teasing him she dropped her voice. 'Are you, now?' It wasn't even that suggestive but he gave her a rueful smile anyway and then, with a quick check that no one was listening, leaned down and with a wink said, 'I am.'

Oh God, she had it bad.

When they were seated – no small feat given that there were nine of them in total but the Lombardi staff were clearly used to big groups and quickly moved a few tables together – there was the usual lively Salvatore family discussion about what everyone was going to have. The majority verdict was that Margherita pizza was a must-have, although Leo changed his mind at the last minute and ordered a Diavola, citing a desire for something hot and spicy. He flashed Lia one of his flirty smiles at this and she grinned back at him, although she couldn't help thinking that, compared to his brother, he was still very boyish. Raph was very much all man.

Lia ordered a Peroni and gratefully sipped the pale golden lager, enjoying the light fizz of bubbles on her tongue. Aurelia had directed the seating plan because the children were squabbling about who wanted to sit next to whom and Lia found herself sitting next to Raph on one side and Leo on the other.

The pizzas arrived piping hot, the cheese still bubbling on top, and they looked every bit as good as had been promised. The soft dough was cooked to perfection and almost melted in Lia's mouth. It was perfectly completed by the piquant tomato sauce and the mellow flavour of the mozzarella. It was quite easily the best pizza she'd ever eaten in her life and despite its size, she had no trouble eating every last bit. The clean plates all round were testament to the quality of the food.

Aurelia and Raph were talking about the summer party when Aurelia broke off. 'Lia, is there anyone you'd like to invite to the party?'

'Me?' Lia asked, her eyes widening in surprise.

'No young man or anything?' Aurelia pressed.

Lia laughed and shook her head. 'Are you sure you want me there? I mean...'

Aurelia scowled, her dark eyes flashing. 'Of course you will be there. All the family will be there. It's always a fun day; we start in the early evening and go on until—'

'Until it stops,' interrupted Ernesto. 'Everyone who is on holiday nearby comes. You must come.'

'Don't worry, it's very informal,' explained Aurelia.

'When is it?' asked Lia, starting to think that actually it would be fun and certainly something to talk about when she got back home.

'Next week. It's wonderful and has become more of a whole weekend event because people start arriving on

Friday evening and some stay through Sunday. Raph, you might have to move into the main house. The children will all be in tents in the garden,' said Aurelia.

'They want to be in tents in the garden,' retorted Raph. 'Eating marshmallows and chasing fireflies.'

'You have fireflies?' Lia's eyes lit up. 'I've never seen any.'

'They are quite magical. Raph, you must take Lia to the meadow, near the stream. They are always there.'

'I must, must I?' teased Raph.

Aurelia's head tilted with regal superiority. 'Yes. Why not?'

'Why not, indeed?' murmured Raph.

'That's settled then. Maybe after dinner when it grows dark? They come out then. It is a beautiful sight. And you can hear the porcupines.'

'Porcupines? Seriously.' Lia wasn't sure whether Aurelia was joking or not.

'Yes,' said Ernesto. 'They are quite shy so you don't see them s often, but they make a lot of noise, grunting. Maybe Raph can take you porcupine hunting too.'

'Do you have any other tasks for me?' asked Raph dryly.

Aurelia beamed at him and said with an overly sweet smile, 'I'm sure I can think of other things.'

'Yes, Mamma,' said Raph with a long-suffering grin. 'I'm looking forward to going home for a holiday.'

'You don't mean that,' she said. 'You see what I have to put up with, Lia?'

Lia laughed and put her hands up. 'Don't bring me into it!' Although she was secretly pleased to be included. Her parents would have loved this place and she wished she could have shared it with them. What were her mum, dad and sister up to at the moment? Even though Lia and Stacey had left home, they still went away for a family holiday for a week in August each year. This year they were supposed to be going to Carcassonne in France. A lump lodged itself in Lia's throat. The three of them would now be going without her. Mum, Dad and daughter. She thought of the text she'd received from her mum just that morning, wanting to talk. She still couldn't bring herself to; she felt so let down by her.

'Lia?' Aurelia's voice pierced her feeling sorry for herself.

'Sorry, I was miles away.'

'I was asking whether you would like dessert? Or will you save yourself for gelato? We have a favourite family gelateria. They make the most wonderful ice-cream.'

'We have to visit Casa Infante. We always go there,' said Giulia in her usual forceful manner. 'Don't we, Papa?'

'Yes, *piccola*' said Ernesto. 'But I think they might have run out of stracciatella ice-cream.'

'No!' Giulia's shocked little face made the adults burst into laughter until it began to crumple with threatened tears.

'I was only teasing, *cucciola*. Don't you worry.'

Giulia pouted. 'I think I should have two scoops because you upset me.'

'I think that one scoop is plenty after pizza.' Aurelia straightened. 'Or,' she said in the sort of voice that suggested she'd just had the most brilliant idea, 'you could stay here, Lia, and enjoy a Limoncello with Raph in peace and quiet, rather than with this noisy lot.'

Lia narrowed her eyes. The earlier question about a 'young man' had reinforced her already growing suspicions. It seemed Aurelia was trying very hard to matchmake her and Raph.

'I'll stay too. I've spent enough time with the brats,' said Leo with a teasing wink at Giulia, before leaning back in his chair, stretching out his legs and putting his hands behind his head. 'I fancy a Limoncello.'

Aurelia's glare bounced off him and beside her Lia heard Raph's quick snort of amusement.

'What?' asked Leo, shooting back upright in his seat. 'Why did you kick me, Mamma?'

Raph snorted again.

'I didn't kick you. You're mistaken, isn't he, Ernesto?'

'But you did,' protested Leo, looking adorably confused.

'Leo, if your mamma says she didn't kick you, she didn't kick you,' said Ernesto. 'Do you know what, I think I will have a Limoncello too.'

Aurelia huffed out a small groan of frustration while Raph's shoulders shook with silent laughter.

Lia couldn't help but smile as well. It seemed Aurelia's matchmaking would have to wait for now.

Chapter Twenty-Five

Her pencil raced rapidly across the page in her sketchbook, making a rough drawing and annotating it with furiously scribbled notes. Her heart jumped with that quick pulse of excitement you get when you know something is coming together. The ideas that had been simmering at the back of her head all day had suddenly burst out on the journey home like a geyser and when they pulled up outside the villa, she excused herself as politely as she could and almost ran back through the shady paths of the garden to her room.

That flash of silver from the fish counters today had been the catalyst for the concept that had been hovering out of reach for the last week. Now it was as if she couldn't get the ideas down quickly enough as she sat at the table on the patio by the pool under the shade of the big parasol. Her brain crackled with energy and she grinned to herself like a fool, thrilled by the heady realisation that this might just be her very best work yet.

As her fingers flew across the page, she began to calm down happy that she had captured what she needed.

After a while, she came to, realising she'd been working non-stop for the last two hours. She reviewed what she'd done and laid down her sketchbook, the rest of the world coming back into focus. That was when she noticed Raph sitting on a nearby sunlounger ostensibly reading a book. She hadn't even realised he was there and had no idea how long he'd been there. Quite some time, judging by his relaxed, comfortable position.

'Better?' he asked.

'Better?'

'Yes, you looked like your tail was on fire when you jumped out of the car.'

'Oh.' She gave a self-conscious laugh, not wanting to sound artisty or precious. 'Just keen to get some ideas on paper.'

He smiled. 'You were so immersed. It must be quite something to be able to lose yourself in something that you love so completely.'

'It is. Sorry, I hope you don't think I was rude... I can be a bit self-absorbed when it comes to work sometimes. But you helped today.'

'I did?'

'Yes, it was the fish.'

'The fish?'

She beckoned him over. 'Come and see.' She had no idea where the urge to show Raph had come from but it was too late to take it back.

'You don't mind me looking?'

'No, and it won't look anything like this when I've finished. This is just the concept.'

Raph came and sat beside her at the table and she pushed the open book towards him. He picked it up, the skin on his fingers bronze against the white paper. Lia studied his hands, desire flooding her as she wondered how they would look on her body. How they would feel.

'Tell me about it,' said Raph.

She stood up and paced a few steps, gathering her thoughts. 'I'm thinking a gastronomic equivalent of the Bayeux tapestry, an unfolding story of food, ingredients and bringing people together. I'll start with the fish in the sea, darts of silver through the waves. The lemons in the lemon groves, tomatoes on the vines, things like that … and then the component parts of a dish: making the pasta, a close-up of the lemons, the fish, the tomatoes and then a family around a table – a bit Last Supperish.' She wrinkled her brow, thinking of her approach. 'I'll have to discuss whether it's divided into separate sections – a bit like the Stations of the Cross – or whether they could display it as one continuous piece, which would be very exciting and completely innovative.' Her body twitched with excitement at the prospect of sending off her ideas. She had so nailed this. 'I'll use silver bugle beads for the fish, diamante chips for the sun sparkling on the sea, and crystal beads for the drops of water on the tomatoes. It's going to have depth and texture. Oh my God, I can't wait to get started.'

This blew her original submission out of the water and now she felt a little embarrassed by how lacklustre her original designs had been. Coming to Italy had reinvigorated her inspiration. Her whole system bubbled with excitement and happiness and…

She threw her arms around Raph and hugged him. She just needed to share the joy fizzing through her veins.

He rose to his feet, the moment her arms went around his neck, his hands coming to her waist, his touch burning though her clothes, and they both froze and looked at each other.

'This time,' said Raph, that crooked smile of his tugging at his lips.

'This time,' she murmured back.

This was it, the point of no return, and after so many near misses, Lia was more than ready to dive right into the kiss. But Raph took it slow, his lips skimming across the corner of her mouth, his hands sliding up her back to bring her closer. Lia's body softened against his and she let out a small sigh – an at-last sigh. She'd been waiting so long for this. His kiss filled that empty longing she'd been feeling for days, suffusing her with warmth, thawing the chill of her loss.

Since she'd discovered that Dad wasn't her dad at all, she'd been adrift, no longer sure where she fitted. With Raph, none of that mattered. He only knew her as she was now, not who she was before. She was just Lia to him.

His kiss deepened, demanding but not overpowering, assertive but not pushy, and his hold was swoon-worthily firm but still gentle. She rose on her toes to meet his mouth, pushing back to gain her own ground. To be an active participant, to kiss him rather than simply be kissed. Gradually, as his tongue sensuously teased hers in a long slow duet, her senses lit up and desire stoked, setting her nerve endings on fire, pulsing with need. His fingers traced her collar bone, trailing kisses beneath her chin, big hands holding her as if he couldn't get enough of her. Her fingers clutched the fine cotton of his shirt, the warmth of his skin burning through the soft fabric, and she pushed it aside to touch him, to skim the smooth satin down to his hips, round to the front to the soft hair leading down.

This man was kissing her. Her. And she wanted him with a bright, fierce need that shocked her. Sex had never been a big deal in the past. With Raph, the red-hot desire consumed her.

'Lia,' murmured Raph, as she tugged at the buttons of his shirt, his hands slowing hers.

'Mm,' she said through her lust-induced haze. Oh God, he wanted to stop. He'd changed his mind. She pulled away, shocked by how lost to everything she'd been. He was going to tell this was a bad idea. Of course he was.

Instead he looked down at her, those blue eyes slightly glazed, a rueful twist to his mouth. She liked the shell-shocked expression on him. Liked it even more when he smoothed one finger along her lower lip, his gaze holding hers, the intimate touch and the scorching tenderness in those blue eyes sending another one of those sparky zings down through her body, bursting between her thighs. Opening her lips she nipped his finger, sucking on it and drawing it into her mouth, watching his eyes darken with desire.

'Bedroom? Yours? Mine?'

She only had one answer: 'Yes.'

'Sure?'

Hell yes, she was sure. So sure, she felt as though her knickers might spontaneously combust at any second.

She nodded.

Taking charge, he began walking backwards, still kissing her, and led her to his room. When the back of his knees hit the bed he tumbled down, taking her with him. The minute she was sprawled on top of him, one leg between his, he eased up her T-shirt and pushed it over her head, tossing it onto the floor.

'You're not going to need that for a while.' His hands went to her shorts. 'Or these.'

'Only fair to do this then.' Her fingers plucked at the buttons on his shirt, already imagining the feel of that gorgeous oh-so-manly chest against hers.

When he'd wrested her shorts from her, he flipped her over onto her back and lay beside her, his head propped on his hand, the other skimming the outside of her ribcage down to her waist as he studied her body. A tiny part of her felt shy, but there was another that felt proud at the keen interest in those blue eyes.

'I've wanted to see you like this for a while,' he said. 'That orange bikini is responsible for a few fantasies. I've imagined you spread out on my bed, open for me.'

'Really?' she blurted with a squeak, the erotic image sending a flush of heat coursing through her. 'I thought you didn't like me.'

'I tried really hard not to.'

She knew she looked a little smug, but why shouldn't

she? The gleam in his eyes told her he liked what he saw. 'I told you lots of people do.'

'You did. I hope lots of people don't see you like this,' he said possessively, running a finger down the valley between her breasts.

She gave him a sultry smile. 'Only a chosen few.'

He leaned down and kissed her nipple through the lacy fabric of her bra, his teeth grazing the sensitive flesh. She arched her back with an involuntary gasp.

'Like that, do you?'

'It's all right.'

'Fibber,' he said and did it to her other breast.

She squirmed, a twist of pleasure spiralling through her. His hand grazed the seam of her knickers, the barely-there touch promising so much more, and she had to bite back another squeak. She moved a hand towards his chest but he pushed it down.

'No,' he said softly, his fingers gently pinching the skin of her inner thigh. 'I'm in charge.'

She arched an eyebrow. She was intrigued.

He leaned forward again and kissed his way down her stomach, his hands holding her hips as his thumbs rubbed over the damp fabric of her pants, teasing her. She lifted her hips but he held them firm. 'You have to stay still.'

Raph spent the next twenty minutes torturing and teasing her, demurring every time she tried to move. When he finally sank into her, she was incoherent with desire and orgasmed almost immediately.

Her reward was a slow, very self-satisfied smile from Raph. 'And that's just the beginning,' he said.

Chapter Twenty-Six

The air conditioning hummed, sending cool air over her naked body. Raph's arm was sprawled across her waist, heavy and warm as his thumb idly stroked her ribs. She felt as soft and pliable as dough and wondered if her legs would hold her if she actually tried to get up.

'Well…' said Lia, 'that was a bit of a revelation.'

Raph grinned at her. 'How so?'

'Who knew you'd be so good in bed?' she teased, even now not prepared to let him have the upper hand.

He gave her another wide smile. 'One does one's best.'

'One might have to try a bit harder next time,' she quipped. 'Show me what you've really got.'

With a growl he rolled over, pulling her on top of his body and nipped at her ear. 'Not complaining, are you?'

'As if I would.'

His hands slid up, teasing the outer edge of her breasts as he stroked her ribcage again. She enjoyed feeling the shape of him, the soft skin, firm muscles and hard bone beneath hers. They fitted. Her body with his. And there was no awkwardness. This was just good sex.

'We ought to get up and go to dinner,' said Raph. 'Although I'd be quite happy to stay here.'

'Oh God. Your mum and my dad!'

'They don't need to know.'

'They definitely do not!' Lia replied. God, that would be embarrassing.

'Although you do realise Mamma would be delighted. This is exactly what she wants. She's been playing matchmaker ever since you arrived.'

'I rather suspected she might be, what with her throwing us together again and again.'

Lia studied his already familiar face and traced a finger down his cheek, her fingertip rasping on the pin-prick bristles just coming through. Smiling down at him, she realised she knew him so well already. 'You're the reliable one and that played perfectly into her plan. The one who'll get the job done properly ... even if you don't want to.'

He scowled up at her. 'Is that supposed to be a compliment?'

She nuzzled his neck and nudged him with her hips. 'There's a lot to be said for someone who gets a job done properly.'

With a laugh, he kissed her again. 'I bet you she'll suggest something for us to do alone together this evening.' A slow smile crossed his face, the blue eyes alight with mischief tweaking her heartstrings. 'What shall we bet?'

After the carb loading of lunchtime pizza, Lia was extremely grateful to find that Aurelia had prepared for dinner a light salad of baby spinach, spring onions and ribbons of courgettes dappled with fillets of fresh anchovies. As usual the whole family sat down under the vine-laden pergola on the terrace, citronella candles burning on the table. Sitting with Bianca and Michael, Lia found herself cross-examined by the music-mad duo about which music venues in London she'd visited. They were sadly disappointed by her lacklustre gig CV, although she did get points for the Roundhouse in Camden. As for her band choices, she was used to Stacey taking the piss out of her but this was a whole other level. Bianca made her feel old, and Leo, listening and chipping in with his observations, laughed uproariously throughout the whole conversation. Apparently he was the cool older brother. Looking round the table, Lia realised that each of the family had their own prescribed role and she wasn't sure where she was going to fit. Clearly her music taste had a lot to answer for and she certainly wasn't going to be the trendy older fashionista sister the girls looked up to. She suspected her make-up bag compared to Luciana's was the difference between a purse and the full 24kg baggage allowance. She had always been the slightly alternative boho one – a bit arty and sometimes flamboyant in her dress sense – compared to Stacey, who would eye her wardrobe with a wrinkle of her nose.

She sighed. What would Stacey be up to, right now? Had she left with Mum and Dad for Carcassonne?

'Would you like some sorbet?' Aurelia's voice interrupted her thoughts and she pushed them away quickly. She was here on the Amalfi coast staying in the most amazing villa – how dare she even think about feeling sorry for herself. She smiled up at her lovely host.

'Yes, please. Are you going to tell me that you made it yourself?'

'But of course. It's so easy.' Her face lit up with a smile and she added, 'Especially when you have an ice-cream maker.'

The delicious lemon sorbet had a sharp citrus tang which not so much cleansed the palate as positively fumigated it. With the first mouthful Lia's eyes puckered in mouth-watering shock. 'Wow! That's lemony.'

Aurelia gave a delighted laugh. 'Everyone says that. It's my own recipe. I don't like to put too much sugar in.'

'It's like frozen *citron pressé*,' said Lia, immediately thinking of her family in France again.

'That's an excellent description,' said Ernesto. 'I shall use it to warn people in future.' He gave his wife a teasing smile to which she responded with a dismissive sniff before giving him an affectionate tug on his ear.

'Now, I've been thinking about another thing you should do while you're here. Raph, you need to take Lia on The Path of the Gods. The views are fabulous but it's a bit too much for me and Ernesto. You could go early so that it's not too hot.'

Raph snorted and exchanged a smug told-you-so look with Lia before saying to his mother, 'Yes, I'm sure it would be at your advanced age, Mamma.' His voice rang with dry sarcasm.

'Yeah, Mamma,' piped up Leo. 'In LA you go to the gym

every other day and you run five kilometres every Wednesdays with Donna and Barbara.'

'Excuse me, Signora Salvatore,' said Ernesto, bristling with indignation. 'Don't include me. I'm in great shape. I could be the next Bond.'

Everyone burst out laughing as he pulled a body-builder pose.

'I'm younger than Daniel Craig,' he protested. 'And he's only just stopped being Bond. I could do that scene coming out of the sea.'

Aurelia patted him on the arm. 'Yes, darling. What I meant was, we have other things to do in the morning when it is best to go.'

'And I don't,' drawled Raph. Lia had to hide a smile.

'You work too much. A day off will be good for you.'

'I had a day off today.'

She huffed out a sigh of frustration. 'Why don't you just do as your mamma asks?'

Raph grinned at her and moved to put an arm round her. 'Sorry, Mamma. Of course I'll take Lia on The Path of the Gods. It would be my pleasure.'

Immediately his mother beamed at him and Raph, turning away from her, winked at Lia.

Looked like she'd just lost a bet.'I feel like my mother's pimping me out,' said Raph as they left the villa a while later and stepped out into the garden. The heat of the day had settled into a mugginess that enveloped them in the shadows of the shrubs and bushes.

'She did seem very keen we left together. Hoping we're overcome by the moonlight, perhaps.'

'I was right.'

'You were right and you win.'

'Remind me what I win.'

'Naked swimming,' said Lia, a quick fizz of anticipation lighting up her hormones like overexcited fireflies. 'She'd be delighted if she knew.'

'She would, but it's worth teasing her a bit longer, rather than let her know her wiles have worked.'

'Have they?'

'Yes. I was doing well resisting your charms until we went out on the yacht.'

She chuckled to herself. Had he looked in the mirror? He had charms in spades, bloody great buckets of them.

'Like I told you, it was that orange bikini that did it. I've been fantasising about getting you out of it. Not something that I really wanted to share with my mother or Ernesto. To be honest I'd rather keep this between us, if you don't mind. I don't want Mamma getting her hopes up. I ought to be honest with you too. Let's just see where things go. I don't know that I'm in the market for a wife the way Mamma is hoping for.'

'I never thought you were,' said Lia. She couldn't imagine Raph wanting anything permanent with her, which was a shame as she liked him, quite a lot more than was probably sensible. But she was in limbo at the moment, not sure which family she belonged to, if either. Until she had a better sense of where she fitted, she wasn't up for making any commitments to anyone.

Raph's gaze warmed her as she descended the steps into the cool water of the pool, his eyes roving over her naked body. She made no move to hide herself from him as he watched her walk towards him. She wasn't one to welsh on a bet. Besides, there was something very erotic knowing that he wanted to see her. Her nerve endings had been dancing with anticipation of this ever since they set off up the path to the guest suites.

Her eyes locked on his as she approached him, a smile on her face as she saw him swallow and his eyes darken. Raph wanted her as much as she wanted him and it sent a thrill of power and excitement dancing through her veins. It was a relief that she could stop fighting the attraction between them and give into the pulsing lust that pumped through her system.

As soon as she was near enough, he pulled her into his arms. 'Come here, you siren.'

'Siren? I thought they sang. You really do not want to hear me sing.'

'Don't I? You were certainly purring with pleasure earlier.'

She laughed as a little shiver of delight rippled down her spine and his mouth drifted along her jawline, his hands finding her breasts just above the water line. The combination of the water lapping around her and his cold fingers on her hardened nipples heightened the sensitivity and she let out a low moan of pleasure.

———

They made love on the poolside, too revved up to make it as far as the bedroom. Afterwards, Raph took her back to his suite, where they showered together and then, wrapped in towels, went back outside to sit with a glass of Limoncello and watch the reflection of the moon ripple across the surface of the water.

'This is lovely,' said Lia with a sigh, pushing her damp hair back over her shoulder.

'Mm,' said Raph. 'But it's not real life.'

'No,' agreed Lia. 'And if it were I'm sure we'd get bored with it. I can't imagine not working.' She paused and poked him in the ribs. 'And I'm not sure you would know how not to work.'

'I can vacation with the best of them. It's just here I'm supposed to be on holiday but Ernesto and Mamma find extra things for me to do like escorting guests on excursions.'

'What a bind. Am I that much trouble?'

'There appear to be some compensations,' he murmured, his breath warm on her skin as he nipped her neck on the soft skin just below her ear. She shivered, tingles running down her body at his touch, even as she laughed.

'Changed your mind about me, then?' she asked.

His mouth found hers and she forgot what she was saying and lost herself in the pleasure of his kiss and the inevitability of finding herself in his bed again.

It was only much later, when he was lying next to her, his breathing deep and even in sleep, that she remembered he hadn't answered her question and wondered if it had been deliberate.

Chapter Twenty-Seven

L ia tied off the final black thread with a sense of achievement and stood back to study the second in her Positano series. This was a smaller piece focusing on the tiled cupola of the main church in the foreground rather than the tumble of houses layering the hillside behind it. A rush of satisfaction bloomed inside her. This was definitely some of her best work.

She tilted her head, considering the picture, trying to define what it was that was different, and identified it almost straightaway. There was a playful element to this piece, something new that had manifested since she'd come to Italy, particularly with this picture. It was perhaps engendered by the pure joy of the last couple of days. She swallowed a quick laugh. She could scarcely look at the little bed in the alcove without blushing.

That first morning after they'd slept together, fired by the coalescing of her ideas, Lia had tumbled out of Raph's bed well before breakfast, keen to get to the studio and

Raph had given her a lift down to the town. Unfortunately, both their plans for a busy working day had gone astray as soon as they stepped over the threshold of the little studio. She laughed out loud to herself remembering how they'd stayed in bed nearly all day, only leaving at four o'clock for a refreshing swim in the sea. Needless to say, she hadn't done any work, and they had agreed that if they were going to get what they needed to do done, she should continue to borrow one of the scooters in future and drive herself. And so each morning she'd puttered down here to start work. Some afternoons, having worked through lunch, she met Raph on the beach for a swim before she returned for a final session in the studio. She'd achieved a lot in the last week.

Her designs for the restaurant had finally come together beautifully and she'd sent them through to her agent, along with the first lemon picture, and they'd been presented to the Braganzis. Photographs of the finished large-scale Positano picture had been posted on her website, although she'd almost be sad to sell it, memories having been woven into the fabric.

Her mobile phone rang and she glanced down at it on the little table next to her. Was that a little ping of disappointment, when she realised it was her agent and not her mother? It appeared that her mother had given up trying to contact her. A fist clenched around her heart. She was so torn. Heartbroken that her mother had kept such a huge secret for all of Lia's life and heartbroken her sister had not been in touch since the impatient, disjointed conversation they'd had at their last meeting just after she'd found out.

Coming back to the here and now in the bright sunshine of the studio Lia could still remember the agonising stab of jealousy that she wasn't part of that unit anymore and the unwelcome realisation of why she'd always felt that little bit different from the rest of her family.

In a daze, she answered the phone to hear her agent's voice full of enthusiastic bonhomie.

'Hey, Lia. I got news. The Braganzis love the designs. You're good to go.'

'Really? That's great.' The news snapped her out of her funk immediately.

'Yeah, they're gonna pay the first half of the commission on the basis of the current designs, but they want to keep it quiet until they make an official announcement as part of their PR launch campaign. I'd say this is your best work yet.'

'I think so too,' said Lia.

'But here's a thing, I got some Italian guy desperate to buy the new picture on your website. Posytawano. He's offered double the asking price.'

'Positano,' corrected Lia with a laugh at his mangled pronunciation. Alec had a dreadful faux American accent, which became more accentuated when he was excited, like now.

'Yeah, you'll never guess who. He's a big movie star name. Apparently he lives there and he wants it.'

'Is it Ernesto Salvatore, by any chance?'

'Yeah, him! That's the guy. How didcha know?'

Lia huffed out a heavy sigh. Where on earth did she start?

'Tell him it's not for sale.'

'What?' Then her agent laughed. 'You want more?'

'No! He's not buying it. I'll give it to him but don't tell him that.' Lia rubbed her forehead. She would happily gift the picture to Ernesto or make a different one for him. There was no way she could take money from him. She was already living free of charge with him and treated like family.

'Kiddo, how you plan to make any money if you give stuff away? Although I guess he's well connected. How do you know him?'

'It's complicated,' she said. 'But I'm staying with him at the moment.'

'You're staying with Ernesto Salvatore! Bloody hellfire on wheels.' Suddenly Alec was very British. 'Go you. No wonder you took off like your knickers were alight. About time too. Celibacy ain't what it's cracked up to be.'

'Alec!' Shock laced her voice. 'It's not like that. His wife is here.' Telling him that Ernesto was her birth father would invite far too much interest and knowing Alec, he'd find a way to leak it to the press at a convenient moment – 'for the good of her career' of course. 'She invited me too. They're … they're old family friends.'

That wasn't a lie. Ernesto was an old friend of her mother's.

'Oh, now you tell me. I thought there was a story there. Although it would be a great story for the press if we could let it be known that your work is being bought by Salvatore. He's got quite an art collection in LA, you know.'

'I didn't, no,' said Lia, grateful for the diversion. 'What sort of art does he collect?'

'He's into all sorts of mediums. Sculpture, ceramics, paintings and now, it would appear, textile art.'

'I'll speak to him myself.' She felt a little guilty doing Alec out of his commission but the second Positano picture was ready to go up for sale, and hopefully that would sell quickly.

It had been another hot, glorious day and although the studio was wonderful for the light, in the fierce heat of the sun it became like a greenhouse. Desperate to cool down, she'd finished a little early and come back to the private pool, hoping Raph might be here. There was no sign of him though and her heart did a little disappointed putter.

At least she had plenty of time for a leisurely swim and a shower before going to the villa to meet Ernesto and Aurelia for what was now an established routine of pre-dinner drinks on the patio.

Aurelia was an amazing cook and delighted in exercising her skills, bringing out favourite local dishes to educate Lia's palate and reinforce her heritage. Not that Lia was the least bit resistant. Her hosts' passion for food was infectious and Lia found her interest growing. Each night she looked forward to finding out what would be served and hearing Aurelia's explanations about the ingredients and how she'd cooked the dish.

She pulled off her dress and stood in front of the

mirrored wardrobe. Should she bother with a bikini? No one ever disturbed them down here.

'Evening.' Raph's low voice startled her.

'Hello.' She watched him in the mirror, her spirits immediately racing into the sky. 'I was just contemplating a swim.'

He slipped inside the room and, skirting the end of the bed, took her into his arms and nipped lightly at her lips.

'Were you?' His hands skimmed her waist.

'Mmm,' she said, her body already softening under his touch. 'But I don't have to.'

She wrapped her arms around him, drawing him closer, feeling the heat of his body through the fine cotton of his shirt as his magic hands slipped the straps of her bra down her arms.

'Missed me?' he murmured, lowering his head to kiss the swell of her breasts.

Her breath hitched with instant lust. 'Might have done,' she said, trying to catch her breath, languorous desire spiralling through her like warm honey.

'Lia! *Tesoro*! Are you home?' Aurelia's voice came from the hallway outside the bedroom.

They both straightened as if they'd been shot, eyes widening with horrified shock.

'Shit!' said Raph.

'Quick!' Lia pushed him into the wardrobe and closed the door, grabbing her dress and throwing it back on as she hurried to the little hallway.

'Aurelia! Hi!' Her voice squeaked into a higher pitch.

'There you are. I thought I ought to come down and check there's nothing you need.'

Lia laughed. 'Aurelia, I think you've thought of everything anyone could possibly want or need. It's the most comfortable place I've ever stayed.'

'I'm so pleased.' She sat down on the bed. 'It's so lovely to have you here. We really are enjoying your stay. You are welcome to stay as long as you like. In fact, we'd love you to come to LA and visit us. There'll always be a room there for you. Raph always comes for Thanksgiving. Maybe you could fly out with him then and stay for a while? He's a good man. I'm so proud of him. I know the two of you … well, I don't think you got off to the best start.'

'What about Leo?' asked Lia, a mischievous imp urging her on. 'Does he go to LA for Thanksgiving?'

'Leo?' Aurelia swallowed. 'Yes, of course but … well, he's Leo. He doesn't take anything very seriously. Not like Raphael. Raphael knows who he is. He's very successful. He worries about people taking advantage of Ernesto and sometimes it makes him a little … unapproachable.'

'Oh, he's fine,' said Lia, horribly conscious of Raph just a few metres away on the other side of the mirrored door.

'Maybe if you spent a little more time with him…'

'You think?' said Lia, perilously close to laughing.

'Oh, yes,' said Aurelia with a guileless smile. 'He's so reliable. Responsible. He'd never let anyone down.'

'My granddad is like that,' said Lia, with all innocence.

Aurelia's face was a picture. 'Maybe not so handsome.'

'Raph is handsome?' Lia frowned. 'I hadn't noticed. Leo is very handsome.' And then she giggled because Aurelia did look quite put out at that. She put an arm on the other woman's shoulder to reassure her. It felt mean to tease her too much, even though she was enjoying herself at Raph's expense. 'Raph is very handsome. And we get on just fine, Aurelia. You don't need to worry. I'm not going to damage him. I find him very entertaining. I'll try not to argue with him so much.'

'Thank you. But maybe the arguing is a sign of passion. Maybe you'll learn there's more to him.' Aurelia gave her a hopeful smile.

'I'll do my best,' said Lia, feeling just a little guilty, but she wasn't ready to share the relationship with Raph with anybody, especially when she had no idea how it might turn out. Neither of them had made any promises.

'I'm sorry, Aurelia. I'm being rude. Would you like a drink of something?'

'That would be lovely but I need to get back to the kitchen.'

With that Aurelia rose and this time left via the patio doors. Lia waited until she was out of sight before opening the wardrobe door.

'You can come out now,' she said, a touch of glee lighting up her face.

Raph grabbed her and pulled her into the wardrobe with a quick teasing kiss. 'Payback is a bitch, Lia.' He kissed her again, his hand grazing her breast, tugging on the nipple. 'Like a granddad, am I?'

She giggled and then swallowed her words in a breathy sigh as his head ducked to tease her breast. He was nothing like a granddad.

Chapter Twenty-Eight

'Sure you don't want to come with us?' Raph asked Aurelia a few days later, all innocence as he took a bottle of water from her and shot a furtive wink at Lia.

'I'd love to but there's so much to do for the party tomorrow.'

'There are caterers coming in,' he said. 'Surely you don't have that much to do? It's a lovely day.'

'I could stay and help if you like,' suggested Lia and he almost laughed.

'No, no,' protested Aurelia, waving her hands at the pair of them, almost shooing them from her kitchen. 'You two go and have fun.'

'I'm not sure hiking The Path of the Gods constitutes fun,' said Raph. 'It'll be hard work, which is why we're leaving so early.' He looked at his watch. Six-thirty on a Friday morning was all wrong. He'd far rather have stayed in bed with Lia for another hour or two.

'I've put some fruit and pastries in the bag for you,' said

his mother, who, even wafting about in her floaty silk dressing gown at ridiculous o'clock, still looked glamorous and far too young to have two grown-up sons.

He kissed her on the cheek. 'Thanks, Mamma. We'll have a wonderful breakfast on the trail. Love you.'

'Love you too, my boy.' She turned to Lia and inspected her, from baseball cap to feet. 'I've put some plasters in the bag too, although your shoes look well-worn.'

His mother's concern amused him especially as he'd discovered among other things that Lia was a runner and he knew that those battered Brooks trainers had racked up plenty of kilometres. He'd also found out she was ticklish, hated her feet being touched, and the little toe on her right foot tucked under the adjoining toe. On her left breast she had a cluster of three moles and there was a crescent-shaped scar on her inner thigh – the result of a tree-climbing accident when she was seven.

'Are you set?' boomed Ernesto, coming into the kitchen clutching his usual demi-tasse of double espresso. He was driving them to Nocelle, after which they'd walk along the trail to Bomerano and then return, this time all the way to Positano. From Positano up to Nocelle there were over 1500 steps, which seemed far too arduous for the start of a walk.

They climbed into the Fiat 500, Lia generously opting to squeeze into the back, and Raph gripped the handle above the door. Ernesto's driving could be erratic and entirely dependent on his mood. This morning garrulity and chattiness prevailed, which Raph could guarantee would affect his ability to concentrate on the road.

Half an hour later, Raph gratefully unfurled himself from the little car, his ears ringing from Ernesto's bellowed conversation to Lia in the back, which had been a challenge with both windows open. The air conditioning still wasn't working as Ernesto had forgotten to arrange to have it fixed, despite three reminders.

He helped Lia out of the back.

'Enjoy the walk,' called Ernesto with a cheery wave out of the window before he shot off with a showy spray of gravel. Raph could only be grateful that he wasn't in the Ferrari.

'Lead on,' said Lia, looking very cute in shorts and a vest top with her hair coming out of the back of her baseball cap in a long, bushy ponytail. Her skin sheened with suncream that smelled of citrus and floral notes.

Quite a few other hikers had gathered at the same point, which was only to be expected at this time of year. It was a popular trail, easy to follow with the red and white painted tiles that identified the correct path, and well worth the walk. They wound out of the town through rustic buildings to the sound of church bells and before long were on the rocky path.

'So how far are we walking, again?' asked Lia.

'Worried you won't be able to keep up?' he teased.

'Not at all.' She smirked at him, a dimple appearing just above her top lip. 'You'll have to carry me if I get too tired.'

He laughed. 'Says the girl who runs 10k for fun. This is only fourteen kilometres.'

'Will you be able to keep up with me?' she asked.

'I've not had any complaints, so far.'

Her laugh pealed out and she shoved him playfully. 'No, you're doing quite admirably.' She gave him an impish grin. 'You live up to heart-throb expectation.'

'Phew. That's a relief.' He grinned at her. She never failed to make him smile or missed an opportunity to take him down a peg. No one had ever been this playful with him or made him feel as relaxed around them. With other people he always had to be on his guard, never revealing too much. They had expectations of him. He was supposed to be smart and serious, and live up to the designer-suit image that had been bestowed upon him by others. He'd drifted into the role, taken on the responsibilities of it and never thought that much about it until just recently. Lia had made him reassess those thoughts, challenging his own view of himself because she didn't take him too seriously. It wasn't so much the proverbial breath of fresh air as a force-seven blast that had blown away his habitual view of himself. With Lia he'd let himself go and let her in, more so than any other woman. Maybe because he knew there was a finite end to whatever this was between them, or at least he'd made that assumption. What if this didn't have to finish with their return to England?

Lia had ducked down to examine a pretty pink flower, her fingers gently brushing the tiny petals.

'Wild orchid, very late,' said a woman passing and Lia engaged her in a conversation about wild flowers before she began taking pictures, clearly delighted with everything around her.

'Ideas?' he asked, already recognising the bright, star-struck glint in her eye.

'Yes. Loads. This is heaven. It makes me want to embroider and applique. God, I've got so many ideas. I might have to come and live here.'

He automatically stiffened at her words, even though they were throwaway and she probably wasn't serious. Ernesto would have taken her at face value. He'd let her move in if she asked.

'It's pretty quiet here in the winter. Cold, too. And wet. Don't forget we're up in the mountains here.'

'Ha!' She laughed and shook her head. 'Raph, if I went to live everywhere that inspired me and took my fancy, I'd be permanently on the road, living out of a suitcase. In fact, I love my little flat and I love living in London, especially at Christmas ... and in the summer and the spring... I guess autumn, too.'

The knot in his stomach eased at her words. When had it become an instinctive reaction to assume the worst? Why assume that Lia would abuse Ernesto's hospitality by inviting herself to stay?

'What do you love about Christmas?' he asked. What put those stars in her eyes at the thought of it?

'The tree in Trafalgar Square. Ice skating at Somerset House. The food hall at Fortnum and Mason. The cold crisp air as you look up at the lights sparkling on Regent Steet. It will always be home, even though I've discovered I'm half Italian. In fact, I don't feel Italian at all ... even though I sort of thought I would when I came out here.'

He reached out and took her hand squeezing it as a pang

of homesickness for his own flat twinged inside him. He missed his life in London too. He'd like to introduce Lia to some of his friends; they'd get a kick out of the way she answered him back and put him in his place.

'It takes a while. I was brought up in London originally; LA never felt like home and I went back to the UK for university and stayed. I've been coming here for the last sixteen summers and even though I speak the language, I'm never completely comfortable with saying I'm half Italian.'

'At least you look the part. The archetypal handsome Italian heart-throb.' She shook her blond ponytail. 'No one is ever going to believe I'm Italian.'

Raph dug his hand into her hair, letting the soft curls trail over his fingers. 'You have beautiful hair.'

She tossed it. 'Thank you.' She beamed at him. 'It's my crowning glory and I'm incredibly vain about it.'

'Vain? I don't think so.' Raph smothered a laugh. If anything, Lia defined low maintenance. He thought of the number of lotions, potions and serums that had invaded his bathroom when Layla had moved in … and the relief when he repossessed his shelf space. And although Ernesto and Aurelia led a relatively simple life here in Amalfi, they were still part of a Hollywood power couple, Aurelia with her own series of highly successful Italian cookery shows, which she produced as well as appeared in, and Ernesto who'd been an A-lister for most of his working life. Raph had grown up in that milieu and it was what he'd become used to. Even trying to stay out of the limelight, his world inevitably contained the same circle of privileged adults. One tended to mix in the same circles, with people of similar experience, because it was safe and you knew those people had as much to lose as you if they were indiscreet.

'Look at that butterfly.' Lia suddenly darted forwards to the edge of the grassy bank, entranced by its bright yellow wings. Everything seem to interest her and he took pleasure from her quick joy.

They walked along the stony path, the cliff face stretching upwards on one side and the sheer drop on the other. Wild flowers grew through the grass while stubby shrubs dotted the landscape, fighting with craggy outcrops to take possession of the sparse ground. The deep blue sea, dappled with paler turquoise pockets around the coastline, stretched away to the distant horizon. They passed ruins encroached on by vines, nimble-footed goats in herds that skittered away, their bells clanging as they went, and the occasional mule picking its way along the path, led by solemn-faced farmers busy with their work, while tourists ambled at their leisure, taking pictures of all they saw.

It was so quiet up here, just the sound of the goats and their bells, the click of loosened stones and the low murmur of voices whenever they passed another group. London and real life felt a very long way away.

They stopped at a small shrine for long gulps of water and a couple of oranges, the sweet juice refreshing and welcome after a couple of hours of walking. As they sat chatting and admiring the view he pointed out the island of Capri and they watched speedboats zipping about, leaving long white trails of churned-up foam in their wake.

'Looks fun,' said Lia.

'Leo-style fun,' said Raph.

'You know, he plays up to his reputation,' said Lia suddenly. 'I think you do, too.'

Raph gave her a startled look. 'What do you mean?'

'No one expects anything of Leo, so they don't make any demands on him. He carries on in his own sweet irresponsible, beach dude and surfer boy way because that's what's expected of him.'

Raph shrugged. That was what Leo was. He'd never knuckled down at anything. He didn't have to. Ernesto gave him a generous allowance and free board both here and in the London house, and there was a room for him in LA whenever he wanted it. Leo had been much younger when their mother had remarried. He didn't remember much about the difficult times before, and Ernesto and Aurelia hadn't wanted him to. She'd spoiled him, spoiled them both, except by then Raph's moud had already been cast. He'd been the responsible one from the moment his father had walked out. Ernesto had given Aurelia back her pride, but before that, Raph's and Leo's father had stripped it from her in an emotionally bullying relationship. In Ernesto she'd found a protector but Raph hadn't trusted him to start with and kept up his role of man of the house for a long while after that. Lia had a point. Maybe it was time he let go and left them to their own devices. He'd allowed them to box him into being Raphael Knight, but what if he tried just being Raph?

Lia laid a hand on his arm and stood on her toes to kiss him on the cheek. 'I like the real Raph a lot more than scary, bad-tempered Raphael Knight.'

'I wasn't that bad, was I?'

'Yes,' she said with a twinkle in her eye.

'Do you want to know something?'

'Always,' she said with another of her beguiling smiles.

'When you turned up at my offices and wanted to talk to me about Ernesto, I thought you were going to claim that you were one of his lovers. Part of my reaction was jealousy.'

'Ernesto hasn't been unfaithful to your mother, has he? Please don't tell me that.' Lia held her hands over her heart as if she were worried it might break.

'No. They adore each other.'

'So why would you be jealous?'

'Because I thought you might be a delusional fan – he does have plenty. The sort that believe because they're desperately in love with him – even though they've never met him – he's bound to reciprocate if he just meets them.'

'You mean … you fancied me?' There was disbelief in her words.

'I'm not sure fancied is the right word. My interest was piqued.'

She pulled a face. 'You fancied me.'

'I was intrigued.'

'You fancied me.' She gave him a superior look and tossed her ponytail.

He lunged at her and pulled her into his arms as she laughed up into his face. 'I did not fancy you. That's what teenagers say. I was attracted to you.'

'You fancied me,' she repeated doggedly, amusement dancing in her eyes before she said, 'I fancied you, too.'

The words jump-started his heart with a little jolt.

'You were all smouldering and tight-arsed Mr Knight in your sexy suit. You gave off repressed-sexuality vibes.'

'I did what?' Now he was laughing. No one had ever described him like that. Or been so open and honest about it.

'You know. Under that severe business attire, there's a passionate man throbbing below the surface.' Her face was wreathed in a teasing smile.

'Throbbing?' he asked, trying to sound intimidating. Unfortunately, it came out as an outraged, very unmanly, broken-voiced squeak

'Oh, yes,' she lowered her voice, mischief written all over her face, 'definitely throbbing.'

He caught her and kissed her soundly again. 'Some people have no respect for their elders.'

'No,' she said with a cheeky grin and kissed him back.

They followed the path to Bomerano, walking through shady trees along the coastline, and stopped at the Café of the Gods.

'I need a cold beer,' said Lia.

Raph looked at his watch. It was only half-past ten.

'I'll take a cappuccino,' he said. However, when the waiter came to take their order, he asked for two Morettis.

'Not being Captain Sensible after all?' asked Lia.

'I'm on holiday today. And a cold beer is exactly what I need.'

Lia made him live a little, which was no bad thing. Maybe he did need to loosen up.

It was definitely the right choice, he decided as the first long gulp of cold beer from the condensation-covered glass slid down his throat. He sighed with pleasure.

'Mmm, perfect,' said Lia, wiping a small foamy moustache from her mouth as she put her half-empty glass down. 'Exactly what I needed.' Her unselfconscious enjoyment made him relax. She was happy in her own skin and didn't try to pretend to be anything that she wasn't. It made being with her easy. With Lia he could be himself because if he did anything she didn't like, she'd be the first to let him know.

After half an hour's break, mindful of the rising temperature, they continued walking.

'The view is better this way and there's more downhill,' he said.

'What are the little islands here?' She pointed to a small archipelago in the Tyrrhenian Sea towards the end of the peninsula.

'They're the Sirenuse. The largest one – Il Gallo Lungo – is shaped like a dolphin, but you can't see it properly from here.' He dug his phone from his back pocket to show her a photo.

'Gosh, it really does. Can you visit it?'

'No, it's privately owned. The dancer Rudolph Nureyev bought it in the eighties and lived there until he died. After that it was bought by a hotelier. I believe you can go and stay there but for a price. It's very exclusive.'

'And the Villa Mimosa isn't?' Lia quirked an eyebrow.

'I suppose it is. I've been spoiled.'

'It's all right.' She patted him on his arm. 'It doesn't show.'

He put an arm around her, pulling her to him as he chuckled in appreciation. With Lia around there was no danger of forgetting that life was fun. He couldn't remember the last time he'd felt this relaxed or enjoyed himself doing such simple activities. London was always a whirl of dinners, events and functions, being on show and appearing at the right things. He was used to being papped, touted as an eligible bachelor and targeted by a certain type of woman. A type of woman who was nothing like Lia. It struck him that he'd been spending too much time with entirely the wrong sort of people.

Chapter Twenty-Nine

By the time they walked down the 1700 steps into Positano, they were both ready for another drink and a cooling swim.

'I wish I'd brought my costume,' said Lia, a look of longing on her face as she looked down towards the busy beach.

'Me too. Let's have a drink and then get a lift back up to the villa. I'll WhatsApp the family group and see if Ernesto or Leo can pick us up. Then we can have a lazy afternoon by the pool.'

'Sounds perfect to me. Lazy being the operative word. No chasing me round the bedroom.' She tucked her arm through his.

'I don't recall having to work very hard to catch you,' he replied, his mouth curving in a smile, remembering peeling her clothes off by the pool the night before.

Her face lit up, her eyes crinkling with delight. 'That's

the problem when you're so damn irresistible.' She kissed him. 'But you probably already know that.'

'Not everyone is worth catching.' And he meant it. Her eyes locked with his and he lifted a hand to cup her chin.

'Am I?' she asked softly.

At her quiet, carefully spoken words, his heart missed its footing for a second, tilting a little off kilter with what felt like an extra beat.

'You are,' he said. Lia was starting to mean a lot more to him. He could imagine spending time in London with her. Her sunny personality bringing new light into his life. Walks in Richmond Park, cooking dinners in his flat, drinks in the local pub on the corner, the one he'd never taken a girlfriend to.

She smiled up at him and took his hand. 'I think you might be too.'

They sat in one of the beachfront cafés drinking Diet Coke, holding hands across the table and not saying much as they watched the world go by. Occasionally catching each other's eyes and smiling in complete accord. Nothing needed to be said and the touch of their fingers seemed to be enough – a bond between them, anchoring them to each other.

For the first time ever, Raph felt like part of a whole. The other sock of a matching pair. Was this what love felt like? He belonged with Lia; somehow the two of them fit together. The only question was, did she feel the same?

Leo tooted the horn and gesticulated out of the window of the little Fiat for them to get in, quite happy to hold up the traffic, waiting in the middle of the road and contributing to the usual traffic chaos of the town, rather than attempting to pull over or park.

'Leo! You're holding everything up,' Raph complained, holding the passenger seat for Lia to climb quickly into the back of the car. The driver in the car behind leaned heavily on his horn and raised his hands in dramatic disbelief.

Leo shrugged. 'The place is gridlocked. No one's going anywhere in a hurry. He can hold his horses.'

'That's because everyone acts like this.' Raph tutted and Leo shrugged again, grinning at Lia, who'd managed to scramble into her seat.

'How was the big adventure?' he asked her as Raph leapt in and slammed the door.

'Amazing,' said Lia with her usual sparkle of enthusiasm while the Fiat kangaroo-hopped a few metres.

'Rather you than me. Far too much effort of a morning. I had a lovely long lie-in.' He stretched languidly, taking both hands off the steering wheel. 'I'd only just got up when I got your message and Mamma was all of a flutter about something, so I scarpered, quick.'

'Great,' said Raph with feeling. No doubt something for him to sort out when he returned.

He felt the soft press of Lia's hand on his right shoulder. Her instant understanding and the subtle gesture of comfort warmed him, a slow glow suffusing through his body. God, this woman. She was everything he hadn't realised he needed. He raised his own hand to graze her fingers with his, pressing them in silent gratitude. Leo, utterly oblivious, was chattering about buying a new paddleboard and asking if Lia wanted to go to the beach later. Her fingers squeezed Raph's shoulder as she told Leo that she planned to stay put in the villa this afternoon.

'I think my tan needs a bit of work.'

'Okay,' said Leo. 'Let me know if you change your mind. Or if Mamma tries to rope you into doing some work for the party. She's in a tizzy about it. I don't why. Everyone always has a good time.'

'That's because she makes sure they have a good time, Leo,' said Raph, irritated by his brother's blithe assumption that parties arranged themselves.

Leo gave yet another one of his laconic shrugs. Sometimes Raph wanted to shake him. He was so bloody laid-back he was in danger of floating off into the ether. It wouldn't even occur to him to put fresh towels out for guests, let alone provide them with bespoke toiletries or check their dietary requirements. Their mamma was the original hostess with the mostest.

'Well, she's in a spin today. If I were you, I'd head straight to your place.'

Raph's fingers tightened on Lia's hand. That's exactly what he planned to do.

'Thanks for the heads-up. Tell you what. Drop us off at the gate and we'll go straight there.'

'Aw man. Then I have to deal with her on my own.' Leo's chagrin made him look so mournful, Raph and Lia began to laugh.

'The difference is, she won't expect you to do anything,'

Raph pointed out. 'Whereas if it's me, she'll expect me to solve whatever crisis it is.'

'Fair enough,' said Leo. 'There are times when I'm dead glad I'm the youngest.'

'You're not the youngest; Giulia is.'

'Youngest, eldest…' said Leo with yet another lift of his shoulders, sticking to his own persistent logic. 'Besides, in devil years, that child is about fifty-three. She's terrifying.'

Raph had to agree with that. Giulia always managed to have the adults at a disadvantage. She had a knack for finding their weakest spot and acting upon it to get her own way. She was going to go far in life.

Leo dropped them at the back gate of the estate and left with a raucous horn salute.

'I didn't know this was here,' said Lia, as Raph produced a key.

'It's so that guests can come and go as they please. There's a key on your key ring.'

'Useful.'

'It's also very useful if Ernesto ever has to avoid the paps or to smuggle people in or out.'

'Does that happen very often?'

'Sometimes attendees come to the party but don't want to advertise the fact they're holidaying out here. The constant attention isn't easy, especially when you're trying to take some time off with your family.' He sighed, remembering the shock of it all when Mamma and Ernesto first married. Facing cameras every time he left the house. People whispering about him at school. Sudden popularity, everyone wanting to be his friend. He hadn't hated it at first

– that had come later, when he learned that it was difficult to know who to trust.

The gate opened with a loud horror-film creak, which made Lia grin. 'Should I be going into the woods with you?' she asked, indicating the narrow path leading through the trees, the dense planting preventing the sun from penetrating the pine needle carpet below.

'I'm the one protecting you,' he said, slinging an arm around her shoulder.

It was only a five-minute walk to the guest lodges and at the front they parted ways to change.

'See you in the pool,' he said opening his front door.

'Last one is a loser,' said Lia, disappearing through hers in a burst of speed and slamming it behind her.

He hurried inside, smiling to himself and grabbing his new swim shorts. He went into the bathroom to change into them and when he came out and crossed to the patio doors he almost fell over the large Louis Vuitton suitcase lying on the bedroom floor, which the bed had obscured from his view. The case was open and its contents spilled onto the floor. A couple of lacy bras, several pairs of high heeled shoes and an enormous toiletry bag were just a few of the things he noted. Raph frowned. The gauzy curtain at the patio window billowed and he went out.

A woman in large sunglasses under a floppy white hat, wearing a white bikini, lay on one of the sunloungers looking at her phone, sipping a cocktail through a straw.

'Raph, darling,' she said as she lifted her head. 'Surprise! What on earth are you wearing?' She stared at his brightly coloured shorts.

'Layla.' Fuck. What was she doing here?

At that moment, Lia in her bikini skittered to a halt in the doorway of her French window and Raph felt the world start to spin.

This couldn't be happening.

'Raph?' Lia's voice, low and thready, came from far away.

Layla smiled, her expression laced with feline satisfaction. She always loved drama.

'Lia, this is Layla…' He was going to get it straight out there. 'A friend of mine.'

Layla rose, the white bikini showing off her assets – which he'd once admired, but now realised made her appear too showy and too obvious. She tossed her glossy brunette hair, the stylised curls artfully falling into place over one shoulder.

'A very good friend,' insisted Layla, coming to stand beside him and laying a proprietary hand on his arm, which he shook off.

Too late, the damage was done. Lia's light had gone out. Her face went blank.

'Hi,' she said with a polite twist to her mouth that some might have mistaken for a smile. Tension knotted his stomach. Damn Layla and her games.

'Lovely place, Raph. Nearly as nice as your apartment. I left the keys with Margery next door and asked her to water the plants.'

He could have strangled her. The villa was nothing like his fucking apartment as well she bloody knew – and Margery Duncan had her own set of keys.

Lia lifted her chin. 'Nice to meet you, Layla. I'm a guest of the Salvatores.'

'Oh, you're here for the party. I couldn't make it last year. I had an acting job, so Raph came out on his own.'

God, she was determined to hammer every last nail in the coffin. She hadn't been invited last year. Regret piled up. Why hadn't he been more insistent about her moving out of his apartment? He honestly thought she'd accepted their break-up and was using the place because it was convenient. He never expected her to come out here.

'Excuse me,' said Lia, 'I was just going for a swim.' She shot a bland smile at Layla and sauntered over to the steps. Raph was desperate to speak to her but first he had to find out what the hell Layla was playing at.

'What are you doing here?' he asked, keeping his voice low and controlled. Layla loved to play up to any emotion.

'I was in the area. Remember I said I was coming out? I thought I'd swing by and say hello. Your mother suggested I stay for the party.'

Raph stared at her. 'Really?'

She gave a tinkling laugh of admission. 'Not really, no. But I explained I'd been living in your apartment and wanted to give you the keys back and I'd called in on my way to see a friend but my friend hasn't answered her phone and now she's texted me that she's in Rome for two days, so I'm a bit stuck. And that's the truth. You know what Sally is like.'

'Jeez, Layla.' He shook his head. Her facility for lying was really quite impressive. But he did know what her friend was like. Unreliable, flighty and with the attention span of a two-year-old high on candy. There was no guarantee that from Rome she wouldn't flit off to St Tropez, Hvar or Marbella.

'Don't worry, I'll leave straight after the party. I just need a place to stay for two nights and then I'll go.' Layla inclined her head towards the pool. 'She my replacement?'

'None of your business.' Tension tightened every sinew of his body. He needed to speak to Lia and explain things.

'Not your usual type,' she said.

'What do you want, Layla?'

'To be friends. Come on, Raph. Play nice.'

Layla had never played nice in her life. She just wasn't that sort of person.

He was grateful that her phone began to ring just then and as she answered it, she immediately launched into a loud, chatty, unselfconscious conversation, leaving him to walk over to the pool. Surely once he'd explained everything to Lia, she'd understand and they could sort things out. Layla could sleep in the spare room and he could move into Lia's suite. Once he'd explained, Lia would probably laugh. Find the funny side of things. Wouldn't she?

Chapter Thirty

L ia refused to show how upset she was and launched into a dogged breast stroke while also keeping a wary eye on Raph.

What an idiot she was. And now the big fat liar was getting into the pool. Did he really think he was going to talk his way out of this one? She put her head down and began to swim a splashy front crawl that made conversation impossible. Raph swam along beside her anyway, with a much smoother freestyle. Damn him. Anger ruined her technique and she ran out of breath quickly. He slowed to swim beside her.

'What do you want?' she asked tetchily, panting slightly, her plan to be cool with him flying out of the window faster than a supersonic jet.

'To explain.'

'To explain what? That you've had a girlfriend this whole time?' She stopped swimming and faced him with a sneer.

'She's not my girlfriend. We broke up just before I came out here. Yes, she's been staying in my flat in London, but we're not together anymore and I certainly didn't expect her to show up here.'

'I bet you didn't. And you didn't think to mention her before now?'

'Because it was over.' He pushed his hair from his forehead with an exasperated move that might once have persuaded her he was being genuine. 'And I didn't think her worth mentioning. She's only here to scrounge a free holiday.'

'Just like me then,' said Lia, with a bright fake smile. God, she was so stupid. Why had she trusted him? He'd lied to her. Just like her mother had lied to her. To make life 'easier'. As if that made everything all right again.

'Nothing like you,' he said with a touch of entreaty, that same desperate plea, reminiscent of her mother over lunch that day, begging her to see her point of view. Lia shook her head. If her mother could conceal something so well for so many years, other people with far less reason could do the same. She was done trusting people.

She ducked away from Raph and swam to the steps nearest her room, hauling herself out of the water.

Wringing out her ponytail, she tossed it with a sniff and stomped into her room.

Anger carried her through her shower and up the path to the villa, where she found Aurelia in the kitchen busy chopping garlic.

Aurelia greeted her with a sheepish smile, laying down

her knife and picking up her wine glass. 'Don't I feel stupid? Can I get you a glass of wine?'

Lia nodded. A whole bottle would go down a treat.

Aurelia poured her a glass, shaking her head. 'I had no idea Raph had a girlfriend. He never even mentioned her. Apparently they've been living together. And here I was trying to matchmake the two of you.'

'I hadn't noticed,' said Lia, trying to sound airy and amused.

Leo, who was sitting on one of the bar stools at the kitchen island flicking through his phone, sniggered. 'I could have told her she was barking up the wrong tree. You're not Raph's type at all.'

Aurelia gave a small sigh. 'I hate to say it but Leo's right. Raph always goes for those glossy girls. All surface and nothing underneath. I don't understand it.'

'Maybe they're easier to be with. They don't make too many demands,' said Leo with surprising insight. Both Lia and Aurelia turned to stare at him.

'What? Just saying. But it's obvious, isn't it? I mean, I know Layla lived with him but it was more of a Hollywood publicist's idea of a relationship than anything else. You know, where they set two stars up just for the media coverage. It's the same with every woman he's been out with. He's not prepared to go all in. He has trust issues.' He paused and sighed and for once Lia saw a serious side to him. 'He thinks that people are only interested in him because of all this.' Leo circled the air with one finger. 'And to be fair, he has been burned a couple of times for that very reason.'

Aurelia winced. 'He found all this difficult to get used to when he was younger but I thought he was better now.'

'He needs to get over it. And get over himself. He's a big boy now. There are worse things that happen every single day.' Leo's mouth turned down in an uncharacteristic display of unhappiness.

Aurelia squeezed his arm and he flashed her a brief, sad smile.

'Never mind, Lia. I can show you a good time. You don't need boring old Raph,' said Leo, his natural sunniness bouncing back.

Aurelia's expression as she looked at Leo was tinged with concern. It made Lia wonder, what was the story there? What had happened to Leo? There was something below the cheery veneer but it was nothing to do with her. She wasn't party to the secrets and history of the family. The realisation served as yet another reminder that she was the outsider here.

'I'm driving to Amalfi to pick up some beer from Melphi's for the party. Wanna come?'

Aurelia rolled her eyes. 'You and your craft beers. He's obsessed. Don't get him talking about the subject, he'll bore you to death. You can help me make pasta if you'd like. I'm making tagliatelle for dinner.'

'There's nothing boring about craft beer,' said Leo and although he smiled there was a definite touch of indignation in his tone.

'I'll take your word for it,' said Lia, who knew absolutely nothing about beer. 'If you don't mind giving me a lift, I'll go down to the studio for a few hours.' Hopefully she could lose herself in her work and not brood about Raph bloody Knight.

———————

Not brooding was easier said than done. After discarding two batches of dyed fabric that didn't quite come out the colour she was hoping for, she focused instead on practising a couple of embroidery stitches that she had in mind for what she now thought of as her Amalfi Coast tapestry.

The sense of disappointment gnawed away at her. Somewhere along the line she'd fallen for the lighter side of Raph that had gradually emerged. Even his dress sense had lightened up, she realised – Layla had spotted it straightaway. Lia scowled to herself recalling the other woman's comment about his shorts. He'd worn the new shirt and she'd noticed a peach one had appeared too. Layla was all wrong for him. He needed someone to show him the colour in life. Suddenly she regretted being so hasty. Coloured by her recent experiences she'd let emotions take over instead of listening to Raph. Maybe she should have heard him out. Leo's comments stuck like a burr, refusing to let go. There was a big difference between the Raph she'd met in London and the Raph she'd got to know here. Leo was wrong: Raph deserved someone who made demands of him. Someone who made him join in. The two of them both deserved to belong somewhere. What if they deserved to belong together? What if the two of them added up to so much more?

Leo was also right that Raph needed to get over his trust

issues. But how could she prove to Raph that he could trust her, when she didn't even trust her own mother anymore? Could she move past the betrayal? Now that she'd met Ernesto and had the emotional break of being here in Italy, she was in a different place mentally. Lia toyed with her phone, wondering if it was time to break her silence and call her mother. But then she put the phone down. It was a conversation that should be done face to face.

For now, she would talk to Raph this evening when she got back. In the meantime she was getting sod-all work done. Locking the studio door behind her, she walked down the maze of alleyways into the town, heading to the gelateria. With ice-cream in hand, scoops of vanilla and chocolate chip, she wandered along to the Chiesa di Santa Maria Assunta. By now she was very familiar with the tiled blue and green cupola that dominated most of the views of the town, but she hadn't actually been inside.

She waited until she'd finished her ice-cream before joining the other tourists visiting the church. Inside, the cool pale walls were decorated with gold trim above the stylish arches and atop the columns. More gold decorated the plasterwork arched ceiling. The ornate touches enhanced the elegant lines of the building, combining simplicity with a touch of decadence, neither overpowering the other. It created a serenity that made Lia sit down in one of the wooden pews just to drink in the quiet atmosphere and observe the detail of the black Madonna and child hanging above the altar, the gold cherubs above the arches and the glass chandeliers suspended below.

As she left she heard a couple of voices that sounded

like a mother and daughter teasing each other. She turned her head but among the many tourists couldn't identify the familiar English accents. It brought a pang. Her mother and Stacey would be in and out of a place like this in a couple of minutes – they were quickly bored by historic buildings, happy to take a look but not keen to linger or ponder – whereas her dad would have joined her in the pew, silently contemplating the splendour and history around them. They'd have wondered aloud about the people who had built the place and what changes the building had seen over the years, and share with each other the bits they liked best. Her dad would have liked the black Madonna, while she would have picked the glass chandeliers.

Loneliness nudged her and she hurried quickly out, back into the sunshine, feeling more lost than ever. Over the last week, Raph had given her a sense of belonging, of being part of something.

She needed to talk to Raph … and maybe give him another chance.

Talking to Raph proved difficult because he'd holed himself up in his study, apparently, and short of knocking on every door on the ground floor of the villa, Lia had no idea where to find him. In addition, Aurelia purloined her as soon as she got back to the house.

'Lia, you've got an artistic eye, would you come and let me know what you think of the bedroom?'

'The bedroom?'

'Yes, we have lots of guests coming for the party. There are several staying but one very important one is arriving today. I'd adore your opinion.'

Lia followed her up the sweeping marble staircase with its carved white balusters and decorative urns tucked into niches along the wall. It was rather magnificent and another reminder that the Salvatores inhabited a very different world from the one she was used to. Tasteful and elegant, the walls were pale sage-green with white plasterwork and cornices. The whole space had Aurelia's understated stamp upon it.

She led Lia along a marble-tiled corridor with bright watercolours punctuating its length. One of the doors was open and Aurelia tutted as they walked past. Lia assumed it must be Leo's room, because clothes were scattered across the bed in a haphazard manner as if a suitcase had just been emptied out and left, until she spotted a familiar pair of eye-catching swim shorts.

'Raph has decided to move to the main house, which is quite annoying because I'd allocated all the rooms already. We've got thirty people staying for the party.'

Lia stopped dead, surprised by this news.

'He's moved here?'

'Yes. Apparently it's all over with this Layla woman. Which I'm very pleased to hear because … well, I know it's a very Italian mamma thing to never think that anyone is good enough for their boy … but I didn't really like her. I mean, it's quite rude to turn up unannounced. Even ruder when she hadn't even told Raph.'

Lia absorbed this information, her pulse picking up.

Had Raph been telling the truth about it being over with Layla?

'And it's even more irritating because I could have put this guest in that suite, which would have been perfect, but never mind. I'm pleased with their rooms.'

They walked along the length of what Lia knew was only one wing of the villa. 'How many bedrooms do you have?'

Aurelia laughed. 'Twenty-two in the main house and one in each of the two guest suites. What do you think?' They'd arrived at the end of the corridor and Aurelia threw open the door.

Lia noticed she seemed quite nervous, twisting her hands together as she spoke.

The room had a lovely restful atmosphere. Its focal point was the large wooden bed with a rattan headboard with a pale wood border. The billowing duvet was covered in an eau de nil fabric with huge wisteria blooms cascading down the middle. Matching rattan cabinets guarded each side of the bed, topped with pretty water jugs and glasses. On one side was a small vase with a delicate posy of flowers in pale pinks, purples and white. A similar posy topped the dressing table on the other side of the room. Full-sized French windows, dressed with voile curtains, led out to a pretty little Juliet balcony overlooking the gardens.

'This is gorgeous,' said Lia, the words bursting out because it was. 'It's so pretty and feminine without being too girly. And I love the cushions.' She moved forward to touch the eau de nil silk cushions embroidered with tiny wisteria blooms. 'What fabulous fabric.'

'You approve then?' said Aurelia, almost sounding relieved.

'Very much. It's quite lovely. And that's a nice touch.' Lia pointed to the little coffee table between two chairs upholstered in pale green velvet. The table held a stack of magazines in English along with a basket of glossy fruit, a small box of Baci chocolates and a cellophane-wrapped plate of cannoli.

'And the bathroom?'

Lia opened the bathroom door to find towels, in the same pale green as the cushions, hanging over a wooden towel rack, as well as wisteria- and lilac-scented toiletries in stylish packaging arranged along a shelf below a big brass-rimmed mirror.

'I think whoever stays in here is going to be very comfortable,' said Lia. 'Are they very important guests?' she asked with a teasing grin.

Aurelia paused for a moment, checking the time on her watch, before answering. 'Yes. Very important. I want to make them feel very welcome.'

'You've nailed it, Aurelia. It looks very stylish but welcoming too. You're an excellent host.'

'*Grazie, bella.*' Aurelia gave Lia a quick hug. 'You're a very good girl. Ernesto is so delighted to have found you and to have such a talented, kind and interesting daughter. You're a very good role model for our girls.'

'I don't know about that,' said Lia. Would Aurelia think that if she knew what she'd been up to with her oldest son?

'It is good to have you in the family.' Aurelia looked at

her watch again. 'Now. I think it is time for an aperitif on the terrace. We should open a bottle of Prosecco.'

Raph and Ernesto were already on the terrace, a chilled bottle at the ready, when Aurelia and Lia joined them. Lia glanced around, relieved that there was no sign of Layla. Raph poured her a glass and they were left alone together for a moment while Ernesto took Aurelia off to go and look at something on his computer.

'Lia,' Raph said urgently. 'Layla and I aren't together. I asked Mamma—'

'I know. She told me. You've moved.' She stared up into his face, her heart softening at the earnest expression in his eyes. 'I'm sorry about earlier,' she said. 'I think I jumped to conclusions without really listening.'

'Maybe I could have been a bit more honest about my past but I never thought Layla would come out here. She talked about it when we were together but to assume like this...' He lifted his shoulders in obvious disbelief.

'Amazing how cheeky some people are,' said Lia.

'I shouldn't be surprised anymore. I should be used to it.' Sadness turned down his mouth in a grim line of resignation.

Lia laid a hand on his arm. 'No, you shouldn't. You deserve better. Not everyone is like that. I promise you. Not everyone is trying to get ahead using other people. Some of us are prepared to put the hard work in to get where we want to go.' She gave him a gentle smile, sad for this man

293

who'd been let down one too many times. She knew what it was like.

When Aurelia and Ernesto returned, Lia and Raph were sitting in the wicker chairs enjoying their wine, chatting about the walk earlier in the day.

'No aches and pains?' asked Ernesto. 'Did you enjoy the views, Lia?'

'I did. It was very scenic. It gives you a very good idea of the landscape and the geography, although I couldn't believe how unprepared some people were. There were a group in front of us who had no water and were in flip-flops.'

'I doubt they got very far,' said Ernesto, glancing at his watch.

Obviously the guest they were waiting on was a big deal. Even Lia was starting to get nervous on their behalf, but also intrigued. She was dying to know who it might be, given that the children were on their best behaviour and Giulia had popped in twice to get her approval on a welcome card she was making.

When the bell at the front door clanged, a charged frisson rippled through the air. Ernesto and Aurelia looked at each other before Aurelia shot another hopeful but nervous look at Lia. With a sudden lunge towards the door Ernesto rushed off to answer it and Aurelia, after waiting a few seconds, trotted after him, her sleek heels tapping on the tiled floor.

Lia exchanged a quizzical look with Raph. Did he know what was going on and who the mysterious guests were?

'They both seem a bit antsy,' said Raph.

'I know. Do you know who's staying?'

'No idea. But they're not usually like this. Don't forget, Ernesto gets equal billing with most big names – it's not a big deal to have celeb guests.'

From the hallway they could hear Ernesto's voice booming with bonhomie.

'Lia,' he announced from the doorway, 'look who's here.'

Lia looked up and almost dropped her drink.

Chapter Thirty-One

'S tacey?'

'Hey sis. Ernesto invited me and I thought it would be a nice surprise. I've never been to Italy and who doesn't want to come to a party?' Stacey gabbled, looking around the room with a wide grin.

She crossed the room to give her sister a hug, whispering in her ear, 'Nice digs, and who's the hottie?'

It was so Stacey that Lia forgot that she'd been keeping her family at a distance and automatically hugged her sister back. 'What are you doing here?'

'You get an invite from an international movie star to stay in his villa and come to his summer party – you say yes! How long have you've been staying here? It's gorgeous. Please tell me there's a swimming pool.'

'Yes and it's lovely. Almost as nice as my private pool,' replied Lia with a mischievous, cocky smile, suddenly delighted to see her sister.

'Shut the front door! Private pool. Get you.' Her sister

hugged her tighter and whispered in her ear, 'You're still going to want to hang out with me, aren't you?'

Lia pulled back and looked into Stacey's face, shocked by the tiny lines of tension around her eyes that underscored the outwardly confident veneer.

'Of course, I am, you donut. Why wouldn't I?' Even as she said the words a sense of disquiet threaded through her head.

Stacey swallowed and her voice wobbled. 'Because of all this. Ernesto Salvatore is your dad now. He's famous. Rich. You'll be all different.'

Lia blinked back her own tears, guilt and regret slamming into her. 'Don't be daft.'

'But you … you…' Stacey's voice quavered. 'You haven't spoken to me or Mum or Dad. You just went. Radio silence. You left us.'

Lia thought of all the unanswered messages sitting on her phone with a twinge of guilt. Her mother had lied to her all of her life, but Stacey was blameless. It wasn't her fault she couldn't relate to the depth of Lia's hurt.

She squeezed Stacey hard, her eyes filing with tears

Over her sister's shoulder Lia saw Ernesto and Aurelia, his arm around her shoulders, both looking as pleased as a couple of cats who'd scoffed down a dozen canaries each. Bless them. They were wonderful, generous people with hearts full of love.

She sneaked a glance at Raph. His thoughtful but unreadable expression made her pause and wonder what he was thinking.

'Why don't you show Stacey up to her room?' suggested

Aurelia, and Lia knew that it was her way of giving the sisters some time together.

———————

'Wow. Just wow. This is awesome,' said Stacey prowling around the bedroom.'I can't believe you're living here.'

'I'm not living here, just staying for a little while.'

'Mum sends her love by the way,' said Stacey, before adding with a heartfelt sigh, 'I'm sorry. I was mad at you for shutting us all out but I get it now. It must be really weird for you. It's weird for me. But you're still my sister, no matter what.'

Lia put her an arm around her. 'I know and I'm sorry too. I just felt overwhelmed by it all and I wanted answers and … if I'm honest, it felt easier to run away than stay and face things. Is Mum okay?'

'Yeah, she's fine. At least she is now. Dad laid down the law. Said it was a big thing for you to come to terms with and we all had to let you do it your way. But then Ernesto got in touch to let us know you were here. You know he invited us all, which was really nice of him, but Mum and Dad decided it might be a bit awkward, so they went to Carcassonne as planned.'

Lia smiled. 'I bet Aurelia put him up to it.'

'She's a sweetie, isn't she?'

'They both are. The whole family is lovely.'

'Especially Raphael – care to tell me what's going on there?'

'Nothing,' said Lia a little too quickly.

'Yet,' said Stacey with a smirk. 'You're obviously losing your touch.'

'He's Ernesto's stepson.'

'Not a blood relative then. Why wouldn't you? I would.'

Lia nudged her sister in the arm. 'You're incorrigible.'

'I know,' said Stacey with a cheeky grin. 'That's why you love me.'

Lia hugged her sister, before the threatening tears could get the better of her. 'I certainly do. I'm so glad you came.'

They all settled down onto the soft linen-covered sofas around the glass coffee table, and a second bottle of Prosecco was opened before dinner. Stacey wasn't the least bit awed by Ernesto and gaily asked him questions about his film career, openly admiring the villa and making it quite clear how thrilled she was to have been invited.

Lia nodded and looked over at Raph. She'd misjudged him so badly, assuming that he was some kind of authoritarian control freak who wanted to keep people away from his stepfather, when he was just trying to do his best and protect his family from unscrupulous people who were out for what they could get.

'Hello. Am I late?' Layla walked into the room wearing a red halter-neck top and flowing white palazzo pants, immediately commanding all attention.

'Oh my God,' said Stacey. 'You're Layla Taylor. I saw you in *Breadcrumbs* at the Lane Street Theatre two weeks ago.'

Layla preened with the recognition. 'Thank you. It's a wonderful part. It's really stretched me as an actress, you know. Do you still do any theatre work, Ernesto?' asked Layla, sinking gracefully into the seat nearest to him.

'No, but I think I would like to return to the stage in London. It would be nice to take the family there for a holiday and to show them the sights.'

'Oh, you should. I'm sure you must get plenty of offers.'

'Some,' agreed Ernesto, modestly.

Catching the wry grin on Raphael's face, Lia guessed that *some* was an understatement of vast proportions.

'Have you thought of investing in the theatre?' asked Layla. 'Becoming a theatre angel. I've always thought it must be so rewarding.'

Lia saw Raph's eyes narrow. 'Don't put ideas in his head,' he grumbled.

Ernesto grinned. 'Raph gets cross with me because I'm always wanting to look at new investments.'

'An investment is supposed to have a return,' said Raph, severely.

'*Sì, sì, sì,*' said Ernesto with a good natured smile, waving away the observation with an airy hand.

'Is everyone ready for dinner?' asked Aurelia, obviously keen to change the direction of that particular conversation, as if it was one that had come up many times.

For the first time, the party was guided into the formal dining room, where the huge square table had been laid with fresh white napkins, sparkling glassware and silver cutlery. On either side of the room were two huge urns set in wrought-iron stands, blousy arrangements of purpley blue hydrangeas, pink roses and lilac lisianthus spilling out. They filled the air with a rich scent of honey and vanilla.

Ernesto invited everyone to sit down and Lia noticed that Layla made a beeline for the seat next to him. Despite the more formal setting the children joined them and Aurelia introduced them all, explaining who Stacey was.

Giulia who'd sat down next to Stacey, peered up at her. 'So you're not my sister but you are Lia's but Lia is my sister. It's very confusing.'

'Tell you what, I can be your honorary sister,' said Stacey.

'Okay,' said Giulia, a little dubious but evidently mollified by this.

'We're all family, *piccola*,' said Ernesto from across the table.

'What if Raph marries Lia? Will Stacey be a proper sister then?'

For a comical moment the table went silent as all the adults tried to work out what this relationship would be.

'Sister-in-law?' mused Stacey.

'Half-sister in law?' suggested Aurelia

'Step-sister in law?' Ernesto offered.

Neither Raph nor Lia looked at each other.

Dinner, despite the unusual formality of the meal being served by staff, was a noisy affair. The children joined in, talking happily with the adults, and the air in the room was punctuated with bursts of laughter, infectious giggles and loud exclamations.

The food was the perfect complement to an already special evening and there was a moment of silent appreciation before everyone tucked into the caprese salad of soft white mozzarella and scarlet tomatoes sprinkled with aromatic basil.

'Whoa,' said Stacey, who'd never been a particular foodie. 'These tomatoes are heaven. God, I might never go home. This is seriously good.'

'And easy to make. Even you could,' teased Lia.

'God, can you imagine saying that to Mum?'

'No!' said Lia, smiling at her sister and imagining their mum eying up the dish. 'She'd take one look and run screaming from the kitchen.'

'Mum doesn't like cooking,' explained Stacey. 'It's a family joke that anything that takes longer than half an hour to prepare is too much time.' She wrinkled her nose, although her eyes twinkled. 'This looks like a lot of chopping would be required.'

'It is very simple,' said Aurelia, her usual evangelical enthusiasm for food surfacing. 'Lia has been helping me in the kitchen.'

'Lia has? Get out of here!' Stacey's dramatic slap of her hand on her chest had the younger children laughing.

'It's true. I learned to make pasta. But not this one,' she said as Patrizia returned with colourful bowls of fresh tagliatelle seasoned with butter and sage, which Lia and Aurelia had spent all morning making.

After a dessert of rich, creamy tiramisu Lia sat back in

her chair and listened to the happy chatter around her. Layla was absorbed in conversation with Ernesto; Aurelia was talking to Luciana, while Michael and Stacey were laughing together. Raph caught her eye and they shared a private smile. It was, Lia reflected, one of the nicest evenings she'd ever had, although she desperately wanted to talk to Raph in private.

When the coffee came out, the children all disappeared and they moved back to the salon, although Layla excused herself. 'I can't drink caffeine at this time of day.' Lia wondered if part of the reason was that Ernesto was now snuggled up next to his wife on one of the sofas and she couldn't monopolise him anymore.

'Would anyone like a Limoncello?' asked Ernesto.

'Sorry,' said Stacey, unable to stifle a huge yawn. 'I'm knackered. Travelling does that to you, doesn't it? Well, maybe not you guys. I bet you have to travel first class so you're not bothered all the time by fans.' Stacey said it with innocent enthusiasm, without envy, just stating a fact.

Within minutes, goodnights were said and only Lia and Raph remained in the room.

'Alone at last,' he said.

Her shoulders sagged. 'I cant believe my sister is here. I've not been great to her but it's ultimately not her fault that my mum lied to me, or that she can't really understand what I'm feeling.' Lia sighed and felt tears prick at her eyes, the familiar sensation of being lost washing over her again.

'Come on.' He pulled her to her feet. 'I've got something to show you.'

Chapter Thirty-Two

T he tiny spots of light winking in and out of existence as the fireflies danced on the clifftop made one of the most magical sights Lia had ever seen. Ragged clouds collected around an almost full moon, scudding across the sky, the shadows dappled with silver.

Entranced she stood hand in hand with Raph in the warm humid air as a light breeze whispered through the Mediterranean pines. It was just what she needed.

'Thank you,' she murmured, breathing in the sharp scent of the trees.

'For what?'

'For knowing that I needed this.' She appreciated the way he understood her and seemed to be able to anticipate what she wanted before she herself even knew.

'You're more than welcome.'

'You've moved back into the main house,' she said.

'I thought it best to give you some space ... and of course I had no intention of sharing with Layla despite what she thought. I honestly don't know what she's doing here.'

'You don't?!' Lia was surprised. It was so obvious to her.

'No. She knows there's no chance of us getting back together. In fact, I don't think she even wants to. I've no idea why she's stayed.'

'Where were you this evening?!' Lia still couldn't believe he hadn't seen it. Layla had Ernesto's influence and money in her sights.

'Worrying about you,' he confessed a little sheepishly. Her heartbeat tripped like it had hit a bump in the road. 'Can I ask a question?'

'Sure.'

'From what I saw tonight, from the way you and Stacey acted to the way she talked about your mum, it sounds as if you're close to your family. What made you go looking for Ernesto? I guess I'm asking … why rock the boat? You lived without him all these years.'

Lia sighed. Putting into words her chaotic feelings felt like looking up at a mountain and knowing the climb ahead would inevitability be hard but ultimately worth it. 'You're right, we're close. But though we get on well, I've always felt like the odd one out.' She gave a satirical laugh, wondering if he would understand. 'Ironically I feel that way most around Mum and Stacey, who are my blood relatives. For one thing I look nothing like them – that's obvious why now. But we're also just so different in temperament. They're both very corporate, working in business doing stuff I don't even comprehend, whereas I've always been the flaky, arty one.'

'Yes, but that still doesn't explain why you were so keen to meet Ernesto.'

'I guess it's because I found out that he was my birth father at the same time as I was having a crisis of confidence about my art. The Braganzis turned down my original commission ideas and rejection is hard. I took it badly and it really rocked me. And then I found out my foundations weren't what I thought they were at all. Added to which, when I tried to find out more, a certain someone was so unhelpful,' she said meaningfully.

'I didn't mean to be. You have to know that there are a lot of chancers out there. I was just trying to protect Ernesto.'

'That may be so, but you didn't even listen.'

'I was doing what I thought was best with the information I had at the time.'

'Hmm,' said Lia, still not quite mollified by this. 'It just added to the perfect storm. I was so pissed off, with you almost as much as with my mum, so I packed a bag, contacted an old Italian friend here and flounced off. That's another example of how I differ from the rest of the family. I'm impetuous and flighty, whereas they're all planners.' She broke off with a small sigh. 'I can guarantee if Mum were here she'd have a list of everything she wants to see. She'd have done her research and would know exactly what restaurants to eat in because she can't bear wandering around looking at menus. She doesn't do spontaneity.'

'She sounds like my kind of woman,' said Raph. 'Ernesto drives me mad, assuming that a restaurant will be able to accommodate all eight of us without a booking.'

'I can see that, but there's joy in checking places out and deciding which you fancy in the moment. You miss out on that if you're uber-focused on sticking to an itinerary.'

Raph shook his head. 'Sounds like a recipe for hunger for me. Or ending up in some crappy place because it's the only one that has a table free.'

'Where's your sense of adventure?' teased Lia.

'Right here,' said Raph and tugged her towards him for a kiss. 'Although if you're going to make me wander around the streets of London looking for a restaurant...'

'What do you mean?' Lia frowned.

He cradled her face in his hands, his eyes darkening, serious and solemn, as they studied her with an undeniable tenderness that made her insides turn to mush. He looked as if he were caught in a starburst, backlit by the fireflies beyond him, and her heart expanded. For a moment she could almost imagine he loved her back.

'How would you feel about us still seeing each other when we get back to London?'

Her breath caught in her chest.

'I'd like that,' she said, trying to play it cool while a flutter of butterflies erupted in her stomach. It was no good: she couldn't be cool. 'I'd really like that,' she said and leaned in and kissed him. And then kissed him again. 'Really a lot. Very much. Very lot.'

He grinned at her. 'Me too. I think we should go public tomorrow.'

'What about Layla? And maybe we should let your mum know first. She's been so desperately trying to matchmake.'

'Don't worry about Layla. I will speak to her and I don't think she's going to mind too much; I'm pretty sure she's been sleeping with her leading man since we split up. However, I will not be giving Mamma a heads-up.' Mischief underpinned his tone. 'I'm looking forward to seeing her face when we walk in together.'

Thank goodness, after tonight he wouldn't have to do this again. He was too old, far too old, to be sneaking around his parents' home, he decided as he left Lia's room early the next morning, hastily tucking in his shirt as he walked up to the main house. But not too old to relish the sensation of blood singing in his veins and the unfamiliar full feeling in his chest, as if his heart wanted to expand and expand until it burst. He chuckled to himself; he sounded lovesick. But whatever the feeling, he liked it. Liked it a lot. Really a lot. Very much. Very lot.

Still smiling he slipped through the French doors on the ground floor and cut through the salon, taking the stairs two at a time up to the room he'd moved into yesterday.

'Up early, bro?' said a dry voice just as he reached for the door handle.

'Bloody hell, Leo. This is a bit early for you, isn't it?' Raph scowled. He was a grown man. He didn't need to explain his actions to his younger brother who was grinning all over his irritating face.

'Couldn't resist the charms of the lovely Layla after all?'

'No, actually.' He grinned at his brother, unable to keep the smile from his face. 'Lia.'

'You sly dog. I wondered if there was something going on there. Nice work.'

'I'd rather you didn't mention it to Mamma just yet. And not while Layla is there.'

'As if I would mention it to Mamma, who is desperate to get you married off.'

'You would.'

'Yeah, I would. It's your turn to take the heat for a change.' Leo's face creased, his eyes crinkling with devilish delight. 'Lia seems very nice, though. You're not going to cock it up, are you?'

'I'm going to do my best not to and yes, she is very nice.' Nice didn't begin to describe it but it was too new and too private to share. Besides, he wanted to hold on tight to these burgeoning feelings and savour them without having them unpicked or interrogated by anyone else. He wanted to stay in the private bubble of happiness that was just Lia and him. It was a new sensation for him.

'Yeah.' Leo's face clouded. 'Sometimes nice isn't enough.'

Raph sobered and clapped a hand on Leo's shoulder. He didn't know all the details as Leo had been very cagey about his short-lived relationship, but he knew his brother was still hurting even though it had been over for a few years.

Leo brightened. 'Sorry, bro. I'm pleased for you. I like Lia. Of course, she's far too good for you and there's every chance she'll come to her senses. Make the best of it while you can.'

An hour later, as he emerged from his study for a coffee, the house quivered with that pre-party buzz as the huge vans parked in the turning circle at the front of the house were unloaded and an army of catering staff moved like ants on the march, efficient and purposeful, carrying silver trays, boxes of glasses, foil-wrapped platters, enormous pans, rolls of carpet and vast bunches of flowers. Raph weaved his way through them to the family kitchen, which was an oasis of calm. At the back of the house, in the commercial kitchen, he knew the well-oiled party machine would be rolling into action.

He found Aurelia sitting eating breakfast, looking serene in a glamorous silk kimono.

'Where is everyone?'

'Leo has taken the kids to the beach and Ernesto is having a meeting in his study.'

'A meeting.' He did a quick mental check of Ernesto's diary. 'That's early. Who with?'

Aurelia frowned. 'With Layla, of course. Didn't you know?'

Raph stiffened. 'No. I didn't know.'

'I thought you did. She...' Aurelia put down her tiny espresso cup looking worried. 'That's why Ernesto agreed to... Oh dear.'

Oh dear indeed. Raph was already striding towards Ernesto's study, his blood on a quick boil.

Calm down, he told himself as he approached the door, there was nothing to be gained from losing his temper, but it was hard to ignore the sense of foreboding mushrooming faster and faster with every step. Outside the door, he deliberately took a few slow breaths and then grasped the handle, easing it open. Layla was sitting opposite Ernesto, a sheaf of paper in her hand. Ernesto, the fool, was nodding and waving his silver fountain pen in the air.

'Good morning,' said Raph, watching as Layla whirled round and Ernesto gave him a welcoming smile.

'Raph!' he called, in his full theatrical boom. 'You're just in time to join the celebrations.'

'I am, am I?' Raph's tone, silky smooth and as dangerous as a viper, made his stepfather recoil. 'And what celebrations would those be?'

Ernesto beamed. 'I've just signed the contract. I'm going to be investor in a theatre show.'

'The contract?' Raph's heart plummeted to the pit of his stomach.

'Yes. Yes. I've agreed to invest in this young lady's production. It's very exciting. A UK tour and then, all being well, Broadway.'

'You've done what?' He stopped dead.

Ernesto beamed at him and Layla gave him a triumphant smirk.

'What the f...?' Raph almost snatched the contract out of Layla's hands except she hastily stuffed it into her handbag.

'Don't worry,' said Ernesto. 'I called Dan in London and he said if you think it's okay then he thinks it's a great idea.'

'You called Dan?' Disbelief spiked in his words. Dan, Ernesto's agent, knew sod-all about Ernesto's financial investment strategy and personal portfolio. Ernesto's face dimmed as Aurelia appeared in the doorway.

'Yes. But I knew you'd approved the investment; Layla said so. You know when it comes to the financial side of things, I trust your judgement.' He gave Raph another one of his confident smiles and Aurelia moved to her husband's side, her eyes pleading with Raph's.

Raph closed his eyes and clenched his fists by his sides, not sure which of the pair of them he wanted to strangle first.

Ernesto was a grown man and could make his own decisions. It wasn't as if he would miss the money, if or when, as Raph suspected, there'd be no return on the investment, but Raph wasn't about to embarrass or emasculate him in front of Layla or his wife.

'Why don't we leave Raph to discuss this with Layla, darling,' said Aurelia, already guiding her husband out of the room. Much as he loved his mother, he knew Ernesto's ego was a fragile thing and she'd made it her job to protect him from this kind of upset. Raph always got to play bad cop.

But Layla – his red-hot temper turned to ice as he turned to her with a contemptuous sneer.

'I see you got what you came for.' He should have known. Layla had used him to get to Ernesto.

'Don't be like that, Raph, darling. Ernesto's doing a wonderful thing, lending his support to the theatrical arts.'

'Ensuring you have a job for another six months, you mean.'

'That too,' she conceded. 'I don't know why you're so upset. It means I can move out of your flat, and it's not like Ernesto can't afford it.'

'It didn't occur to you that I might not like being used? You told him *I* approved of this deal.'

She lifted her shoulders in an elegant shrug. 'I implied it. To be fair, I thought going out with you would open a few more doors.' With a roll of her eyes, she added, 'You're not exactly Mr Fun Guy. Bit too stuffy. Do you ever let your hair down and actually enjoy yourself? I mean you look good, but the sex – you're a passionless fuck.'

'Thanks, but I wasn't looking for points.'

'Six at best, sweetie.'

'Nice to know.'

'Look, no hard feelings. It was mutually beneficial. You got some hot eye candy to shore up your image as the sophisticated financier about town. I bet it didn't do your business any harm either. And as for me, I made a good contact … eventually. It would have been nice if you'd invited me here at some point, instead of me having to blag my way in, but I guess you were too busy banging that Lia chick.'

Raph gritted his teeth, determined not to show the hits were landing. He'd never imagined that he was in love with Layla, but this cold dissection of their time together felt like a betrayal and her casual reference to Lia infuriated him.

'Don't talk about her like that.'

Layla threw back her head and exhaled loudly. 'There's one born every minute. Don't tell me you're in love with her.'

Her words brought back the warm glow that nestled inside him at the thought of Lia, her soft body that he'd left just over an hour ago. Someone like Layla would never understand that connection, the feeling of completeness.

'She's no better than me. It's not like she didn't used Ernesto's name to get the commission to do the artwork for the Braganzi restaurant.'

'You're talking rubbish.'

'Am I? I read it just this morning in one of the showbiz columns.' Layla held up her phone and read from the screen. 'Lia Bathurst, daughter of Ernesto Salvatore, has secured a commission worth a cool half million to provide the artwork for the new Braganzi restaurant and hotel in London.' Her voice ended on a high note of triumph. 'You're telling me she'd have secured that commission without playing the family card? A fancy outfit like that wants a name, not a nobody. Plain old Lia Bathurst wouldn't have got a look-in. Wise up, Raph. How come she was in Italy at just the right time?'

'You don't know what you're talking about. You're just trying to justify what you've done.'

'Oh, fuck off, Raph.'

With that Layla turned and marched out of the study.

Chapter Thirty-Three

L ia carefully inserted the wooden dowels at the top of the fabric and held up the length of silk, which rippled slightly in the breeze coming through the windows of Aurelia's sitting room. She'd borrowed an iron from Patrizia to give the full-length picture of Positano a final pressing.

'It's so beautiful, Lia. Your father is going to be so so happy,' said Aurelia, pressing her hands together. 'You are very talented. He will love it.' Her faint Italian accent deepened with emotion.

'I know he wanted to buy it, but I wanted you both to have it as a gift. It's the least I can do for making me feel so welcome.'

'We will hang it in the ballroom as a surprise this evening. He will be thrilled.' Aurelia clasped Lia's hands, tears shimmering in her eyes. 'You have brought us so much joy, coming here this summer.'

'And I haven't said thank you for inviting Stacey. That was really kind of you.'

Aurelia kissed her cheek. 'I knew you were hurting. It's a shame your mamma and papa couldn't come.'

'You wouldn't have found it strange, them being here?' Lia asked.

'*Cara*, it was a long time ago. I worry for you.'

'For me. Why?'

'Because it is not good to have this distance from your mamma. Stacey told me you're not speaking to her. That makes me very sad. Family is everything and more.'

Lia frowned. 'But she … she lied to me. There were so many times when she could have told me.'

'When?' asked Aurelia. 'When you were a little girl? Would that have helped then?'

'No. But maybe when I was older.'

'Sixteen. Eighteen. Twenty-one. Twenty-five. When would have been a good time?'

Lia pursed her lips. 'Okay, I can see that maybe there never would have been a good time. But she should have told me at some point.'

'And what if you'd never found out?'

'But I did find out.' Even to herself, Lia sounded like a petulant toddler. 'And now I don't know what to feel. It's so confusing. I'm so angry with my mum and with myself. I'm mad at her because everything I thought was true isn't. It's like I'm walking on a cloud and any moment I could fall through, and it wasn't like that before.'

Aurelia pulled her into a hug, stroking her hair. 'Aw,

honey. I'm sad for you but … I'm sad for your mamma as well.'

Lia tensed, the guilt like a woodworm picking more and more holes in the fabric of who she was.

'And you really didn't mind me coming here? The child of another relationship your husband had.'

Aurelia, with that ability of hers to empathise and know when to change the mood, wiped a weary hand across her brow. 'To be honest, *bella*, it's been very difficult. I quite fancied the role of the wicked stepmother. It's so hard playing nice.'

Despite the emotion churning in every last bit of her, like a relentless cement mixer, Lia burst out laughing. 'Nice try, Aurelia. You don't have a mean bone.'

'Ah, *cara*, you are a delight. It has been so lovely having you join the family. You must come for Thanksgiving. I wouldn't ask your mother to forgo you for Christmas but please come to LA in November.'

'Thank you. That sounds rather wonderful.' Especially if she and Raph were still together then.

'And now I must get ready for the party. There's so much to do.'

'Can I help with anything?'

'Yes, you can go and lie by the pool and have a lovely relaxing day. When I say there is so much to do,' Aurelia winked, 'I mean for the catering team. All I have to do is give them orders, and, to be honest, Patrizia knows everything. We will have drinks on the terrazza at six for the household, and the first guests arrive at six thirty.'

'How many people are you expecting?' asked Lia.

'A hundred and thirty-three,' said Aurelia.

Lia stared at her, the words in her mouth dissolving on a near choke. She didn't know that many people well enough to invite to a party.

'I know, we try to keep it select but what can you do?' Aurelia lifted her shoulders in a guileless expansive shrug as Lia struggled to keep a straight face. 'Ernesto is very popular and lots of people plan their holidays in Italy so they are available. Luckily we have a really good concierge service that arranges the helicopters. It can get very busy. In fact, I made Ernesto move the helipad to the far side of the estate because it was too noisy.'

Lia just stared. Because Ernesto and Aurelia were so down to earth, it was easy to forget who they were and the world they inhabited. No wonder Stacey had looked so impressed yesterday.

'Now that's very interesting.' Aurelia had moved to the window and was holding back the lace curtain.

Through the glass Lia could see a black Mercedes with an open boot and Layla handing the driver a huge suitcase.

'She doesn't look very happy,' observed Aurelia rather blandly and Lia almost laughed. Layla, in huge black sunglasses and spindly heels unsuited to the gravel surface, stomped, as best she could, around the car before hurling her handbag and an expensive-looking vanity case into the backseat with scant regard for the contents. She threw herself into the passenger seat and yanked the door shut. The tinted windows of the executive saloon sealed her off from view as the car drove off.

Aurelia beamed at Lia. 'Maybe now that she's out of the picture, Raph might see what's under his nose.'

Lia laughed. 'You never give up, do you?'

'He might be a six foot strapping man, but he'll always be my boy. And if he's too stupid to see that it's time he found a lovely woman, what sort of mother would I be if I didn't give him the nudge he needs?'

Lia's expression was as bland as she could make it. 'Who's the lovely woman you have in mind?'

Aurelia shook her head with an exasperated tut as Patrizia appeared in the doorway, a phone to her ear, which she held out to Aurelia. Lia took advantage of the interruption to make an exit.

———

'Did you know Julia Roberts is coming tonight?' asked Stacey as they sipped Limoncello spritzes on the balcony of San Pietro di Positano.

Lia nodded. She'd brought her sister out to get away from the party preparations and to show her some of Positano.

'And George and Amal Clooney are flying from Lake Como,' said Stacey, her eyes wide with star-struck anticipation. 'And Ernesto Salvatore is your birth father. Oh God, can you believe Mum slept with him? Mind-boggling.'

'I'd really rather not think about it.'

'But it's cool.'

'What are you going to wear?' Lia asked shutting the subject down.

'I've bought a really gorg Temperley dress. I'm hoping it will be posh enough. What about you?'

'Bloody hell, that must have set you back a bit.'

Stacey shrugged. 'Not every day you get to go to a Hollywood party. And I'm worth it.'

'I bought an amazing skirt in Naples.' Rather, Raph had bought it and she'd nearly died when she'd seen the price, although it was so gorgeous she wouldn't have been able to walk out of the shop without it. She'd insisted on paying him back. It might have been a nice gesture, but she was a financially independent woman who could afford to buy her own clothes, even expensive ones.

'Can I do your hair?' asked Stacey.

'If you want,' said Lia. 'Why don't you come to my room to get ready?'

Stacey shared a grin with her. 'Will you do my make-up? I can never get my flicks as neat as you do.'

'I know,' said Lia a touch smugly. 'Artistic hand.'

'Yes, well, I'm better at hair than you.' She gave Lia's curls an envious glance. 'Now we know where the curls came from. And I always thought it was the milkman.'

'Stacey!' Lia laughed.

'It's going to be one hell of a party. We need to look our best.'

'I'm not sure anyone is going to be looking at us,' said Lia.

'I don't know; Raphael seemed very keen yesterday evening. Couldn't take his eyes off you,' said Stacey, before adding, 'and I noticed him taking a very early walk of shame this morning.'

Lia gave her sister a dirty look.

'What? He's definitely all man. Bet he looks good in the buff.'

'Stacey,' she hissed.

'So, what's the score with him?'

Lia couldn't help but revel in the little glow of happiness that was radiating through her. She gave a small smile. 'We're … seeing each other. Seeing how it goes when we get back to London.'

'That's so cool, although what is he? Your step-brother?'

'Yes,' said Lia.

'Now, that's what I call keeping it in the family,' Stacey joked.

'I wouldn't get ahead of yourself – and don't say anything. We haven't said anything to Aurelia and Ernesto yet. We decided we'll go public this evening at the party.' Just saying it out loud had Lia's nerves fluttering. She hadn't seen Raph since this morning but they'd agreed to meet at the family gathering for drinks before the party started. Aurelia was going to be pleased but, that aside, she couldn't wait to be with Raph again and to be able to be with him openly.

Chapter Thirty-Four

Lia admired herself in the mirror as she did a quick twirl. Stacey had done an amazing job on her hair, carefully drying the curls into corkscrews, which she then teased out into a mass of individual ringlets. A white silk halter-neck top, cut very low at the back, accompanied the silk and chiffon skirt Raph had bought her in Naples. The effect was elegant and feminine and she felt sexy and very female as the skirt swished around her tanned legs, the warm breeze brushing across her bare back.

She couldn't wait for Raph to see her all dressed up.

Picking up her clutch bag, she gave herself one last check in the mirror, blew herself a kiss and walked up the path to the villa. Guests had been arriving all afternoon and since Layla's unexpected departure, Stacey had moved in next door. Impatient to be at the party before it even started, Stacey had left twenty minutes ago with a bad case of FOMO.

A champagne reception to kick off the party was being held in the loggia, which ran along the side of the villa and made the most of the commanding view from the cliff top. There was a palpable air of excitement in the main hallway as Lia cut through the house. The cool marble hallway was full of flowers; the doors were open and two white-gloved, penguin-suited butlers stood at the door in readiness to greet the arrivals, while a gaggle of maids in neat black dresses and white aprons gathered to guide guests to the powder room, the cloakroom and the main party out on the terrazzo.

Aurelia was a party mastermind and her organisational and logistical skills would have been the envy of NATO. She had everything under control and had achieved it with peaceful diplomacy, commanding the staff with quiet dignity and unhurried calm. They all adored her, and it was no wonder. Lia thought she might just be one of the kindest and best people she'd ever met – inviting Stacey to join them had been such a thoughtful thing to do.

Lia smiled to herself, delighted that she was about to give Aurelia something she wanted, someone to love her son. Raph's mamma wasn't the only one who could hand out the surprises! She picked up her pace, anxious and excited to see Raph.

The room was already full when she arrived and she wove her way through the crowd, taking a proffered glass of champagne and searching for Raph. She spotted him, his back to her, talking to Aurelia and Ernesto. Her heart did the little bump she still hadn't become accustomed to and she wriggled her way past several other people that she knew she didn't know even though they looked very familiar.

'Ah, Lia,' said Ernesto, greeting her. 'Max, this is my daughter and the very talented artist who created this.' He pointed to her picture hanging on the wall. Raph was talking to his mother and hadn't shifted, and Lia, impatient to greet him, had to smile and nod politely at the tall thin man Ernesto was insistent on introducing her to.

'Lia, this is Max Albertini. He's the owner of the Brunelleschi Gallery in Firenze. He likes your work very much.'

Lia's eyes widened. Albertini's gallery was one of the most prestigious in Europe. Her agent would be thrilled to know she'd met him.

At that moment Raph turned around, just as Albertini took her hand with both of his. 'Miss Bathurst, I am delighted to meet you.' His heavily accented voice and extravagant gestures almost made her giggle but then she caught sight of the cold condescension on Raph's face, sobering her immediately. It took her a second to realise that she was the icy focus of his gaze. Swallowing the sharp spike of foreboding, she dredged up a smile for Albertini, who was still talking.

'This is quite the most exquisite piece of work. I'd be very interested in talking to you about an exhibition.'

'What a stroke of luck,' purred Raph. 'Signor Albertini being here on the very day that you gave Ernesto this piece of work.'

She shot him a startled glance, shocked by the rumbling malice in his voice. Inside part of her crumbled. Raph couldn't possibly mean what he was saying. He knew her better than that, didn't he? A flash of temper struck harder. How dare he even think that. 'Wasn't it just?' she said to him, lifting her chin and squaring her chest.

'Your career's really taken off since you hitched your wagon to Ernesto.'

Aurelia put a warning hand on Raph's arm but he shook it off, which incensed Lia further.

'You think?' She gave him an insincere smile.

'Raph,' pleaded Aurelia. 'Not now. Not here.'

He gave his mother a mutinous look and for a moment Lia thought he was going to walk away but instead he took her arm. 'Excuse me, Lia and I need to talk.'

With fury washing inside her like the waves at high tide, she allowed herself to be led through the French doors onto a terrace overlooking the gardens and the pool.

'When were you going to tell me about the Braganzi commission being finalised?'

Lia stared at him. 'What do you mean?'

'There's been an announcement in the media. It's featured on several websites.'

'How do you know that?'

'I have a search set up on Ernesto's name. A press statement has been released, announcing that Lia Bathurst, Ernesto Salvatore's long-lost daughter from a previous relationship, has secured the commission to provide artwork for Braganzi's London venture. Apparently father and daughter are spending a summer together enjoying their reconciliation.'

'But ... they ... don't know the connection.'

'Don't they? So they regularly shell out half a million pounds to starving artists?'

'It's not a half a million pounds,' she snapped. 'It's half of that.'

'I imagine even a fraction is more than most artists earn in a lifetime, let alone for one gig. No one would blame you for using every means at your disposal to make sure you were picked. The Braganzis haven't been slow to leverage it. I'm not sure their restaurant would have received quite so much publicity at this juncture without the mention of Ernesto's name.'

'That was nothing to do with me.'

'You seriously expect me to believe that? The timing is just a little too perfect. It sounds like when they rejected your initial designs for the commission and you discovered you had a famous father, you immediately came to find your famous father whose name might just open a few doors…'

'I don't need Ernesto's name.'

'But it's worked out just fine for you, hasn't it?'

'If that's what you think, I'm not going to change your mind. You never really trusted me, did you?'

'I…' She saw it in his face even before he admitted it with a careless lift of his shoulders. 'No, I guess I didn't.'

'So these last few weeks … they meant nothing?'

'Clearly not to you. Or maybe it was an added bonus.'

'You weren't that good in bed.' As soon as she said it, she wished she hadn't. It was bitchy, unnecessary and totally untrue. Striking back left a sour taste and she was ashamed of it.

His lips turned white. 'Funny, that's exactly what Layla said the minute she'd got Ernesto's signature on a contract to invest in her play.'

A cold chill spread across her body and she hurt for him. Knowing she'd struck a direct, spiteful hit, she immediately put her hand out to touch Raph and he flinched. 'I'm sorry, I shouldn't have said that. It's not true.'

But the damage was done. It had been inflicted a long time ago and his innate assumption that people were only interested in what his stepfather could do for them had once again been reinforced, just as it had by serial offenders over the years.

'I've no idea what the truth is with you, Lia.' He turned away. 'I thought you were different but you're no better than Layla. Although, to be fair, at least she was honest in the end.'

'Oh, fuck off, Raph,' she said and walked away. If he thought that about her, he could go boil his head.

Chapter Thirty-Five

Lia lay on the sunbed, eyes shut tight, ignoring the sound of flip-flops heading her way.

'Here you are.' Her sister's voice was far too loud and cheerful.

'Mmm,' she said, not bothering to open her eyes or remove the sunglasses, resigned to the fact that there was no hiding or getting away. She'd been lying here listless and hot since she'd woken up.

'Hangover?'

'Mmm.' Her headache had as much to do with misery than alcohol. A sleepless night and a broken heart compounded the sensation of being as limp as a rag after a 1800rpm spin in a washing machine.

'Aurelia insisted I brought some breakfast down to you.'

Lia's stomach turned over and she prised open one eye to see the plate of pastries Stacey held out. She winced at the smell of vanilla and chocolate.

'Ouch, you really are feeling rough,' said Stacey, helping

herself to a croissant and to the sunlounger next to Lia. 'I didn't think you'd drunk that much.' Lia's stomach protested some more with a savage twinge as she watched her sister take a big bite of the flaky pastry, crumbs cascading down her blue T-shirt.

'I didn't at the party.' It was the pity-party bottle of Prosecco she'd downed out here on her own after everyone else had gone to bed, while overanalysing every last word Raph and she had said to each other over the last couple of weeks. Her mood ranged from mad to sad to furious again. How could he possibly think that she'd slept with him to further her career? And as if it wasn't insulting enough that he didn't think she had her own merit, he'd rejected everything they'd shared. Her submission had been some of her very best work. How dare he take that away from her? Make her doubt her ability? She was glad she'd told him to eff off. She would live off the look of shock in his eyes for a very long time. Damn him.

'You and Raph carried on partying, did you? It was noted that you were both missing in action this morning. I didn't say anything. I guess you two decided not to go public last night.'

'Mmm,' said Lia, grateful for her sunglasses as she felt a stupid tear gather in the corner of one eye.

'Man, that was a kick-ass party. I talked to… Lia, are you listening?'

'Sure,' said Lia, swallowing. Maybe she should go and talk to Raph. Explain he was wrong.

'I kept seeing people I thought I knew. I'd said hello to a couple of people and they said hi back before I realised I didn't know them. I guess it happens all the time as they didn't seem to mind. I had a really long conversation with a totally hot guy; I think he's in something on Netflix, although he never mentioned it.'

Lia let her sister chatter away, all the time holding her own internal dialogue, one that had been on repeat for the last twelve hours. As soon as she'd come back to her room, she'd fired up her laptop and searched her own name, finding the words Raph had thrown at her repeated verbatim several times, all clearly taken from the same press release.

Despite it being nearly one in the morning, she'd phoned Alec.

'Hey, honey.' He'd answered almost immediately. 'Where are you?'

'I'm still in Italy. Did you know the Braganzis have made an announcement?'

'Shit. No. Christ, nobody told me. What the crap is going on?'

'Apparently I got it.'

'You did! Well, that's fuckin' A. Well done, honey. That's great news. I hope you got a bottle of something to celebrate.'

'Did you tell the Braganzis that I was Ernesto Salvatore's daughter?'

'No. Are you? You told me he was just an old family friend.'

'Yes, and somehow they found out. It was in their press release.'

'You're kidding me.'

'I wish I was.'

'Well, it's not done any harm. And yes, it mighta helped, but I think this is your best work and you nailed their vision – *that's* why they chose you. You need to celebrate. This is mega. A big step up. I'm proud of you, babe. This is really going to put your stuff on the map. I guarantee you're going to go stratospheric now. Now go celebrate and I'll speak to you tomorrow.'

He'd hung up before she could say another word but what else was there to say? Alec was pushy when it came to selling her but he was also supportive and she believed him when he said he hadn't told Stella and Vincent Braganzi. She trusted him. He'd always had her back.

'Lia? Are you listening?' Stacey's voice interrupted her thoughts.

'Sorry. Did you know I got the Braganzi commission?'

'Get out of here! For the new restaurant? Oh my God. That's amazing! Seriously. You have to get me a table there. Do you know the one in New York is booked up three months in advance?'

'Yes, I did.'

Stacey launched herself at Lia and gave her a hug. 'Have you told Mum and Dad?'

'Not yet,' she said evenly. Her conversation with Aurelia yesterday had opened up a new seam of guilt, which her conscience was mining for all it was worth.

'They're going to be made up.'

They would, she knew that. It was one of the reasons she'd been so desperate to win the commission: it was a tangible sign of success that they could recognise and appreciate.

'I bet Ernesto has been to Braganzi in New York.' Stacey took another pastry.

'Yes,' said Lia dully and stood up, not really sure what she wanted to do but feeling restless. Maybe if she grabbed her phone, which was still charging beside her bed, she could scroll through the announcements to cheer herself up.

'Lia, you're a right misery this morning.'

'Yeah, thanks.' She began to walk to her room, Stacey jumping up to follow her.

'I know a great hangover cure,' she said.

'Do you?' Lia couldn't have cared less.

'Yes,' said Stacey. 'This.' With that, she pushed Lia into the pool.

———————

Half an hour later, she was walking up the path to the house with her sister. The impromptu dip had washed away her self-pity and her usual spirit had reasserted itself. There was no damned way she would let Raphael bloody Knight spoil her moment of glory. He could go stuff his head up his backside where it belonged. She'd worked flipping hard for this job and she was going to celebrate her triumph in spite of him and the taint he'd tried to bring to her win. Like Alec had said in their phone call, this was some of her best work and Raph wasn't going to take it away from her.

Ernesto and Aurelia were gathered on the terrace,

sipping coffee while the children, none the worse for a late night, were playing in the pool.

'Lia,' bellowed Ernesto, oblivious to the wince of Aurelia sitting next to him. 'Did you enjoy the party?'

'It was wonderful, thank you,' she said, putting on her best smile, grateful that the sun was so bright it justified her keeping on her shades.

'Lia's got some news,' interrupted Stacey, pushing Lia in front of her.

'The Braganzis have announced that I've been commissioned to provide artwork for their new restaurant.'

There were universal cries of congratulation from everyone.

'Well done, Lia.'

'Fantastic.'

'You clever girl.'

'This calls for more champagne,' said Ernesto, leaping to his feet and disappearing before Aurelia could stop him. 'I knew Vincent had excellent taste.'

'You must be thrilled, *cara*,' said Aurelia.

'I am. It was definitely worth coming to Italy for inspiration.'

'I'm so pleased. It's a shame Raph's not here, I know he'd be pleased for you.'

Despite all her good intentions that she was going to ignore Raph and any mention of him, she couldn't stop the question rolling off her tongue. 'Where is he?'

'He's had to go back to London. Some emergency with his company. He took an early flight from Naples.'

Lia's heart contracted in her chest, shrivelling into a tiny, hard, walnut-like lump. That was the end of that then. It was over and he'd gone without saying goodbye. Well, sod him. He could go … to hell. Benefit of the doubt, chance to explain – obviously neither appeared in his dictionary. It just went to show, she shouldn't have trusted him after all.

Chapter Thirty-Six

One month later

L ondon should have been grey and overcast, but instead it was vibrant and bright with cerulean cloud-free skies that constantly reminded Lia of being in Italy. She spent every minute she wasn't sleeping working on the Braganzi commission, which had now been given the official name of 'The Italian Diary'. It had given her a legitimate excuse not to have Sunday lunch with her parents and she'd been able to fob her mother off with a couple of 'snowed-under, speak-soon' types of texts, although her dad's GIFs continued, always eliciting a smile and that dull thud of guilt. Stacey visited the studio the day after she had returned from Italy, seen the amount of work Lia needed to do and had backed her excuses up to their mother.

A month after her return and a mere four days before

the restaurant opened, she was putting the finishing touches to her creations.

She stood back from her work table tilting her head, considering whether to add another bead, another stitch to this final section.

'Oh, bugger it,' she said out loud, voicing the frustration she felt with herself. All week a sense of dread had been building. Memories of Italy, of Raph, were woven into the very fabric of the piece, and the thought of handing over the two completed lengths of material made her feel physically ill. Bereft. If she were honest, the work was complete, had been for days, but she couldn't stop tinkering with it, couldn't stop running her fingers over it, couldn't stop looking for flaws. It was without doubt her best work and irrevocably tied to Raph. She'd refused to let herself think about him, but with every stitch, embellishment and dye colour he was in her mind.

She'd stayed on in Italy for another week after the party, finalising the details of the commission with her agent and the Braganzis. Time was tight to complete the work for the restaurant opening and she'd reached the point where she really needed to be back in her own studio – or at least that's what she'd told Ernesto and Aurelia. The truth of the matter was that she'd reached the point where she knew Raph would not return to Italy and certainly not while she was still there. Every day he didn't come deepened the hollowed-out sensation she felt. It became harder and harder to hide – even though she spent every waking minute in the studio in Positano, apart from the afternoon Leo had called to take her to the beach.

She remembered answering the unexpected knock and flying to the door, hope dancing in her chest. Raph had come back. He'd realised he was wrong.

'Leo!' She tried to resurrect the smile on her face, feeling it dimming second by second as she stood there staring at him.

'Hey, Lia. Thought you might like a break. Come to the beach.'

'I … I've got work to do and I don't have a bikini.'

Leo held up her orange bikini with a cheeky grin. 'Yes, you do. And you need a break and gelato!'

She paused.

'Stracciatella. Just think of it. Cold in your mouth. Little starbursts of chocolate.'

God, she was so bored of being miserable.

She grabbed the bikini from his hands. 'Give me a minute and you can buy the ice-cream.'

'*Sì, sì, signorina.*'

They ambled to the gelateria near the busy seafront and then took their ice-creams onto the beach, finding a space in the crowded public area.

They'd been eating in easy companionship when Leo said, 'Giulia sent me.'

'Giulia?'

'Yes. She's worried because you're sad. She told me I had to take you for some ice-cream. Apparently, "Girls eat ice-cream when they're in love and sad."'

Lia arched an eyebrow, unable to speak because of the lump sitting in her throat. 'Sh-she said that.'

Leo nodded. 'Funny little thing. She notices stuff. I think

it's because she's the youngest. She's always trying to catch up, so she pays close attention.'

He turned to look at her. 'It's Raph, isn't it?'

There was no point denying it, so, wrinkling her nose, she nodded and looked out over the waves to the distant horizon, scanning the people in the shallows, standing chatting, enjoying themselves in their brightly coloured swimwear. The scene registered in her brain, another potential picture, which she focused on instead of the pain that nestled in her chest like a hard nut.

'He's an idiot. I'm sorry.'

'Thanks.'

'Being in love sucks sometimes. Want me to talk to him?'

Lia stared at him from behind her sunglasses, studying his handsome face, uncharacteristically serious for once. She could see the sea and sunshine reflected in his lenses, his eyes shielded by the sunglasses.

'I am capable of falling in love,' he said with a shrug as he turned his face away from her. 'I just choose not to. It hurts too much.'

For the first time, she noticed the tension in his taut jawline.

'If it's any consolation, I think Raph loves you.'

'It's not,' said Lia, keen to shut the conversation down. 'And no, I don't want you to talk to him. I'm quite able to tell him what I think of him. But thanks for the offer anyway.'

'What are you going to do?' asked Leo, leaning back on his elbows, looking as if the answer didn't matter to him.

Lia had a feeling it did. There was a forced casualness in the question.

'I'm going to go home, work hard and forget all about him.' She picked up a small stone and tossed it from hand to hand. The weight of it dropping into each palm anchored her to the moment and her decision. It was the right thing to do.

'Or you could give him a chance.' Leo spoke softly and Lia turned to glare at him, surprised by his quiet determination.

'He's the one that walked away.'

'And you're the one that let him. Do you know why he walked away?'

'Yes, and he's wrong.'

'Of course, he is. That's a given.' Leo flashed her one of his charming smiles. 'Even more reason to give him a chance. He's too dumb to realise what he's done.'

'Oh, he knows,' said Lia. 'He knows.'

'Okay, he's too dumb to sort it out.'

'That's his problem.'

'Yes but … you're sad. I think he's sad.'

'I'm not sad, I'm mad. Mad as … as a mad thing.'

'He upset you.'

'More than upset me. He questioned my integrity, my talent – everything I've worked for. He can go stick his head up his own bottom.'

Leo laughed. 'I look forward to telling him that.'

'I'd really rather you didn't. I know you're being kind, Leo, but I need to move on. Raph isn't going to change his mind about me. His issues are too deep-rooted. He believes what he believes, and to be honest, it's not surprising. Look what Layla did. He thinks I'm the same. There's nothing I can say to make him change his mind. He has to be able to trust me and come to that decision by himself.'

She'd replayed that conversation on the beach nearly as many times as she'd replayed the final conversation with Raph. She lifted her chin as she thought of her final words. Okay, it hadn't been her finest hour and her temper had got the better of her, but Raph deserved them. It was rare she lost her temper, very rare. And to swear like that... Her mum would not have been impressed. In hindsight it had been very childish even if it had given her immense satisfaction. But she hadn't been the one in the wrong. Unfortunately, that thought still didn't give her much comfort four weeks later.

———————

She locked up her studio an hour later, having tidied up and taken a few last panoramic pictures and videos of the two completed pictures. Each one was over five metres long and last week she'd been to the restaurant to check the final measurements. The pictures would be stretched onto purpose-built frames and mounted on opposite walls, each one running the length of the room and then curving around a corner. As she walked along the dappled pavement in the heat of the sun, she thought about how her work would look and whether Raph would ever see it. Would he think of her, if he ate at Braganzi? Would he eat there? Or would he boycott it?

As she approached the tall Victorian terrace that housed her flat, she noticed a familiar figure sitting on the short flight of stairs up to the front door. Her footsteps slowed and her heart bumped uncomfortably in her chest.

It was too late to turn and run; he'd seen her. She took in a breath and carried on walking. At the sight of his face, she contained the 'What are you doing here?' that threatened to spill out.

Dark circles shadowed his eyes and his skin stretched over his cheekbones. He looked gaunt. Knots tightened in her stomach and it felt as if it were full of stones. She swallowed; she'd been punishing him. Like a child instead of a grown woman.

'Dad.'

'Hi, sweetheart.'

Immediately she wanted to cry. She'd missed him so much. Instead she stood there, awkward, shifting from one foot to the other.

'Do you want to walk?' he asked.

She nodded.

'The Heath?'

She nodded again. They walked in silence until they reached the Heath and carried on up the hill across the grass.

'I've missed you,' he said as they crested the top.

With a swallow, she managed in a very small voice, 'I missed you too. Did Mum send you?'

He laughed. 'No, she didn't. She's feeling far too guilty and determined to give you the room you asked her for, even though it's killing her.'

Lia felt her stomach hollow out with guilt and regret. There was nothing she could say in her own defence.

'Stacey says Ernesto has quite a place.'

'Yeah. Him and his wife, they were really nice to me.'

'That's good.' He took her hand and squeezed it. 'Really good. I'm glad for you. I'd have hated for you to be disappointed.'

Her heart turned over with a slow clunk. That was so like him. The gentle soul in the family, who took a step back to let his wife and daughters shine. He didn't do emotion; he let the women in the family take care of that. He was always steady, even-keeled and solid. The wall around their family that had kept them safe and protected.

He stopped and gestured to a nearby bench. 'I always knew, you know, but it never made any difference to me.'

Lia took a sidelong glance at him. He was gazing at the skyline of London, as if studying the skyscrapers in the distance, but he held her hand, his fingers tightening very slightly as if it were the only way to let the emotion leak out under control.

'You've always been my daughter.' He spoke in a matter-of-fact tone but Lia knew baring all was hard for him. 'She told me she was pregnant when we first got together but I didn't mind. I wanted both of you and it's never mattered to me that you were created by someone else. I've always thought of it like gardening. Someone else planted the seed but I've done the nurturing. I've been there every step of the way. You're *my* daughter. Always will be. I just wanted you to know that. In case … well, in case you didn't.'

A tear slipped down Lia's cheek. She'd been so wrapped up in how she felt and what had been done to her that she'd been in denial about the impact on her dad. The realisation broke over her, a wash of guilt, regret and utter shame. How could she have treated him so badly?

When she burst into tears, he put his arms around her and hugged her.

'Hush, sweetheart. Hush.'

'Oh, Dad, I'm so sorry. I've been an absolute cow. I was so mad at Mum. I'm so selfish. Thinking only about myself. It was such a shock and I couldn't understand how Mum had kept it a secret all this time.' She sobbed into his shirt, soaking the thin fabric with tears, but now she'd started she didn't seem to be able to stop. All she could think of was how horrible she'd been.

Eventually her sobs quietened.

'I'm sorry, Dad. Really sorry. I need to see Mum. Talk to her properly.'

'She'd like that. She's been trying to give you space but it's... She's unhappy. She feels she handled it wrong, but I promise you it wasn't done for her benefit. It was always because she loves us. All of us. And she didn't want to do anything to jeopardise our family bond. Your mum didn't want to take that away from you.

'We talked about how we might explain about your birth father. I suppose talking about him like that made him less significant. Less of an intrusion into *our* family. We talked about it so many times, I can't tell you. But there was never a right time to tell you. Never.'

He paused and Lia saw the glistening of tears in his eyes. It made her feel sick.

'I don't want to lose you, Lia.'

'You haven't lost me, Dad.'

'Haven't I? Stacey said you got on really well with Ernesto and his wife.'

'They were lovely. You'd like them. Genuinely kind people and very generous – they made me feel really welcome but…' – Lia wiped away the tears under her eyes with a sniff – 'You'll always be my dad.'

'Good,' he said and patted the hand he held.

They sat for a minute or two, both of them contemplating the scene before them, the distant swish of traffic in the background, while birds carolled in the nearby trees. A small sparrow hopped around their feet in search of crumbs under the watchful eyes of several greedy pigeons.

'I'm sorry, Dad.' She wasn't sure she was ever going to be able to say it enough. How did you get over making such a big mistake?

'I know, sweetheart. I understand. You were protecting yourself from getting hurt.'

'No, I was being a self-absorbed brat and only thinking of myself. Can you … can you forgive me?'

He laughed and hugged her. 'I think you need to forgive yourself.'

And just like that, with the love of a parent, he set her free.

She squeezed her dad back. 'Thank you.'

'For me, there's nothing to forgive. It was self-preservation on your part. You were like a tortoise backing into your shell, keeping your distance because you thought it was safer. You were protecting yourself from the fear that you meant less to us, less than Stacey, less to me, less to your mother. But you don't. Nothing has changed. You have to believe that.

'At the same time, your mum was also trying to protect you, she wanted to keep you safe from those fears and those doubts. Maybe she was wrong. Maybe she was right. But never doubt that she loves you very much.' Typical Dad. He could talk about her mum's emotions far more easily than his own.

A bit like Raph. Had he been protecting himself? Layla had let him down, and friends before that. Now she had some distance, Lia could see how it must have hurt for him to think that their relationship was a castle built on the sand of her ambition. Could she forgive him for making a mistake? For jumping to conclusions?

She leaned her head on her dad's shoulder. 'Thanks, Dad,' she said and they sat there for a while longer as the sparrow continued to hop around their feet, still on the lookout for food.

Chapter Thirty-Seven

A
s Raph's cab turned the corner, he caught a glimpse of someone going the other way and butterflies leapt in his stomach at the sight of the bright sun lighting up a mass of blond curls. Before he could look properly, she was out of sight and the cab sailed up the street to his office. He clenched a fist on his thigh, irritated that the memory of Lia still had the power to get to him.

He slammed the door of the taxi with more force than was necessary and marched the few steps along the pavement to his office. He almost walked past the door, feeling the need to keep moving to relieve some of the pent-up energy fizzing through his body. Maybe he should; his staff might be grateful for it.

As he paused just before opening the door, through the open window he heard, 'Hard hats on, the Prince of Darkness is back.' With a grim smile he stepped into the office, spotting the guilty expressions on the faces of his PA and the company receptionist as they both hurriedly did that look-busy thing.

'Afternoon,' he said. 'How is everyone?'

'Hot,' said Heidi, his assistant. Her hair stuck to her forehead and her smile was weary.

'I think we need ice-creams,' he said, digging into his wallet and pulling out a couple of notes. He had a brilliant team and he'd tried hard to rein in the vile temper that had been riding him for the last few weeks but clearly he'd not been doing that well. 'I'll go back out and grab a couple of packs of Cornettos.'

'I'll go. You'll buy the wrong ones,' said Andrea, bobbing up from behind the reception desk, snatching the cash from his hand and darting towards the door, despite the heat.

'I'm not sure you can have the wrong sort of ice-cream in this heat,' drawled Heidi.

'Raph's boring, he'll go for vanilla not chocolate,' complained Andrea over her shoulder as she left in a flurry of jangling bracelets and flying skirts.

'Don't know where she gets her energy,' said Heidi. 'Good meeting?'

'Very good. And I heard the Prince of Darkness comment.' He raised an eyebrow.

'Good,' said Heidi.

'Have I been that bad?'

'Grouchy, I'd say. We're getting used to it.' She leaned back in her chair and swiped at the sweaty tendrils at her temples. In her mid-forties, she'd been with him for the last four years and seemed to have united in a pact with Aurelia to be his London-based mother. They regularly had lengthy chats on the telephone before Heidi put his mamma through to him.

'By the way, you had a return visitor. She didn't want to make an appointment but she left you a note; I've put it in your office.'

Raph's pulse quickened too eagerly, his body responding before his brain, adding one and one and making ten in one go. It couldn't be Lia. Why would she come here? Despite logic telling him that, he still hurried into his office.

The white envelope lay in the middle of his desk. Without pausing to read the writing on the front he ripped it open.

You are cordially invited to a preview of the opening of Braganzi on Thursday 1 August.

Drinks and Canapes from 6.30pm

RSVP e.benson@braganzi.com

In a fluid scrawl on one corner of the stiff card was written, *Hope you can come, Lia.*

Baffled, he stared at the invitation, batting it against his other hand, the flapping noise loud in his office. Why on earth would Lia invite him to come? The last time he'd seen her, she'd told him in no uncertain terms where to go.

What could she want from him now? Apart from to drive him mad. He'd been trying to solve the puzzle of her since the night of the party. Thoughts of her intruded night and day, and even though he shut them down as quickly as he could, she still crept in. The enigma just grew bigger and bigger, with him trying to prise it apart. He couldn't equate the woman that had constantly challenged him with someone who took a free ride. From day one she'd been different, contrary and difficult, never impressed by him or who he was. He'd guessed it was for the money, although she'd never seemed that materialistic. There were too many contradictions to fathom and now here was another one. Why was she inviting him? And why now?

He laid the invitation in the centre of his tidy desk, taking a moment to square it up parallel with the lines of the leather inlay, as if that might help the disordered jumble in his brain. Actually, he didn't care that he couldn't make sense of things. He was fed up with the constant effort of trying to forget her. No one was perfect and she was undeniably talented. She deserved a chance to shine. If she'd used Ernesto's name to get there, he couldn't begrudge her. People did far worse things every single day.

He clicked on to her website looking for contact details, but the only number available was for her agent, Alec McClure.

'They look fab-u-lous. Your best work, although the Positano collection exhibition is getting a lot of pre-publicity. Max Albertini is practically frothing at the mouth. You know Ernesto is loaning him the original?'

Lia, with a mouthful of pins, was carefully attaching the last metre of fabric to one of the two specially customised three-metre-long frames. She simply nodded and let Alec's prattle wash over her head. She'd been working non-stop for the last month and felt emotionally and physically drained. The last thing she wanted was to tear the delicate fabric at this late stage.

'Want a drink in a minute, Lia?' asked Stacey, standing beside her, supporting the last bit of material.

'God, yes. I've just got this final section to attach. I'd love a large Coke with a ton of ice.'

'I'll get one too,' said Alec. 'There's an open tab at the bar; order what you like, Stacey. I've got to step outside to make a couple of calls. The signal in here is crapadocious.'

He disappeared and Lia drooped a bit. With this heat all she wanted to do was wilt and melt into a puddle on the floor.

'You look knackered,' said Stacey, taking in her baggy eyes and downturned mouth.

'Thanks a bunch.'

'You need a holiday,' said Stacey. 'A proper holiday.'

'Don't even think about it,' warned Lia. 'I'll be giving the Amalfi Coast as wide a berth as possible for quite a while.'

'But why?' whined Stacey. 'Ernesto said you *and me* could visit any time. Even if they're not there. You've got Patrizia's number. You can go any time you like.'

'I'd rather go somewhere else.'

'You could just call Raph, you know. Clear the air. Maybe he's calmed down now and you can explain.'

Lia weighed things up before she spoke. 'I invited him to the opening.'

Stacey stared at her. 'What brought that on? I thought you hated him.'

'I've forgiven him.'

'But...' Stacey looked confused. 'He dissed you.'

'When I spoke to Dad, he made some good points about forgiveness and hurting.'

'I'm bloody glad he did and that you and Mum are speaking again.'

'We weren't not speaking; I just needed some space,' said Lia, the familiar rush of shame dousing her.

'Okay. Whatever. I'm just glad everything is back to normal and we're now related to a famous and rich family.'

Lia gave her a bemused smile. '*We're* related?'

'Aurelia told me to consider myself part of the family. Besides, if you and Raph got together we would be. They'd be my in-laws. In fact, I think you two should get married.'

Stacey sauntered off in the direction of the bar as Lia gently tacked the last piece of material into place.

She took a step back, relaxing slightly, the tension leaving her shoulders. Her Italian diary was a triumph, one of her best pieces of work yet. The painstaking hours dyeing the silk, embroidering and embellishing had paid off.

'It looks wonderful,' said a voice from behind her.

A shiver ran up her spine at the familiar low timbre and she closed her eyes. He was here.

Raph.

Adrenalin raced through her with an explosive rush, making her a little shaky and stealing her breath. For a moment she savoured the exquisite knowledge that he was behind her, that he'd come to her.

She exhaled a long quiet sigh, trying to calm the burst of emotions zipping about like pinballs, and turned around, her eyes avidly inventorying every bit of him. With his rumpled dark hair, the white shirt stuck slightly to his broad chest and his jacket hooked oh-so-casually on one finger over his shoulder, he looked every inch the sexy corporate pirate. Her mouth went dry as the image of his naked torso flashed into her brain and she took a helpless step towards him, her palms upright, the need to touch him burning into every pore. Her knees were trembling and she prayed he couldn't tell.

'I got your invitation,' he said, his eyes searching her face. She caught something in them that gave her hope and her lips curved into a tremulous smile. How had she forgotten how gorgeous he was? Or how much she longed for his touch? God, she was so in love with the sod.

'The invitation was for the day after tomorrow,' she said just a touch tartly. He'd ruined everything, turning up looking all sexy and rumpled when she was soaked with sweat, her damp, not-washed-for-two-days hair twisted up in a messy bun skewered with a couple of pencils and wearing baggy, paint-stained dungarees over a vest.

Those luscious lips that she desperately wanted to kiss turned up at the corners. 'I couldn't wait that long.'

Everything inside her shimmered with feeling like bright butterflies fluttering and she thought she might evaporate with happiness on the spot.

'You do realise you've ruined everything.' Mean, but she felt a dart of satisfaction at the sudden shock in his eyes. She wasn't going to make this too easy for him.

'I know I was a dick. I came to apologise.'

'You're supposed to wait until the opening night when I will be wafting about in a semi-transparent killer dress and porn-star shoes and my hair will be sensational. *I* will be sensational and you won't be able to get near me through the crush. I will give you a couple of cool, dismissive looks through the evening…' Lia pouted and then burst out, 'And instead you come now when I'm all sweaty, quite possibly smelly and not expecting you.

'What are you doing here, Raph?' She sounded like a temperamental two-year-old.

He laughed. 'One of the things I love about you, Lia, is that you never ever give me an inch. Not even when I'm here to grovel.'

'Are you?' She tilted her head.

'Yes.'

'Anything else you love about me?'

He stepped forward and grasped both her hands. 'Dozen of things but mainly I just love you.'

She reined back the instinct to throw herself into his arms; she wasn't about to let him off the hook just yet. After all, he had kept her waiting for a month.

'Well' – he folded her arms – 'you took your time getting around to saying it.'

She couldn't help her mouth quirking or her eyes crinkling just a little.

He knew. He knew that she was almost smiling at him.

'What can I say? I'm an idiot.' He spread his hands wide.

'I agree.'

His eyes twinkled now. 'Now it's your turn.'

'My turn?' She arched her eyebrows.

'Aren't you going to tell me you love me? Isn't that the age-old convention, now that you've brought me to my knees?'

She paused, swallowing, before asking very quietly. 'Have I?'

His arms slipped around her waist and he looked down into her eyes. 'Oh yes, Lia. You'll be pleased to know that you have.'

'Good,' she said, not being quite as cool as she pretended. Her arms were shaking as she gripped his shoulders.

'Why did you send me the invitation?'

'So you'd know I've forgiven you.'

'Thank you.' He touched his forehead against hers and she felt his relief as the tension in his muscles faded away. 'I didn't know how to come back. As soon as I saw it, I had to see you. Luckily your agent's office is very indiscreet. They said he was here and I figured if he was you must be.'

'Excellent detection.'

'I have other skills.'

She lifted her head. 'Do you think you could remind me?'

'I'd be happy to.' He ducked his head and his lips closed over hers. The familiar burst of firework happiness exploded and she sank into the kiss, her arms enfolding him, her body welcoming his home.

Epilogue

Lia's pictures were drawing lots of attention, as was she. Raph looked over to where she stood surrounded by a crowd of photographers, reporters and Vincent Braganzi and his wife Stella.

She looked stunning in a striking confection of turquoise silk and chiffon, which draped artfully over her body. It wasn't the semi-transparent number she'd threatened – thankfully – but he still looked forward to peeling it from her later that night.

'She looks lovely,' said Aurelia at his elbow.

'Mamma.' Raph bent to kiss her on both cheeks. 'How was your flight?'

'It was great, although it was sad to say goodbye to the children.'

'You're going to see them again in a couple of days. Although I'm still amazed you entrusted Leo to get them home to LA.'

'Don't be like that to your brother. He's a good boy.'

'Boy being the operative word. Is he ever going to grow up? He needs a job. Some kind of focus.'

'Didn't you know? He's applied for a special traineeship with a brewery in Prague.'

'You're kidding.' Raph frowned at Aurelia but her face was perfectly serious.

'It's true. If he gets it he will go and stay there for a few months.'

'Oh, well … if that's what he wants to do.'

'Apparently he really does. He's spent every day for the last month travelling to the Melphi Brewery in Amalfi to learn as much as he could about making craft beer. He wants to make his own.'

'Good luck to him,' said Raph, surprised by this news but more interested in celebrating Lia's evening. 'Have you spoken to her yet?' He nodded towards Lia.

'No, she's been so busy since we arrived and everyone wants to speak to her,' said Aurelia.

'Where's Ernesto?'

'Over there. With Max.' She pointed at the two men on the fringe of the group around Lia. Ernesto looked up just then and, grabbing two glasses of champagne, moved towards them and handed his wife a glass.

'Raph. Nice to see you and nice that you're supporting your stepsister.'

Raph had taken a sip of his drink and almost choked. 'What's he doing here?' He used his glass to indicate Max Albertini.

'He couldn't stay away. He wanted to see the pictures.' Ernesto signalled to Max to join them.

'Simply exquisite.' Max sighed. 'I'm so excited for the exhibition. Ernesto, I owe you.'

'So you keep telling me,' said Ernesto. 'But I will not sell the Positano picture. Not for any price.'

'I know,' said Albertini mournfully. 'I am very grateful that you have loaned it to me. The exhibition is already creating great interest.'

'Lia's exhibition?' asked Raph.

'Yes. Despite the prices, I've already had a couple of sales.'

'I guess Ernesto's daughter can command a premium,' said Raph, pleased for Lia. She couldn't help who her relatives were, he supposed, and if it helped her art career, then who was he to disapprove?

Max's laugh was quick and dry. 'She doesn't need Ernesto's name. It was very fortuitous for me, to meet her in person. I have been wanting to exhibit her work for a very long time. It's unique and so distinctive; she's one of the only artists to be working in this style and is one of Europe's foremost textile artists. You do know her work is on display in the Moco in Amsterdam, don't you, and that she's one of the very few Western artists to have her work displayed in the Itchiku Kubota Museum in Kawaguchi in Japan?'

Raph felt a tectonic shift in his brain. 'So, Lia is quite … quite famous?'

'In the textile world, she's the queen. She's built quite a reputation in the last five years. But textile art is a specialist field, so most people would not have heard of her.'

'Yes, Vincent was very impressed when I told him Lia was my daughter,' said Ernesto preening slightly.

'You told him?' Raph asked sharply.

'Of course. What a small world, eh?'

'When did you tell him?'

'When I saw Lia's website. Vincent had said he was commissioning a young textile artist last time I saw him in New York and I'd never heard of such a thing. So when I saw Lia's work, I emailed him to say what a coincidence it was that my daughter is a textile artist and we realised it was the same person.'

Raph shook his head. Lia had never needed Ernesto's help or influence because she was already well established. He now realised that her gifting the picture to Ernesto had been an inordinately generous gesture.

Raph scrubbed the heel of his hand against his forehead, cursing himself. No wonder she'd been so incensed and told him where to go. He'd insulted her to an even greater degree than he'd realised. Oh boy, had he insulted her.

And yet … she'd forgiven him. He was going to be spending the rest of his life making it up to her but, all things considered, that didn't sound such a bad deal. He had a few ideas of how he might make a start.

'There's Stacey,' said Aurelia. 'And they must be Lia's parents. We should go and say hello. Come on, Ernesto. And you, Raph. They ought to know more about the family their daughter is involved with. Are you going to tell them who you are?'

'Aurelia, the boy isn't going to tell them that he's her lover.'

For the second time in one evening Raph's drink went down the wrong way. 'I beg your—'

'Raphael, you think your mamma doesn't know when you're in love with someone? I have eyes, you know.'

He laughed. 'Yes, Mamma.' He followed her over to the trio standing looking a little lost.

'Mary,' said Ernesto, swooping down on Lia's mother. 'It has been a very long time.'

'Ernesto, hello.'

'This is my wife, Aurelia, and her son Raphael.'

'I'm so pleased to meet you,' said Aurelia. 'Your daughter is absolutely delightful. It has been a pleasure getting to know her.'

Raph, slightly off centre, saw Stacey wink at him but his attention was quickly drawn to Lia, who had managed to extract herself from her fan club and was walking their way as if she knew he needed rescuing. The fabric of her dress flowed around her lithe figure and he felt the same punch of attraction as he did the very first time he'd seen her. Then he'd been horrified because he hadn't wanted to feel that way. Now he welcomed it and his heart thumped harder when she came straight to him and linked her arm though his.

'Hello,' he said huskily.

'Hello. Missed me?' She leaned up to kiss him and everything in him sighed. All was right with the world.

'Mum, Dad, I'd like to introduce you to Raph.'

Behind her, he saw his mamma's beatific smile and the quick satisfied look she and Ernesto shared, as if they'd been entirely responsible for the match.

Raph turned to meet Simon and Mary Bathurst. 'Lovely to meet you.'

'And you. Lia's told us a lot about you.' Simon Bathurst gave him a shrewd look. For a mild-mannered-looking man, there was a fierce glint in his eyes.

Lia gave Raph's arm a quick reassuring squeeze.

'Dad,' she warned. Simon's face relaxed, although there was still a threat in the soft grey eyes. 'I'm glad you've sorted your differences,' he said.

With a laugh, Lia leaned forward and kissed her father on the cheek. 'You can stand down now.'

Her mother stepped in front of her husband after giving him a fond glance. 'It's very nice to meet you. You must come to lunch.' She turned to Aurelia and Ernesto. 'How long are you in London for? You must all come to lunch.'

'That would be lovely,' said Aurelia. 'We would like that very much.'

Simon, Stacey and Lia all stared at Mary, who blushed bright scarlet. 'Or maybe we could go out.'

'Why don't you all come to me?' suggested Raph. 'And Lia and I will cook pasta for you.'

'Yes,' said Aurelia, clapping her hands in delight. 'She's quite the expert now.'

'But she did have the best teacher,' said Ernesto, putting his arm around her as he beamed at Mary. 'I remember you very nearly poisoned me once.'

Everyone went silent for a moment and Aurelia rolled her eyes and stood on his foot. 'I'm so sorry, Mary. What can I say? Men are idiots. Especially mine.'

Mary smiled at her before glaring at the hapless Ernesto.

'Thank you for reminding me of that, Ernesto,' she said, giving him a severe look before her eyes twinkled as Simon laughed and kissed her.

'Thankfully I didn't marry you for your cooking,' Simon joked.

'Just as well,' said Mary. 'But I recognise it's a considerable skill that has always eluded me… Maybe I should give it another go.'

'You should come to Italy,' said Aurelia. 'I will show you how to make pasta.'

'This isn't strange at all,' muttered Lia in Raph's ear.

He shook his head. 'It's my mamma's way of showing acceptance. If she offers to teach someone to cook in her kitchen, she's welcoming them into her home and her heart. She's always been brilliant at knowing which ingredients work best together.' He smiled down at her.

'That's lovely,' said Lia, taking his hand and lacing his fingers with hers.

'I didn't stand a chance really. I think she knew we were the perfect combination; it just took us a little longer to catch up. The minute she took you into the kitchen and taught you how to make my favourite pasta sauce, I knew I was in trouble.'

She grinned up at him. 'And now?'

'Well, we Italians like to keep things in the family. I wouldn't change it for anything.'

'Just as well.' She squeezed his hand. 'You're stuck with me now.'

And he wouldn't change it. 'You're stuck with me and my family – they all adore you.'

'That's okay, I adore them too.' She lowered her voice. 'Although not as much as I adore you.'

Warmth blossomed in his chest, spreading throughout his body, and he was lost for words as happiness suffused him. He'd never thought he'd feel like this about someone. He brought her hand to his mouth and held it to his lips as if the touch could convey his emotion. As she stood there before him, her blond hair rippling down her back, her eyes bright with joy, he realised he'd found what his mother had found with Ernesto all those years ago. The emotions were just too bright and shiny to articulate at that moment, much as he wanted to.

Lia looked at him, her hand still pressed to his lips, and with that canny way she had of understanding him, she whispered, 'Me too.'

Acknowledgments

Romance books don't always get the love from the wider public and I've had people ask when I'm going to write a 'proper' book. However, recently I've been so touched by messages from readers who have thanked me for writing my books and for helping them through difficult times. There is no higher compliment that I could possibly receive and I'm so touched by the thought that my words can transport people and give them a respite from real life. If I can do that for one person, that is enough and I don't need to worry about writing 'proper' books.

So for all the readers that have enjoyed my books, a big thank you to you for giving your time to read and your hard earned money to taking a chance on this and every other book.

I also don't take for granted the team of people behind each book – they are the ones that bring the polish and the sparkle, my fabulous, legendary editor, Charlotte Ledger and the incomparable, Broo Doherty, much beloved agent. A big shout out to the unsung people behind the scenes, the sales team, the rights team, especially Rachel McCarron, copywriters and proofreaders, as well as the brilliant editorial team at One More Chapter, Bonnie Macleod,

Arsalan Isa, Chloe Cummings and Emma Petfield, all of whom help bring a book to life.

The author and One More Chapter would like to thank everyone who contributed to the publication of this story...

Analytics
Abigail Fryer
Maria Osa

Audio
Fionnuala Barrett
Ciara Briggs

Contracts
Georgina Hoffman
Florence Shepherd

Design
Lucy Bennett
Fiona Greenway
Holly Macdonald
Liane Payne
Dean Russell

Digital Sales
Lydia Grainge
Emily Scorer
Georgina Ugen

Editorial
Arsalan Isa
Charlotte Ledger
Federica Leonardis
Bonnie Macleod
Jennie Rothwell
Tony Russell
Kimberley Young

International Sales
Bethan Moore

Marketing & Publicity
Chloe Cummings
Emma Petfield

Operations
Melissa Okusanya
Hannah Stamp

Production
Emily Chan
Denis Manson
Francesca Tuzzeo

Rights
Lana Beckwith
Rachel McCarron
Agnes Rigou
Hany Sheikh
Mohamed
Zoe Shine
Aisling Smyth

The HarperCollins Distribution Team

The HarperCollins Finance & Royalties Team

The HarperCollins Legal Team

The HarperCollins Technology Team

Trade Marketing
Ben Hurd
Eleanor Slater

UK Sales
Laura Carpenter
Isabel Coburn
Jay Cochrane
Tom Dunstan
Sabina Lewis
Erin White
Harriet Williams
Leah Woods

And every other essential link in the chain from delivery drivers to booksellers to librarians and beyond!

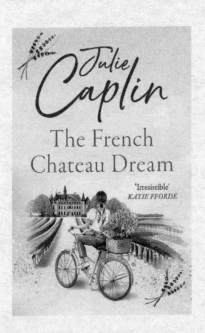

You are invited to a summer of sparkling champagne, warm buttery croissants and a little bit of je ne sais quoi

With a broken heart and a broken spirit, Hattie is in need of a summer escape. So when an opportunity comes up to work at a beautiful, stately chateau in the Champagne region of France she books her flights quicker than the pop of a cork.

Romance is the last thing Hattie is looking for but then she wasn't expecting gorgeous Luc to stroll into her life. Hattie starts to wonder if a holiday fling – or maybe even something more – might be just what she needs.

Available now in paperback, ebook, and audio!

Escape to the snow-peaked caps of the Scottish Highlands and a romance that will melt your heart...

Izzy McBride had never in a million years expected to inherit an actual castle, but here she was, in the run up to Christmas, Monarch of her own Glen – a very rundown glen in need of a lot of TLC if her dream of turning it into a boutique bed and breakfast was to come true.

But when Izzy's eccentric mother rents a room to enigmatic thriller author Ross Adair and the Scottish snow starts to settle like the frosting on a Christmas cake, it's a race to get the castle ready before they're all snowed in.

Available now in paperback, ebook, and audio!

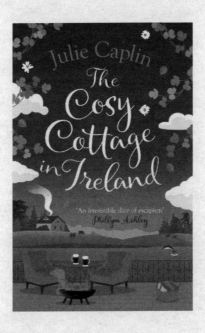

Snuggle up in your favourite armchair and take a trip across the Irish sea for comfort food, cosy cottage nights and a heartwarming romance...

Talented lawyer Hannah Campbell wants a change in her workaholic Manchester life – so she books herself a place at the world-renowned Killorgally Cookery School in County Kerry. But on her first night In Ireland, sampling the delights of Dublin, Hannah can't resist falling for the charms of handsome stranger Conor. It's only when Hannah arrives at her postcard-pretty home at Killorgally for the next six weeks that she discovers what happens in Dublin doesn't quite stay in Dublin...

Available now in paperback, ebook, and audio!

ONE MORE CHAPTER